FROM THE CRADLE

FRIENDS OF THE YREKA LIBRARY
719 FOURTH STREET
YREKA, CA 96097

OTHER TITLES BY LOUISE VOSS AND MARK EDWARDS

Killing Cupid

Catch Your Death

All Fall Down

Forward Slash

OTHER TITLES BY MARK EDWARDS

The Magpies

What You Wish For

Because She Loves Me

OTHER TITLES BY LOUISE VOSS

To Be Someone

Are You My Mother?

Lifesaver

Games People Play

LOUISE VOSS
AND
MARK EDWARDS

FROM THE CRADLE

This is a work of fiction. Names, characters, organizations, places, events, and incidents are either products of the author's imagination or are used fictitiously.

Text copyright © 2014 Mark Edwards and Louise Voss
All rights reserved.

No part of this book may be reproduced, or stored in a retrieval system, or transmitted in any form or by any means, electronic, mechanical, photocopying, recording, or otherwise, without express written permission of the publisher.

Published by Thomas & Mercer, Seattle

www.apub.com

Amazon, the Amazon logo, and Thomas & Mercer are trademarks of Amazon.com, Inc., or its affiliates.

ISBN-13: 9781477825273
ISBN-10: 1477825274

Cover design by bürosüd° Munich, www.buerosued.de

Library of Congress Control Number: 2014940618

Printed in the United States of America

Prologue

It was an emotional nuclear explosion. A few seconds of innocent calm, perhaps a faint falling whizz, the silence as Patrick opened the front door and everything was too quiet . . . Knowing instantly that something was wrong, but not yet having a clue as to how much, how complete and irrevocable that wrongness was.

It had been a particularly long day. Detective Inspector Patrick Lennon had been stuck in a windowless interview room for seven hours with an uncooperative drug-addled thug called Dean Kervin, who had a face like a potato that had been boiled several days earlier. Despite the fact that several witnesses and two CCTV cameras had seen Dean smash the window of the sporting goods outlet and beat the security guard to death, he was stubbornly denying it. All he kept repeating was 'It wasn't me. I wasn't there.'

Patrick had been desperate all day for some fresh air and a non-stewed coffee, but what was really keeping him going was the thought of walking back into his warm, baby-scented home, and the sticky embrace of his five-month-old daughter Bonnie. A glass of wine in one hand, Bonnie cradled in the crook of his other arm, then a Chinese takeaway in front of a movie with Gill, once Bonnie was fast asleep. He had almost laughed at the thought that such an image would be so welcoming. His teenage self would have ripped the piss out of him so mercilessly – wine and babies? A takeaway in front of the telly? Pathetic.

No. Not pathetic. Happiness, security, the purity of family. What life was all about.

The only spanner in the works on the domestic front was that Gill had been very down recently. Everyone knew it was hard, staying at home all day with a tiny baby, especially when you'd had a responsible and demanding career. Gill was a barrister, never happier than when she was tearing apart – eviscerating with words – some lowlife like potato-faced Dean. She did it with such aplomb. Patrick hoped she'd soon regain her spark. Sociable and friendly though she naturally was outside of court, the whole NCT cabal thing, gangs of breastfeeding mums taking over coffee shops and attending baby-music classes, just didn't do it for her. She had tried, but every time came home complaining that if she had to listen to any more chat about mustardy nappies she would scream . . .

Patrick smiled at the thought as he reversed their bronze Toyota Prius – something else that his teenage self would've had a word or two about – into the short driveway of their boxy little townhouse in West Molesey. When he was trying to impress people, he told them he lived 'near Hampton Court', whereas in truth West Molesey was a mile and a half away, the poor sibling of the much grander East Molesey with its conservation area and plethora of two-million-pound properties. He thought that he had never been so happy to be home. He had even stopped at Tesco Metro and bought a bottle of wine and a bunch of gerbera daisies, Gill's favourites.

Later, he'd wonder if he'd known it from the second his key turned in the lock, or if he'd imagined that he knew.

What he did instantly pick up on, though, was the silence. They were surely at home, because the buggy was in the hallway, and all the lights were on. Had they just popped round to a neighbour's? Unlikely. The neighbours in their little close had turned out, disappointingly, to be remarkably unfriendly, and Gill hadn't made any friends in the immediate vicinity. Usually Radio 2 was blaring away, the TV showing *CBeebies* with the sound switched off. The tumble dryer churning, kettle boiling, the familiar noises of Gill clattering around in the kitchen, starting dinner for her and Patrick. There were none of these sounds.

'Hello?' Patrick called as he stepped inside and closed the front door behind him. 'Gill?'

Nothing. Patrick frowned. He took off his leather jacket, hung the car keys on the key rack in the cupboard by the door and put the flowers and wine carefully onto the hall floor. They must be out, he thought – then hesitated. Something told him that they weren't out. Gooseflesh swept up and down his body, even though he had no reason at that stage to fear anything.

'Gill, where are you?' he repeated uneasily, and walked towards the back of the house, down the hall to the kitchen. As he passed the foot of the stairs, a movement made him jump out of his skin.

Gill was sitting on the third stair, an expression on her face the like of which he had never seen on anyone in his life. Her usually pink face was waxy and drained, and her eyes were two dead pools of horror. She was clutching Bonnie's favourite toy, a knitted Peppa Pig, and rocking soundlessly back and forth.

Patrick gasped, and grabbed her by the shoulders, half-hug, half-challenge. 'Gill! Sweetheart, what's the matter!' He fell to his knees on the stairs in front of her and held her tightly, rocking with her. 'What's happened? Has someone died?'

That was Patrick's first thought – because if something had been wrong with Bonnie, Gill wouldn't have been sitting on the stairs, she'd be sitting by the cot.

Gill didn't reply. She didn't acknowledge him, or even seem to realize that he was there. 'Talk to me, darling, what's happened? Gill, please!'

She seemed to Patrick to be half her normal size, diminished by shock and this awful, inchoate grief.

'Where's Bonnie?'

Gill immediately stopped rocking. Stopped breathing, clamped her mouth closed, those sensual lips that Patrick had fallen in love with before he even properly met her. She closed her eyes and tightened her fingers into Peppa Pig's soft pink body.

Then she started moaning. The sound grew in pitch and intensity from moan to groan to bellow and then, opening her mouth again, up into a roar of primal pain that bounced up the walls and sucked every shred of peace out of the house, forever.

Patrick jumped up, a sob already escaping from his throat. 'Oh my God. Gill, where is she? What's happened? *WHERE IS SHE?*'

He pushed his wife to one side and even though it had just been a light push, she toppled sideways and fell down the two remaining stairs to the floor, where she lay motionless, still making the same unearthly howling noise. He raced up the narrow staircase, legs like a marathon runner approaching the final mile, the breath jagged in his chest, and tore round the banister and into Bonnie's tiny bedroom.

At first he thought that there was a doll lying in her place in the cot; a strange, swollen, purple doll. He took a step into the room and realized that the doll *was* Bonnie. Her limbs were twisted into unnatural shapes and she had clear marks around her throat. Fingermarks.

With a roar louder than his wife's, Patrick released the side of the cot and bent over his lifeless daughter, gasping air into his lungs so that he could try and breathe it into her tiny still ones. With two gentle, shaking fingers he massaged her sternum, praying that he was doing it right, trying desperately to remember the correct steps from the baby CPR course that Gill had insisted they both attend in her pregnancy. *Push, push, breathe. Push, push, breathe.* Bonnie was still purple. She was still warm. That was good. *Push, push, breathe.* His tears dripped onto her closed eyelids.

Push, push, breathe.

He didn't know how long he did it for. Time spun into a horrible vortex that seemed to be dragging him down further and further until finally there was the tiniest mew. Bonnie's eyes opened a crack, and closed again. Her chest, not much bigger than a bag of sugar, heaved very slightly.

Patrick flung himself backwards against the bedroom wall, hyperventilating and sobbing. He grabbed his mobile out of his back pocket, dialled 999, howled for an ambulance. Everything for the next half hour was a blur of movement; cradling Bonnie, rubbing her back to keep her baby breaths coming, wondering if she was brain damaged, crying, letting the ambulance men in, watching them clamp a tiny oxygen mask over his daughter's face.

It was while they were doing this that Patrick walked on shaky legs over to his wife, who was still curled in a foetal position on the hall floor, moaning and clutching Bonnie's toy.

He put his arms around her, lifted her up to a sitting position, cradled her close to him in the same way he had just done to his daughter. She smelled metallic, of fear and sweat. He picked a stray long brown hair off the shoulder of her sweater, and waited till his breath was regular enough to speak. He put his lips to her ear:

'Gillian Louise Lennon, I am arresting you for the attempted murder of Bonnie Elizabeth Lennon. You do not have to say anything, but anything you do say may be taken down and used as evidence in a court of law . . .'

Chapter 1
Helen – Day 1

'Hurry up, Hel!'

Helen could hear Sean jangling his keys in the hall, no doubt checking his watch and tutting.

'I'm nearly ready!' Helen called back down the stairs from the bathroom, trying to keep her tone light. This was their first date night in weeks and she didn't want it to start off on the wrong foot.

Frankie was in the bath, playing with her bath toys, three brightly coloured water-squirting plastic vehicles. She squirted a long stream of water at Helen and giggled so hard that she lost her balance and slipped backwards under the bubbles. Helen lunged for her and hoisted her back up, holding her breath for the imminent cries, but Frankie just looked surprised and then, realizing she now had a Regency-style wig of bubbles on her head, laughed even harder. Helen laughed too, even though her vintage silk blouse now had a long wet streak down the front.

'Come on, time to get out. Alice is going to read you a story. You promise to be a good girl for her?'

Frankie nodded vigorously, sending bubbles flying around the steamy bathroom. Helen was privately slightly bemused by her three-year-old daughter's devotion to her surly teenage half-sister. Alice had the sort of grudge against humanity that made Pol Pot seem positively benevolent and, worse, since she'd started dating Larry, there was more than a faint whiff of booze around her. Alice's beautiful caramel-coloured skin was permanently caked beneath a thick layer of dark foundation to hide spots that were barely visible to start with, and her soft black curls had taken on a limp defeated appearance.

'Teenagers,' Sean often said, definitively. 'They're all the same.'

But were they really? Helen wondered. She lifted Frankie out of the bath, with the towel twisted in front of her body to form a tight handle so she could lift her without touching her – a favourite game. She giggled again as Helen set her down on the bathmat and hugged her wet body close. Her almost-black hair was plastered in spikes to her head, and her brown eyes laughed as she hugged Helen back. Like Alice, Frankie had caramel skin, a shade lighter than Helen's. Sean was the only Caucasian in the family, something that confused people when they learned that the two girls were half sisters – as if it did not compute that a white man could choose not one but two black women as mothers to his children.

For a second Helen thought of those two other sets of parents, both within three miles of their own house, who no longer heard their babies giggle, could no longer feel their dense fragrant warmth in their arms. It was unspeakable. For the dozenth time she felt anxious about leaving Frankie with Alice.

'HELEN!' bellowed Sean from the front door. 'They'll have given away our reservation if you don't get a move on! Let Alice do it – Alice, can you go up and take over, please?'

Helen had already persuaded Frankie into her Dry-Nite pull-ups and brushed cotton pyjamas. She was rubbing her daughter's hair dry and helping her clean her tiny teeth by the time Alice finally dragged herself away from her beloved iPad and the endless supply of humorous YouTube videos and old episodes of *The Big Bang Theory* which was all she ever seemed to watch.

Frankie's face lit up when she saw her big sister. 'Ali! You read my story, yeah?'

'Alright, trouble. Come on, let's go and choose a book. Only one, mind, and no fuss when it's finished.'

Frankie wriggled off Helen's lap and dragged Alice away towards her room.

'Alice?' Helen called, unbuttoning her shirt to change it for a dry one. 'If you let the cat out the back door, make sure you—'

'—lock it again straight away. I *know,* Helen. Chill out! I'm not stupid.'

'We won't be late back, no later than about half ten anyway. Have you got revision to do?'

'Nah. Only Drama left, and I don't need to revise for that. It's a practical.'

'Call us if anything at all doesn't – well – seem right.'

It sounded crazy. Alice had babysat loads of times in the past year or two – but it was only in the past month that two small children had been abducted in the area . . . Alice rolled her eyes to indicate that she held the same opinion – that it did sound crazy.

'Um – one more thing . . . Larry's not coming over, is he?'

Alice squared up to her, with Frankie still clinging on. 'So what if he is? Don't you trust me to look after Frankie properly?'

Helen took off the damp shirt and hung it on the heated towel rail, turning back to Alice in her bra. Alice looked contemptuously up and down at her body. The look was enough to make the most confident woman wither. Helen wasn't as slim or pert as she had been before Frankie, her belly softer, gravity and pregnancy having launched a twin assault on her figure.

'It's not that. Of course I do. And I don't dislike him, Alice. I just think that on a school night . . . Plus you know your dad doesn't like him being here when we're out.' She braced herself for the fight, but to her surprise, Alice conceded.

'He's not coming round, so don't get your knickers in a twist.'

'Good.'

'STORY, Ali!' Frankie reminded her, kicking her thin legs against Alice's hips.

'Stop it, squirt,' she grumbled, and carried her away.

'Hurry up!'

'Oh Sean, for God's sake, I'm *coming*, OK?'

Just as soon as she'd kissed Frankie goodnight.

Later, in the restaurant, both their moods had mellowed after a bottle of silky Merlot, and a very nice *coq au vin*.

'This is lovely,' Helen said.

'It certainly is, my sweet,' Sean agreed, in his comedy Del-Boy voice. '*Mange tout, mange tout.*'

She laughed, and studied him affectionately. 'You've been saying that for years.'

'Ah but it never gets old, does it? Unlike me.' He rubbed ruefully at his bald head, now kept shaven to draw attention away from the large hairless spot at the crown. The stubble made a small scratchy sound under his fingers. Sean had great cheekbones, but a slightly unfortunate cone-shaped skull. He didn't look *bad* with a shaved head, but Helen had to admit he'd looked better with hair.

'You're still gorgeous,' she said, smiling at his spikily fringed dark green eyes.

'You're not so bad yourself, doll-face.' He winked at her and they clinked glasses, but Helen couldn't help wishing that he would occasionally return a compliment with something a little more romantic than a silly accent.

Her phone buzzed, and she immediately picked it up from the table, where she'd kept it throughout the meal. But it was only an electronic notification of someone's move in Words With Friends, and she sighed with relief. For once, she had actually remembered to charge her phone before going out, something she was hopeless at. Sean was always nagging her about it.

'Perhaps I should call to see how it's going,' she said, phone still in hand. Sean reached across the table and gently took it from her. 'Relax, Hel. If there was a problem Alice would've called. You know she would. She might be a lazy madam but you know she adores Frankie. Besides, there's no way she'd deal with a pile of vomit or too much screaming on her own if she knew we were only ten minutes away, so we can be certain that nothing's amiss. Why are you so jumpy all of a sudden? You haven't been this paranoid since she was a baby!'

Helen felt annoyed with him again. 'You know why. Liam McConnell and Izzy Hartley, that's why.'

Liam and Izzy were the names of the two stolen children. Helen's friend Elena took her child to the same nursery Liam had been enrolled at, and knew his mother. The poor woman was a total wreck apparently, dragging herself around hollow-eyed with Prozac, on permanent tenterhooks for the smallest morsel of news of her son, news that so far – almost a week in – hadn't materialized. Both children had vanished seemingly into thin air, within two days of one another.

Sean bristled slightly at the implied criticism, as he always did when it came to his daughter. 'Alice would never let that happen. '

Helen poured them both another glass of wine, to try and dispel the image of little dark-haired chubby bespectacled Liam – his photo was all over the papers – being unstrapped from his car seat and removed. CCTV in the supermarket car park showed a single glimpse of a muffled-up person carrying him away, but there was no trace of where and no indication whatsoever of who it was. Liam's mum had only nipped back into the supermarket to retrieve some dry cleaning she'd forgotten. She was gone barely two minutes.

Sean gave Helen one of those long, impenetrable gazes where he could be thinking anything from 'This is the woman I really, really love', to 'Wow, you make my life a living hell.' She didn't really think it was the latter, but by the same token, she did find him unreadable sometimes. It wasn't that she didn't feel loved by him – perhaps just not loved as much as she'd have liked. Not loved as much as he'd loved Alice's mother, all those years ago. Helen had given up fishing for information on that score. She had long realized that the shutters clanged down the moment she even mentioned the woman's name. The dreaded dead perfect first wife – pretty much impossible to live up to that ideal, so Helen had stopped trying, and Sean never spoke of her.

'I just can't stop thinking about those children – both younger than Frankie. Hardly more than babies . . . Let's change the subject – what shall we talk about?'

Sean smiled properly at her. His smile could still make her heart quicken. He took her hand across the table, sliding her phone into his pocket so she couldn't keep checking it. 'There was something I wanted to run by you, actually,' he said, and she was puzzled at the slightly shy tone of his voice.

'You're not going to beg me to let you buy a new car are you?'

'No . . .' He took a deep breath and gazed into her eyes. 'Hel, I know I was joking about the nightmare of having two screaming babies, but Frankie's almost four now and—'

She felt a sudden sharp pain of love and excitement in her belly.

'—do you think it's time we had another one? It would be so nice for Frankie to have a little brother or sister. Alice would love it too.'

Helen's smile broadened into a beam, and she squeezed his hand tightly to stop tears of joy spilling down her cheeks. He'd been anti the idea of a second child for so long that she'd given up hinting.

'Really? You're ready?' Every atom of her danced when he nodded slowly back.

'Yeah,' he said. 'Actually I think I am.'

They were a lot later getting home than Helen had originally told Alice they would be. She'd insisted that they celebrate with two glasses of champagne, and after they paid the bill and left, they decided to walk the long way home. They went through the locked park, climbing over the gate to get in like two giggly teenagers, enjoying the crisp summer air. They kept stopping to kiss, the way they used to when they were first together and couldn't keep their hands off one another.

By the time Sean turned the key into the lock of the front door, it was 11.25 P.M. All the lights were still on downstairs, and Helen sobered up enough to tut when she heard the sound of the TV coming from the living room. Alice should have gone to bed an hour ago.

She dumped her handbag on the bottom stair. 'Ali? We're back. Sorry we're later than we – oh!' She walked into the living room to find Alice fast asleep on the sofa, and immediately dropped her voice, as Sean followed her in. 'Look, Sean, she's sparko, bless her!'

'Have you checked to make sure Larry's not hiding under the coffee table?' They both laughed softly. 'You wake her up, darling, while I go and check on Frankie.'

Helen climbed the stairs, smiling to herself. She didn't usually like to make love late at night – too tired to feel suitably receptive – but the prospect of a baby banished her tiredness. She went into the bathroom and chucked her unopened contraceptive pills straight into the swing bin. Then, even though she was dying for a wee, she came back out and crept down the hallway to Frankie's bedroom. The cartoon dinosaurs around her magic lantern threw soft violet and peach shadows around the room as she pushed open the door, waiting to see the hump of her in her toddler bed – she always manoeuvred herself into a sort of prone kneeling position when she slept, as though praying to Mecca.

But there was no hump. At first, Helen thought she was just lying uncharacteristically flat under the duvet, which was pulled up, as though she was hiding. Fear flooded her entire body, as though dropped on her out of a bucket above her head. She ran over to the bed and whipped back the duvet.

Frankie was gone.

Chapter 2
Patrick – Day 1

He was hallucinating children. There, in the space between lamp-posts, a shadow thrown against a wall by the headlights of a passing car. Another at the entrance to an alleyway, submerging into the darkness like a night-swimmer going under, slipping from sight. A small figure in the rain, weaving between legs in a crowd. A white face against a smudged bus window. A city of little ghosts. Then he would blink and rub his eyes and the child would be gone.

'You look shattered.' His partner, DS Carmella Masiello, looked over at him. It was just past eleven P.M., and DI Patrick Lennon was giving Carmella a lift to the new-build apartment she shared with her *other* partner, Jenny. He wondered if she knew how much he envied her. His own home life couldn't have been more different.

'Your eyes – they look a little like a basset hound's.'

'Thanks, Carmella. You really know how to make a guy feel good about himself. I was told once that I have sleepy eyes, and that it's sexy.'

He temporarily angled the rearview mirror towards himself so he could see his own eyes. He did look knackered. He hadn't been taking care of himself, not the way Gill used to – she was always buying him eye serums and moisturisers that he felt embarrassed using. 'But you don't want to ruin your good looks,' she would say, further embarrassing him. He was six foot two, with brown hair and matching eyes, and he'd been told he looked more like an alt-country singer than a cop. He didn't believe it though – he didn't think he was anything special and neither, apparently, did his partner.

Carmella's laughter drowned out a whole chorus and half a verse of the Cure song that was playing on the car stereo. 'There's a difference between sleepy and knackered,' she said when she finally got hold of herself.

'There's also a big difference between having me as a partner and having Winkler.'

'You wouldn't!'

He smiled, then remembered what they'd been talking about, and why he was so tired, and the smile vanished into the shadows with all the ghosts.

Seven days ago on June 2nd, three-year-old Isabel Hartley, known to the public as Izzy since the tabloids had shortened her name for the sake of their headlines, had been taken from the living room of her family home in Richmond, where she was watching TV. Isabel's dad Max had been out the front, waxing his beloved car. Then he got an important call from work on his mobile and went inside, leaving the front door open, and up the stairs to his office to dig out some papers. He was up there for twenty minutes. When he came back downstairs, Isabel was no longer in the living room. She wasn't anywhere to be found.

Max Hartley was something in the City, loaded, the kind of person who, according to common perception, had little devil's horns beneath his hair and a pointy tail concealed beneath his Hugo Boss suit. The mother, Fiona, was a former catalogue model who counter-balanced her husband's profession by organizing charity fund-raisers. They lived in one of the best postcodes in the country, the kind of place where nothing bad happened. The Hartleys never thought that their child would be taken from their front room in the middle of the afternoon, certainly not on a street like the one they lived on.

Two days later, June 4th, another child had been abducted. Liam McConnell was two, a cheeky, chunky little boy with poor eyesight that forced him to wear glasses. His mum, Zoe, had left him in the car in Twickenham Sainsbury's car park, strapped into his child seat, after realizing she'd forgotten to pick up her dry cleaning. She was only gone for two minutes, she insisted, though Patrick was sure it was more like five, maybe more. The woman in front of her in the queue had been arguing about a stain on her cashmere cardigan and Zoe, a freelance marketing consultant, described how she'd shifted impatiently from foot to foot, eager to get back to the car, on the verge of abandoning the dry cleaning when it was finally her turn.

She had locked the car, could clearly remember the *thunk* as she depressed the central locking. But when she got back to her white Audi A4, the back door was open and Liam was gone. An hour later, when a uniform had asked to see the car key she hadn't been able to find it. Then she remembered, on her way back into Sainsbury's, bumping into a man who had almost knocked her over. The car key had been in her jacket pocket. Patrick was certain that the man who had bumped into her had taken the key – unless Zoe was making the whole thing up, that she had forgotten to lock the car and had concocted the story to stop her husband, Keith, who ran his own recruitment company, blaming her.

Patrick had personally scoured the CCTV footage from the car park. One camera had caught the briefest glimpse of a man in a dark jacket carrying a child who looked like Liam, but it was impossible to see the man's face or where he'd gone. Zoe insisted that the man who'd bumped her had been wearing a black jacket, but she had barely looked at his face, the photo-fit they'd put together from her patchy memory likely to be 90 per cent imagination. This hadn't stopped the picture from being printed on the front of every newspaper in the country, sparking hundreds of calls from members of the public saying the man looked like their neighbour, their boss, their husband. Every single one of these unfortunate men had been eliminated from the investigation.

Patrick wouldn't say the last week had been the hardest of his life – he'd had much darker weeks – but they had been long, frustrating and exhausting. Huge pictures of Isabel and Liam hung in the incident room. Their images were burnt into the retinas of every man and woman on the team. But so far, though Patrick would never admit this in public, they hadn't got a bloody clue what had happened to the two kids or where they were.

It was as if they had evaporated.

A red light caught them and Patrick saw another phantom infant flash before his eyes, running between the stopped cars. His whole body thrummed with the need for sleep.

'When you were younger,' he said, 'did you ever think you'd be spending your evenings locked in a room with a paedophile with a comb-over and halitosis?'

'Oh god, don't remind me. It's in my nostrils. What causes that smell?'

'Rotting gums. They should send him round schools as a warning to children about cleaning . . . Or maybe not – what the fuck am I saying?'

The interview had been a waste of time. Chris Davis was sixty now and had served his time for the abduction of a little girl thirty years before. But as he lived only a few streets away from Isabel

Hartley and her family, he was on the list. But he hadn't done it. He had an alibi for the disappearances of both Izzy and Liam.

It had been almost a week since Isabel had vanished, and five days since Liam. The chances of finding them diminished with every passing day – no, every hour.

'What do you think they should do to people like Davis?' Carmella asked. 'Chemical castration? String 'em up? You should hear me ma, the things she says about child murderers. Like Baby P – she was on one of those Facebook groups calling for his stepdad to have his balls ripped off in front of a baying crowd, and salt rubbed into his bleeding, empty . . .'

He winced. 'Carmella! Please!'

'Sack.' She grinned wickedly. 'With respect, Sir, you're a lightweight! All those muscles and tats, everyone thinks you're such a hard man, don't they? But they don't know what I know – you're a sensitive little flower at heart, aren't you?'

He made a mock-scary face at her and she laughed, then looked serious. 'But I want to know – what *do* you think?'

Lock them up in the dark forever. Put a bullet through their skulls. Make them pay for the pain they've caused. But he didn't say that. He said, 'I don't care what happens to them afterwards. My job is to catch them.'

Carmella raised a dubious eyebrow. She was a pretty woman, thought Patrick. Actually, that wasn't the word. 'Pretty' was a well-kept suburban garden. Carmella was more like a wild meadow into which someone had chucked random handfuls of seeds, with her corkscrewing auburn hair, dark Italian eyes and Dublin accent.

Patrick's mobile rang.

'Oh shit.' All he wanted – *all* he wanted right now – was his bed. His body screamed at him to ignore the chiming phone.

'Can you get that?' he said, nodding at the dashboard where the phone vibrated on the plastic.

She studied the display. 'It's Mike.'

DS Mike Staunton was another member of the MIT and part of the team investigating the abductions. He was young, keen, good at his job, slightly irritating.

Carmella held the phone against his ear.

'Mike.'

'Sir. Where are you at the moment?'

'Driving home. Why, what's happened?'

'I just got a call from the station – someone's phoned in and reported seeing a man with a couple of little kids going into an abandoned building on the Kennedy Estate in Whitton. They reckon they can hear kids crying. It's probably nothing but thought I'd better call you – want me to check it out?'

'The Kennedy? We're about five minutes from there. Leave it with us.'

Carmella sat up in her seat. 'The Kennedy?'

'Yeah. My favourite place to go just before midnight.'

He fiddled with the CD player, looking for something to buoy his spirits and wake him up. *Inbetween Days* came on and he turned it up.

Beside him, Carmella groaned. 'Not this lot again. Haven't you got anything current?'

He drummed the steering wheel and nodded his head. Passing a bus stop he saw a toddler dash in and out of sight. Another hallucination. 'Carmella, I'll make a Cure fan of you if it's the last thing I do.'

The Kennedy Estate was one of those places where the police went in pairs, where, in his less politically correct moments, Patrick thought the *Jeremy Kyle Show* must hold their castings. A snakepit, where the most poisonous and dangerous members of society slithered, but also a sad place, where elderly residents barricaded themselves away, where children were born not with a silver spoon but its opposite: rusty, burnt, smack-stained. Hope didn't come to die among these ugly high-rises and piss-stinking underpasses, because hope had never dared venture here.

'JFK would be so proud they named this shithole after him,' Carmella commented as they drew up outside a dark building on the edge of the estate.

They got out of the car and looked up at the building. Most of the windows were boarded up. Not a single light shone in the remaining flats. It was, it seemed, abandoned, ready for demolition, or perhaps the council would wait for nature to do its work, let it crumble, or leave it for future civilisations to marvel at. In the meantime, it provided a haven for squatters.

'Is it always this quiet around here?' Carmella asked.

Patrick looked about. 'It does seem unusually tranquil.'

From within a nearby tower block, a dog howled and a man shouted for it to shut the fuck up.

Carmella said, 'That's the word I would have used. Tranquil. Reminds me a little of the place Jenny and I went on honeymoon.' She sighed.

'Most people who live here are too afraid to come out after dark.' He lifted the boot and took out a sturdy torch. If he was an American cop he would have a gun, but he had no weapons with him at all. Still, the intention here was to investigate, that was all. The first sign of danger and he would call for back-up, although this wasn't remotely reassuring – it only took a second for a finger to pull a trigger, or a hand to plunge a knife . . . 'Stay close behind me.'

The front door of the building collapsed from its hinges when he pulled it, almost landing on his foot.

'That was the first booby trap.'

They went inside and were instantly hit by the stench of shit and rot. Patrick tried the light switch. Of course, it didn't work. They paused in the stairwell next to the lift, the doors of which stood open, revealing several bags of stinking rubbish.

He gestured for Carmella to follow him up the stairs, the torchlight bouncing off the graffiti-defaced walls. Lots of pictures of penises. Big ones, small ones, hairy ones, spurting ones. Mostly big, hairy, spurting ones. It was enough to give a man a complex.

'This place smells worse than Chris Davis's breath,' Carmella whispered.

'It smells like a Glastonbury toilet.'

They stepped into the first floor hallway, the torchlight illuminating a row of doorways, a few of which stood open or lacked doors entirely. In the deep silence, Patrick's ears whistled faintly, his tinnitus a war wound from attending too many gigs when he was younger. Nowadays, the silence reminded him of those loud, sweaty, exciting nights, and his older self wished he'd worn ear plugs or not stood so close to the amps.

'I can't believe that whoever took Izzy and Liam would bring them here. It has to be—'

Something shot out of a doorway and Carmella gasped, grabbing Patrick's arm.

'It's just a rat,' he reassured her.

The rodent paused on the path before them and sniffed the air before sauntering back into the flat.

Carmella laughed. 'That scared the—'

Patrick grabbed her upper arm and put his finger to his lips. 'Hear that?'

'If you're going to make some wisecrack . . .'

'No, listen.'

They stood in the silence and Carmella cocked her head and stilled her breathing.

'I can't hear—'

'There.'

She stared at him. 'Oh my god.'

From somewhere above them, so faint it was barely audible, came a child's cry. They paused for another few seconds, and it came again. *Waaah.*

'It's coming from one floor up,' Carmella said. She took out her phone, the screen glowing in the darkness.

'No. Let's check it out first.' He took a few slow steps back towards the stairwell, his partner just behind him.

'It didn't sound like a toddler,' she said. 'More like a baby. A newborn.'

'That's what I thought.'

'What do you reckon?' she whispered. 'Some junkie mother who's squatting here with a baby?'

'We'll know in a minute.'

They crept up the concrete steps to the next floor. The smell was even stronger up here, a blend of urine and damp and rotting food. A dog barked in the distance, but when it fell quiet the sound of the baby crying returned, closer this time.

Patrick pushed open the door, which squeaked like a squeezed mouse, and stepped through, shining the torch along the row of doors. They were all shut, except the third one along, which was slightly ajar. He took a deep breath, through his mouth, and trod as lightly as he could towards the door.

From within, he heard someone cough.

He looked back at Carmella, who had her phone out, ready to call for back-up at a moment's notice.

Patrick went through the door, into a pitch-black entrance hall. There was a large hole in one wall. Something crunched beneath his feet and he shone the torch at the floor. A syringe. He gestured for Carmella to be careful.

The door to what must be the living room was shut. From the other side of this door he heard it again: the cough, and then the faint crying sound of a baby. He couldn't figure out why it was so faint. It sounded like it was locked in a box.

He held up three fingers, then counted them down: three, two, one.

He went in, calling, 'Police.'

He swept the room with his torch. A figure sat slumped in the corner, cloaked in darkness, not moving. Beside the figure, a pram – the old-fashioned sort. And from within the pram came the muted baby's cry.

He thought the figure in the corner was unconscious from the way the head drooped – until it jumped up and screamed at them.

Words leapt over one another, barely legible, but two words stood out from the jumble: *My baby. My baby.*

He shone the light into the face of a woman, an old woman with lines clawed in her face by decades of rough living, crooked yellow teeth, the witch from Hansel and Gretel brought to life. 'Not my baby!' she screamed, pulling the plastic doll from the pram and clutching it against her.

Patrick had figured it out almost as soon as he'd entered the room.

'Hello, Martha,' he said. 'Don't worry, we're not going to hurt your baby.'

Five minutes later, Patrick and Carmella were back in the car.

'Don't tell anyone,' Carmella said. 'But when she jumped up and started screaming at us, I almost sprang a leak.'

Martha – no-one knew her surname, or if Martha was even her real first name – was well known in the area. The locals sometimes called her Mother Hubbard or just the Crazy Baby Lady. She could often be seen pushing her ancient pram, mostly in and around the cemetery, a pram that contained many dolls plus one particularly life-like one that Martha treated as if it was a real baby. Her child. She had been around for all of Patrick's career – a decade and a half. Despite appearing to be insane, and to fully believe that the doll was real, she had been replacing its batteries for years, so it continued to cry and occasionally say 'Mama.'

'Any idea why she's like that?' Carmella asked.

Patrick switched on the car lights. It was beginning to rain, a light summer drizzle come to gently wash the streets. 'There are lots of rumours. That she lost her baby in a house fire, or that she accidentally let her own child drown in the bath. Who knows? Maybe she never had a real baby of her own.'

'So sad.'

Patrick nodded. 'I really need to sleep,' he said, as much to himself as Carmella.

Which was when his phone rang again. The moment he answered it and heard the words 'Another child's gone missing' he knew he wasn't going to be getting any sleep that night – or, indeed, for days to come.

Chapter 3
Helen – Day 1

Helen sank to the floor, landing on the fluffy pink and yellow rug by Frankie's bed. She squeezed her eyes shut, trapping her tears.

The police. This was real. It was actually happening to her, the worst thing that could ever happen to a parent. The very worst thing. In the papers, they talked about child abduction as 'every parent's worst nightmare', a cliché so well-used it had lost its power. But here it was.

For a moment, as she'd charged into Frankie's room after she and Sean got home, she had thought that her initial fear was unfounded. She wished she could return to that moment now. Freeze it, live in it . . .

She often found Frankie asleep on the carpet when she climbed out of bed at night, and there was a dark shape on the floor on the far side of Frankie's toddler bed. Blaming the alcohol, she cursed herself for being so melodramatic and bent to lift her up, but as she walked around the bed she saw immediately that it wasn't Frankie at all, but her huge Tigger soft toy, the one her godmother had given her. There was a blanket over him – presumably Alice and Frankie had tucked him in down there as part of Frankie's bedtime routine.

The smile had fallen off her face and Helen had flung aside the toy, as if Frankie might have been hiding underneath. Her panic was back, stronger than ever. She'd lunged for the overhead light switch and the room had flared into harsh white light, diluting the magic lantern's lazy whirls down to nothing.

'Frankie?' she'd called, not loudly, not yet, part of her still thinking how foolish she'd feel when she threw open the wardrobe door and there she was, or how scared Frankie would be to hear her yelling . . . but she wasn't there. Helen had run along the landing, looking in the bathroom and the two other bedrooms on the first floor, then pounding up the narrow twisty attic stairs to Alice's room in case she'd sneaked into her bed.

'Frankie!' Louder this time, loud enough that Sean had heard her from the living room.

'What's the matter?' His voice had sounded faint – and irritated, which upset Helen. Obviously there was a problem, if she was shouting for their daughter at almost midnight!

'She's not here! Sean, she's not here!'

Helen took both flights of stairs two at a time, almost slipping on the bottom one as she'd swung around the newel post and pushed past her husband. Sean tried to grab her but she slipped out of his reach and ran over to where Alice was still fast asleep on the sofa.

'Alice – Alice! Where's Frankie? She's not in her bed, I can't find her. Where is she? Wake up!' She shook her stepdaughter's shoulder but even though Helen was yelling in her ear, Alice had just groaned and buried her face in the sofa cushions.

'Wake *up*, you stupid, irresponsible little—'

'Helen!' Sean barked. 'That's not helping. Alice – wake up sweetheart. We need you to wake up.' He too had shaken the girl's shoulder, softly at first but then with more urgency as she still didn't open her eyes.

'Hel, she looks really poorly,' Sean said, rolling her over onto her back. 'Why won't she wake up?' He had patted her cheek gently and bent over her, sniffing, presumably for alcohol or drugs. Helen had to clench her fists behind her back to prevent herself actually slapping Alice awake.

'Oh Sean, what if she went outside? Alice was passed out, she could've just wandered out into the street, anything could have happened. What do we *do*?'

The last word rose on a wail of increasing panic. Helen's head was full of images of people carrying away children; the grainy hooded figure caught on CCTV unstrapping Liam from his car seat and running; the faceless thief who had taken Izzy from her house . . .

'It's him!' she had gasped, unable to breathe at all. 'The same person who took Izzy and Liam, I know it. I *knew* something bad was going to happen, I felt it, and now look – ALICE, WAKE UP!'

She had bawled into her ear, and Alice moaned and thrashed on the sofa. It was true, she did not look at all well, but at that moment Helen felt nothing but frustration and irritation. Every moment spent trying to get her to wake up was a moment when Frankie could be further away. She dashed through the open plan living room into the kitchen, filled a glass of water and ran back, throwing it right into Alice's face, the water rushing through Sean's fingers as he instinctively raised a hand to stop it.

The girl had finally opened her eyes and squinted up at them, water streaming off her cheeks and eyelids. She spluttered as some went in her mouth. 'Wha . . . wha?'

'Talk to her, Sean,' barked Helen. 'I'm going to check the garden and the garage.' Later she would be glad that Alice had been sufficiently out of it not to have been aware of the tone of her voice. She hadn't meant to sound so harsh.

She left Sean tenderly wiping the water off his daughter's face with his sleeve, and tore towards the garden. The patio doors were locked, so she ran to the kitchen door – despite her explicit instructions, it was unlocked. Flicking on the deck lights, she flung open the door and ran in mad circles around the garden, searching every dark bush and flowerbed, even up the old pear tree, in the shed, the garage, under the table tennis table, calling Frankie's name so loudly that lights began to pop on in the bedrooms of the neighbouring houses.

She'd run back inside, where Alice was now sitting up on the sofa, rubbing her face, dazed.

She could hear Sean's footsteps upstairs, as if he was repeating her search, like he wouldn't believe Frankie was gone until he'd seen it for himself.

Helen had stopped still for a moment, as if the enormity of the situation had landed on her like an anvil, pinning her to the spot. Then nausea had begun to erupt without warning from the pit of her stomach, and she turned to run for the downstairs loo. She didn't make it – her hand was on the door handle about to pull it but the force of the explosion made any further movement impossible. Vomit had gushed all over the patterned carpet runner on the hall floor, filling up the gaps between the floorboards and splattering all over the loo door, a dark red despairing stain of *coq au vin, crème brûlée,* champagne, red wine, a reverse celebration, a mockery of the joy she had felt just an hour earlier now dripping down the walls.

Sean hadn't paused to rub her back or coo blandishments, the way he normally did when she was sick – but that was fine. She'd have screamed at him if he'd tried. He was on his mobile and out of the front door, shouting Frankie's name amongst the dark shapes of parked cars, behind front fences and up driveways.

Helen staggered into the kitchen, not even thinking of clearing up the mess she had just made. She wiped her face with kitchen towel, panting with terror and nausea, then made herself sip some water straight from the tap. When she bent her head to drink, her pulse pounded so hard in her temples that she had to hold onto the sink to keep herself standing upright.

'Don't panic, don't panic, she'll be fine,' she muttered in the direction of the fridge door, decorated with Frankie's daubings. 'She has to be. She's just wandered off. Not taken, no. Not taken.'

She gave an involuntarily whimper. When the dizziness had subsided enough for her to stand almost straight again, she realized she hadn't searched the kitchen, and ran around flinging open every single door – utility room, airing cupboard, washing machine, kitchen units – even the smallest one on top of the oven's extractor fan, as though she might find Frankie curled up in there with the Tupperware and spare light bulbs. She left them all gaping, her kitchen on display like the contents of her stomach, and climbed wearily back up the stairs to Frankie's room where she stood in the doorway, high on some terrible drug that she couldn't escape from, unmoored.

She heard Sean come charging back into the house, his footsteps steady and hard until a pause when he circumnavigated the puke in the hall, then up the stairs to find her.

'Nothing,' he said. He put his arms around her tightly. 'The police are on their way.'

Helen just gaped at him. Then she slumped against the doorframe and slid to the floor, sobs racking her body.

And she was still there now, on the fluffy little rug, unable to gather the strength to move. Waiting for the police. Waiting for someone to come and help them, to make it all better.

'Come on, sweetheart,' Sean said, bending to take her arm and help her up.

'This rug needs cleaning,' Helen said.

He blinked at her.

'Look at it!' She was aware that her voice was loud, that she sounded on the verge of hysteria. 'All these little clumps . . . Look.

Frankie knows she's not allowed to eat sweets in her room. I bet Alice sneaks them to her.'

'Helen, come on . . .'

The doorbell rang.

Helen leapt to her feet. Someone bringing Frankie home? Good news? Hope swelled inside her as she ran down the stairs, two at a time, almost falling. Sean was a step behind her.

She yanked open the door to find two uniformed police officers, a man and a woman, and as the female officer opened her mouth to speak Helen felt a chill go through her, a premonition. She was never, ever going to see her beautiful little girl again.

The policewoman led her, sobbing, back inside her house.

Chapter 4
Patrick – Day 1

Sean and Helen Philips, the couple who had reported their child missing, lived in Teddington, in a street of large Victorian houses with a probable combined value greater than the GDP of Luxembourg, a stone's throw from Bushy Park. Not, Patrick mused, that people round here would throw stones. What would they throw – teacups, dirty looks, barbed comments? Patrick rubbed at his eyes, feeling slightly delirious. The truth was that he felt more comfortable in places like the Kennedy. At least there he knew exactly what people would throw, would be too busy ducking to enjoy the luxury of a muse.

He and Carmella approached the house, a chunky double-fronted red brick with a wisteria-covered portico over the door, and a neatly landscaped front garden. It was one of those houses that looked too smart to live in, gleaming glossy paintwork on the front door and around the windows, and not a pebble out of place on the gravel driveway. He would put money on them having a weekly organic 'vegbox' delivered, and that there'd be skis in the garage and a Polish cleaning girl coming in twice a week.

When Isabel was taken, Patrick had initially been convinced that a ransom demand would imminently follow, but none came.

The same with Liam. When a child is taken from a well-off family, the first assumption is that money must be the primary factor. But so far there was no evidence of that, which made these cases not only less fathomable but more frightening. Over the past week, the people in this part of south-west London had become jittery, as though the local branches of Starbucks had been accidentally serving up coffees containing quadruple shots. More than jittery. The people of the borough of Richmond-upon-Thames were terrified.

And the pressure on the police, on MIT9 in particular, was like nothing Patrick had experienced before, even when there'd been a serial rapist-and-murderer slicing lives apart in Sutton, or during the James Lawler case, when a gang of white kids had beaten a black schoolboy to death at 4:30 in the afternoon. With intense media and public interest, this case had immediately been classified as a critical incident, the most high-profile investigation Patrick had been involved in. This was the kind of pressure Bowie and Queen sang about, and the last couple of nights Patrick had gone to bed with that insistent bassline bouncing inside his skull.

He checked his watch. 00:29. As he knocked on the door, his body tapped into its adrenaline reserves. *Here we go*, he thought. *Here comes the rush.* He closed his eyes for a second, let it wash over and through him, like a blast of minty air that made his veins tingle and his skin prickle. He cast off his tiredness like a snake sloughing its skin. He was ready now.

Beside him, Carmella yawned.

He shot her a look. 'Whatever you do, do not yawn in front of this family.'

'Sorry, sir.'

A uniform opened the door, an expression of mixed recognition and relief passing across her tired features at the sight of Patrick and Carmella.

'Evening, sir. PC Sarah Hayes, and this is PC Viv Mortimer . . .' She looked as though she was about to say more, then stopped, embarrassed. For a moment, Patrick thought she was going to thank him for coming, as though she was hosting some sort of grim drinks party. PC Mortimer was lurking awkwardly in the hallway, and Patrick hoped that the pair had displayed more confidence than this in dealing with the Philipses. From the living room he could hear the low rumble of a man's voice, the rising and falling tremolo of a woman's.

'I asked them to stay in there, sir,' said PC Hayes. 'Till we had a chance to brief you.'

He gestured for the uniforms to accompany him back through the front door, out of earshot of the family.

'Brief away.'

PC Hayes had a notepad in her hand, but didn't refer to it. 'Sir, we have Sean and Helen Philips. They went out for the evening, leaving their daughter – actually, she's Sean's daughter and Helen's stepdaughter – to babysit. The daughter is called Alice.'

'How old?'

'Fifteen, sixteen in August.'

'And what about the other child, or children – who was she babysitting?'

'Just one, sir, the abducted. Three years old; Frankie. She's the daughter of both Sean and Helen. Like I said, they went out, for a meal at a restaurant called Retro.'

'Very nice,' said Carmella.

'They got back here at 23:25 and found Alice asleep on the sofa. Mrs Philips says she went straight up to check on Frankie – and she wasn't there. The first thing they did was wake Alice up, who had no knowledge of Frankie's whereabouts. They searched the house, then Sean went out and looked in the gardens, front and back, and the immediate street, then called us. That was at 23:35.'

'Any sign of a break-in?'

'We haven't touched anything in the house, sir, but the Philipses told us the back door was unlocked. Mrs Philips is sure the door was locked when they went out – and she says she told Alice to lock it again if she let the cat out. Alice swears that she didn't see the cat all evening and hasn't been near the back door.'

Patrick gestured to the front door. 'This door was locked?'

'That's what they say.'

He groped in his inside jacket pocket and produced the electronic cigarette he always carried around with him. He'd been quitting and re-starting smoking for a decade, and this was his latest attempt at giving up. Unfortunately it was a bit like having sex with a blow-up doll – he imagined – or eating quorn bacon. Still, it delivered a hit of nicotine and he needed one now. He sucked on it, noticing that PC Hayes smirked slightly at the way the end lit up green.

He exhaled a cloud of water vapour and said, 'OK, I want to talk to the family. Carmella.'

She followed him into the living room.

The three family members were occupying separate parts of the three-piece suite. On the left, farthest from the door, Sean Philips perched on the edge of a cream armchair, casting anxious glances at his wife, who sat on the far right, in another armchair. Between them, the teenage daughter was collapsed on the sofa, slumped back into the cushions, a stunned expression on her face.

Both Sean and Helen stood up as he entered the room, Helen moving closest to him, Sean just behind.

'Good evening, Mr and Mrs Philips, Alice. My name is Detective Inspector Patrick Lennon and this is my colleague Detective Sergeant Carmella Masiello. You must be frantic with worry, so let's not waste any time.'

The first thing Helen Philips said was, 'Is it him? The man who took Izzy and Liam?'

She was shaking, her fists clenched tight by her sides, and she was giving him that look, the one he knew so well. The kind of look dying people give surgeons – desperate, hopeful. He couldn't help but think that she was going to look great on TV, that the papers were going to love putting her picture on the front page. The beautiful, haughty mixed-race woman, huge brown eyes, sharp cheekbones, Cupid's bow lips. And there, on an antique sideboard, were rows of framed photographs, among them a solo picture of a little girl, a photo that must have been taken in a studio by a pro. A gorgeous kid with her mum's huge eyes and soft wispy dark brown curls. The papers were going to love putting her on the front page too.

Patrick crossed to the sideboard, fingers hovering over the picture. 'May I?'

Helen looked away from the photo as if it burned her eyes, but Sean nodded.

Patrick held up the picture. 'This is Frankie?'

'Yes.'

Sean's voice was flat and low. There was a trace of Estuary in his voice, Essex or north Kent. He was a few years older than Patrick, late thirties, and he looked like he kept himself fit – slim with a firm jaw. He seemed to be trying very hard to keep it together right now, as if even being in this room was killing him. He wanted to be out there, searching for his little girl.

Tears rolled down Helen's cheeks and Sean tried to put his arm around her but she shrugged him off.

'You didn't answer my question,' Helen said. 'Is it him?'

Patrick replied in a voice that was firm but with a velvety nap of softness. 'We have no way of knowing that yet, Mrs Philips. Right now, we're keeping all options open. It's only just over an hour since you discovered that Frankie wasn't in her bed. We need to keep an open mind.'

'No!' Helen shook her head vehemently. 'She hasn't just wandered off. She's been taken.'

Sean joined in. 'Shouldn't you have roadblocks up, helicopters out there, search teams? I should be out there searching. Not standing around here chatting.'

He took a step towards the door. Carmella moved into the centre of the doorway, blocking the exit. Sean made an exasperated sound in his throat.

Patrick said, 'Mr and Mrs Philips, the first thing we need to do is talk to you, establish exactly what happened.'

'We got home, our daughter was gone. That's what happened,' Sean said.

Helen was chewing her index finger, staring at the floor. She looked up at Patrick. 'At least she's got Red Ted with her.'

Patrick waited for her to continue.

'She's had it since she was born,' she said. 'She never sleeps without it. Ever. I searched her room and it's not there.' The last few words were stifled by a sob.

Patrick gave her a few moments, during which she allowed her husband to put his arm around her. A thought of Bonnie and her grubby Peppa Pig flashed into his mind. Peppa was his daughter's Red Ted equivalent. 'Mr and Mrs Philips, I need you to come to the station.'

'No way,' Sean interjected. 'What if someone brings her back? We need to be here.'

'We'll have officers here. But we need to examine the house, look for evidence.'

'Forensics?' Sean said.

'Among other things. We can't do that with you in the house, I'm afraid. And I would appreciate it if we could talk to you tonight. While it's all fresh in your heads.' They stared at him, unblinking. 'I promise you – we are going to do everything we can to find Frankie.'

They acquiesced. As Carmella prepared to lead them from the room, Patrick turned his attention to the girl who had thus far remained silent. She had stood up and slipped her hand into her dad's. She kept her head down, and her hair fell around her face so he couldn't see her properly. But while he'd been talking to Sean and Helen he'd sneaked glances in Alice's direction. She'd been watching him too, wide-eyed, staring at the tattoos visible on his forearms, although he couldn't tell if it was with approval or disgust. Above all, she looked worried and scared. But her body language, the way she hugged herself and flinched whenever her father and stepmother spoke? That told him that of the three of them, she almost certainly had the most useful story to tell.

Once Carmella had left to escort the Philipses to the station, Patrick checked that the SOCOs were on their way, along with the other members of the team. There would be a lot of disgruntled spouses left sleeping alone tonight. That was one of the good things about being single – to all intents and purposes at least. No one to make him feel guilty.

He trod through the silent house, going into the kitchen first, thinking about how the media were going to go crazy when they heard about this one, about the panic that would ensue. And the pressure on his team, which was intense already – it didn't seem possible that it could get worse, but he knew it was about to. It was like going from 2-0 to 3-0 down in the first half of a match you couldn't afford to lose.

Three children in one small area of London within a week. A living room, a car and now a bedroom. The person the press were calling the Child Catcher was getting braver, daring to go upstairs now, like the urban fox that had caused almost as much hysteria when it crept into someone's house and tried to drag their baby out. Of course, he shouldn't assume that it was the same person in all three cases. But unless it was a copycat – and Patrick had never actually come across a copycat criminal in over a decade of police work – or some kind of insane social phenomenon, this had to be the work of the same person. A person whose need to commit these crimes was escalating rapidly.

He slipped on a pair of disposable gloves and examined the back door, peering through into the darkness of the garden.

Something thumped against the glass and he jumped. It was a cat, a ginger specimen, jumping up at the door, trying to get in.

'Better catch yourself a mouse tonight, mate,' he said.

The keys were in the lock. He made a note in his pad and looked around the kitchen. A lone wine glass stood on the draining board. A takeaway pizza box poked out of the bin. There was a very faint smell of cigarette smoke. Was that what had happened? Alice had opened the back door to have a crafty fag while her parents were out? And she was too frightened to admit it? Patrick could understand that if it was the case. He still didn't smoke in front of his parents – not even his fake fag.

He left the kitchen and, after a brief look round downstairs, went up to the first floor. Frankie's room was the second door on the left, immediately identifiable from the picture of a cartoon fairy on the door. Pushing it open gently, he went inside and looked down at the bed. Unmade, a small dent in the pillow, a pair of teddies at the foot of the quilt, presumably neither of them the treasured Red Ted. Forensics would need to do a thorough examination of this room – assuming Frankie didn't turn up in the next few hours – so he didn't want to disturb anything, but his eyes were drawn to a little desk beneath the window, with an equally miniature chair. An art desk, piled high with crayons and felt-tips and a big pile of colouring books.

There were a few sheets of paper in the centre of the desk, pens left next to them with their lids off. With everything else in the room so neat and tidy, Patrick wondered if Frankie had done these drawings since her mum and dad went out.

He picked up the top picture, holding it between gloved fore-finger and thumb. A picture of what he thought was supposed to be a cat, drawn in orange. The very cat that was miaowing outside the back door now.

The picture beneath this one, though, was more intriguing. He crouched down to look at it better. A large square, with a cross through it – the universal child's rendition of a window. In one corner of the window, an imperfect circle. A circle with two more circles inside it, a line and a curve.

Eyes, a nose and a mouth.

It was, Patrick realised, a picture of a face looking through a window.

But looking out – or in?

Chapter 5
Helen – Day 1

'What was your name again?'

Helen squinted at the detective as though she'd never seen him before, even though he had been in her house not half an hour earlier. She had automatically asked his name – cooperative, polite, the well–brought up girl who knew her manners . . . as if good manners would make any difference! Fuck it, she would have shattered every pane of glass in the building with her screaming, if screaming was the way to return her daughter to her.

What was she doing here, at 1 A.M., in this weird lemon-painted room, when she should have been sated and snug in bed with Sean, in the deep sleep of the wine-tipsy post-orgasm? She longed to be able to rewind time to that moment before she'd stepped into Frankie's room, back when everything had been alright. Further than that, to the moment when she and Sean had gone out. She would rewrite the script, change the future. But this was real life, and time could not be rewound, reality could not be altered. At that second, she felt in every cell of her body that if any harm had come to her baby girl, she would kill herself. Continuing to live just wouldn't be an option.

'DI Lennon,' he said, lighting up one of those water-vapour fake cigarettes.

'Can I call you Helen? Sorry for the inhospitable time of night.'

'Helen's fine,' she muttered, watching the end of the plastic fag glow green as DI Lennon sucked hard on it. She had to sit on her hands to try and stop them from shaking, and she could feel the imprint of the diamond from her engagement ring digging into the underside of her left thigh.

She pressed harder, welcoming the pain.

'I'm sure you appreciate that the sooner we can build a complete picture of what we're dealing with here, the greater the chances are of finding Frankie quickly.'

The sound of her daughter's name spoken by this man sent a current through her body. He had a nice voice, deep and kind, with a softening trace of a West Country accent in there somewhere. Patrick seemed to notice the tiny little involuntary jerk she gave, and she saw the sympathy in his face.

Under normal circumstances, she thought, he would make her feel flustered. A woman in uniform walked in and handed her a coffee that she didn't recall asking for, and as she sipped it, she worried irrationally that he looked more like the bass player in a rock band than a detective: hard-bodied, if slightly slope-shouldered. She focused on his face instead and saw that, under the handsomeness, it was still boyish, and kind – the sort of man you can visualize in a school portrait, aged about five, looking exactly the same but with more hair, softer skin and smaller teeth.

'Do you have kids?' she blurted, leaning forwards, willing him to reply in the affirmative. He paused before nodding his head, and her aching eyes filled with fresh tears.

'But even if I didn't, I would still do everything possible to get Frankie back for you, Helen,' he said, and the kindness and urgency in his voice made her tears spill in two straight lines down her cheeks and drip off her chin. 'Let's make a start, shall we?' He clicked on a voice recording machine.

'Could you run through your movements again for me this evening, Helen? I know we talked about it at the house, but we need to get it down on record. Have a particular think about whether anything unusual happened – if you've spotted anyone hanging around, or coming to the house . . .'

Helen wiped her face and took a deep breath. She recounted the events of the evening, although had to stop several times to compose herself. The thought of her and Sean enjoying wine, celebrating, kissing and laughing, while Frankie was . . . Frankie was . . .

Nobody knew where Frankie was.

'What did Alice say when you got in?' Patrick asked her casually, and she felt irritated.

'As I told you already, she was fast asleep. We had to chuck water at her to wake her up, she was so out of it.' Seeing DI Lennon's eyebrows ascend, she began to gabble. 'But she's very tired at the moment, she's just finishing her GCSEs and she had a dance class today too, so she was bound to be tired. Plus, we were about an hour later than we'd said we'd be.' Helen looked away.

'Oh? How come?'

Helen's lip trembled. 'We were celebrating. Sean said he was ready for us to have another baby, and I was so happy – it's what I've wanted for ages.'

DI Lennon smiled, but with his lips pressed together so it looked more like a grimace than a congratulatory expression.

'How long have you been married?'

Helen sat harder on her diamond, remembering Sean sliding it onto her fourth finger on that white hot beach in the Seychelles, a strange, tender, fierce look in his dark green eyes. 'Four and a half years. I was three months pregnant with Frankie. But we always wanted to get married anyway. We'd been together for two years before that. You know I'm not Alice's mother? Sean was married before.'

'I didn't know. She looks like you. So, Alice was how old . . . ?'

'Ten, when we married. She was a flower girl at our wedding. Eight, when we met.'

'Awkward age for a girl to accept her dad wanting to marry someone other than her mother,' Lennon said casually. 'Is she close to her own mother, Sean's first wife – assuming they were married?'

Helen wanted to scream at him: '*How is this relevant? Just FIND FRANKIE!'* She bit her lip. 'Sean's first wife died in a car crash when Alice was three.'

Lennon wrote something in his notebook. 'Did Sean date other women before you met him?'

Helen shrugged. Tears sprang into her eyes again – with every question he asked, Frankie could be quarter of a mile further away from her. 'I know you need to ask these questions, DI Lennon, but can't they wait till tomorrow? Surely the most important thing for now is to be out on the streets trying to find Frankie?'

Lennon patted her hand, but without condescension. 'I can see how you think that, Helen, but please know that we have a lot of bodies out doing just that, plus more officers scouring CCTV footage from around your house. My job is to build up a picture of your lives together, and I assure you that it's just as important.'

He handed her a tissue and she blew her nose.

'Sean had a couple of girlfriends, I think. He did a bit of internet dating. But when Alice was about six she started to object to him going out and leaving her with babysitters. So he didn't see anyone for a couple of years, then he met me. We met at Alice's school summer fair. I was there with my friend Samantha whose daughter Celia is my god-daughter. They'd roped me into helping her on the face-painting stall. Sean and Alice came along and we got chatting when I was painting Alice as a tiger. He checked that I wasn't married, then asked me out for a drink.'

Helen remembered that first look at Alice's pretty little face then, back when it had been a blank canvas, no tiger whiskers or stripes of hidden resentment and secret fury. How she'd been so attracted to this sexy dad that she could barely paint the orange marks on Alice's cheeks in straight lines.

'And how did Alice cope with you going out with her dad?'

Helen sighed. 'Not brilliantly. Tantrums and so on. It wasn't easy, and if I hadn't been so in love with Sean I might have given up. But we persevered, and now Alice and I are basically fine.'

'Basically?'

'She's fifteen. Everything's a drama. She's not afraid of having a go at me – or at Sean. But she adores Frankie, and would never do anything to hurt her. She'll be devastated that she's missing. How long will you need to keep her here?'

'Just till we've got her statement too. She's what we call a Significant Witness. Your neighbours, Mr and Mrs—' He consulted his notes. '—Jameson, have kindly offered to put you all up when we take you back. Your place is a crime scene for the moment, I'm afraid.'

'Pete and Sally. Oh. That's so kind of them. But OK.'

'So, tell me, Helen, has Frankie ever wandered off before?'

Helen sat up straight, gritting her teeth with sudden fury. 'Before? What do you mean, *before*? She's never wandered off, full-stop, and certainly wouldn't have done tonight! Once she's asleep she rarely wakes up till dawn. There's a stairgate at the top of the stairs that she can't open, she can't reach the front door Yale lock, and even if the back door had been left unlocked, she couldn't have got out through the garden gate.'

Lennon's reaction was calm, unruffled. He wrote a note in his black notebook, in such small squiggly writing that Helen couldn't make out what it was. Then he gazed into her eyes again.

'I didn't mean anything. Some kids are wanderers, some aren't. We just need to know that Frankie isn't.'

'She's not,' said Helen, visualizing Frankie fast asleep in her toddler bed, her cheeks hot and red in slumber, a snail trail of contented drool linking the corner of her mouth to her flannelette sheet, clutching Red Ted under one arm. The pain was like a knife in her stomach; she felt eviscerated by it.

Lennon stood up, walked across to a small table in the corner of the interview room and opened a cardboard folder.

'When did Frankie draw this?' he asked, removing a slightly crumpled piece of paper with one of Frankie's crayoned efforts on it. Helen took it and frowned.

'I've never seen it before.'

'Really? It was on the desk in her room when we searched it, under a drawing of a cat.'

Helen looked more closely at it, and her hand flew to her mouth when she realized what it was. 'Someone looking through a window at her? Oh my God!'

'It might not mean anything sinister,' Patrick reassured her. 'Frankie's bedroom window was still locked – we're certain no-one came in that way.'

'What if they put a ladder up, to look in?'

'Well, there isn't one there now. It's probably nothing relevant, but we just need to document everything.'

'I tidied up her room before we went out. There were definitely no drawings on the table then – she must have done them after her bath. When Alice was meant to be looking after her . . .'

'What makes you think she wasn't?'

Helen's hand shook as she held the drawing. 'Because Alice loves drawing too. She *always* helps Frankie with her drawings, adds background, does the bodies around the faces she draws, that sort of thing. They draw maps together too – funny little maps that

Frankie calls 'naps'. She dictates the landmarks and Alice draws them. They look so sweet when they get stuck into an art session, their heads together, tongues sticking out . . . She didn't really like drawing without Alice there.'

Her voice trailed away.

'Maybe Larry did come over after all,' she said eventually.

Lennon looked up from his pad. 'Larry?'

'Alice's boyfriend. She's not supposed to have him round when we're not there.'

The detective arched an eyebrow. 'You don't approve?'

'Oh, no, it's not that. But . . . well, I knew that if he was there Alice would be . . . distracted. When she was supposed to be keeping an eye and ear out for Frankie.'

Helen clenched her jaw as she watched Lennon scribble more lines in his fancy notebook. Why had she ever entrusted the care of her precious daughter to Alice? And what was all this about the drawing? Someone looking through the window . . . A wave of nausea hit her and it took all her strength to stop herself being sick.

She swallowed and looked up at the detective. When she spoke her words came out strangled. 'Please find her. You have to find her.'

His expression as he returned her gaze was understanding and his words heartfelt: 'Rest assured, Helen, I will move heaven and earth to get your little girl back safely.'

But it didn't make Helen feel any better.

She keeps staring at me, shrinking away like she's going to catch something. It's irritating me, as are the flies buzzing around the van, three big fat buggers that keep bouncing off the windows and evading me. This morning I woke up to find one of them sucking on my arm, which almost made me vomit. I guess I smell like shit, being stuck in this van for the past 24 hours, sticky from the heat and the excitement and fear. I keep fantasizing about showers, but I'm going to have to wait. Patience is something I'm good at, after all.

'Come on,' I say, offering her a bottle of Fruit Shoot. 'Have a drink.'

She screws up her pretty face and shakes her head.

'How about something to eat? Look, I bought you some chocolate.'

It's so hot in the van that when I unwrap the Freddo Frog, half of it squidges onto my fingers, the irritation this causes making my eardrums pulse.

'Drink,' I said, my voice firmer, pushing the purple bottle towards her. 'Drink, or I'll get cross.'

She looks at me with her big eyes, those beautiful lashes taking my breath away, just like they did the first time I ever saw her, and reluctantly takes the bottle, sucks from it.

'That's a good girl.'

I bought the sugary drinks and the chocolate and all the other food – the crisps and Haribo and fairy cakes – at the supermarket, scanning it all through the self-service machine, one of those wonderful inventions that makes it so easy to live without attracting attention. Okay, I had a brief moment of anxiety when there was an unexpected item in the bagging area, but the member of staff zoomed over and swiped her staff card without even looking at me.

It's growing dark outside now. Shadows creep into the van. I can hear music thumping somewhere in the distance, probably a party somewhere out there in someone's garden. You expect the countryside to be silent, just the hoots and scuffling of animals. But even out here, you can't get away from everyone. I need to keep moving, but I can feel London pulling me back, like I'm attached to it by a piece of elastic.

The Fruit Shoot has given her a burst of energy that makes her tremble. She asks me for a piece of paper and a pencil so she can do a drawing. She draws a house with stick people smiling from the windows.

Then she cries for a bit, sucking her thumb. 'Red Ted,' she says. 'I want Red Ted.'

That's about the hundredth time she's mentioned her teddy bear. I should have brought the bloody thing with me.

I suppress my irritation, helped because the flies have stopped bashing themselves against the windows, and tell her it's time for bed. I lift the quilt cover and she slips under, facing away from me, her hair splayed on the pillow.

I slip under the quilt with her, though there's barely enough room for both of us.

'Come on,' I say, and I put my arms around her.

Chapter 6
Patrick – Day 2

The first thing Patrick wondered when he woke up was why his pillow felt like it was made of wood. He opened his eyes at the same moment he realized he was still in the office, asleep at his desk. A stream of dribble trickled towards the framed photo of his girls. In it, Gill was gazing joyfully at the baby, back when Bonnie still had milk spots and a tuft of blonde hair that was as soft as kitten's fur. It was probably the last time he remembered seeing Gill truly happy and, like some kind of weird karma, the picture scraped at his heart like fingernails on a blackboard. He kept meaning to put it away, to replace it with a solo portrait of Bonnie now she was almost two. But he couldn't bear to.

He tilted his head from side to side, listening to his neck crunch. He poked the space bar on his keyboard and the screen sprang to life. If only he could wake up as quickly as the computer. It was 8:07 A.M. He must have fallen asleep at around 5 A.M.

'The guv wants to see you.'

He turned to see Carmella, looking fresher than a daisy on a dewy spring morning, holding out a Starbucks cup.

'You're an angel,' he said, before burning his top lip on the scalding coffee.

He texted his mum on the way to DCI Suzanne Laughland's office, and she replied with her customary swiftness, telling him that Bonnie was fine, that she'd slept through the night and was at this very minute carpeting the dining room floor with Weetabix. Bonnie was eighteen months into her messy phase and the thought of his mum stooping yet again to scrape soggy cereal off the floor, lift the toddler out of her seat and keep her entertained, change her nappies and deal with her tantrums, made him flinch with guilt. But Mum insisted she enjoyed it – as did his just-retired Dad.

It was not a conventional set-up, living with his parents at thirty-five, with his little daughter and without his wife, but right now it was the only thing that worked. The only way he could continue to do this job.

'Patrick, come in.'

He entered DCI Laughland's office and took a seat.

'You look knackered,' she said.

'Don't you start. I'm going to brave the shower in a minute.'

'Rather you than me.' The office shower was a pathetic, hastily installed addition to the unisex toilet, with water temperature that veered straight from scalding to freezing and back again. It was only ever used in times of dire need.

'And you've got a pink mark on your face that looks like the edge of a mouse mat.'

He rubbed his cheek. Suzanne Laughland and Patrick had worked together for a long time, stepping up ranks in tandem over the last ten years, Suzanne always one rung above him. She had ash-blonde hair, tied back neatly, and huge blue eyes that made her look years younger than her true age, despite the worry-lines on her brow and the deepening crinkles around her eyes. She wore the lightest touch of make-up, no jewellery apart from her wedding ring.

She had a picture on her desk too: of her and her husband, Simon. They had no kids. Patrick had never asked her why she'd chosen not to be a mum, or if she had indeed chosen it.

'I need you to give me an update,' she said, 'before we go in and brief the team.'

He told her about the interview with Helen Philips, and the subsequent interview with her husband, Sean.

'Any conflict in their testimonies?'

'Hmm. Not really. They both described the evening very similarly. They only disagree when it comes to Alice, the teenage daughter.'

Patrick watched Suzanne push a strand of hair from her face.

'Helen thinks there's a strong possibility that Alice had her boyfriend round – one Larry Gould. Carmella says that Sean is adamant she wouldn't do that without telling them. I should mention that Helen is Alice's stepmother.' He briefly described the family history.

'So Dad thinks Alice is a little angel who can do no wrong?'

'Exactly. I'm talking to her this morning. Their neighbour's agreed to come in and be her appropriate adult.'

Suzanne's mobile beeped and she glanced at it, her face creasing with irritation. Simon, Patrick hoped, enjoying the thought that his boss would be in a grump with the smug git.

'Alright, good,' she said. 'Keep me posted on that. I assume the FLOs are with the family now?'

'Yes. Sandra Godden and Li Chen. They're the most experienced FLOs we've got left. The others are with the Hartleys and the McConnells. The Philips family are staying with the next-door neighbours until the SOCOs are done.'

Suzanne came round the desk and perched on the edge of it, Patrick avoiding looking at her legs.

'Find out what you can from Alice. But don't spend too much time on it.'

He bristled. 'You don't need to tell me how to do my job, guv.'

'I know.' Her tone softened. 'But we are surely thinking this is connected to the other two abductions, which means the Philipses are not suspects.'

'I haven't ruled anything out yet.'

'But surely—'

'Yes, I know. It's either the Child Catcher—'

Suzanne winced. This was what the tabloids had started calling the unknown offender after a child at Sainsbury's who'd seen *Chitty Chitty Bang Bang* had reported seeing a man with 'a long nose' in the supermarket the day Liam had been taken.

'Sorry. Or it's a coincidence. Either way, Alice Philips is our most important Sig Wit and if her boyfriend was there, he's one too.'

'Let's go and talk to the team.' She paused before the door. 'We've got three missing kids now. Three! If we thought the public were panicking before . . . This is like a pandemic.'

'No, it's not.'

'What?'

'A pandemic is when a virus crosses international borders. All of these crimes have occurred within the same borough. It's an epidemic.'

She rolled her eyes and sighed. 'You're a fucking smart-arse, Patrick Lennon. Go and have your bloody shower and I hope it freezes your nuts off.'

But he was sure a smile flickered on her lips as they left the room.

As Patrick stood naked under the ridiculous trickle of alternately tepid, boiling and freezing water, he felt the ball of tension growing in his belly. Even now, after being the lead detective on a baker's dozen of cases, he still experienced an icy dread whenever he had to face the team, ten pairs of eyes on him. A psychologist he chatted to at a party once had told him that the feeling you get when you do something that scares you – like public speaking – caused the reptilian part of your brain to scream 'fight or flight', releasing all that intoxicating adrenaline into your system. The feeling he got when he stood up to talk to a crowd was, apart from his enduring love of The Cure and Brighton and Hove Albion, the last thing that linked him to his schoolboy self. He dismissed the memory of himself as a schoolboy by glancing in the mirror above the basin – the shower wasn't nearly hot enough to cause it to steam up. If he'd had those tattoos and muscles when he was fourteen, he doubted he'd have had the sort of problems he'd suffered at school when he'd been a skinny white misfit.

He replayed Suzanne telling him he was a smart-arse and the little smile that had appeared on her lips. It was the kind of exchange they would never have in front of anyone else, when they were strictly professional. It was difficult for men and women to be friends at work without rumours spreading about them, especially when one of them had authority over the other. It was irritating, just as it was irritating that some Neanderthals in the Force were resentful of women with higher ranks than them. Gill had asked him once if he minded that his superior officer was a woman and then joked that he liked to be given orders by powerful women. He smiled to himself. Maybe there was some truth in that.

He just about managed to get enough water over him to clean off the grime, and stepped out of the cubicle, drying himself with the tiny towel he'd had in his gym bag. It was hardly rejuvenating, but it was enough to make him feel halfway human again. He couldn't help glancing nervously at the toilet door to make sure it was locked – the last thing he needed before a briefing was one of his team to walk in and catch him naked, muscles or no muscles. Old habits died hard. Besides, they'd never take him seriously again.

Five minutes later he was in the incident room, aware that his team were staring at the damp hair curling onto his collar as he wrote the names on the whiteboard – Sean, Helen, Alice, Frankie – and described to the team what they already knew. He had to dismiss a brief uncomfortable thought that they would all know he'd been so recently naked at work, chiding himself for the moment of self-consciousness when there was so much else at stake.

Someone had already hung an enlarged photo of Frankie alongside the pictures of Izzy and Liam, and Patrick let his gaze linger on it for the moment, inviting everyone to do the same. *This* was their focus. These children, their families. Sometimes, in the din that reverberated around cases like this, it was easy to forget that.

MIT9 was one of the Met's twenty-four Murder Investigation Teams, all coming under the Homicide and Serious Crime Command. Despite their name, the MITs were not only responsible for investigating murder, but much of the other nasty shit that made Patrick wish his fantasy career as a rock star had got beyond a handful of terrible gigs in south-coast pubs. Manslaughter, serial rapes, infanticide, mass disaster – and missing persons cases where there was, to use the official language, 'substantive reason to suspect life has been taken or under threat'. This was one line he would never repeat to the parents of the missing kids.

'Right,' he said. 'You all know the drill by now.' He nodded at DS Staunton. 'Mike, I want you to coordinate house-to-house. Remember, we want any suspicious or strange activity over the last week – anyone seen hanging around, checking out the Philipses' house, anyone spotted sitting in a car or van outside the house. I don't even need to tell you this.'

Mike said, 'If it's anything like the other two, no one will have seen a bloody thing.'

'We might get lucky,' piped up DI Adrian Winkler. Six-foot-two, with shoulder-length black hair, longer and thicker than Patrick's own, and good-looking enough to complete the set of what most women were supposed to be interested in, Winkler was one of the other DIs on the team. His nickname was, inevitably, Fonzie, although it was more a sarcastic reference to the fact he thought he was the coolest man on earth than because he shared a surname with the actor who played the Fonz. 'There might be a curtain-twitcher living next door. Nice shower, by the way?'

'Better than nothing, thanks, Adrian,' Patrick said flatly. 'I want you coordinating the search teams, along with Preet.'

Winkler shot him daggers. 'Oh come on, Pat, not the fucking *search teams*. All those do-gooders tramping through the park looking for clues when you know most of them would rather be forming a lynch mob. DC Gupta and I have a lot better things to do with our time, you know.'

Patrick almost smiled, until Winkler added, 'When a lynch mob would actually be a much better idea. Help clear out some known sex offenders, get the nonces off our patch.'

'No problem, sir,' said DC Preet Gupta, stepping in before things got too heated. 'Come on, Adrian, they're just jealous we'll be out in the fresh air.'

But even the prospect of spending time with Preet, easily the prettiest of the detectives in the room, couldn't appease Winkler. Patrick had heard whispers over the last few days that Adrian was unhappy with how he, Patrick, was conducting the investigation. They'd had run-ins before, usually over Patrick's methodical way of doing things. Winkler was the kind of cop who preferred to drop bombs then sift through the fall-out. Patrick knew he was going to have to watch him.

Patrick continued dishing out responsibilities. CCTV for DC Sarah Trentner, DC Martin Hale checking social networks and phone records. The third DI on the team, Leanne Cornish, had the job of continuing to eliminate known offenders, not just in Richmond but all surrounding areas, including the parts of Surrey that came outside the Met's jurisdiction. None of it was a surprise. On day one of the investigation, after Isabel had vanished, the energy in the room was fizzing, like a team of hounds straining at their leashes. Now, though, everyone was tired, concussed through banging their heads against the brick wall of this case. The truth was, they had no leads. No idea at all what had happened to these children.

'Right, listen up,' Patrick said, forcing himself to make the speech. 'We've now got three sets of parents relying on us. Three *desperate* sets of parents. We need to keep our focus. We will find these kids. We will find the person who's taken them. We just need one stroke of luck, one little crack to appear in the case and then we can . . .' He wasn't quite sure where he was going with this. 'Put our fingers into the crack—'

Winkler smirked. Patrick could see ten pairs of raised eyebrows.

'—and prise it open. Um, prise that crack wide open until we see daylight.' He paused, gathered himself, ignoring the staring faces. 'So let's get out there. Team.'

He turned to the whiteboard and rubbed his eyes. Suzanne, standing by the door, gave him a curious look. He felt a little stab of resentment. She should be the one doing the motivational speeches. But then she gave him a little reassuring smile and he forgave her.

As the team dispersed, he walked over to her, gesturing for Carmella to join them. Before he could reach her, Winkler stepped in to his path.

'Do I really have to look after the fucking search team?'

'Yes. You do.'

Winkler opened his mouth to protest again, then some gears appeared to grind in his head and he changed tack.

'Alright, sir. Thanks for the speech by the way. We'll prise that crack open for you. You don't have to worry about my motivation.' He looked into Patrick's eyes. 'I mean, you know how I feel about people – men or women – who hurt their kids.'

He exited, leaving Patrick clenching his fists and counting to ten.

Winkler was one of those people who specialized in finding weak spots and poking them. Well, he had just got himself assigned to search party duty for the rest of this investigation. An image of Winkler crawling across Bushy Park on his hands and knees, dodging used condoms and dog shit, made him feel a lot brighter.

'I'll call a press conference for later this morning,' Suzanne said. 'The media are already going bonkers. We've got Sky News running a ticker about the case – they're camped outside here and the Philipses' house. Same with the BBC, ITV, all the papers.'

'Don't tell me, Perez Hilton is flying over to cover it too.'

Suzanne ignored him. 'Let's get a statement from the parents, read it out.'

'I can handle that,' said Carmella. She looked fresh this morning, Patrick thought enviously. *She* had probably had a nice long leisurely bath with lots of scented bubbles and a cup of tea brought to her by her wife.

'OK, good.' Suzanne nodded at Patrick. 'You were right. We will find them.'

Before he could respond, Mike poked his head around the door. 'Sir, your witness is here.'

Before going in to talk to Alice Philips, Patrick went to the Gents to splash some cold water on his already clean face, try to stop the tiredness pulling him into its murky depths. The shower hadn't done the trick. As he dried his cheeks on a scratchy paper towel, one of the cubicles opened and DI Winkler emerged.

'Keeping you up, are we?' he said, standing at the basin next to Patrick.

As Patrick moved towards the door, Winkler stepped into his path.

'Why'd you have to give me the search teams? Total waste of my skills. You know that.'

'Stop moaning, Winkler.'

The other man narrowed his eyes and drew himself up to his full height so Patrick was forced to look up at him.

'Must be handy having a wife in the loony bin,' Winkler said.

'What?'

'Yeah. Loads of opportunity to invite *Suzanne—*' he said her name like a ten-year-old teasing a classmate over a girl '—round to discuss tactics.'

'What the fuck are you insinuating?' Patrick tried to stay calm, his pulse accelerating.

'Oh nothing. Just a little word of warning. It must be very nice being the DCI's pet. But fuck this case up and you'll be in the doghouse.'

Patrick shook his head. 'Was that really the best you could come up with?'

He pushed past Winkler, their shoulders rubbing together. Before he left, he heard Winkler say, 'Poor kids.'

He span round. 'What did you say?'

Winkler held his hands up. 'Oh nothing. Just feel sorry for these kids, that's all.'

Patrick exited the Gents before he did something he regretted. Winkler had managed to press three of his buttons in one brief exchange. He looked down and realized his fists were clenched, his nails digging into his palms, leaving a row of little crescents.

Alice Philips was dressed all in black, with dark eyeliner, shiny boots and her naturally raven hair tied back with a scrunchie. She sat with her arms folded across her black T-shirt, obscuring the name of a band that Patrick was sure he wouldn't have heard of anyway. He had to face it: he was out of touch. Most of the CDs he bought these days were deluxe reissues of albums he'd loved twenty years ago. God, even buying CDs marked him out as a dinosaur. But he liked to think that he and this teenage Goth – or was she an emo? – had something in common, even though she would no doubt cringe if he told her that he used to dress like her, had long hair that he'd back-combed and dyed to make it look like hers.

Beside Alice sat her appropriate adult – the neighbour, Sally Jameson, a woman in her late fifties who reminded Patrick of Camilla Parker-Bowles, vaguely aristocratic, who kept shifting in her seat like she couldn't believe she was here, in a room in a police station that smelled like farts, when she should be eating strawberries and cream at Wimbledon. Sean and Helen had asked her to accompany Alice, understandably unwilling to spend any more time in an interview room.

Patrick opened his notepad while Carmella set up the video camera.

'How are you feeling, Alice?' he asked in a soothing voice.

She shrugged, then said, 'Sick.'

'You're not well?'

'No. Sick with worry about Frankie.'

The whites of her eyes were bloodshot, from tiredness or crying, perhaps both. Her body language was defensive, her arms wrapped tightly around her torso like she was freezing cold, despite the sticky warmth in the room. She would barely make eye contact, though that was normal for teenagers talking to cops. Beneath the desk, she jerked her legs up and down in a way that reminded Patrick of himself. Even today, his mum was always complaining about his restless leg syndrome.

'We just want to ask you about last night.'

'I don't know anything,' Alice blurted, hugging herself even more tightly.

Carmella said, 'Alice, there might be something that you don't know is important. So we need to go through everything. Is that okay?'

She said, 'Yeah,' looking straight into the camera.

'Alright,' Patrick said. 'Tell us what happened last night. From the point your mum and dad went out.'

'She's not my mum.'

'Sorry, your stepmum.' He made a mental note of the way she'd spat those words out.

'Helen,' she said, putting the emphasis on the first syllable.

'Go on, Alice,' Sally prompted. The girl nodded, like she was having a conversation inside her head, then said, 'So . . . Dad and Helen went out at about seven. I read Frankie some stories – she's obsessed with dinosaurs so pretty much all her books are about T-Rexes and velociraptors and stuff – either that or fairies – and then put her to bed. She's a good girl for me – she went down without making any fuss.'

'Was her bedroom window shut?'

'Yeah. Well, to be honest I didn't really look. I closed the curtains and I don't remember it being open. Oh my days, was it open . . . after?'

Patrick shook his head. 'No, I was just checking.'

'What, you think someone might have got in earlier and been, like, hiding in there? Someone could have been in her wardrobe or something while we were reading?'

'Alice, don't panic. We have no reason to think that.'

Sally reached over and tried to squeeze Alice's hand but she snatched it away.

'It's not my fault,' she said. 'She's my little sister. I love her to bits. Do you think I would do anything to put her in danger?'

Patrick could feel this interview wriggling fish-like from his grasp. But maybe it was good to give this girl space – because if she did know something, at this point it seemed pretty likely that she was going to blurt it out. He didn't reply, confident that Alice would feel the need to fill the silence.

She sat and twirled the silver skull ring on her finger.

'OK,' Patrick said at last. 'What happened after you put her to bed?'

'Nothing. I had dinner, watched telly.'

'No revision?' asked Carmella.

'I've finished all my exams, except one.' A hint of a smile. 'I'm almost free.'

Patrick checked his notes. Alice was an August baby, meaning she would have just taken her exams at the age of fifteen, one of the youngest in her year.

'Did you watch TV in your room or the living room?'

'Why?'

Patrick couldn't help but smile to himself. One day Bonnie would be like this.

Carmella replied. 'Alice, we need to know your movements within the house so we can work out what time the intruder might have got in, and their entry point.'

'Alright. Well, I had dinner straight after Frankie went to bed. So that was around eight. I ate it in the living room in front of the TV. Then I went up to my room for a bit to, like, listen to music and stuff. Then there was a film on that I wanted to watch so I went back downstairs. It started at ten.' She swallowed. 'But I fell asleep while it was on and the next thing I knew Helen was chucking water in my face.'

Patrick asked, 'Did you have the music on loud?'

'Eh? Oh, in my room. Not really.'

'Was it too loud for you to be able to hear if someone came in and went up the stairs?'

'Hmm. Yeah, I guess so.'

'What about if Frankie had made a noise – started crying or called out?'

'I would have heard that. I always hear her, even if I have my headphones on.'

Patrick understood that. There was something about the human brain that was designed to pick up children's cries, although he had always thought it was only one's own children you could hear.

'Did you leave your room at all between eight and ten?'

'No.'

'Not even to use the toilet?'

She looked at him as if the idea of this middle-aged man asking her about her visits to the loo was the most gross thing she'd ever heard. 'I've got my own bathroom.'

En-suite. Very nice. Patrick scribbled another note. 'When you left your room at ten and went downstairs to watch TV, did you check in on Frankie?'

She stared at the table. Next to her, Sally scrutinized her carefully. Alice's tone, when she replied, was defensive. 'No. I was sure she was asleep. I didn't fucking expect some fucker to waltz into our house and snatch her, did I? Otherwise I would have camped outside her room with a knife.'

'Alice, calm down,' said Sally, who had flinched at Alice's f-word double whammy.

Patrick adopted his most soothing voice again. 'We're not judging you. Alright?' Although he couldn't help thinking that this sort of bad language was pretty unusual, from a well-brought-up fifteen-year-old from an upper middle-class family in Teddington.

She nodded, refusing to meet his eye.

'OK. So, did you see or hear anything unusual at all?'

'No. Nothing.'

'Have you seen anybody or anything out of the ordinary near your house recently?'

'Like what?'

'Like, for example, people hanging around. Watching the house. Men you don't recognize.'

She wrapped her arms even more tightly around herself. 'Oh god, that's too creepy. No, I haven't.'

'Did you have anybody over last night?'

A second's hesitation, and her eyes flickered briefly up and to the right. 'No.'

Patrick, who had been acting as casually as he could when he asked her that question, looked up from his notepad and said, 'Are you sure?'

'Yeah, of course I'm sure. I'm not senile.'

'You didn't have your boyfriend round?' asked Carmella. 'Larry?'

'No! Who told you that?'

Carmella raised her palms. 'No one. I was just checking. I mean—' she leaned forward conspiratorially, '—I was a teenage girl once. I'd always have friends round if my parents went out.'

Alice sniffed. 'Well, I didn't. And I don't see how any of this could help find Frankie anyway.'

'We just want to know if there were any other potential witnesses,' said Patrick. 'Did you speak to anyone?'

'I might have talked to Larry on the phone briefly. Yeah, I did. And I Snapchatted Georgia. That's my best mate.'

Patrick had a vague idea this meant sending a photo that almost instantly deleted itself.

'And did you drink anything? Alcohol, I mean.'

She lifted her chin defiantly. 'I had a little glass of wine. Dad lets me have wine at home. He says most British teenagers turn into binge drinkers because they see alcohol as something forbidden. I'm not like that.'

'What about drugs?'

'Does my dad let me take drugs? Of course not.'

'I meant, did you take anything, smoke anything, last night?'

'For fuck's sake – sorry – no, I didn't.'

'What about cigarettes? You didn't pop out for a fag at any point?'

'I don't smoke.'

'Did you know the back door was open when your dad and Helen got home? Did you open it?'

'No.' Her eyes were wide.

'Are you absolutely sure? I'm sure your parents – I mean your dad and stepmum – aren't going to care right now if you went out the back and had a crafty cigarette.'

'I didn't. I swear.'

'You definitely didn't open the door?'

She looked sick. 'No. Listen, do you really think I would hide anything? All I want is for my little sister to come back. I want you to find her. I'm not going to tell you lies. I didn't . . .'

She started to cry and Sally gave Patrick a withering look, pulling Alice into a hug.

'End of interview,' Patrick said. Carmella switched off the video recorder.

'She's lying about the boyfriend,' Carmella said, as soon as Alice and Sally had gone.

'I know. But why lie about him coming round? That little speech she gave at the end sounded pretty convincing.'

'I expect she thinks that he didn't see or hear anything either, and she doesn't want to get into trouble. Her dad isn't going to be impressed if Frankie was taken while Alice was in her room shagging her boyfriend. But let's talk to him, see what his story is.'

'He won't want to talk to us. According to the info Helen gave us, he's seventeen and Alice is under age. He's going to think we'll do him for statutory rape.'

Patrick rolled his eyes. 'We'll have to convince him we don't give a shit about that. Unless we can use it in some way. Right, you get his address and, in the meantime, let's sort out this press conference.'

As they left the interview room, DS Staunton hurried around the corner towards them.

'Sir, there you are.'

'Mike?' Patrick asked, but from the expression on Mike's face he had a horrible feeling of foreboding.

The detective sergeant lowered his voice. 'They've found a body. A little girl.'

Chapter 7
Larry – Day 2

'Hey, could one of you do me a big favour, please?' Larry had put on his politest face, the one he used for the headmaster. The *butter wouldn't melt* face, his mum called it. He casually slewed his bike sideways in the wide alley running alongside Sainsbury's, and addressed the two schoolboys coming towards him in black blazers and stripy ties – from that nobby stage school across the Green, Larry recognized. They came to a halt, glancing at each other from under their fringes, but with curiosity rather than fear. The tall one was literally two feet taller than his mate, but something about them told Larry they were probably in the same school year, maybe 9 or 10.

'What, bruv?'

Bruv? Larry almost laughed out loud. This lanky posh twat had actually called him bruv? He matched his own language accordingly.

'Yeah, sweet – can I borrow your phone for a minute? Need to call me mum, innit, see if she's home as I ain't got a key and some tosser nicked my iPhone yesterday.'

The tall one hesitated, but the tiny one immediately put his hand into his blazer pocket and pulled out a phone. 'No worries, pal,' he said, smiling earnestly at Larry. 'As long as she don't live in Australia!'

They all snarfed politely. Larry took the phone. 'Galaxy S4,' he said, turning it over. Then he did two things simultaneously: popped the phone's back off, whipped out his flick knife and pressed the open blade menacingly but discreetly against the waist of the tall one, under his blazer.

'Sorry about this, but needs must, eh?' he said conversationally. 'But being decent, I'm letting you keep your SIM – take it out and I'll be out of your hair. Unless you want me to take the whole thing, you'd better be fucking quick about it.'

The mouths of both boys gaped open in shock and outrage as Larry handed the phone back to its owner. He applied a little pressure to the knife handle. 'Quick, I said.'

Panic in his eyes, the tall one removed his SIM card and reluctantly handed the phone back to Larry.

'Good boy,' Larry said, pocketing it and, still holding the knife, turning his handlebars towards the end of the alley. It was at that moment the smaller boy seemed to wake up out of his terrified trance. He gave a high-pitched yell, a girly sort of squeal, and made a lunge towards Larry, swinging at him with a small fist. Larry laughed, and kicked hard at him, his foot connecting with the boy's kneecap. The boy's yell turned into a howl and he doubled over. The tall one made a similarly ineffective pass towards Larry, but Larry could tell it was only done because he didn't want to look like a pussy next to his tiny mate.

'Oh, give over, you twats,' he said, pushing his feet up on the pedals of his bike and surging away towards the end of the alley. 'It's only a fucking phone. Get mummy to claim it on the insurance.'

Half an hour later Larry arrived at his next destination, the piss-stinking echoey grey concrete Kennedy Estate in Whitton. He had cycled hard all the way there, to try and quash the nerves – bordering on terror – that he always felt whenever he came to visit Jerome. But, as he'd said to the schoolboys, *needs must.* He needed the money that Jerome would give him for the four purloined mobiles currently swinging together in the inside pocket of his jacket as he stood on his pedals and rode as hard as he could. That way, he could blame his pounding heart on the exertion from the exercise and not on the sight of Jerome's mean, yellowish face as Jerome opened the steel door to his flat and narrowed his eyes at him, as he always did.

Larry carried his bike up to the eighth floor – no lock, and he knew it would be nicked in a nanosecond if he left it downstairs. Plus, it gave him another reason to be panting acceptably.

'What you got for me, Lawrence?' said Jerome with no preamble, through a crack in the door.

'Awright Jerome?' Larry patted his jacket pocket, and Jerome jerked his head to indicate he could come in.

'Leave the fucking bike, mate. Don't want no mud and shit on me carpets.'

Larry reluctantly propped it outside the flat, figuring that at least it was less likely to be stolen this far up. He followed Jerome inside, surprised and unnerved as always at how tidy and minimalist the place was. It was like bachelor pads he'd seen in movies set circa 1985, all chrome and smoked glass, grey and black patterned wallpaper on one wall, pale grey paint on the others, and a framed monochrome print of all those 1920s construction workers in New York eating their lunch on a girder thousands of feet up on a half-built skyscraper. The only thing currently out of place was the chunky black girl in a crop top and Day-Glo orange leggings sprawled on the sofa smoking a big spliff. She didn't acknowledge Larry at all, and Jerome didn't introduce her.

'Let's 'ave 'em then,' he said impatiently.

'Three Galaxies and an iPhone 5,' Larry said, trying not to sound smug. He quashed the mental image of the phones' former owners, the terror on the face of the middle-aged woman on the top deck of the bus at the sight of his blade, the expression of pain on the schoolboy, the bemused businessman on the Tube, the young girl pushing a pushchair, startled and afraid as he'd simply plucked the phone from under her chin where she'd wedged it as she walked along chatting. His mum would be so upset with him if she knew. But they were only phones.

He felt a flare of anger at his mum. Why couldn't she get a job? She wasn't some useless chav; she was a nice lower middle-class woman who'd been a housekeeper for the same family for fourteen years. Since they made her redundant a year ago – the kids were all grown up now and they didn't need her anymore – she hadn't been able to find anything else. The pile of red bills on the windowsill behind the telly was getting so high that it would start blocking out the fucking light soon.

None of his mates knew how tight cash was for him and his mum. The two of them lived in a terraced cottage in a nice area of Teddington, decent enough that he sometimes had people over, when his mum went out. He'd never had Alice round, though. He felt too intimidated by her poshness and the size of her folks' place, and he wanted to impress her. The relationship was still new enough that he feared she might drop him for someone richer if she saw where he lived.

Jerome's chin jerked briefly upwards in a nod.

'Three of them have SIMs in,' Larry gabbled. 'That one don't.' He pointed at the schoolboy's phone.

'Whatever,' Jerome said, bored. 'I'll give you forty pounds for the lot.'

Larry forced himself not to look disappointed. This was less per phone than the last time, but he was too scared of Jerome to point it out.

'Sweet,' he said wearily.

Jerome took an enormous bundle of notes out of the side pocket of his combats and peeled two twenties off the top. Larry held out his hand to take them, and at the last minute Jerome snatched his own hand back again. Suddenly he was looming right up into Larry's face, his terrifying greenish pallor giving off some sort of rancid scent – or was that his breath? His teeth were disgusting, crumbling and bright yellow, and his eyes dead and flat. Larry had always assumed that Jerome was in his late twenties, maybe early thirties, but up close he could see that he was probably younger – maybe only a few years older than himself. Larry's legs wobbled but he forced himself to stand his ground.

'What?'

Jerome tipped his head slowly and menacingly to one side, scrutinizing Larry from mere inches away. 'You tell that evil little slut that I'm on to her. She owes me, more money than anyone's ever owed me before and lived. Tell her to watch her fucking back cos, make no mistake, I am gonna *hurt* her. Now piss off out of here.'

Larry obliged with alacrity, running so fast down the stairs that he bashed his bike handlebars on every corner, and almost fell several times in his haste to be as far away as possible. *Shit shit shit,* he thought at every step. She's really done it now.

Chapter 8
Patrick – Day 2

The sun was shining in the park in which the body had been found. Patrick and Carmella stepped out from beneath a canopy of horse chestnut trees and the strong sunshine caused spots to dance before Patrick's eyes. He paused, took a drag on his e-fag and almost swooned as the nicotine and bright light hit his exhausted brain. Shadows swayed and stretched on the cracked earth at his feet and he stood still, focusing on the trunk of the nearest tree, waiting for his vision to return to normal. His left ear was whistling crazily, his tinnitus turned up two notches.

'If this is Frankie Philips or Isabel Hartley,' Patrick said, 'by the end of today this place is going to be the centre of the biggest shit storm south-west London has ever seen.'

'I've got an umbrella in the car,' Carmella said. She looked almost as sick as he felt. For the past week, he had known this moment would come. In cases like this, when seven days had passed, there were only two outcomes. A body. Or nothing, ever.

There were three unmarked cars and a van full of cops waiting behind them, and the Home Office pathologist had been alerted. But Patrick and Carmella were going in first.

'You're going to need the biggest umbrella ever when the media get wind of this,' he said.

For the past couple of years, the existence of the travellers' encampment in Crane Park in Twickenham had been one of the hottest – no, most incendiary – topics among locals. It was rare for the local paper to run without a story about the travellers, who had been blamed for everything from a dip in property prices to a surge in petty crime, with endless miniature moral panics whipped up by journalists, whether it was down to sanitation or the travellers' dogs crapping in the park, taxpayers' money being spent on benefits or the cost of towing away abandoned vehicles that had been dumped outside the encampment, rumours of 'drug-dealing gypsies' selling weed to local teens, or people complaining that they feared letting their children play in the park.

Personally, Patrick wished people would leave them alone. This was partly because moral panics and witch-hunts always made him bristle – he had a natural fear of mobs, whoever the target – and partly because he witnessed every day the very worst of what went on in the so-called respectable world, the city outside the camp's walls. But he knew that if the Crane Park encampment and the Child Catcher case collided, it would be the local equivalent of the president of South Korea going on TV and accusing Kim Jong-un of using his nuclear missiles as a tiny penis substitute.

A young man was waiting for them at the gates – deeply tanned, with thick black hair and a checked shirt gaping open to reveal a hairy chest. He wore a solemn expression and, without speaking, tipped his head to indicate that Patrick and Carmella should follow him.

They walked through the camp: mobile homes set up in a jumbled formation; cars in varying degrees of nick; men and women sitting around in the sunshine, kids running about in shorts, dogs sniffing at wheel rims. To look at, it reminded Patrick of a music festival – but the atmosphere was very different. The air was charged, rippling with barely suppressed hostility as they walked past.

The young man walked with his hands in his pockets, not talking, until they reached a large, gleaming mobile home at the centre of the camp.

'Mickey's waiting inside,' he said, knocking on the door.

They stepped up into the vehicle where a man with wiry grey hair, a flat nose and forearms like Popeye's stood waiting for them. They shook hands and the man introduced himself.

'I'm Mickey Flanagan,' he said, gesturing for them to sit down. The man had testosterone coming off him in great musky waves. He was around fifty but looked fit, like a retired boxer. They sat opposite him around a small table. Mickey picked up a can of Dr Pepper and took a swig, but didn't offer one to his guests.

'It was you who reported finding a body?' Patrick asked.

Mickey nodded. 'It was.'

'And where is she now?'

The other man paused. 'I want you to know straight up that it was no one in this community. I can promise you that.'

'Just tell us the facts, Mr Flanagan.'

Mickey thumped the table. 'This is a decent community. You think we don't know what they say about us out there? What they're going to say when they discover a babby was found here?'

Patrick waited, keeping eye contact with the other man.

Eventually, Mickey sighed. 'Alright, so. It was that bloody little idiot Wesley. He found her.'

'What's Wesley's full name?' Carmella asked. Patrick noticed how she accentuated her Irish accent when talking to the traveller's leader.

'His last name's Hewson.'

'And where is he now? It's better if we hear it from him.'

Mickey stared at Carmella and muttered something under his breath. He stood up, went over to the door and leaned out. A minute later, a man of around eighteen or nineteen came in to the mobile home. He was wearing a white polo shirt with baggy jeans and had gelled-down hair that accentuated his jug ears. He held himself straight, trying to give it some attitude, but the moment Patrick fixed him with his steeliest glare the façade of bravado crumbled away.

'Tell them what happened, ya eejit,' Mickey said.

The moment Wesley spoke it was clear he wasn't the brightest star in the firmament. In Patrick's childhood, they would have called him remedial. He wouldn't look anywhere near them as he spoke.

'I found her round the back, by the bins, like. She'd been—' He screwed up his face '—just left there, you know, with a, like, black bin liner over her. There were all flies buzzing about. It was minging.'

Patrick swallowed. 'Her?'

'A little girl. Just a tiny little thing, you know. About the same age as my daughter.'

Mickey nodded. 'Wes here is a father of two.'

'When was this?' Patrick asked, expecting to hear the time of day.

'Monday.'

It took a second for the reply to sink in. He and Carmella exchanged a look of shock.

'*Monday*? That was six days ago.' So it wasn't Frankie.

Wesley hung his head like a dog who'd been caught stealing Christmas dinner and Mickey said, 'He was hiding her.'

'Where?' Patrick asked. The heat was making him sweat and he felt sick, dizzy with dread. Carmella had gone a shade paler too.

'Tell them,' Mickey said, cuffing the teenager around the back of the head.

'Round the back of the camp, behind where the bins are, there's this, like, old building.'

'Used to be public toilets,' Mickey explained.

'I put her in there. Covered her up with this old, like, tarpaulin. I'm sorry. I'm really sorry.'

Patrick stared at the boy. There had been few times in his career when he'd been lost for words, but this was one of them.

'Listen,' Mickey said, stepping in front of Wesley. 'He may be a fucking eejit, but he did it because he knew exactly what people would think. Travellers – murdering those little kids that have gone missing. He panicked. Decided to hide her till he'd figured out what to do.'

'And, what, it took him six days to decide to—'

'Tell me. Yeah. And I called you straight away.' Mickey looked as sick as Patrick felt. 'That little babby needs to be buried by her family. And you need to catch the sick bastard who did it.'

'I'm so sorry,' Wesley said again.

An hour later, Patrick propped himself against the bonnet of his car, swigging from a bottle of water and trying to ignore the growing buzz in his ears, a buzz that echoed the noise of the flies in the abandoned public toilets. The SOCOs were in there now. The whole encampment had been sealed off and Wesley was on his way to the station in the back of a police car.

Carmella came up and put her hand on his arm. 'Hey, you OK?'

How could he answer that? He had just lifted the crinkly green tarpaulin to stare at the naked body of the three-year-old girl he had spent the last week praying was still alive. He knew without a doubt it was Isabel Hartley. He took another gulp of tepid water.

'Somebody needs to tell the Hartleys,' he said, thinking not just of them but the other two families. Of how their terror would ramp up to a higher pitch when they heard this news.

'The FLOs can do that.'

'And we need to sort out what to say at the press conference. DCI Laughland is setting it up now.' He looked at the fence of the encampment, scrawled with graffiti: GIPPOS FUCK OFF. In the distance he could hear squeals of excitement from the children's playground. The shit storm really was about to descend on this place. 'And I want every man, woman and child in the camp questioned. What did they see? What do they know? Wesley's story is stupid enough to be true. But he's still our only suspect right now. And right behind him are all the other people on this camp. They—'

He broke off, rubbing his face.

'You're going to conduct the press conference?' Carmella asked.

'Of course.'

She raised an eyebrow. 'With respect, you look like a tramp I gave a quid to on the way in this morning. And smell only marginally better – that shower obviously didn't work. Why don't you go home, take a proper shower, get changed?'

'Are you my mother?'

'No, but I reckon she's the only one who'd be able to sort you out right now. Go home, Pat. See your daughter, give her a cuddle.' She put her hands on her hips and he squinted up at her. 'Rinse the taste out of your mouth.'

Patrick let himself in to his parents' house – he couldn't bring himself to call it home, even though it was where he had been brought up – to be greeted by the sound of Bonnie howling from upstairs and the cajoling tones of his mother trying to be heard over the noise. 'Come on now, petal, we're going to playgroup soon, and you can't wear your pyjamas to playgroup now, can you? All the other boys and girls will be dressed. You don't want to be the only one in pyjamas, do you now?'

As he passed the open living room door he saw his dad Jim sitting in his favourite chair, frowning at his iPhone, doubtless either playing Scrabble or reading the BBC website app. It seemed to be all that Jim did each day, that, and the Sudoku on the back page of the Guardian. Jim had retired from the civil service two years earlier, ostensibly to help Patrick's mother Mairead with baby Bonnie, although Patrick never saw him lift a finger. It made him feel even more guilty about the burden he had placed on Mairead's shoulders – despite the fact she robustly denied that the care of her only granddaughter was in any way a burden.

Bonnie screeched back. 'YES I WANT TO BE THE ONLY ONE IN PYJAMAS NANNY!'

'What are you doing home so early, Pat?' Jim barely glanced up from his phone.

'Flying visit,' Patrick grunted in reply, dispelling the mental image of Isabel's tiny broken body. In his mind, her face had morphed into Bonnie's, the way it had looked on that terrible day he'd come home to silence and to Gill's unravelling.

He went upstairs, desperate to see his daughter. There was a small stand-off taking place in the tiny study that had been hastily converted into Bonnie's room. Bonnie stood with her arms folded and eyes narrowed, glaring at her grandmother. '*No*!' she said, and stamped her feet at the little summer dress that Mairead was holding out to her. She was indeed still wearing her Peppa Pig pyjamas.

'Hello, Bon-Bon,' Patrick said, crouching down to her level and tapping her on the shoulder.

'DADDY!' she shouted ecstatically in his ear, twining her arms around his neck. Her dark curls tickled his face, soft as cobwebs. 'You came home!'

He laughed and picked her up, the solid warm weight of her almost bringing tears to his eyes. 'Yes I have – I will always come home to you! This time it's just a quick visit to say hello, and then I need to have a shower and go out again. But I'll be back later, I promise. Let's get you dressed so Nanny can take you to playgroup, shall we?'

He took the sundress and a tiny pair of cotton pants out of his mother's hand, as she gave him a grateful smile and a kiss on the cheek. He tried not to notice how tired she looked as she went back downstairs, more like seventy-eight than the sixty-eight she'd turned last month.

'Right, you. Here's what we'll do. You put your big-girl pants on, and then you can put your Peppa PJ shorts back on – but only if you also wear the dress. Fair enough?'

Bonnie wriggled to be put down, then scrutinized him suspiciously. 'Is that a deal, Daddy?'

'I reckon that's a very good deal. What do you and Peppa Pig think?'

Bonnie sighed with her whole body, spreading her little palms wide and letting them flop against her sides. She consulted her knitted Peppa toy. 'We say yeh,' she said reluctantly and allowed Patrick to kneel down and dress her. Then she brightened. 'Daddy take me playgroup?' Patrick smiled at the way she pronounced it; *pwaygwoop*.

'I can't, Bon-Bon, I'm sorry, not today. Daddy's got to go back to work.'

He winced, anticipating the bank of TV cameras, the shouted questions, the barely suppressed hysteria – and then, inevitably, the way that the public would recognize him as 'that cop off the news' and hold him personally responsible for any lack of breakthrough or developments in the case . . . And then, the painful conversations he'd doubtless have to have with a panic-stricken Sean and Helen Philips.

'Why?' She squished his cheeks between her hands, forcing him to look in her eyes. She smelled so sweet, a mixture of soft baby skin and apple juice.

'Because it's my job, darling. I help people. And today I have to help the family of a little girl a bit like you.' *Only not dead, thank God.*

'I doan like your job.'

He smiled at her. 'Sometimes I don't much like it either, but I have to do it. Now, let's go and see if Nanny will play tea parties with you for ten minutes while I have a shower. Then, I tell you what, I'll give you and Nanny a lift to playgroup in my car, how about that?'

'Yeah!' she shouted, and Patrick sagged with relief that she seemed to have accepted the compromise. He carried her downstairs into the living room, not failing to miss the very slight exasperated eye roll from his dad at the imminent interruption to his peace.

'Play with Gramps for a moment, he really wants to play tea parties,' Patrick said sweetly, depositing Bonnie in Jim's lap where she immediately made a grab for his iPhone, which Patrick knew always annoyed Jim. Jim deftly extricated the phone and wrapped his arms around Bonnie in a big bear hug to distract her. Patrick left them like that, hoping that Jim wouldn't immediately go and find Mairead and dump Bonnie back on her so he could get back to his online Scrabble. It was a familiar, unacknowledged, gripe. As Patrick stripped off and climbed under the pathetic dribbly shower – that was another thing he missed, the power shower he'd installed himself in his and Gill's house – he tried to quash the gripe. Jim and Mairead had both agreed to take him and Bonnie in, and Jim had always been lazy. It would be naïve to assume that he would suddenly become a child-minding housework-blitzing dynamo once he retired. It was so good of them to help out when the only alternative would have been extreme stress for Pat himself, and a string of au-pairs and nannies.

Feeling marginally better after a good wash and brush-up – no time for a shave as well – Patrick dressed in a suit and clean shirt, selecting a tie from a collection of almost identical ones all jumbled together in a shoebox under his bed. He loathed having to wear a tie, and consequently made sure that if he did have to, it was unobtrusive and skinny to the point of anorexia.

Along with the box of ties and all the other dust-coated junk beneath the bed were several fat books that he'd bought in the weeks following Gill's breakdown, thinking they might help him understand, see what he'd missed, what he could have done better. *Post-Natal Depression: A Guide for Partners. Women Who Harm: The Psychology of Female Violence.* Then there was one called *The Snapping Point*, a huge brick of a book by Dr Samuel Koppler. This was the one he'd found most helpful, that gave him some understanding how Gill must have felt in those black days. Ultimately he had shoved the books beneath the bed. They made him feel too guilty, convinced that he should have seen what was going on at home. But he had been so busy, tired all the time. Having a baby was such relentless hard work that his senses and instincts were dulled to the point that he hadn't been thinking straight. That was his excuse, anyway. It didn't make him feel any better.

He was sweating again by the time he got back downstairs, where Jim was back in his armchair and Bonnie in the kitchen 'helping' Mairead make cheese sandwiches.

'I have to get back. I told Bon I'd drop you both off at playgroup on the way, but we'd have to leave now,' he said to his mother, swiping at Bonnie's buttery hands with a damp cloth. A greasy butter stain on his suit was the last thing he needed right before the press conference.

'Thanks love, right, I'll take the sarnies with us then,' said Mairead, getting out a roll of clingfilm from a kitchen cupboard. She had never learned to drive, and Jim hadn't got around to changing the flat tyre on their ancient Peugeot 107, so she had to walk everywhere with Bonnie in a pushchair, unless Patrick could give them a lift. Patrick looked at his watch. 'Don't want to rush you, Mum, but I have to leave RIGHT now,' he said. 'Got a press conference at two.'

Mairead's head jerked up. 'What for?'

'You'll hear it on the news later – but we found Isabel Hartley.'

His mother's hand flew to her mouth. It was clear from Patrick's grim tone that it hadn't ended well. 'Oh that poor, poor mite. And her poor parents!'

'She was found on the traveller camp in Twickenham. Although we don't know if she was—' he mouthed the word *killed* '—there, or just dumped there afterwards. Keep it to yourself till after the news tonight, won't you.'

That particular nugget of information would cause immediate chaos at Bonnie's playgroup, if Mairead let it slip, he thought. But he knew his mother was discreet enough not to leak it. Everyone would know soon enough.

'Go and find your shoes, Bonnie, there's a good girl. You can have your sandwich in the car as a special treat.'

Bonnie ran out into the hall, and Mairead turned to face her son. 'Oh Pat. That's just awful.'

He nodded. 'I know. And this is just the start of it. There are still two kids missing out there.'

Chapter 9
Helen – Day 2

Helen knew that many people would find it odd, suspicious even, that she had come to do a workout today, but she'd had to get out of their temporary refuge, their neighbours the Jamesons, next door.

At the gym, in this air-conditioned artificially lit space, pounding hard on the treadmill, the pain in her lungs and the thud of her heart muted the desperate voice in her head, the voice that cried out Frankie's name in a perpetual anguished loop.

The terror of someone harming the perfect flesh of her only child was unendurable. What would she do, if that was the case? What if the next tiny body found dumped like rubbish, like Isabel Hartley's had been, was Frankie's?

She missed Frankie so much that she thought her head would explode. And now the terrible news about Isabel made everything twenty – no, a hundred times – worse.

The woman with the frizzy greyish hair had told them. Sandra? Sarah? Helen just thought of her as the FLO, the Family Liaison Officer, a faceless but well-meaning police woman who apparently now had to hang around them, getting in the way and making sure – what? Making sure they weren't keeping Frankie captive in the garden shed? Making sure they weren't sneaking out under cover of darkness to bury her stiff body?

'Just to make sure you're OK,' the woman had said when she first moved into the Jamesons' place with them. As if they could be OK, with Frankie missing, and their own house a taped-off crime scene.

So now Sean and Helen spent their nights clinging miserably to opposite sides of the Jamesons' strange, slippery spare bed. Sally and Pete Jameson had diplomatically gone to stay with other friends. Alice was in the second spare room, and the FLO squeezed into a single bed between a home office shelf and desk unit and an old exercise bike, in the room that, on the other side of the party wall, was Frankie's bedroom. It was strange, thought Helen, being in a house the mirror image of their own, but without any of its comfort and familiar possessions.

And worst of all, without Frankie.

She'd had so many calls and messages from friends, which she should have found comforting, but she didn't want to hear from anyone except the police, telling her they'd found Frankie. Earlier that morning she'd taken a call from Liz Wilkins, a former colleague who Helen always got on well with, and who she was sure Sean had a bit of a thing for. Liz wanted to double-check her address because everyone at work had clubbed together to buy a bunch of flowers. Helen thought that was weird, because Liz knew their address very well – she'd been round for a dinner party at which she and Sean had flirted so outrageously that Helen had made him sleep on the sofa that night. As Liz told her how everyone was thinking about her 'and poor Sean', Helen had felt her anger heating up and had hung up on her.

Helen increased her pace, pushing against the wall of pain, staring at her increasing heart rate on the screen. Earlier, after hearing the news about Izzy, she had locked herself in the bathroom and sobbed for what felt like hours. When she came out the FLO was hovering.

'Let me make you a cup of tea,' she'd said briskly. 'It's been another shock, I know.'

'I want to watch our press conference,' Helen said. 'It must be on the BBC news website or something.' She hadn't been able to face watching it earlier, when it went out live, hearing her own words read out in a flat respectful monotone by DI Lennon.

'I'm not sure that's a great idea,' said the FLO. 'It will only upset you more.'

Helen stared at her. 'I couldn't be any more upset than I am right now,' she said, knowing even as she spoke the words that they weren't true. If DI Lennon came round to tell them that it was Frankie who'd been found on the travellers' site instead of Izzy Hartley, then yes – she would be a *lot* more upset.

'I'll watch it later,' she conceded abruptly.

They went back down to the kitchen where Sean and Alice sat at the table, Sean staring blindly at the sports pages of *The Guardian*, a can of beer beside him, even though it was only lunchtime. Alice's fingers pecked listlessly at her mobile. She looked wan and unhappy, but somehow that realization only made Helen feel even angrier with her.

'Alice,' she began, ignoring the alarmed warning look from Sean, whose head had shot up at the tone of her voice.

'What,' said Alice, a statement not a question. She might as well have added . . . *ever*.

'Nothing,' Helen replied flatly. She had an awful feeling that if she started on Alice, she'd never stop. But even though she hadn't said anything further, Alice, affronted, still pushed back her chair, its legs making a loud grating sound on the stone floor.

Sean jumped up too, and in the panicked way he had whenever Alice kicked off, ran across to her and wrapped her in the sort of huge bear hug that Helen wished he'd bestow on her, his own wife, more often.

Alice, however, wriggled out of his grasp. She was crying, fat tears rolling down her cheeks, her pale face reddening with outrage as she faced Helen.

'I know what you were going to say,' howled Alice, working herself up into the full tantrum, fists clenched at her sides like a six year old. 'You really don't trust me at all, do you? In fact, I bet you blame me for Frankie being kidnapped, don't you? Of course you fucking do! I was babysitting, it was my fault, that's what you think, isn't it? Why don't you just have the guts to come out and say it, you horrible—'

'Alice!' said Sean and the FLO simultaneously. The FLO abandoned her tea-making mission and sprang into action, rushing over to try and calm her down. She had no idea what a futile gesture that was, thought Helen. Once Alice was in full-on meltdown, there was nothing anyone could do.

'I just wanted you to swear on Frankie's life that Larry didn't come over that night,' Helen said, taking the bull by the horns. At that moment she didn't care if Alice never spoke to her again, or how cross Sean was with her for 'upsetting' Alice.

Alice made a frustrated sound, half scream, half angry expostulation, pulled the FLO's hand off her, grabbed her phone off the table and stormed out, slamming the Russells' front door. The FLO rushed after her.

Helen's heart sank, hearing the commotion that this caused amongst the four or five paparazzi on the pavement outside the front gate. She could hear the cameras clicking from the kitchen, and the sound of male voices: '*Alice, what's the matter?*' '*Alice, how are your folks feeling about the news about Izzy?*'

She turned to Sean, craving the security of his embrace, but his face looked like thunder.

'You shouldn't have done that,' he said flatly, when she came to him.

'Oh come on, Sean! There's something she's not telling us, I know there is!'

He looked at her. 'You *know* there is? What the fuck does that mean? Because what it sounds like to me is that you're desperate to make Alice the scapegoat, so you've got someone to blame . . .'

Helen gaped at him. 'Sean! That's just not true, and I think it's grossly unfair of you to be so unsupportive. I just can't sit around here doing nothing while Frankie's still missing, I can't!' Her voice rose. 'Let's go outside and make a statement of our own to those photographers. Come on. It's got to help, surely.'

'No,' Sean said, putting his hand on her arm to restrain her. 'No, Helen, it's not the right way to do it. Maybe later, a formal press conference with that cop, Lennon, you know, the one who's just done Isabel's . . .' He trailed off.

'I haven't seen the one about Isabel. I'll watch it tonight on the nine o'clock news.'

'Don't,' said Sean, his eyes filling with tears. 'Don't watch it, Hel. And please don't go outside now. If you want to appeal on TV, let's organize it properly. But I don't want to go on TV so you'd have to do it by yourself.'

He sounded reticent, almost embarrassed. Helen frowned at him. 'What? Of course I'm not doing it on my own. It would look so weird if you weren't there! Why on earth wouldn't you want to do it, if it might help us find Frankie?'

Sean just shrugged and turned away. 'I need to find Alice, make sure she's OK,' he said. 'I'm going upstairs to ring her.'

He had left the kitchen and, finding herself alone, Helen had felt the urge to flee. She grabbed her car key and headed out. At the gym, she had bought a whole new kit and towel from the little shop. The gym was in a hotel, Grant's, by Richmond Park, and she often came here when Frankie was at nursery so she could work out before relaxing for a while in the hotel lounge with a coffee. With no family or work pressures, these were the only moments she got to herself.

She was beginning to slow down her pace when she heard someone say her name. She looked up – it was Marion, a friend she'd met here at the gym a few months ago. Sometimes, when Helen wanted solitude, the presence of a friend at the gym was a nuisance, but most of the time it was nice to have someone to chat to about stuff that wasn't related to children or domestic duties.

Marion was another mixed race woman, like Helen, with a white mum and a dad who, Marion hinted, was a well-known musician, though she'd never revealed who he was. She didn't have any kids of her own and Helen was envious of her skinny body and free-and-easy life. *Your life can be easy like Marion's now*, a cruel voice whispered inside her skull, and she shook her head violently. She would never ever complain about the nursery run or the endless chores that came with having a small child ever again.

'What are you doing here?' Marion asked, wide-eyed, stepping onto the treadmill beside Helen's.

Panting, Helen answered, 'I had to get out.'

Marion nodded seriously. 'Has there been . . . any news?'

'No.'

Marion started to run. Right now, Helen wished she would either go away or talk about something else. Tell her some stories about her pop star dad or moan about her manicurist. Just for five minutes, that was all. Give Helen's brain something else to think about before it ate itself.

'I heard about Iz . . .'

Helen didn't give her a chance to finish the sentence. 'I have to go.'

She slowed the treadmill to a halt and began to walk away. Then, feeling guilty, she turned back.

'I'm sorry, Marion. I just can't talk about it.'

'I understand. You poor thing. But I'm sure she'll turn up, safe and sound. Just wait and see. Everybody is looking out for her. I saw it on Facebook – a special page.'

'I didn't know about that.'

Marion nodded. 'It's got thousands of members. The whole country wants to find her, Helen. We're all praying for you.'

As soon as she got home Helen went onto Facebook and searched for her daughter's name. Within moments she was on the 'Find Frankie' page that some well-meaning local had set up. Her heart skipped a beat at the sight of Frankie's little face in the photograph, and she reached out and touched the screen with her fingertip, stroking Frankie's cheek. There were already 43,000 'likes' of the page. To comfort herself, she began to scroll down through the hundreds of comments, needing to know that other people cared about Frankie too, that she wasn't alone.

The first few did help: 'God bless that little mite, and keep her safe. Please share her photo so that everyone can look for her,' 'My heart goes out to the family, hope she's found soon,' and many similar. But the next one made Helen catch her breath: 'Those comments below should be deleted, they're horrible. How can people be so cruel?'

What comments?

Fresh tears welling, Helen considered closing the laptop lid and walking away – but she knew she couldn't, not without looking.

She scrolled down, and the vitriol she discovered in the next few remarks made bile rise in her throat.

'I blame the parents. What were they thinking, going out and leaving a child to look after that little girl?'
'Frankie's mum and dad should be in prison – they DISGUST me. Leaving that child at home with a 15 year old'.

'Someone told me they reckon the parents done it and they buried the body of that poor little baby in the park. THERE'S NO SMOKE WITHOUT FIRE!!!'

Her head sank onto her arms, and in the silence the only sound she could hear was the blood pounding in her ears.

After what could have been another minute or ten, unable to stop herself, anger coursed through her, replacing the lethargy of grief. She sat up straighter and started writing a post on the Facebook wall, telling them who she was, typing so fast that her brain couldn't keep up with her fingers.

'It shocks and appals me that people, strangers, can come on here, people who know nothing about me or my family, and cast judgement upon us. Do you think we deserve it? That our beautiful little girl deserves to have been taken? Yes, I wish more than anything in the world that I hadn't gone out that night, that we had never left her with her half-sister (although it's completely legitimate for us to have done so. Fifteen is a legal and acceptable age to babysit other children, particularly family members). I fantasise that I have a remote control that will rewind time, take me back to the other evening and instead of going out with my husband – which I was perfectly entitled to do! – I had spent the evening cuddling my daughter and protecting her. Thank you to all the people who have offered support and sympathy – please, I urge you, to look for Frankie. To the people who slate me and my husband – I hope you are ashamed of YOURSELVES.'

She hit 'enter' before she could change her mind.

Within seconds, the page went crazy, comments flooding in, most agreeing with her, some questioning her identity, others backing up the words of the original trolls, berating her as if they were barely literate moral guardians of the universe. She sat back and watched the list of comments grow through teary eyes.

As she sat there, a blob of red appeared to signify that she'd received a private message.

She opened it, and her whole body went rigid with cold.

Chapter 10
Patrick – Day 2

Air. He needed air. But he was unable to tear himself away from the wall where pictures of the three missing children were posted. He corrected himself – two missing, one missed. He hadn't seen the parents of Isabel Hartley since they'd been told the terrible news, was saving that particular ordeal till the next day. How would they cope? Isabel was their only child and he knew the answer to his question: they wouldn't. How could you cope with something like that? Sure, they would probably carry on living, most likely for another fifty years. They might go on to have more children, together or with new people. They would go on living – but their lives as they knew them had ended this afternoon when one of Patrick's team had sat them down and spoken to them with a soft voice.

The press conference had ended an hour ago. The room had been silent apart from the click of cameras, the sounds of shuffling and the reporter from *The Sun* hacking away with a dry cough. But as soon as Patrick had finished speaking, the *Sun* reporter, whose name was Harry Carlson, asked if it was true that Isabel had been found on the Crane Park gypsy camp, as he put it, and the room erupted. Now it was all over the web and the hotline was going crazy. There were nineteen official traveller sites in Surrey plus a lot more private and illegal encampments. People who lived around every one of them were now calling in with reports of seeing travellers with small children in tow.

Patrick sat down at his desk and plugged his headphones in, bringing up his iTunes playlist and choosing one of The Cure's lighter albums, *The Head on the Door,* the music helping to soothe his mind and get his neurons firing. Listening to the tracks he'd loved when he was a teenager made him feel young. It was as if he was tricking his brain into believing it was the agile mind of a nineteen year old, but with the experience and knowledge of a man twice that.

He took out his Moleskine notepad and opened it to the next blank page. His colleagues smirked when they saw it, and he knew it was an affectation, but it still irritated him when Winkler called him Dickens, or sometimes JK – the only bloody writers he had heard of, probably.

The notepad was full of scribbles, thoughts, questions, a tangle of information that had become so knotted and jumbled that he felt lost. He needed to step back, make some clear notes to sort out what he knew and, more importantly, what he didn't yet know.

On the blank page, he started a list.

1. Isabel + travellers
2. Liam/Sainsbury's
3. Frankie + family

He tapped the page with his pen, listening to Robert Smith sing about how yesterday he had felt so old, and began to write down the facts beneath the first heading, starting with Isabel's disappearance, the fact she had been taken from her house, and then what he knew so far about her fate. But after a few lines he stopped, frustrated.

Yes, he knew she had been found by Wesley on the edge of the encampment six days ago – one day after she disappeared – and that she had been naked. From what he had seen, there were no obvious signs of how she had died, no visible wounds or injuries. He also knew that neither Wesley nor Mickey, whose details had been run through HOLMES, had any convictions beyond one twenty-year-old charge of GBH for Mickey when he had been involved in a fight in a pub. At the moment, two DCs were crunching the names of everyone else in the camp through the system, and so far nothing had come up.

He wrote 'Need to eliminate travellers' and underlined it. His gut told him that Mickey Flanagan was right: that the body had been left there deliberately to shift attention onto the travellers. There were two possible reasons for that. Reason one was that it was someone with a vendetta or some other reason to want to cause hellfire to rain down upon the travellers. But how did that tie in to the other missing children? Were they about to find the other kids' bodies dumped on other traveller sites? He made another note to get that checked out, his stomach clenching as he wrote it, knowing how that would look, to both sides.

The vendetta idea seemed unlikely. Which left the most obvious reason: a diversionary tactic. The only problem with that was that it seemed so obvious and ill-thought-out. He drew a large, elaborate question mark on the paper. He needed to talk to the forensic pathologist, Daniel Hamlet, and was waiting to get the call from the mortuary.

He moved on to the second page. Liam and Sainsbury's. It still astounded him that someone had managed to remove a child from a car in a busy supermarket car park without anyone noticing. No doubt they would be receiving calls right now from people claiming to have spotted a 'dodgy gypsy' lurking by the trolleys. But they had already been through the CCTV, which didn't cover the McConnells' car nor, to Patrick's dismay, the entrance or exit of the car park. They had also been running appeals on TV and in local papers for anyone who had been in Sainsbury's between 10 A.M. and noon on June 4th who had seen anyone carrying a small child to come forward, so far with no useful leads.

Finally, as the album neared the end of what would have been side one when he had originally bought it on cassette, when he was at school, he turned to another page and wrote FRANKIE AND FAMILY.

The SOCOs had turned up nothing useful at the house. No prints, no DNA, nothing at all. The field team had been going from door to door all day and had come up with one potentially useful fact. An elderly man who lived opposite, and who had opened the door to let his cat in just as the ten o'clock news was finishing – 'I bloody hate the amusing story they always have on at the end,' he had grumbled – had seen 'a lad cycling away on a pushbike'. He hadn't seen this lad coming out of the Philipses' house but there was a strong chance that this was where he'd been.

Patrick wrote down Larry's name on the paper. Patrick didn't think for a second that this teenage boy was responsible for abducting his girlfriend's half-sister, but he wanted to talk to him. If Larry had been in the house when Frankie had been taken, or just before, he was an important witness. He made a note to ask Carmella to go and find him. She had a way with teenage lads.

There was also Sean Philips. In the madness of the day, he hadn't personally interviewed Frankie's dad yet, although Carmella had taken a brief statement from him. That was another job for tomorrow.

Finally, he wrote down 'Frankie's picture'. The child's drawing, stored now as evidence, made Patrick's skin feel like hundreds of tiny baby spiders were crawling across it. When had Frankie seen someone peering through her window, if that was what the drawing signified? And why hadn't she alerted her sister if she'd seen a face at the window? Surely, that's what any small child would do? He double-underlined the question just as his phone vibrated on his desk. He pulled his headphones down around his neck and said, 'Yes?'

Daniel Hamlet was the most serious person Patrick had ever met. He was a black man in his mid-forties and, while on TV forensic pathologists tended to employ gallows humour to make what they did more bearable – just as Patrick and many of his cop colleagues did – Hamlet was like his Danish namesake in that he was intense and not known for his sense of humour. He didn't even smile when faced with the 'Alas, poor Yorick' quote for the 10,000th time in his life. But then, thought Patrick, who could blame him?

He followed Hamlet through the brightly lit corridors of the mortuary, wondering as he always did if the lighting was so intense because it was the only way to keep ghosts from creeping into the shadows. Or perhaps that was just him. If he was religious he might pause to reflect on all the souls that had passed through this building. Actually, that wasn't right, was it? By the time you got here your soul had already departed. They were just bodies. Meat and bone and hair. Whatever it was that made you a person was gone, alive only in the memories of those left behind, in the genes you'd passed on.

He hated this fucking place.

'My full report will be ready tomorrow, Detective Inspector,' Hamlet said when they reached his office.

'I understand.'

'But we want to catch this bastard as soon as, don't we?'

Patrick was taken aback. He had never heard Hamlet swear before, or show anger. He followed the line of the pathologist's vision to a framed photo on his desk. A little girl with chubby cheeks and a grin that contained everything that was absent from this building.

'We do.'

'I watched a little of the press conference on the TV earlier. Looks like everyone in the country is rather keen for you to find them.'

'What can you tell me?'

He laced his fingers together. The fingers that had wielded the scalpel that had cut a little girl open that afternoon. 'There are no signs of external damage. No wounds. I checked her throat for signs of strangulation but there is no bruising.'

Patrick pictured an adult's hand on a small child's throat and shuddered, trying with all his mental strength not to connect this case to his personal life.

'But her lungs tell us a story. They are spongy and contain water.'

'She drowned?'

Hamlet inclined his head. 'It's exceedingly difficult to tell with certainty if a person drowned. If a body comes to me that was found in water, we might assume they drowned but it could be that the person, for example, suffered cardiac arrest. It's possible that this child swallowed a large amount of water but then died by some other means.'

'But in your opinion?'

'She drowned.' As Patrick thought about this and what it might mean, Hamlet asked, 'When was she found on the traveller's encampment, exactly?'

'Last Monday, the third. At roughly ten in the morning, according to the idiot who found her.'

'Hmm. You know that in cases like this, when days pass between death and the autopsy, it's difficult to estimate the date of death.'

Patrick nodded. 'But I think we can surmise that she was left there during the night between the second and third. There are lots of joggers and dog-walkers around in the early morning, passing the encampment, so it's most likely that she was dumped under the cover of darkness. Which means she was killed very shortly after she was taken from her house.'

He had figured this out already. Isabel had gone missing at 3.45 P.M. on the 2nd. If her body was found the next morning, unless Wesley was lying or mistaken about the day, it meant that whoever had taken her had murdered her within hours.

'Is there any evidence that suggests that Wesley has given us false information about when he found her?'

Hamlet frowned. 'No. Like I said, it's very difficult for me to give an exact time of death but I would say that, from the condition of the body, a week seems correct.'

Patrick made a note in his pad and waited for Hamlet to continue. In his pad, he already had details of what she had eaten for her last meal: macaroni cheese with peas, and melon for dessert. He asked Hamlet if there were any other foods in her stomach and was told that there weren't.

He waited for Hamlet to reveal the piece of information he most needed to know, but dreaded. He braced himself.

'There are no signs of sexual activity whatsoever,' Hamlet said.

Patrick looked up, surprised. 'Really?'

The pathologist said, 'Yes. No sexual penetration, no semen on the body or in the mouth, no signs that her genitals had been touched at all.'

At the same time that Patrick felt relief, he experienced more confusion. The fact that the first two missing children were different sexes had always made the team wonder if paedophiles were involved. Most paedophiles preferred one or the other, boys or girls, but that had shifted their thoughts onto a gang – a paedophile ring, possibly traffickers of children. But if there was no sexual assault, why was that? Had something happened that had panicked the abductor?

Why go to all the trouble and risk of abducting a child from her home and murdering her almost immediately if sexual assault was not the motive? Or maybe, Patrick realized, it *was* the motive but the abductor had not, for whatever reason, had the chance to carry out their vile aims.

'It will be of some comfort to the parents,' Hamlet said. 'A crumb. There's one more thing.'

He brought out a pile of clothes, which Patrick recognized as the ones Isabel had been wearing: a pair of jeans, a lilac T-shirt and a white cardigan, stained with filth. The clothes had been left beside the body.

'Smell them,' Hamlet instructed.

Patrick did as he was asked. They smelled smoky, like she had been close to a bonfire.

'What is it?' he asked. 'Wood smoke?'

Hamlet tilted his head. 'I'm not sure. I think it's smoke, yes, but I'm not able to say from what. Not cigarettes. Possibly a bonfire.'

'It probably got on her clothes at the encampment. OK, Daniel, thanks again. I'd better get back.'

Hamlet nodded. 'Well, I'll be seeing you.' He caught hold of Patrick's arm and looked him in the eye. 'Please catch him.'

As Patrick walked back to his car, he tried to work it out in his head. If not a paedophile, then who? What was the motive? Had Isabel been targeted specifically because of who she was? Had the killer done it to get at her parents, to cause them the greatest pain possible? And if so, did that mean that the targets in all three cases were the parents?

Perhaps it was the families they should be looking at. Maybe it was there, in some connection between the sets of parents, that they would find the motive – and the killer.

He turned the key in the ignition and drove slowly out of the car park, heading back to the station. Isabel Hartley had been killed very soon after she was taken. If he, Patrick, was one of the parents of the other two kids, Liam and Frankie, that fact would ram a shard of fear into his heart. Because the likelihood was, the two other children were already dead. Their bodies were out there somewhere, waiting to be found.

He prayed he was wrong.

The kitten won't stop meowing and its piss is leaking through the bottom of the cardboard box. But I'm sure she is going to love it. All little girls love kittens.

She's been very quiet since she's been here. Barely spoken at all. When she's not knocked out or locked away for her safety, she mostly cries. I want to see her real self, and I reckon the kitten will help. It was a stroke of luck, finding it. I was chucking away some rubbish and when I lifted the lid of the wheelie bin, there they were – three little kittens. Of course, I didn't want three so I left the other two where they were and grabbed this one. It's a tabby, and its head appears to be slightly too large and heavy; it flops like a newborn human baby's.

I picked up a paper while I was out too. So they've found Izzy's body. I wondered how long it would take them. It said in the paper that the police were looking at forensic evidence and that a number of people are helping them with their enquiries.

Poor Isabel. Shame she had to die. She was a great help to me. Little Liam too. I hope they don't find him too quickly.

I love children, but of all the children in the world, none are as precious as the special girl who lifts her head and looks at me with doleful eyes when I open the door of the van, which I've moved several times today, keeping moving so no one notices it.

'Look what I brought you,' I say, setting the box down on the pull-out table.

'A kitty cat?' Her face lights up as she registers the incessant meowing.

'That's right. A kitten. Just for you.'

'What colour is it?'

'Let's open the box and see, shall we?'

I open the lid and the cat springs out before I can get hold of it, a blur of fur and claws. I try to grab it but it scratches me and hisses pathetically. I swipe at it, knocking it to the floor, its oversized head causing it to pitch forward and roll over before skittering back to its feet.

'Stop, stop.' She's squealing.

The cat dashes around the floor like a cornered rat. I'm cursing it, trying to scoop it up, and I finally manage to grab it. Just as I lift it, it squirts out a geyser of shit, the foulest-smelling gunk in the history of foul smells. To add insult to injury – or should that be the other way round? – it bites my finger and scratches my wrist.

I drop it, and before it can get away, I stamp on the wretched thing's back.

'Stop that fucking noise,' I yell at the girl. 'Stop it, or I'll fucking stamp on you too.'

She's hyperventilating now and I regret being so harsh. The kitten is still alive, though its back must be broken. There's shit all over its fur. What a fucking great idea that was.

I grab it and chuck it out the door like it's a soft toy.

Now I have to deal with a distraught child.

'Mummy, mummy,' she sobs, taking long fragmented breaths. 'I want my mummy.'

'It's OK,' I say. 'It's OK. We'll get you another kitten. I can get you one right now.'

It's when she starts to scream, that boiling old-style kettle noise that is so high-pitched I can only just hear it, that I have to clamp my hand over her mouth, push her into the tiny cupboard. I don't have any choice. I can't risk anyone hearing her. Not now.

Not ever.

Chapter 11
Jerome – Day 2

Jerome Tyson Smith stood at the window in his snow-white jockey shorts, pushing out his pecs and rubbing his abs with the flat of his hand, and gazed out over the piece-of-shit estate he called home.

From way up here he could see the pramfaces heading home with their Iceland bags weighing down the back of their buggies. He watched an old man with two sticks make his agonizing way to the entrance of the tower block opposite. Over there, Jerome could make out a couple of his boys hanging, keeping watch. He wondered if they could feel his gaze falling down upon them like the eyes of God. That was a chunk of his power right there: his men knew, whatever they were doing, Jerome Tyson Smith was watching.

'What ya doing, babe?'

He turned and looked at the naked woman on the bed. Carla. She had a sheet draped over her, one vast boob almost spilling loose, a foot with gold-painted toenails on display.

'Hey, princess,' he said, crossing to the bed and bending down. For a moment, Carla's eyes lit up – until he ran a hand across the warm flank of the Staffordshire terrier that sat thumping her tail against the mattress.

He crouched and scratched the dog's ear. Rihanna. She gazed at him with adoration and rolled onto her back so he could tickle her belly.

'Yeah, you like that, RiRi. That's right. *That's* right.' He inserted his long fingers beneath her sparkling collar and scratched, making the staffie groan with pleasure.

'Why don't you come over and do that to me?' Carla pouted, lowering the sheet to give him an eyeful of her admittedly glorious nipples.

'Give the dog a bone, huh?' he said. She looked hopeful. No self-respect. 'Nah. I'm gonna take RiRi out for a patrol.'

'Ah, Jerome, you love that dog more than you love me.'

There was no point responding to that. Carla had got *way* too comfortable, was starting to act like his goddamn girlfriend or something. It was time to bin her. He was Jerome Tyson Smith and he just had to click his fingers and bitches came running. White, black, Asian. Private school princesses and council estate skanks. They all wanted a piece of him. One nine inch piece.

'Come on RiRi,' he said, smiling as his best and only friend jumped down to the floor and trotted over to him, little nails clacking on the hard floor. They headed for the door.

'Hey Jerome,' Carla called from the bed.

'What?'

'That dog – it went for me earlier. Mean lil' bitch only tried to bite me when I come out the bathroom.'

He looked down at his dog. 'Good girl.'

Two minutes later Jerome and RiRi stepped out into the muggy air. They walked around the estate. He had grown up here, him and his mum and a string of men who either wanted him to call them dad or just wanted him to stay the fuck away so they could fuck his mum. A friend of his, Leonard, had told Jerome how his cousin had been molested by one of his mum's new boyfriends, and after that the eleven-year-old Jerome had slept with a knife under his pillow and a razorblade in his pants. Fortunately, none of his mum's friends had ever tried it on with him but one of them, a bug-eyed motherfucker, literally, called John Johnson had murdered her, strangling her in her bed while the fifteen-year-old Jerome listened to the new Beyoncé album through his headphones in the next room.

In an alternative, fairy-tale version of Jerome's tale, he had an aunt who lived out in the country and she would take him in and teach him about being a respectable citizen and engender him with a love of healthy pursuits and he'd end up at Oxford or some shit. But no, his Aunt Jacqui, who wasn't really his aunt but someone his mum had gone to school with, lived in the flat next door, in the same stinking tower block, and she'd taken him in. On his second night with her he'd realized that she wanted to take him in literally and, although he'd already been with plenty of girls at school by this point, he soon understood what it meant to receive the love of a good woman – or rather, a woman who was really good at blow jobs.

At sixteen, when he left school, she kicked him out after she discovered he'd pawned an engagement ring she'd been given when she was eighteen, that she'd somehow managed to hold onto all these years. He'd moved into another flat in the block opposite.

He missed his mum sometimes, and even occasionally missed Jacqui and her pierced tongue, but since those days he had started to make something of himself. He was an entrepreneur. He liked watching *The Apprentice* and *Dragons' Den*, all those shows about business, even though most of the people on those shows were sad fucking losers. Because Jerome had figured out long ago that there were only three ways to get rich quick in this city: be shit hot at music or football, become a banker or turn to crime. He couldn't sing, was a mediocre football player and even though he'd always been the brightest kid in his class, his education wouldn't get him a job in the tatty branch of Barclays round the corner, let alone in the City. Which left crime.

And he'd done alright. He had kids all over the borough nicking iPods and jacking sat navs and car stereos – but that was small change next to phones. He was turning over 100 phones a day now, more on weekends, mostly iPhones and Galaxies. Candy from babies, that's what it was. He did a little drug dealing too, but he'd figured that was much riskier and the competition fierce and vicious. He wasn't quite ready to take on some of the big gangs yet.

He was starting to feel like a big fish in a shitty little goldfish bowl though, swimming around in his own filth. At night, when he looked out of his window, he could see all the lights stretched out across London and he knew he wanted more. He needed to step up. And to do that, he needed more capital than the phones and stolen gadgets brought in.

The question was, where was it going to come from?

He and RiRi approached a couple of Jerome's foot soldiers, Curtis and Milo. When they weren't stealing iPhones off soft college kids they were a rap duo who totally sucked ass. He lifted his chin in greeting and the two rappers did the same.

'Alright, Jerome. Alright RiRi.'

The dog sniffed Curtis's leg then lay down on the hot asphalt with her legs stretched out before her.

'Yo, look at that,' Curtis laughed. 'Bitches always be lying down for the Ty Master.'

At this, Milo made a desperate 'cut it' gesture at his rap-mate, but Curtis was high on something and laughed loudly at his own joke.

Jerome took off RiRi's chain, stepped behind Curtis and slipped it round his throat, pulling hard. Curtis made a satisfying choking sound, desperately attempting to get his fingers beneath the chain.

'Apologise,' he said calmly.

Curtis rasped and Jerome loosened the chain a little.

'I'm sorry, Jerome, man. I didn't mean no disrespect.'

'Not to me. Say sorry to Rihanna.'

Jerome pulled the chain tighter. Milo gawped at his friend as his face turned purple. Jerome felt his biceps flex satisfyingly as he increased the pressure. Then he let go, the other man dropping to his knees, clutching his throat and gasping.

'Say sorry to her.'

Curtis crawled towards the staffie, who lifted her chin and regarded him imperiously.

'I'm . . . sorry . . . Rihanna,' the rapper said.

They watched the dog, Curtis trembling with fear as he waited to see what the terrier would do.

RiRi hauled herself up and trotted in the opposite direction.

'Apology not accepted,' Jerome said. The blood was pounding inside his head now. It felt good. Better than being inside Carla, better than one of Aunt Jacqui's BJs, better even than getting paid.

As he hauled the pleading Curtis around the back of the block, the chain swinging from his free hand, RiRi walking beside him, he remembered someone else who needed to be taught a lesson. That little rich bitch. He'd told Larry to give her the warning but hadn't seen or heard from either of them since.

He made a mental note to do something about it. To get a message to her. Just as soon as he'd finished with this muppet who'd dissed his dog.

Chapter 12
Patrick – Day 3

The woman who opened the door of the narrow terraced two-up two-down had probably been beautiful once. It was there in the way she held herself, a sense memory from her past in which every man she encountered would look her up and down. Life had worn her down, though, as surely as the tide turns pebbles to sand. She had blonde hair with the roots showing and her eyes were dull behind thick-framed glasses.

'Yeah?' she said.

Patrick showed her his warrant card, Carmella echoing him. Patrick said, 'Detective Inspector Patrick Lennon. Trisha Gould? We're looking for your son, Larry.'

She hesitated and Patrick cut off the lie. 'We know he's in, Mrs Gould. We just saw him come in the door. Unless you have another teenage boy visiting.'

'What's it about?'

Carmella stepped forward. On the drive over, she had been unusually quiet and the whites of her eyes had a pink tinge as if she'd been crying or had a sleepless night. He knew he should have asked her but he was bloody useless at things like that, about delving into the touchy-feely. Gill had always laughed at how he would do anything to swerve away from conversations about emotions. If he wanted to say something important to her, tell her he was hurting about something, he would put a record on that covered the way he was feeling, hoping she would take the hint and find some magical way of making it better.

'We need to talk to your son,' Carmella said in her most no-nonsense tone, and Trisha Gould sighed and beckoned them in.

Larry Gould was slouched on the sofa with a paperback novel in his hands. He turned his face towards them, a picture of innocence. He was seventeen, a handsome lad, with short hair and a gold earring. His expression was neutral, like he'd been expecting them. Patrick guessed that Alice must have told him they'd been asking about him.

His mum stood behind them as Patrick said, 'What's the book? Any good?'

Larry held it so they could see the cover. *To Kill a Mockingbird.*

'Great book,' Carmella said warmly. 'Is that homework?'

Larry looked like he was about to say yes when his mum said, 'No, he loves reading. Always got his nose in a book,' and Larry squirmed with embarrassment. Patrick knew that, for teenage boys like Larry, reading was considered somewhere down there with being fake – this generation had, in Patrick's limited experience, an obsession with 'keeping it real' and being 'true to yourself'.

They sat on the armchairs opposite Larry, with his mother standing behind the sofa.

'Larry, we want to ask you a couple of questions about the night of the ninth, the day before yesterday,' Carmella said. She leaned forward, her eyes wide, transformed from the quiet, sad person she'd seemed on the way over. Patrick saw Larry's eyes flick to her chest for a nanosecond.

'You mean the night Frankie got snatched.'

'That's right.'

The teenage boy was making a tremendous effort to sit still. Patrick could almost see balls of tension and energy bouncing around inside him. Larry said, 'You are going to find her, right? She's such . . . such a sweet little kid. Alice is in bits.'

Carmella was right on the edge of her chair and she reached out and touched Larry's forearm. 'You think a lot of Frankie?'

'Yeah, course.'

'Then maybe you can help us find her.'

'What do you mean? I don't know anything.'

Patrick said, 'Where were you on Sunday night?'

Larry said, very quickly, 'Out with my mates.'

'Doing what?'

'Just, you know. Hanging around. Chatting.'

'You didn't go round to see Alice?' Carmella said. 'She's your girlfriend, isn't she?'

'Yeah, she is. But no, I didn't go round.'

Carmella smiled. 'She's a very pretty girl, isn't she? Stunning.'

Larry did his squirming thing again, but there was a hint of pride in his expression. *That's my girlfriend you're talking about.* 'Yeah. She is.'

'And you knew her parents were going to be out?'

'No. No, I don't think so.'

Carmella chuckled. 'Really? We wouldn't blame you if you went round there Larry. Whatever you got up to, we don't care.' As she said this she looked blatantly at his groin and he blushed. 'If you're worried you're going to get into trouble because Alice is underage, I can assure you we're not concerned about that.'

He was bright pink now while, behind him, his mum had gone pale. 'I didn't go round there. And even if I had, I don't see what it would have to do with Frankie disappearing. I didn't snatch her or nothing. As if!'

'We just want to know if you saw anything.'

'No, I didn't.'

'So you *were* there?' Carmella said.

'No. No, like I told you. I was with my mates.'

'But, Larry, a neighbour saw you there. Cycling away.'

'That can't have been me. Probably some other teenage boy on a bike.' He tried to make a joke. 'I hope Alice didn't have some other bloke round there. I'll kill her. I mean, I wouldn't . . .'

Patrick stood up and crossed the room quickly so he was standing over Larry, crowding him. 'If you *were* there that night, whatever you were doing, you're potentially an important witness. That little girl is missing. I guess you heard about Isabel Hartley? About how we found her dead yesterday? I assume you don't want the same thing to happen to Frankie, do you?'

Larry's Adam's apple bobbed. 'Of course not. But I wasn't there. I swear.'

The room fell silent.

Patrick exhaled through his nose. 'Come on, we're wasting our time.' He took his business card out and flicked it onto the sofa. 'If you remember that you were there, even if you can't think of anything that might help us, call that number.'

Back in the car, Patrick thumped the steering wheel with the flat of his hand and winced. There was a tangy smell in the air, the odour of a coming storm. He pictured a rippling swimming pool on a tropical island, somewhere peaceful and far away. But before he could enjoy the vision, a child's body floated into view in his imaginary pool, eyes closed, a tiny Ophelia, and he gasped as if he were the one drowning.

'I think he'll crack if we keep leaning on him,' Carmella said.

Patrick shook away the image of the drowned child.

'It's not worth it. I say we forget about Larry Gould – even if he was shagging Alice that night, he probably didn't see anything useful. Let's follow the leads we've got.'

His partner hesitated before nodding. 'OK. We'll follow the leads we have. Which are?'

Patrick took his Moleskine notebook out of his pocket and waved it at Carmella. 'Have you had breakfast?'

'Yes, I had a bowl of muesli.'

'Well, all I had was half of piece of toast and jam that Bonnie chucked on the floor. I'm ravenous. Let's go to Diners' Delight.'

'Oh god, just stepping in that place makes me break out in zits.'

Ten minutes later they took a table at Patrick's favourite greasy spoon and while Carmella played it safe with bottled orange juice and a round of toast, Patrick went for the full English and a bucket of tea.

'Everything alright with you?' he asked.

She looked up from her OJ, surprised. 'Yes. Why?'

'Oh, just checking. This is a tough case. Wanted to make sure it's not getting to you.'

'If I say it is, will I get a week's leave?'

Patrick's navvy-sized breakfast was plonked down before him and he squirted it with watery ketchup that had been poured into a Heinz bottle, giving it ideas above its station. 'Er – no.' He jabbed a corner of toast into his fried egg, breaking the surface and causing the yolk to ooze across the plate. Carmella wrinkled her nose. 'Everything OK at home, yeah?'

Her shoulders drooped. 'Everything is rosy.'

'Cool. I just thought you seemed a bit . . .' Could she tell how awkward he felt? 'Emotional.' He cringed at his choice of word.

'Hmm. Well, I am a *woman.* We tend to get a bit emotional every now and then.'

'Sorry.'

She smiled at him. 'Everything's fine, honest. Nothing for you to worry your pretty big head about. Let's talk about the investigation, can we? I thought you had all the answers in your magic notebook.'

He gulped tea and looked around to make sure no one was ear-wigging. 'I wish. But, so far, what has this case turned up? No DNA, no decent witnesses, no suspects.'

'What about the travellers?'

'We'll carry on interviewing them all, but I believe Wesley Hewson when he says Isabel was dumped there and that he hid her because he knew the travellers would get the blame.' He took a bite of sausage. 'We need to know the motive. What connects the children? The amount of risk the abductor took tells me that these kids weren't selected randomly.'

Carmella shuffled her chair as an old man with whiskery ears squeezed past, the chair legs scraping painfully on the hard floor. 'But all the children are so different. Two girls and a boy. None of them look alike.'

'The only thing they have in common is area, and their ages. They live in a three-mile radius of each other. They're all between two and three. And all their parents are well off.'

'No ransom demand, though.'

Patrick sat back, fighting the urge to burp. 'We need to find where the lives of the three families intersect. If we draw a Venn diagram of everything we know about the Hartleys, the Philips family and the McConnells, there might be something in the point where they meet that tells us why these kids were targeted.'

'I'm guessing you've already got a Venn diagram drawn in your notebook.'

He smiled. 'Yeah. But there's nothing in any of the intersections.'

They sat in silence for a few moments, watching punters come in and out of the cafe. A copy of *The Sun* lay on the next table and

Patrick grabbed it. Isabel's smiling face was on the cover along with that morning's headline *The Sun Offers £100k to Find Izzy's Killer.* Two days after Isabel's abduction, against the advice of the police, who knew it would bring forth every nutter in south west London, the Hartleys had offered a hundred grand to anyone who could help bring their daughter home safely. Now the newspaper was replacing that offer with a reward to find the murderer.

'Let's go talk to the families now. I'll go to the Philipses, you can go and see the McConnells and then I'll go and talk to the Hartleys too. Get them to brainstorm everything they can remember. Get them to go back through their diaries, their Facebook pages, their phones, their photos – anything that will prompt memories of what they've done and where they've been over the last three months.'

They left the greasy spoon and Patrick drove Carmella back to the station so she could pick up a car.

'Good luck,' she said, stepping out into the heat of the morning.

As he was about to drive off, his phone beeped. It was a text from his mum, reporting on what Bonnie was doing. They had been to a petting zoo and Bonnie particularly loved the goats, apparently. Then a second text came through.

I wasn't going to say, but B keeps asking about her mum. I don't know what to tell her.

Patrick sighed and fired off a reply. Let's talk about it later.

He had known this time would come but had been burying his head in the sand, ostriching, as his mum put it. But it was something he had to deal with. What to tell his daughter about the mother who had tried to murder her – and whether to let Gill see Bonnie. If she wanted to see her, that was. He had no idea. It was another thing he tried not to think about.

Chapter 13
Helen – Day 3

Helen felt as though her brain could be divided into two lobes, not left and right, but Frankie and That Message. She had thought of nothing else for the past ten hours, lying awake the entire night fretting about it, resenting Sean for the scant sleep he had managed, even though for most of the time she knew he was awake too, lying silently next to her. Occasionally he rolled over and cuddled her tightly, almost fiercely, but it was of no comfort. Several times she almost blurted it out to him, asked his advice. They were a team. Surely she had to tell him that there was someone out there claiming they knew where Frankie was? But it was too risky. *Tell no-one*, the message said. It was from a woman called Janet Friars. What if she did tell Sean or that detective, and Frankie suffered for it?

Also, their FLO had made a dismissive comment that had stuck with Helen, as the FLO had unpacked milk and bread from the corner shop. She'd said that Izzy and Liam's parents were being hounded by 'nutters on Facebook' insisting they knew stuff: psychics, hippies, the mentally ill, the attention-seeking . . . 'Wasting police time like that,' the FLO had tutted. 'Diverting valuable resources. Shameful. You ignore them, if you get any.'

But what if she ignored it and Frankie suffered more? Helen felt the sword of Damocles hover over her, hanging by a single hair, about to cleave her in two – and for a moment, she thought she would have welcomed it. At least it would be an end to this intolerable nightmare.

She had been spending a lot of time on Facebook recently, obsessively checking the page Marion had told her about at the gym, reading the kind comments and obsessing over the nasty, critical ones. She had messaged Marion about it and her friend had fired back a message telling her to 'Ignore them – they are stupid trolls.' Then Marion had added, 'I'm sorry. I wouldn't have told you about the page if I'd known about the trolls.'

It was easy for Marion to say, wasn't it? Ignore the trolls. Helen felt compelled to read the vile comments about what a bad mother she was, how she would burn in hell for letting that 'sweet little angel' out of her sight. In the rare moments that she slept, she dreamed about them, about a mob screaming abuse at her, pointing their witchy fingers and taunting her.

The endless night finally morphed into a reluctant peach sunrise, and a morning bringing the mixed blessing of getting out of bed in their own house again. On one hand, it was a relief to once more be surrounded by the familiar scents of home and their own belongings, knowing where everything was . . .

Everything but Frankie. And that was the other hand. It was a particular sort of mental torture, to be there without her, seeing her finger paintings on the fridge and her toys tidied, unplayed with, in the basket in the conservatory. Photos on the piano and her tiny stripy wellies in the hall. At least being in the Jamesons' house had spared them that. They had been allowed home late the night before, and gone straight to bed, too distraught to focus on anything but the vain attempt to sleep.

When Helen came downstairs on the morning after their first night in the house alone without Frankie, she found Alice and her friend Georgia already sitting at the kitchen table, looking at YouTube clips on Alice's laptop, empty cereal bowls in front of them.

'Oh! Hi, Georgia. We don't usually see you this early.'

'Hi Helen,' said Georgia through her fringe. With what was clearly a vast amount of effort, she muttered something else that Helen didn't catch, but which made Georgia's pale cheeks flush scarlet. Alice looked embarrassed too.

'Sorry, what was that?' Helen tied her dressing gown belt tighter, suddenly aware of how terrible she must look – hair like a bird's nest, sleep in her eyes and creases on her face. At least it was only Georgia.

'I said, I'm really sorry about Frankie and I hope they find her soon,' the girl blurted in a rush, staring at the tabletop. 'Everything will be fine. I'm sure it will,' she added half-heartedly.

Helen smiled wanly and came over to give Georgia a hug around the shoulders. Helen had always thought that Georgia was the most beautiful of all Alice's friends, with her long wavy red-blonde hair and flawless skin. She looked like a perfect English rose – but, according to Alice, had already slept with three boys, and managed to get herself an ASBO last year for jumping on and damaging the roofs of three cars late at night after one too many Breezers. Apparently she was mortified, though, and voluntarily wrote letters of apology to all three of the cars' owners . . . Even so, Helen had thought at the time that she was glad Alice was her stepdaughter, rather than butter-wouldn't-melt Georgia. She didn't *dis*like Georgia's mother, a mouthy posh woman called April, a writer of bonkbusters, apparently, and every time they met, one of other of them would say, 'we MUST go out for that glass of wine soon' – but somehow they never did.

'Thanks, honey.'

'Did you watch the press conference?' Alice asked Helen. Helen was surprised at the question – it was the first time Alice had spoken to her since she had stormed out yesterday.

'Yes, I watched it on the ten o'clock news.' She flicked on the kettle and put a teabag into her favourite mug, one that Frankie had – with some help – decorated for her at one of those paint your own pottery places. Her hand trembled as she added sugar, feeling the need for the sweetness. 'It was awful. Isabel's poor parents. I can't imagine what they're going through.'

Although she could.

'Do either of you want tea?' she asked, but both girls shook their heads. 'It was weird, hearing our statement read out. I'm glad they didn't show our pictures though – or worse, ask us to read it out ourselves. They showed that photo of Frankie. And one of Liam O'Connell. I thought that detective did a pretty good job.'

'John Lennon,' said Alice, and immediately corrected herself. 'No, Patrick, isn't it? I was thinking of the Beatles.'

Helen managed a brief laugh. 'He's coming over this morning. He wants to talk to me and Sean again.' She tried to keep her tone neutral, aware of the dangerous ground she was now treading. 'Might be helpful if you could stick around, Ali, just in case . . .'

She tensed, waiting for the next instalment of yesterday's outburst, but Alice merely looked at Georgia. 'Don't think I can come to Kingston with you then, if I have to stay here. Go without me. Say hi to the others.'

'Are you sure, babe? We could go tomorrow instead?'

'Nah. Not really in the mood for shopping anyway.'

Helen felt relief swoosh through her. She made the tea, turning briefly away so the girls couldn't see her face.

'Have you finished all your exams, Georgia?' she asked, taking her steaming mug across and sitting down next to Alice at the table.

Georgia nodded. 'Yeah. Glad I'm not doing Drama, otherwise I'd still have one to go, like poor old Alice.'

'I won't have to do it though, will I, Helen?' Alice asked anxiously. 'The school said they'd put in for mitigating circumstances.

I don't care about Drama anyway, I'm shit at acting. I only took it 'cos I thought it would be easy, but it isn't.'

Helen sighed 'Well, I'd say these counted as Mit Circs, yes.'

Alice brightened. 'In that case, I've finished my GCSEs!' An expression of half-guilt, half-delight flashed across her face, making her look sly.

Helen had to bite the inside of her cheek hard to prevent herself making an extremely snide comment. The doorbell rang, and she groaned. 'Don't tell me he's here already . . . Ali, please could you get that? I'm not dressed.'

Alice slouched with bad grace to the front door. She objected on principle to doing anything that Helen asked her to do.

It was Lennon. He followed Alice back into the kitchen and Helen saw him take in with interest the sight of Georgia sitting at their kitchen table. Georgia stood up immediately and put on her denim jacket. 'Anyway. I better get going. I only came over to see if Alice wanted to come to Kingston with us.'

Georgia vanished out of the kitchen before Helen had the chance to say goodbye, Alice close behind her.

'Something I said?' Patrick Lennon asked, raising his eyebrow. He sat down at the kitchen table uninvited, which irritated Helen slightly, although she made sure not to let it show.

'I doubt it. That's teenagers for you. Tea?' Helen asked.

'Thanks. No sugar, please.' He took out a black Moleskine notebook – rather poncy for a copper, thought Helen.

'Is Sean about? I need both of you for this – and Alice, if that's OK,' he added, as Alice returned, hovering uncertainly in the doorway.

'He's upstairs. I'll get him,' she said, retreating. '*Da-ad!*' they heard her shout up the stairs.

'He's probably in his study,' Helen said. 'I haven't seen him all morning.' She couldn't quite keep the bitterness out of her voice. She yearned for Sean's support, to feel that they were in this hideous nightmare as a team, bonded together as tightly as two halves of a walnut in its shell – but Sean had retreated from her, emotionally and physically, to the point that she almost felt she had lost a husband as well as a daughter. He always had been a bit of a tortoise, retracting his neck into a silent unreachable place as a response to difficult emotional situations. Helen supposed she thought, when they met, that she could change him.

Every woman always thinks that, she thought now. *And they never can.*

Alice's footsteps stomping back down the stairs were joined by Sean's quieter ones. Helen took out two more mugs and re-boiled the kettle.

'DI Lennon just wants to ask us a few more questions,' she said to him, taking in his unshaven, grey face and bed-head hair, even though it was ten thirty and he'd been up for hours – his side of the bed had been empty since about six A.M. Her heart squeezed with pity for him, forcing herself to understand that he felt as bad as she did. He just showed it in different ways.

'Yeah, I know,' he replied shortly. 'Alice told me.'

'Sorry we're not dressed,' Helen said. She felt embarrassed at the state of both of them – Alice was the only one who looked halfway presentable.

'Right, thanks, folks,' Lennon said, once they were all seated with cups of tea in front of them. 'The main reason I'm here is because I'm asking all three families for a comprehensive list of places you've taken the kids in the last six months. Not just nurseries or clubs, but parties, coffee shops, toyshops even, if you can remember. Outings you might have had locally. Trips to the swings. Santa's grottos, if you can remember that far back.'

'What's this for?' Sean asked. 'Trying to find somewhere the children might have been . . . spotted by the bastard who took them?'

DI Lennon nodded and they sat for ten minutes or so, compiling a list on the back of an A4 envelope that had contained a travel brochure. It helped, thought Helen, having something concrete to do, and something that united them, even just for a short time. They all called out suggestions, which Alice wrote down in her careful cursive. Helen wished she could write down all the memories of Frankie that each suggestion conjured up.

'Nursery – it's Ladybirds Nursery in Church Road. She goes – went – every morning. And the playgroup at the church, All Saints in Fulwell. We sometimes go to their Wednesday afternoon session. She likes it there. Mostly because they have homemade cheese straws.'

'How about that soft play centre we took her to in March, at Syon House? Remember, she spilt my cappuccino all over herself.'

'Archie Fuller's birthday party the other week – Dad, you took her there, didn't you?'

'Well remembered, honey. Yeah, I did. And there's the Dads' Club in Bushy Park on a Saturday morning – when I was desperate.'

Sean cracked a smile, and Helen put her hand on his knee. 'He hates Dads' Club,' she explained.

'All those bloody earnest left-wing Teddington dads talking about quinoa and private school fees.'

'Swimming lessons at the Lensbury.'

Alice scribbled away.

'Where do you do your grocery shopping?' Lennon asked.

They all looked at him. 'Not Sainsbury's,' Helen said. 'We go to the Waitrose in Twickenham, usually . . .' She paused. 'Have there been any leads on poor Liam?'

Lennon shook his head. 'Not yet, but we're still assimilating all the information.'

Alice started doodling on the envelope, thick cross-hatched shading on the inside of the outline of a church, next to the word 'Church playgroup' on her list. She leaned her head slowly onto Sean's shoulder, and he hugged her tightly. Helen tried not to feel jealous.

She opened her mouth to tell them about Janet Friars' Facebook message – then stopped. Suddenly her decision was made. She *was* going to tell no-one. She was going to reply to Janet Friars herself. It was almost certainly a hoax, but if that was the case, there would be no harm in not telling Sean. And she could feel that she was doing something practical herself, even if it was just ruling out the woman, without causing any more stress to anybody else.

It made her feel a tiny, tiny bit better. As soon as Lennon had gone, she was going to reply.

Lennon began to say something else when the drill of the doorbell sounded, long and loud, and they all jumped.

'What fresh hell is this?' Sean grumbled. 'If it's another fucking journalist, I'll—'

'I'll go,' Lennon said, pushing back his chair, and Helen felt grateful to him. The family liaison officer had made herself scarce for a couple of hours, presumably taking some time off while the DI was on the premises instead. It was so intrusive, having non-family members in the house, but Helen supposed that it did have a few advantages – like having an on-site bouncer.

'Oh my God,' said Alice, 'could they, like, ease off the doorbell?' But the bell went on and on, one continuous sharp sound like an alarm, right up to the point that Lennon opened the door.

'Who the 'ell are you, and where's my son?' came a querulous female voice with a thick Essex accent, almost as high-pitched with fury as the doorbell had been.

The three of them still at the kitchen table put their heads in their hands as one. 'Oh no – not bloody *Eileen*,' said Helen and Sean in tandem. Helen couldn't help herself and started to cry.

Alice spoke in a flat monotone. 'Just when we thought things couldn't get any worse . . .' They all listened with dread to the footsteps approaching down the hall. Seconds later Sean's mother, puce with sorrow and fury, burst into the room.

'How could you let this happen and why did you not think to let me know? I had to see it on the bloody telly! Do you have ANY idea how traumatic that was for me?'

'Hi, Granny.' Alice got up and left the room, going around the other side of the table to her grandmother so as to avoid embracing her. 'Haven't seen you for, like two years. That's probably why Dad didn't tell you.' She turned back to Helen and Sean. 'I've changed my mind. I'm going into Kingston to meet Georgia. See you later.'

Eileen took her coat off and started to sob. 'Frankie, my poor little mite. Oh darling, where is she?' She grabbed Sean around the neck and kissed his head, but he moved away. 'As if you care, Mum,' he said, and slid his hand into Helen's.

Perhaps it wouldn't be so bad after all that Eileen had turned up, thought Helen, blowing her nose on a piece of kitchen roll.

Lennon opened his notebook at a new page. 'Mrs Philips, I take it?'

'Last time I looked, yes,' said Eileen, 'Sean love, make your old mum a cuppa while I talk to this nice detective. It's alright, we've already been introduced.' Sean rolled his eyes at Helen but got up and refilled the kettle. Helen wiped her eyes and slipped out of the kitchen – Lennon would be busy with Eileen for the foreseeable future, and there was something she felt she had to do.

Noticing with despair the large suitcase sitting by the bottom of the stairs – *that woman is staying here over my dead body* – Helen went upstairs to the bedroom and opened the laptop she'd left on her bedside table.

She read the message again: `I know where the lost children are. Can we meet? 2pm on Thursday in`

Teddington M&S café. I'm being watched. Can't tell you over the Internet. DELETE THIS AND TELL NO-ONE.

'Janet Friars' profile gave away little information. As they weren't friends on there, Helen couldn't access her wall, but her profile picture was of a dog – a white Scottie – and there was no personal information to give Helen any clue about who this woman was.

She quickly typed a reply:

If you know something, you should go to the police.

She sat and waited for a reply, but none came.

Chapter 14
Patrick – Day 3

Fiona and Max Hartley opened their front door together, arm in arm. But it was less a demonstration of solidarity and support than a necessity, Patrick thought. They were literally holding one another up while everything about them sagged with grief – shoulders, eyes, mouths. Fiona Hartley could barely drag her hollow red-rimmed eyes up to meet Patrick's. She looked even worse than when Patrick had last seen her, when Isabel had still been missing. He was glad he hadn't been the one to break the news that Isabel's body had been discovered.

'Come in,' Max Hartley said flatly when Patrick told them he was there to try and piece together Isabel's movements over what had ended up being the final few weeks of her life. When he mentioned her daughter's name, Fiona twitched briefly and clutched more tightly on to her husband.

Their wide hallway had sheets of plastic taped to the wooden floorboards and an old avocado-coloured toilet and basin leaning against the wall near the front door, alongside unopened boxes of new bathroom accessories and old broken tiles. Patrick had to step over the same length of copper pipe that he had negotiated last time he had been in the house. He remembered Max saying that his brother and he were doing the renovations themselves.

'I don't suppose you've done any more on your bathroom.'

As soon as he said it, he winced internally. Of course they hadn't – why would they be doing DIY at a time like this?

The couple paused and glanced at one another. Max spoke in a low voice. 'I doubt we will now. It's our guest bathroom. We were refitting it for the Spanish au-pair who was meant to be moving in at the start of next month. I had to email her last night and tell her that we wouldn't be needing her now after all . . .'

His eyes filled with tears and he sobbed, a single loud harsh sob. For a moment, and to his abject horror, Patrick felt tears rise in his own eyes. He blinked, and had to take a deep breath before he could speak.

'Oh God. What a terrible email to have to write.'

He was going to add 'I can't imagine' – but the truth was, he could. He could absolutely imagine it. *Get a grip*, he yelled at himself.

They walked into the kitchen, where Fiona immediately slumped at the huge farmhouse table and lit a cigarette.

'No need not to smoke in the house any more either,' she muttered, offering the pack to Patrick. He almost reached his hand out to accept – the muscle memory of a reaction to stress – then shook his head. 'I smoke the fake ones now,' he said, showing her his e-cig and having to clench his teeth to resist taking a drag on it before shoving it back in his pocket.

'Coffee?' Max asked, and Patrick nodded.

'Thanks. White, no sugar.'

The coffee, when it came, was bitter and the milk had small oily lumps floating in it. The kitchen bin was overflowing and the cat litter tray by the back door badly needed a clean-out.

'Don't you have your Family Liaison Officer with you anymore?' Patrick asked abruptly. Not that the FLO's remit would be to clean out the cat's litter tray, but here was a couple that clearly needed a bit more help. The FLO could organize that. Fiona made a face.

'We told her to go. We don't want someone we don't know hanging around looking sympathetic. It's hard enough as it is.'

Patrick noticed that all Isabel's paintings had been ripped off the fridge. He hoped for Max and Fiona's sake that they had saved them in a folder somewhere and not torn them up and thrown them away in a storm of grief.

He took out his notebook and started to prompt the couple to come up with a list of the places they had been with Izzy. For a few minutes, as with the Philipses, they seemed glad of the distraction, and came up with a fairly comprehensive list – Patrick had to write fast to keep up with them. But then their voices petered out into silence, as if they had only just realized the significance of why they were doing this.

Fiona stood up abruptly, stubbing out her cigarette into an overflowing ashtray on the table. She looked as though she was sleepwalking as she drifted over to a fruit bowl next to the fridge. Opening a cupboard above the counter, she took out a small flowery pink plastic bowl, ripped a banana from the bunch in the fruit bowl, peeled it, then took a dessert spoon from a cutlery drawer. Her husband gasped and half-rose in his chair. 'Fi—' he said hopelessly, watching her use the edge of the spoon to slice the banana into the plastic bowl. Tears rolled down his cheeks as he and Patrick then watched her take out a pot of Hundreds and Thousands and shake the colourful sprinkles all over the banana segments.

Fiona shook more and more, until the banana was totally buried and the sugar sprinkles dusted the kitchen counter. There was something hypnotic, almost ritualistic about the way she did it. It made Patrick think of someone dropping earth on top of a coffin in a grave. A small white coffin . . .

For a moment they were all silent, until another audible sob from Max cut through the silence. Patrick jumped up and gently removed the now-empty cake decoration container from Fiona's trembling hands. He took her by the shoulders and led her back to the table, helping her back into the chair.

'Was that Isabel's favourite snack?' he whispered, forcing himself to look into her blank eyes.

She nodded and looked away.

'Right, let's see what we've got.'

Patrick and Carmella sat down together in the incident room back at the station, the pictures of the three children staring down at them from the wall, silently urging them on. Patrick still felt shaken from the meeting with the Hartleys, but at the same time was even more fired up, a cocktail of anger and sorrow making him utterly determined to catch the bastard who had done this. The prospect of seeing Frankie and Liam's parents going through what the Hartleys were now suffering added a layer of desperation to his determination.

DS Mike Staunton entered the room carrying a cardboard tray of coffees from the Costa down the road. Mike was the very definition of a decent, solid cop. Recently married to the beautiful Aurelie, Mike talked about his wife more than any man Patrick had ever met. It was sweet. He hoped the long hours and occasional horrors of the job didn't wreck the futures of the happy couple.

Mike handed Patrick his. 'Vanilla latte, double shot. Carmella, extra flat and wet.'

She grinned up at him. 'Let me guess, regular filter coffee for DS Staunton.'

'You know me so well.'

Patrick and Carmella spread out their lists on the table. Mike looked over their shoulders. 'Why don't you put them all into the computer and sort them alphabetically?'

'This is quicker,' Patrick said, his eyes scanning the three lists. He felt shaken from his visit to both families, but particularly the Hartleys. He thought he was never, ever going to forget the image of Fiona Hartley slicing banana and sprinkles for a little girl who was never coming back. All the way through the interview, Patrick had kept thinking *It was so nearly me*. He dreamed about that afternoon, when he had come home and found Gill sitting on the stairs, every week, but in his dreams Bonnie didn't come back to life, and he always woke up trembling and cold, relief sending him rushing into his daughter's room to confirm that yes, she was still alive. Still here. Unlike poor Izzy.

He read through the list out loud. 'Different nurseries . . . The Hartleys go to church but the other two families don't . . . No common holiday or day trip destinations . . . Two of them have been to The Playbarn, that soft play place in Teddington but the McConnells haven't . . . Two go to this thing called the Eleven O'Clock Club in Bushy Park . . . Only the McConnells shop regularly at Sainsbury's . . .'

The door opened again and DCI Laughland came in. As always, when she walked into the room, Patrick's blood stirred; everything else in the room grew a little dimmer compared to Suzanne.

She came over to the table. 'Any progress?'

The strain of the case, the pressure from the media, and those higher up, showed on her face. As well as wanting to find the abductor for the children and their parents, Patrick wanted to do it for Suzanne too. Not just to repay her faith in him but because, at the most basic human level, he wanted to make her happy.

He told her what they were doing and she pursed her lips. 'Can I have a word?'

Patrick followed her to her office. 'What's up?' he said, as she shut the door behind them.

'How close are we to making an arrest?'

'An arrest? You know we haven't got any real suspects yet.'

All the warmth that was normally in her voice when she talked to him was absent. 'What about this traveller? Wesley Hewson?'

'He's not the murderer. I'm sure of it.'

'But he failed to report the body. He fucking concealed it.'

Patrick was surprised to hear her swear.

'Why are you so sure it's not him?'

Patrick tensed. She was the SIO but he was the lead detective on this case. 'There's no motive, and his explanation for why he did it makes perfect sense. Suzanne—' She raised her eyebrows. 'Sorry. *Ma'am.*' He knew she hated being called that but he was pissed off now. 'We could pursue Hewson but I'm convinced it would be waste of time and effort.'

She prowled round the back of her desk. 'I don't think you realise how much pressure I'm under to show that we're getting somewhere with this. I want you to arrest him for perverting the course of justice.'

'Why? He didn't intend to obstruct the case.'

Her face was pink. His probably was too, he realised. 'Why are you sticking up for this cretin?'

'Because it's a waste of time and energy. We need to concentrate on—'

'You can multitask, can't you?' she snapped. 'Obviously you need to concentrate on finding out what the kids' lives and routines have in common, and all the other . . . *stuff* . . . you're doing.' She waved her arm as she said this, as though 'stuff' was a pointless exercise in futility. 'But I'm ordering you to arrest Hewson too.'

Patrick didn't speak. His heartbeat thumped in his ears, the blood feeling thick and hot in his veins. It should be up to him whether Hewson was arrested. It was his investigation. Suzanne was completely disregarding his opinion. Eventually he said reluctantly, 'If you think that's for the best, boss. Why don't you send Winkler to do it? He'd enjoy it.'

'Very well. I will.'

Patrick hated this. He wanted to say something to make things good between them. But he was angry and couldn't think of a single thing to say except, 'Are we done?'

Back in the incident room, he found Carmella and Mike poring over the lists. Patrick sipped at his coffee and winced. Stone cold. Ruined. An apt drink for the way he was feeling right now.

'There's nothing,' Carmella said. 'Not a single place where their lives intersect. How can that be? I thought I had it for a moment, that Frankie went to a playgroup that's attached to the Hartleys' church – but it's a different one. And there doesn't seem to be anything else.'

Patrick sat down and scrutinized the lists again. Something popped out at him. 'What's this? Dads' Club. Carmella, didn't you say that Mr McConnell took Liam there occasionally. What is it?'

'I don't think he told me.' Carmella said.

'Don't think? Well, fucking call him and find out.'

She stared at him with wide eyes. She and Mike exchanged a look and he knew exactly what they were thinking – that he'd just had a bollocking from the SIO.

He would apologise later, but for now he watched Carmella call the McConnells, turning into the corner of the room to speak to the father of missing Liam again. After a couple of minutes she hung up and came back over, picking up the Hartleys' and Philipses' lists.

'The Dads' Club is a place where dads can take pre-school children on a Saturday morning. It takes place at the Eleven O'Clock Club in the park.'

There it was. Like three gold bells falling into line on a fruit machine.

'Jackpot,' Patrick said.

Another park, more happy children's voices floating across from the playground, little yelps of excitement from the swings and slides and sandpit. Bonnie came to this park most days with her nan, or Patrick sometimes brought her on his days off. He and Gill used to come to this park too, way back when, before she got pregnant and had Bonnie. Back before everything changed. Patrick remembered long, baked summer's days spent lounging on the grass with a newspaper and a picnic. Slow kisses on hot afternoons. He remembered one day early in their relationship when, concealed by trees, he had slipped his hand beneath her skirt and brought her to a silent, gasping orgasm.

It seemed like a lifetime had passed since then. That happy couple didn't exist any more. But there was one good thing remaining: Bonnie.

'I broke my leg falling off a swing when I was a wee girl,' Carmella said.

'You were a daredevil, I bet.' He had apologised for his outburst, and she assured him the incident was forgotten already.

'A little minx, according to my dad.'

Patrick smiled. 'I was always scared of things like that when I was little. Heights, danger, anything that might make me fall over and hurt myself. I've got a lot better now but Bonnie takes after me, unfortunately.'

'I'd say she's pretty fortunate to take after her dad.'

Rather than her mum. The words hung unspoken and Patrick said, 'Right, let's go check out this place.'

The Eleven O'Clock Club was based in a squat prefabricated building next to the playground in the south-west corner of the park. It closed its doors at one but Patrick had called ahead and someone had agreed to meet them and talk to them. He could see her now, an attractive black woman in linen trousers and a white T-shirt, waiting by the door, staring at her phone.

'Jemima Walters?' Patrick asked, shaking her warm hand. 'DI Lennon, DS Masiello. Thanks for agreeing to meet us.'

She nodded. 'Are you investigating the child abductions? Oh those poor—'

'Can we go inside, where it's private?'

'Sure, sure.'

The interior of the building looked like the inside of any nursery or playgroup. A couple of small slides and a miniature climbing frame in the shape of a train in the centre, toy cupboards all around the edges, posters of Teletubbies and Peppa Pig stuck up around the walls. To the right was a counter where, Patrick imagined, the staff served cups of coffee to exhausted parents and orange segments and triangles of toast to energy-burning pre-schoolers.

Jemima pulled up some plastic chairs and sat down on one, gesturing for Patrick and Carmella to do the same.

'You're the manager here, is that right?' Patrick asked.

'Uh-huh.' The woman's legs bounced with nervous energy. She made Patrick feel like grabbing her knees and forcing her to stay still. 'I can't believe it. Those poor babies. Little Isabel. You know, I thought I recognized her. I said to my husband, I know that pretty little face. But we get so many children here.'

'Mrs Walters, you do understand this conversation is confidential? We need your discretion. It could be vital.'

Her eyes met his, a little flash of excitement to go along with her distress. She was important. Trusted.

'You have my word,' she said.

'Good. Can you tell me a little about this place first?'

She explained that the Eleven O'Clock Club was a centre run by the council, her employer, to provide a place for parents to take babies and pre-school children every weekday morning. 'It's hugely popular. Sometimes I think we're the very heart of Nappy Valley.'

'And on Saturdays you run the Dads' Club?'

'Mmm. Although that's not its official title, you know. That's just what everyone calls it. Mums and grans and granddads are welcome too. Anyone. But we get a lot of fathers on Saturday morning, giving their wives a break from the little ones.'

'I'll have to check it out,' Patrick smiled. 'I've got a daughter who's just about to turn two.'

'Oh, please do.'

'Do you keep records of everyone who attends on Saturdays?' Carmella asked.

Jemima stood up, went behind the counter and fished out a book from a drawer. 'This is the signing-in book. To be honest with you, we don't enforce it, but everyone who comes in has to sign in and out, and give their name, the names and ages of their kids, their postcode and phone number. Plus there's a voluntary two-pound fee that goes towards snacks and drinks.'

'Can we borrow this?' Patrick asked.

'I . . . don't know.'

'We'll look after it.'

'Why do you need it? Why are you here?' Her knees were jiggling faster than ever now.

Patrick leaned forward, slightly concerned he might get hit by a jerking knee. 'Jemima, we believe that all three of the children who were abducted were regular visitors here. We're simply following all lines of inquiry. It's nothing for you to fret about.'

'OK . . .'

'We also need a list of all your staff, including cleaners, any temp staff, anyone who has worked here at all over the last six months.'

'That will be difficult for me to get on a Saturday.'

'You know that Liam and Frankie are still out there somewhere, Mrs Walters?' said Carmella. 'Someone has them. We can't afford to waste any time.'

Flustered, Jemima said, 'Of course, yes. OK, I can get that for you but it will take a couple of hours.'

'That's fine,' Patrick said. He gave her his card and scribbled his email address on the back using a felt-tip that was lying on a nearby art table.

'It can't be anyone who works here,' Jemima said, to herself as much as the police. 'It just can't be.'

As they walked out of the building into the bright sunshine, Patrick's phone rang.

It was Suzanne.

'Any news from the Dads' Club?' she asked.

He immediately felt irritated again. 'Are you checking up on me? You know I'll report back as soon as—'

'No, Patrick, I'm not checking up on you. DS Staunton just brought me some interesting news.'

'Right?' He watched a little girl clamber up the slide in the playground and slip down on her belly, giggling with delight. Her dad stood nearby, ignoring her, thumbing his iPhone.

'We've had a call. A witness who says they saw something in the Sainsbury's car park. I want you to go and talk to them right away.'

Chapter 15
Helen – Day 3

As soon as Helen could escape back up to her and Sean's bedroom, she checked to see if Janet Friars had replied. Nothing – just a message from Liz Wilkins, her former colleague, asking how she and 'poor Sean' were coping, which Helen deleted angrily. Her own message to the woman remained unopened. She deleted Janet's message as instructed then sat and waited, staring at the computer screen, hoping that the little tick would appear saying at what time her last one had been read. Nothing. Janet Friars obviously wasn't online.

Who was she? How could she know where Frankie and Liam were, and not have told the police – unless she was either a nutter, or the kidnapper herself?

Helen wondered idly if she'd be in trouble with the police, for not telling them about the message. She didn't care. They were bound to think it was a hoax, and it would break her heart if they didn't look into it. The FLO's words 'nutters on Facebook' kept ringing around her head, but she knew that she would personally respond to every single message she received from anyone saying they knew anything about Frankie's whereabouts.

Helen half-listened to Eileen's voice, floating up through the floorboards, somehow managing to sound both lilting and grating, going on and on, first to Lennon – God knows what the DI had found to ask her about when she hadn't seen her granddaughter for over eighteen months of Frankie's short life, and knew nothing about her routine or likes and dislikes – and then, after Lennon left, to Sean. Helen could tell, by the hectoring tone that had entered Eileen's voice. She gritted her teeth. Poor Sean. The one thing that united her small family more than anything else was their mutual antipathy towards her mother-in-law, the racist cow. Her own late mum, Winnie, had refused to ever speak to Eileen again after their first meeting when Eileen had informed Winnie that 'the blacks' were taking all the good jobs.

This antipathy was reconfirmed when Sean came stomping up the stairs. Helen softly called out to him, and he came into the bedroom and sat heavily down on the unmade bed next to her. His face was white and exhausted.

'As if things aren't already disastrous enough,' he said, rubbing his face vigorously with the palm of his hand as though washing it. '*She* has to turn up. She's a vulture! I bet she loves this – did you see what she was wearing? That's her best suit, the one she only wears to weddings and parties. She's only showed up because she thinks she'll get to be on TV. I'm surprised she wasn't wearing that fucking awful hat that goes with it.'

Helen hadn't seen her mother-in-law frequently enough to know what her best suit was, but she had been vaguely aware of the monstrous purple nylon floral two-piece that Eileen was wearing.

'She'll never forgive us for not inviting her to the wedding, will she?'

Sean sat on the end of the desk and put his feet up on the side of Helen's swivel chair. 'That was five years ago. She needs to get over it. *Your* folks forgave us, didn't they? So why can't she?'

'They weren't happy, but yeah, I think they were grateful we spared them the cost of two flights from Cape Town. I wish Mum could've been there, though. If I'd known she wouldn't even be around to meet Frankie . . .'

Helen glanced across at the framed photo on the desk of her and Sean on their wedding day, barefoot on a beach in the Seychelles, a warm sea-breeze whipping her hair across her tanned face, Sean smiling down at a ten-year-old Alice who stood between them, clutching a posy of pink roses. It had been a perfect wedding, just the three of them plus a couple of witnesses plucked from by the pool at their hotel, the sun setting behind them as they said their vows to the grinning Indian minister. Helen remembered the feel of the cool damp sand between her toes as she promised to love Sean forever.

Sean put his hand on top of hers, and she was shocked to see tears flood into his eyes. He never cried.

She snatched her hand away and jumped up, shocked. 'You don't think they'll find her alive, do you?'

He bit his knuckle like a little boy would, and she stared at him, this man she adored but who was a closed book to her, as his shoulders heaved. 'Oh darling, come here,' she said, tenderly taking him into her arms even though she wanted to punch him for doubting that they would get Frankie back again . . . 'It's OK, they will find her,' she soothed, as much for her own benefit as his. 'They will, they *have* to . . .'

They stood like that for five minutes or more, arms wrapped around each other, Sean's breath hot on her neck and his tears wetting her skin. 'Don't push me away, Sean,' she begged softly into his ear. 'We can get through this together. I need you. Mum's dead, and I can't talk to Dad. You're all I've got.'

'I need you too,' he muttered back. Then he extricated himself from her embrace and scrubbed at his face. 'Right, better get dressed. What are we going to do with the old dear? I can't send her back to Braintree on the next train – she'd probably try and sell a story to the tabloids saying we've buried Frankie in the back garden—'

'*Sean!* How can you even make a joke out of it?' Helen's lip trembled, although she knew he had only made the flippant comment because he was mortified about her seeing him cry. *Men*, she thought. *Why are they so pathetic?*

He tutted, but had the grace to apologise. 'You know what I mean. We'll let her stay for a couple of days but no more. Are you OK with that?'

Helen sighed. 'I suppose so. It's more than she bloody deserves, though. Why couldn't she be a proper granny to Frankie when she was here?'

'She *is* my mother,' Sean retorted weakly. 'I'm going for a shower.' He stripped off his clothes, and Helen gazed at his body, as familiar as her own, a T-shirt tan and the skin underneath fish-bellied pale and hairy, his flaccid penis small and vulnerable. She felt a rush of affection and lust, craving the oblivion of sex, the comfort of arousal. She was just contemplating following him into the shower when he turned at the bathroom door.

'Have you told your dad, by the way? About Frankie?'

As if there was something else more important.

Helen sighed. 'No. Not yet. Don't want to worry him.'

'You should, you know.'

'I know. But there's nothing he could do. And God forbid he suddenly show up on our doorstep too. One troublesome in-law's enough, surely.'

The thought of her dad was enough to successfully quell any burgeoning lust she had vaguely entertained. Sean had gone into the shower, and she left him to it. As soon as she heard the water running, she dashed back to Facebook and refreshed the screen. A new message from Janet Friars! She clicked on it.

'It's difficult at the moment as I have no money and they're watching me, can't go to police. I will meet you on Thursday at 2.'

Helen's heart sank. So that was most likely it – Janet Friars was already mentioning money. She was bound to be some callous chancer trying to extort cash from her. Thursday was two days away and she couldn't wait that long. She wrote a message back:

You know The Sun have offered a £100k reward? Why don't you tell the police what you know, then you might get that? Wouldn't that be a better way to go about it?

Then she deleted it, holding her finger on the back arrow key and watching the letters be swallowed up by the thin black cursor. It made her feel sick, to think that she was potentially bartering for her daughter's life. She typed a new sentence.

How do I know you are genuine? If you really do have information, why haven't you told the police?

Duh, she thought, and deleted it again. If the person was genuine, then they really would be in fear of the repercussions of talking to her. She wrote one final sentence: Give me some proof before we go any further, or I'm telling the police, and sent it.

What has my life come to? she thought. This time last week she was taking Frankie to feed the ducks and wondering when her next editing job would come along so she could get back to work, to escape the long, slow company of toddlers. Now she knew she would gladly never work again, just to have Frankie back. Even if Sean's salary evaporated into nothing and they were on the poverty line, she wouldn't want to let Frankie out of her sight, ever again. She would forget about her career. She would watch *Dora the Explorer* on a continuous loop, play hundreds of games of *I Spy* and read board books all day until her eyeballs bled, the ones that she always thought of as 'bored' books and which previously made her want to die of boredom. *Anything*, she begged the God in which she had long ago stopped believing. *I'll do anything to get Frankie back again.*

She gritted her teeth and forced herself to get dressed instead of waiting in front of the computer screen. When she came – reluctantly – back downstairs, Eileen was sitting at the kitchen table knitting something revolting-looking. Frothy hanks of pastel wool cascaded off the edge of the table and her hands moved so fast that they were a blur. She knitted as though she was accusing someone of something terrible, Helen thought.

Eileen gave her a look that said 'and what time do you call this to get dressed, when your mother-in-law's here, and your baby is missing?' Helen decided to at least attempt a charm offensive.

'Eileen, thank you so much for coming. I'm sorry I didn't say hello properly before, it's all been a bit . . . overwhelming, as I'm sure you can imagine.' She leaned over and gave Eileen a brief hug. 'It's really kind of you.'

'Thank you, Helen, love, of course I had to come. I couldn't sit at home doing nothing with that little lamb God knows where, and now the news of poor little Izzy Hartley . . .' She dissolved into loud snotty sobs, and Helen tore off some kitchen roll and handed it to her. She had aged since they last saw her, Helen thought, studying her mother-in-law's broken veined cheeks and sunken eyes. Too much smoking had left fissures all around her mouth, and a general dissatisfaction at the way her life had gone had etched crevices in her forehead and carved deep frown lines between her eyebrows. She was sixty-five but looked more like late seventies.

'I know. It's unspeakable,' Helen said. 'But we just have to keep hoping and praying the police will find her.' She was amazed that she managed to keep her voice steady and her eyes dry, but she found that Eileen's hysteria helped keep her detached.

'So, how have you been? It's been ages.'

Eileen stopped crying and glared at her. 'That's because you haven't invited me to anything.'

Helen sighed. 'Eileen. You have an open invitation to see us whenever you want, you know that. I wasn't having a go, just making conversation. But we do have this family liaison officer staying with us at the moment, so it's a bit of a houseful what with the police coming and going, and Alice's friends in and out . . .'

'Are you saying I can't stay?' Eileen pursed her lips, deepening all her wrinkles further.

'No, not at all, as long as you don't mind sleeping on the zed bed in the office. I'm just saying sorry that the spare room's not free . . .' Helen chickened out of imposing the three-day maximum time limit. Let Sean do that, she thought. 'Anyway, you must be hungry, let me get some pasta on. Sean's just having a shower. He'll be down in a while.'

When the pasta was done, and Sean had reappeared with spiky wet hair, the three of them sat down. Frankie's empty booster seat was still attached to the fourth chair at the table, like a reproach. There was a tomato sauce stain on the strap of it that Helen didn't want to clean off. She and Sean picked at a few tubes of pasta each. It was the first meal that she had cooked in three days, the FLO having made several others that none of them had touched. Helen found herself hoping the FLO would come back soon, so at least then Eileen would have a captive audience that wasn't herself and Sean.

Eileen ate with gusto, wittering on about people 'back home' that Helen knew Sean had no interest in hearing about. Helen switched off completely. All she could think about was whether or not Janet Friars had replied again, and as soon as she could reasonably leave the table, she got up abruptly. 'Leave the bowls. I'll clear up later,' she said. 'Just going to call the station to see if there are any updates.'

Once back in the study with the door firmly closed, she approached the computer as though it might detonate at any moment.

There *was* a new message, and she shivered as she read it: I can't tell the police, he'll kill me and the little ones too. But he didn't take Izzy. Just Liam and Frankie. Frankie's wearing fairy PJs. That enough proof for you? See you Thursday.

Helen moaned. Frankie had indeed been wearing her Tinkerbell pyjamas, but she was sure that this had been mentioned in the press conference – hadn't it? Then she couldn't remember if it had, or if she'd imagined it. Her hand hovered over the telephone, and she knew in a flash that she was now well and truly out of her depth. She was an idiot to think she could handle this herself. She *would* call the police. She dialled the number of Sutton police station and, once she got through the automated options to a real person, asked for DI Lennon.

'He's out, I'm afraid. Who shall I say is calling?'

She hesitated. 'It's Helen Philips. I need to talk to someone senior on the team investigating my daughter's abduction. It's urgent.'

After a maddeningly long pause, long enough for Helen to realize that Sean was going to be really pissed off with her for corresponding with Janet Friars without telling him, she heard a bored-sounding voice:

'DI Winkler. Can I help you?'

She explained the situation and read out the Facebook message thread bar the specific instructions about meeting, almost whispering to prevent Sean and Eileen eavesdropping.

'I see,' said Winkler. 'Have you told DI Lennon about this development?'

'No. I didn't want to waste anyone's time. Our FLO said we'd be bound to get loads of hoax messages on Facebook,' Helen replied sheepishly. She was surprised at Winkler's reaction:

'Well, Mrs Philips, I'm a firm believer in leaving no stone unturned. I'm on my way over now – please can you remain at home until I arrive? I'll only be ten minutes.'

Helen put the phone down and tried not to feel too optimistic. She closed her eyes and hugged herself, imagining she was holding Frankie, tears rolling over her cheeks and onto her baby's soft hair. This DI Winkler sounded like a man of action, like someone who could get things done. She was glad she'd been put through to him instead of Lennon.

Chapter 16
Patrick – Day 3

Entering the Hollisters' enormous house in St Margaret's was like walking slap bang into the middle of an explosion of noise and fur and utter, absolute mayhem of almost cartoonish proportions. There were kids everywhere: a boy running down the stairs with no shirt on, a girl plonking discordantly at a piano, a toddler in a nappy chasing a cat around the living room, another boy mowing down zombies at full volume on an Xbox. Two red setters and a Yorkshire terrier appeared to be engaged in some kind of doggy ménage-a-trois in the kitchen. The smell of dirty nappies and dog fur assaulted Patrick's nostrils as he stepped over a pile of wooden bricks and almost skidded on a yachting magazine that had been left on the wooden floor.

'Welcome to the madhouse,' said Liza Hollister, the mother of the child who had seen something in Sainsbury's car park. She was almost six feet tall, with scraped-back blonde hair and clothes straight out of the Boden catalogue.

Patrick introduced himself just as the shirtless boy of around eight dashed up and yelled, 'Mum, Coco's put Saskia in the toilet again.'

'Oh for goodness sake.' Liza stomped off and returned a few moments later with a wriggling toddler under one arm and a drenched cat under the other. She tossed the cat through the open French doors and Patrick watched it saunter off as if nothing had happened.

'Daisy, stop banging that fucking piano,' she shouted. She picked up a wooden spoon and banged it against a small gong that she obviously kept for such occasions.

'Daisy, Dominic, Sebastian – go and play in the garden. And take Coco with you.'

'Aw, mum, it's boring,' moaned Sebastian, the older boy who'd been playing on the console.

'Go on the trampoline. See how high you can bounce. Go on!' She turned to Patrick and muttered through clenched teeth. 'Try not to land on your neck on the way down.'

The four trooped out through the French doors into the size-able garden, followed by the three dogs, who ran around their feet and tripped the toddler over.

'That's better,' Liza grinned. 'Right, Detective Inspector. Coffee? You look like you could use one.'

'That would be fantastic, Mrs Hollister.'

She leaned forward, giving him an eyeful of cleavage. He vaguely recognized her – then it struck him. She used to be on TV, presenting some late-night 'yoof' programme. She had been a ladette, always falling out of nightclubs with her knickers on dis-play, boozing for England. She had married that rock star – what was his name? The one who played guitar in an indie band then went on to become a dance music producer.

She clattered about the kitchen making coffee – proper coffee, that she had to grind – and Patrick scanned the bookcases while he waited. There were a lot of books of erotic art. Then he noticed a photo of Liza hanging on the wall – it was her on the cover of FHM ten years before, naked, her nipples airbrushed away but her bottom on show.

Oh god, he thought. *I bought that issue.* He had taken it into the bathroom with him . . .

'You alright?' she asked, coming back with a steaming mug of coffee. 'You look a bit hot.'

'It is very hot in here.'

She nodded at the *FHM* portrait. 'Ah, those were the days. The older kids find it terribly embarrassing having pictures of their half-naked mum hanging up, but fuck it. I was a looker in those days.'

You still are, he almost blurted. Instead, he said, 'What do you do these days?'

She gestured around her. 'This. I look after this bloody lot. Danny is in the studio most of the time, or DJ-ing. Leaves me looking after his spawn.' That was his name! Danny Hollister. 'But I've just had an offer to go on the next series of *I'm a Celeb* and between you and me I might just do it. See how he copes for two weeks without me. Ha!'

Patrick sipped his coffee. 'Which of the children thinks they saw Liam McConnell?'

Liza frowned, the mood in the room changing instantly. 'That's Bowie. He's up in his room. Let me get him.'

He expected her to go up the stairs but instead she shouted, 'Bowie! Can you come down here?'

'I've been over it with him,' she said. 'I wanted to be sure he wasn't making it up, or had dreamt it. But I swear he's not.'

'I'd like to hear it in his own words,' Patrick said. 'But can you tell me why it's taken so long? Did he only just remember?'

'Oh, we were away. We'd stopped off at the supermarket on our way to the airport. We have a villa in the south of France and we were taking the kids there for the week. We're heading back over there in a fortnight.' She gestured out of the front window at the people carrier parked on the driveway. 'We were in that thing – the tank, we call it. I went into the shop leaving Danny with the kids. I'm sure it was bedlam as always, the kids fighting and complaining. Danny would have been trying to get them to stop squabbling. But Bowie is quieter than the others. He usually sits still and reads books or looks out the window, daydreaming. We reckon he's going to be a writer when he grows up.'

A skinny boy of seven came into the room. He was the spitting image of his mum, with long blond hair and big blue eyes. He looked nervous.

'Babe, this is Detective Lennon. Lennon, meet Bowie.' She paused, then started to giggle. Patrick laughed too – he couldn't help it – but the boy didn't crack a smile. His pale face remained serious, anxious, and Patrick remembered what he'd been like as a child. Just like this: scared of strangers, always 'away in the clouds', as his mum put it, preferring to sit with a book when his friends were out playing football.

Liza put her arm around her son's shoulders and led him over to the sofa. He stared at Patrick, chewing his fingernails. Patrick sat down on a floor cushion to ensure the boy's eye level was above his, to make him feel less uneasy.

'Bowie.' He felt daft saying the boy's name. He'd probably change it to Joe or something when he was older. 'Your mum tells me that you saw something when you were in the car park at Sainsbury's just before you went on holiday.'

Bowie nodded almost imperceptibly.

'I just need you to tell me what you saw.'

The boy spoke, his voice surprisingly clear. 'It was him, that boy who's in the newspapers. Liam. I saw his picture on the front of the paper when we got back. They said the Child Catcher got him.'

He looked over at his mum, then back at Patrick. 'But it wasn't the Child Catcher. It was a lady.'

Patrick could hear his own heartbeat. 'A woman? Tell me what you saw.'

'I was just, like, sitting looking out of the tank window, watching what was going on. This guy with dreadlocks had just dropped a bottle of drink and it had smashed and there was red liquid everywhere, and he was jumping about, so I was watching him. Then I saw this car – an Audi—'

'You remember the type of car?'

'He loves cars,' Liza interrupted. 'He knows all the makes and models. Knows a lot more about them than I do.'

'Yes, it was a white Audi, one of the saloon models. I could see a little kid sitting in the back seat, his face pressed against the glass, like he was looking for his mum and dad.'

'Then what happened?'

'I saw this woman walk past the car, and then she did . . . what's it called when you see something without realizing and then you stop and turn around?'

'A double take?'

'That's it. She did that. And she walked back to the car window. She had her back to me. But then she opened the car door and lifted the little boy, Liam, out of his booster seat and carried him away.'

'How did he look?' Patrick didn't want to ask leading questions.

'I don't know what you mean.'

'I mean, could you see his face? Did he look happy, sad?'

Bowie thought about it. 'He just looked kind of relaxed. He wasn't struggling or anything. Or crying. I thought she must be his mum or auntie or something because otherwise I would have told my dad.' He bit his lip. 'I'm really sorry.'

'Bowie, you have nothing to be sorry about. It's great that you saw something and that you're telling us. Did you notice if the woman had a car key? Did you see her unlock the door?'

He pursed his lips. 'No. But she had her back to me. She might have had the key in front of her. I guess it would have been a remote one.'

Patrick nodded. 'Did you see where they went?'

Bowie stared at the floor. 'No. Because then Mum got back and she had ice lollies and everyone went a bit crazy. I mean, even crazier.'

'And what about the woman. Would you recognize her?'

'I think so.'

'Could you describe her? I don't mean right now – I mean, if you sat down with an artist, could you tell them what the woman looked like so they could draw her?'

'I could try. She had sort of frizzy dark brown hair. She was short.'

Patrick smiled. In every investigation, you need a break, a stroke of good fortune. This could be his: finding the most observant seven-year-old in London.

He addressed Liza. 'I'd like you and Bowie to come down to the station so he can sit with a sketch artist. It's important to do it as quickly as possible.'

'That's fine. I just need to get someone to babysit. I'll go and ask Sandy next door.'

She zipped out of the room, towards the front door, and Patrick found himself sharing an uncomfortable silence with Bowie. The boy stared at the rug and Patrick groped for a topic of conversation that this kid might be interested in. Cars, that was it. But then he couldn't think of anything to say about cars. He was still fishing about in his head when Bowie said, 'I expect he's dead.'

Patrick looked up.

The boy glanced at the window to see if his mum was coming back. 'The lady who took him. My brother said she's a witch. She steals kids, sucks their life from them, then dumps their bodies.'

'No, that's not—'

'And now I've told you I've seen her, she'll come for me.' His voice trembled but Patrick could sense he was trying to be brave. 'Please catch her, Detective. Before she gets me.'

Patrick stared at the computer, his head filled with the image of a witch with yellow, gluttonous eyes and a mouth full of sharp teeth designed for tearing and chewing children's flesh. A woman. Bowie had said that Liam had been taken by a woman, and he was in with the sketch artist now, describing her. The news had raced around the station like chicken pox round a nursery.

And he'd said that Liam hadn't been scared, had looked at her like he knew her. He picked up the sketch Frankie had made of the face at the window (*the witch?*) and asked himself, again, why the Philips girl hadn't cried out or told her sister about it.

While he'd been out, Carmella had been through the book from the Eleven O'Clock Club and entered each of the parents' names, and Jemima Walters had sent over the names of the staff. He scrolled through the lists. Each of these names was being run through HOLMES to see if they had a record, along with the Violent and Sexual Offenders Register, ViSOR.

Patrick squinted at the list. He really needed to see an optician; the edges of the letters were blurred, the words not quite in focus. Or maybe it was tiredness, though he didn't feel tired at this moment. His whole body was popping with adrenalin.

He was about to get out of his seat and go to talk to Carmella, when a name on the list caught his attention. Denise Breem. Why did he know that name? He opened his web browser and Googled it, remembering in the split second before her image appeared who she was and what she was notorious for.

'Fuck,' he whispered. He jumped out of his seat and dashed out of the room, calling Carmella as he went.

Chapter 17
Alice/Larry – Day 3

'Seriously, I've had it with living here. Can't we get a place together?'

Even as Alice said it, she knew she didn't mean it. Larry smelled far too bad for her to want to actually live with him. She, Georgia and Larry had only been in her bedroom for five minutes and she was dying to open the window. She leaned into his neck, experimentally inhaling his smell of sweat, weed and old socks, and wrinkled her nose. Would it be uncool to ask him to have a shower next time they went to bed together? Last time she had been almost gagging whenever his armpit came near her face. Shame, because she really loved him. He was so nice to her, and the first one she had ever Done It with. Besides, all boys stank, didn't they?

'Sure, darlin', if you got a spare twenty-five grand a year to rent a one-bedroom flat round here . . . That's a shitload of weed to sell,' he replied, putting his arm around her shoulder.

'That much?' Alice and Georgia chorused, shocked. Then Alice giggled. She was a little high, she realized. 'Actually I changed my mind. I wanna live with *you*, Georgie.'

'Course you can, babes,' Georgia said through narrowed eyes as she blew a neat smoke ring. 'My mum fucking loves you. You could move in tomorrow.'

'Really?' Alice sat up. 'I'm going to open the window, I'm boiling.'

'Yeah. Wouldn't that be cool?'

'Yeah. And you smell so *gooooood,*' Alice opened the hopper window then flung herself on top of Georgia on the bed and they rolled around together, half-wrestling, half-hugging.

Larry watched, reaching out a hand to Alice's black nylon-clad thigh under her short school skirt. 'Always fancied a threesome,' he snickered, although his touch was tentative and his fingers shook slightly. Alice noticed the flicker of relief across his face when she pushed him off and sat up. 'No chance!'

'So why don't you want to live here anymore?' Georgia scrolled through the songs on Alice's iPod, settled on a Lil Wayne track and replaced the iPod in the speaker dock. 'I mean, obviously it must be shit, with Frankie gone . . .'

'It's *really* shit,' Alice said with feeling. 'Helen's in a total state the whole time. Dad's gone all quiet and won't talk to anyone, the police are in and out – well, that Family Liaison Officer's only just left us alone, she was there for days, like they were worried we were all going to, like, I dunno, *stab* each other or something . . . Which Helen and Dad probably would do if they got the chance. They totally think it's all my fault that Frankie's been taken. And now, to top it all off, my bloody Nan turns up.'

'Don't you like your nan?' Larry enquired.

Alice snorted. 'She's a horrible interfering old cow. Even Dad doesn't like her, and she's his mum. She only turned up 'cos she thought she might have a chance to be on TV. She keeps going outside and talking to the paparazzi, offering them "exclusives". It's so embarrassing. Dad and Helen have even gone out for a drive just so they don't have to talk to her. Still, at least it means we can hang out here without them hassling us . . .'

'Do you really miss Frankie, babes?' Georgia asked.

Alice had to grit her teeth not to snap back. 'Of course I do! It's so quiet here without her. And it's just so horrible, not knowing what's happened to her, whether or not some fucking paedophile's doing . . . you know . . . stuff to her.'

Her voice cracked and two big tears dropped straight from her eyes on to her flowery Cath Kidston duvet cover.

Larry looked simultaneously mortified and concerned. He hugged her, and this time Alice felt comforted by his odour.

'But they don't give a shit about me, about how *I* might be feeling. I mean, don't they realize how freaked out I am that someone came into my house, while I was here, and took my sister? How do they think that makes me feel? I could've been killed, but does that occur to them? No! The thought of some stranger in my house, taking Frankie out of her bed and out the house – it makes me want to puke. I don't want to stay here anymore. I'm gonna run away somewhere, I mean it. They wouldn't even notice for ages, probably. All they care about is Frankie.'

'Don't do that, Al,' said Georgia, tears now in her own eyes. 'Please don't do that.'

Alice felt comforted by the solid presence of her friends, one on each side of her, and at all the attention. She sniffed and swiped her hand under her nostrils.

'Who's this?' asked Larry, keen to change the subject. A new track had come on the iPod.

'Biggie Smalls,' said Georgia.

Larry laughed.

'What?' Alice felt pissed off that he was laughing while she was in such distress.

'It's funny. Biggie Smalls, Lil Wayne. Got any Tiny Tempeh?'

'No, but she's got some Little Richard,' Georgia said.

'Medium Sean.'

'You're making that up! There's no Medium Sean!'

Even Alice giggled, which quickly turned into that hysterical sort of gasping, heaving involuntary laughter that was hard to stop, long after the joke had ceased to be funny. The three of them clutched at one another and laughed until Georgia said, 'Stop! A little bit of wee just came out!' and they all laughed even harder.

There was a sharp rap at the bedroom door, and the locked door handle jigged. 'Hold on,' Alice called out, hastily concealing the ashtray containing the roach under the bed, and sprayed a generous whoosh of body spray around to disguise the smoky smell, filling the room with a cheap cloying scent. Larry made a mock-vomiting face. *That's rich*, thought Alice, *coming from him*.

Alice opened the door a crack. Eileen stood there frowning at her. 'What's all that racket?'

'Just having a laugh with my mates, Nan.'

'And don't call me Nan. You know I hate it!' snapped Eileen. Alice looked pained and blushed. All her friends called their grandmothers 'Nan', but Sean, Helen and Eileen insisted on 'Granny'. Why did they have to be such snobs? Fake snobs at that. When Granny wasn't concentrating she sounded like she was off *The Only Way is Essex*. Alice turned and glanced over her shoulder to see Georgia and Larry making faces at each other.

'What is it you wanted, *Nan*?' she said, through the gap in the door.

Eileen put her hands on her hips. 'It's not right, Alice Philips, you and your friends messing around and laughing when your sister's been kidnapped.'

Alice rolled her eyes. 'For God's sake. Do you expect me to sit in silence all day? Am I not allowed to try and take my mind off it for a bloody second?'

'Don't you use that tone with me, madam.'

Eileen was working herself up into a righteous frenzy, but Alice banged the door shut in her face. She pulled the iPod from the dock and grabbed her denim jacket, purse and mobile. 'Come on, let's go. I'm not sticking around to be harassed by that old bag.'

'We'll go and see Jerome down the estate,' said Larry. 'Got a bit of business to do – you two can come with me.'

'Jerome? Do we have to?' Georgia said.

'Yeah,' Alice agreed. 'And I'm sure he shags that dog. He's totally in love with it.'

Georgia giggled and Larry pulled a face. 'You're sick.'

'Thanks,' said Alice.

He swiped at her. 'Not *that* kind of sick. But he wants to see me. Can't not go, can I?'

Georgia and Alice exchanged a look. Alice said, 'I suppose not. You go, then, Laz, and we'll catch you this evening. I've totally got enough stress in my life without having to deal with that freak on top of everything else. Let's go to your place, Georgia, yeah?'

Alice opened the door and barged past her grandmother.

'Awright, Nan?' asked Larry, in a neutral tone that could either have been just barely polite, or downright mocking. Alice saw him look Eileen up and down, taking in her man-made fibres and bad perm. Eileen was definitely far more of a Nan than a Granny.

'How dare you talk to me like that, young man?' Eileen's already red face was puce with rage.

'Hiya Mrs Philips,' muttered Georgia, trying to be conciliatory, but it was too late.

'You're grounded!' Eileen shrieked, pulling at Alice's sleeve.

Alice turned and faced her. 'You've got to be fucking joking! Call yourself my granny? You're a stranger to me! We don't want you here. None of us do – not me or Helen or Dad, so why don't you just sod off back to your Essex caravan site or estate or wherever that horrible place you live is, and leave us alone?'

The three of them ran down the stairs, out the back door, and through the garden gate into the back alley, to avoid the two bored photographers still hanging around at the front.

'Laters, Lazzer,' Alice said, hugging Larry round the waist. He kissed her deeply, as Georgia averted her eyes and lit a cigarette. 'Don't get eaten by Rihanna, will you?'

Larry hesitated in the doorway outside the dirtiest of the tower blocks that littered the estate, as though they'd been dropped there randomly from outer space. The wire-reinforced glass doors were so filthy that even he, who could hardly describe himself as fastidious, didn't want to touch anything. Heart in mouth, he reluctantly slipped into the lobby just as the lift doors pinged and slid open.

Jerome stood there, looking equally intimidating and ridiculous in huge gleaming metallic trainers, freshly shaved head, a silver leather jacket, and jeans of such thick, new stiff denim that Larry thought they would stand up by themselves if Jerome's short legs hadn't been in them. The dog had a matching silver collar and lead and was snarling softly.

Larry's mouth went dry and he felt suddenly preppy and immature in his OBEY sweatshirt and Vans, even though he wouldn't be caught dead wearing the sort of gear Jerome was sporting. 'Alright Jerome?'

'What are you doing here?' He gestured threateningly towards him and the dog upgraded its snarl to a sudden growling bark, straining towards him on its designer lead.

'You texted, said you wanted to . . .' but Jerome didn't let Larry finish.

'I hope you ain't brought me no more phones. I ain't doing phones no more, so don't pester me with that shit. I'm upgrading into something much fucking bigger.' He looked around to check no-one was listening, then dropped his voice. 'Got a contact for some really good shit. Skunk. And as it goes, I might need a few more kids who can spread the good news around the local colleges an' that. You interested? Better cut for you than for the phones, innit.'

'Maybe. I'll need to think about it.'

'Whatever,' said Jerome, making a face to imply that only pussies ever thought about anything. 'I'll give you ten minutes to think about it, since I'm in a good mood, so I'll let you come with me while I take RiRi for her morning constitutional, and we can talk business. Let's go.'

Larry followed Jerome meekly as they processed around the estate, stopping at every corner for the dog to sniff and squat. Eventually it took an enormous crap, which Jerome of course left in a steaming pile on the ground near the estate's pitiful excuse for a playground – one rusty swing and a roundabout with most of the railings snapped off it. Despite his nerves, Larry had to suppress a grin at the idea that Jerome would ever have pulled a roll of poo bags out of his silver leather jacket, picked up the dogshit and disposed of it in the nearest bin. As if!

'What are you smirking at, you tosser?' Jerome snapped at him.

'Nothing!' Larry said hastily.

Jerome came right up to him, so close that he could see the tinge of his pallor and the open pores on his nose. 'You disrespecting me?'

'No, Jerome.' Suddenly Larry really wished he'd gone with the girls back to Georgia's place.

Something caught Jerome's eye over Larry's shoulder and he jerked his head up, laughing cruelly. 'Oh man. My day just got a whole lot better. Look who it is – the Crazy Baby Lady.'

Larry glanced behind him to see a very small, very wide old lady swaddled up, despite the heat of the day, in so many layers of drab clothing that she could hardly walk. She had dirty silver gaffer tape holding her shoes together, and her scalp showed through a few remaining wisps of candyfloss hair. The lady was pushing – or, rather, hanging on to – the handle of a very old-fashioned rusty pram that was full of something Larry couldn't quite make out at first.

'She's *well* old,' Larry commented. 'Why's she got that pram?'

'Cos her "baby"'s in there, innit. All her babies.' Jerome laughed meanly and a shiver ran up Larry's back. What sort of babies would that homeless-looking woman have? Dead foetuses? Mangy old cats, perhaps. Frankie's innocent face flashed through his mind, and he shivered again. There were so many weirdos in the world.

But at that moment, he'd have chosen the Crazy Baby Lady over Jerome, any time.

Jerome pimp-rolled over to the old woman and her hooded red eyes flashed with fear and fury.

'Git aways from me!' she screeched, trying to turn the heavy old pram. She pointed at him with a shaky finger. 'You're a bad man!'

Jerome mimicked her in a high-pitched mocking voice. Then he stuck his face close to hers and dropped his voice two octaves. 'You is right. I is a *BAD* man.' He was showing off, thought Larry with disdain.

Jerome darted his hand into the pram which, Larry saw with a brief shock of cognizance that he felt physically in his belly, was full of dolls. Dirty, charity shop sad cases, rag dolls with stuffing spilling out, naked Barbies with matted hair, blank Bratz dolls wearing nothing but stilettos and bras. They were all piled on top of each other, reminding Larry of when they studied the Holocaust in Year Nine, the unforgettable images of naked gassed bodies in unspeakable heaps that, although he never admitted it to anyone, gave him nightmares for weeks afterwards.

But Jerome seemed to know exactly what he was looking for in his sinister lucky dip. He grabbed at the doll on the top, a slightly cleaner, better-cared-for one in a stained pale blue Babygro. They were supposed to be able to blink, those dolls, although this one had one eye stuck open, and the other stuck shut.

The old woman wailed, a heartrending screech of pain.

'Give it back, Jerome,' said Larry, without much conviction.

'Fuck off, you little twat,' Jerome responded, waving the doll around by its foot, like a lasso, taunting his dog with it as though the doll was a juicy steak. The woman clutched at Jerome's arm and he batted her away in disgust. 'Get your filthy claws off of me, you old hag.'

'Give me my baby!' she screeched in a cracked voice. RiRi the dog was working herself up into a frenzy, sensing the tension and aggression in the air, which was doubtless Jerome's intention, as he kept smiling down at the dog and barking back at it. Then he somehow activated the doll's crying mechanism, and its thin mechanical high-pitched wail could be heard above the rest of the commotion. Jerome found it hilarious. Larry had had enough.

'I'll do it,' he said abruptly, 'but in a couple of weeks, yeah? Got a lot on right now. Catch you later.' He started walking away as more kids gathered, at a safe distance, watching the entertainment with blank faces.

Loud screams broke out behind him and when Larry turned around he saw the old woman on her knees trying to reach into RiRi's jaws, where the dog had hold of the doll and was violently shaking it into several separate bits, limbs flying, the head rolling off and bouncing on the tarmac.

Jerome stood by with his arms crossed, laughing as though it was the funniest thing he had ever seen. Then he kicked the pram over, scattering all the other dolls.

Oh man, thought Larry. *What have I let myself in for?*

Chapter 18
Patrick – Day 3

Patrick gathered together all the members of the team in the incident room, with a couple of notable exceptions; Winkler was missing – no one was sure where he was but Patrick was hardly cut up about it – and the DCI, as he was trying to think of her, was in a meeting with the Deputy Commissioner. But everyone else was here, all focussing intently on the large square photograph pinned to the centre of the board.

'Denise Breem,' Patrick said. 'Everyone recognize the name?'

Mike was first to respond. 'Caspar Doyle's missus.'

The name Caspar Doyle sent a shudder of revulsion through the room from both sexes. Seven years ago, Doyle had been convicted of abducting and murdering ten-year-old twins, Lucy and Kelly Draper, who had been on their way home from school. He had brutally raped them before stabbing them to death and attempting to bury them in the back garden of his terraced house. Fortunately, a neighbour had heard him digging up his lawn at midnight and called the police. Two days later, after refusing to speak in interviews and threatening to go on hunger strike, Doyle had hanged himself in his cell.

The police had always suspected that Doyle's girlfriend, Denise Breem, had helped him abduct the girls by luring them to the house. She, or someone matching her description, had been seen hanging around the school in the days immediately before the two girls were murdered. But there was no evidence, she denied everything and, with Doyle dead, it was impossible to make a case against her. To the sickened frustration of every officer involved, they'd had to let her go. With no charges, she wasn't on any registers and her record was clean.

'What do we know about her?' Patrick asked. 'She was twenty-four at the time, so she's thirty-one now. Brought up on the Kennedy Estate, both parents on long-term sick, her dad, by all accounts, a violent, drunken scumbag. Denise left school at sixteen, no qualifications, a couple of convictions for shoplifting to her name.'

'Wasn't there some . . . incident with her sister?' Carmella asked.

'Well remembered. Yes, when Denise was fourteen, her ten-year-old sister was taken into care after social workers discovered that a friend of her parents, a guy called Steve McLean, had sexually assaulted her. McLean was living with the family at the time as their lodger. According to the reports from the time, the whole family blamed the little girl, as if she was some kind of Lolita and he was an innocent victim.'

Heads shook and voices murmured darkly around the room.

'But the social workers didn't think Denise was in any danger after McLean was put away, and Denise denied that he'd touched her too. When questioned about it when she was being interviewed about the Boyle case, Denise said her sister was "a little slut who was asking for it" . . . But none of that matters right now. All that matters is that Denise is the only person with any kind of record we can find on the list from the Eleven O'Clock Club that all three of our abducted children attended.'

'What the hell was she doing there?' Mike asked.

'I'll come to that in a moment,' Patrick replied. 'First, this afternoon I interviewed Bowie Hollister—'

He ignored the sniggers.

'—a seven-year-old boy who says he saw Liam McConnell being taken from his mum's Audi . . . by a woman.' He explained the rest of what Bowie had said and as he spoke he could feel it: that buzz in the air, as it seemed that finally they were getting somewhere. 'Bowie has been with a sketch artist here this afternoon. And this is what he came up with.'

Enjoying the theatricality of it, Patrick lifted the enlarged sketch from where it lay face down on the table and pinned it to the board beside the photo of Denise.

'Fuck! It's her,' Mike said, as most of the other detectives in the room made similar noises.

'It *could* be her,' Patrick corrected him. 'The woman in the sketch appears to have the same dark, frizzy hair, the same shaped face, similar features.'

'The same cruel lips,' Carmella interjected.

'Very poetic, Carmella. Perhaps. But there are a lot of women who look like this.'

'I've been out with a few of them,' wisecracked a DC from the back of the room.

'I need a detective to go through the CCTV from Sainsbury's again, looking for Denise. Preet, can you do that please?' He made a mental note also to ask Preet Gupta if she knew where Winkler, her supposed partner, had got to.

'Also,' Carmella continued, 'Zoe McConnell said that she thought a man bumped her on her way into the supermarket, which was how we assumed she lost her car key.'

Patrick said, 'Mike, can you talk to Mrs McConnell again, find out if she is certain the person who bumped her was a man? I don't think she'd be mistaken about that though – in which case we can assume there were two of them working together. The man bumped Zoe, then passed the key to his female accomplice.'

Mike was deep in thought. 'If McLean is out of prison now, which I guess he would be if it was ten years ago, maybe he and Denise have hooked up – he has a hold over her from when she was a kid. And now she's helping him procure other kids . . . a cycle of abuse.'

'It's a theory,' Patrick agreed.

With the room buzzing, Patrick explained what Denise had been doing at the Dads' Club. He caught Carmella's eye. 'Let's go and find Denise Breem.'

The Helping Hands Agency was based in a cramped, dingy office above a KFC in Whitton, the smell of fried chicken hanging in the air and making Patrick's stomach growl. He told the woman who ran the agency, which provided temps for manual work – cleaning, menial factory work, jobs on building sites, and so on – who they were looking for and watched her press her lips together until they turned white.

'Hounding that poor woman, are you?' The owner, Sarah Mason, was in her early fifties with dyed pillar-box-red hair.

'You know about her past?'

'Yeah, of course. She told me all about how the police tried to stitch her up.'

'And you sent her to work as a cleaner at a club for *children*?'

Sarah Mason's eyes were full of contempt, a look that bounced off Patrick like a bullet off Kevlar. 'She loves kids. Just because she made the mistake of going out with a scumbag.' Her eyes watered, and Patrick understood why this woman felt empathy for Denise Breem. She saw them both as women who'd been let down by men, nothing more.

Carmella leaned in. 'Ms Mason, we don't have time to chat about this all day. We need to know where Denise is right now.'

'And before you argue,' Patrick added, 'and start going on about rights and privacy and whatever, save your breath. This is a murder investigation. You might be the one in a million who thinks Denise is Snow White, but if the tabloids find out you tried to protect her, I don't think you'll have many clients wanting your helping hands any more.'

Walking out, Patrick felt no pride, just grim satisfaction. This, right here, right now, was the point in the investigation where the ends justified the means. The only thing that mattered was finding those kids.

They pulled up outside Freshtime Foods, a hangar-shaped architectural carbuncle based on the edge of an industrial estate in nearby Feltham. Patrick took off his sunglasses as he got out of the car, sweat prickling his armpits, the air thick and chewy. Carmella followed him into the building, appearing cool and fragrant as always, even as they pushed through the hanging plastic slats across the doorway into the stifling heat of the factory. Patrick had worked in a place like this once, during the summer holidays when he was a sixth-former, back at the height of his Goth days, when he always went out wearing make-up. He'd made the mistake of forgetting to remove his eyeliner before coming in to work one day. The meatheads who staffed the factory had loved that, giving him the nickname Rambo. Leaving that factory after a summer picking black cornflakes off a production line had been one of the happiest moments of his life.

A man wearing a foreman's uniform approached immediately.

'We're looking for Denise Breem.' As the foreman frowned, Patrick said, 'She's a temp.'

'Wait here.'

The foreman walked over to the centre of the factory floor, where pots of jam were boxed and stacked on pallets, a group of women standing either side of a conveyor belt wearing blue and white caps and shapeless smocks.

'That's her,' Carmella whispered.

Patrick squinted. Carmella was right. At the far end of the conveyor belt, down which pots of jam trundled, was the woman they were looking for. And at the same moment Patrick recognized her, the foreman spoke to one of the women, who pointed at Denise – and she bolted.

She ran towards the back of the factory and a row of huge cylindrical vats.

'Come on,' Patrick yelled, and he broke into a run, just as a forklift truck sailed into his path. He skidded to a halt, swearing at the man driving the truck, who lifted his ear protectors questioningly.

Ignoring him, Patrick and Carmella dashed around the back of the truck and ran past the conveyor belt towards the vats. There was no sign of Denise.

A door led out into a yard where dozens more pallets were stacked up. The two detectives went out into the bright sunshine. The yard was deserted.

She had to be hiding behind one of the stacks. Patrick gestured for Carmella to go down the left hand side of the row, while he took the right. His heart was thumping fast with excitement.

He crept along the row of pallets, Carmella doing the same on the other side. He could feel the sun burning the top of his head.

There was no sign of their quarry.

'Where the fuck is she?'

Carmella was about to reply when Patrick saw her. She was crouched behind a forklift truck at the far end of the yard, her blue cap just visible.

'Looks like we've lost her,' he said loudly, walking slowly towards the forklift, keeping his eyes averted. Then as he drew level with the truck, he shot off to the left, Denise popping up and starting to run, but he had the momentum – and grabbed hold of the back of her factory smock as she made a half-hearted attempt to get away.

'Get off me!' she yelled. 'I'll have you for assault.'

Patrick rolled his eyes. 'Come on Denise. Why were you running? Something to hide?'

She narrowed her eyes at him and spat, 'What am I supposed to have done, eh?'

'We can talk about that back at the station.'

'I ain't done nothing.'

'Denise, we just want to ask you some questions,' Carmella said in a soothing tone.

Denise flicked her eyes up and down Carmella's body. 'Don't call me Denise. It's Miss Breem to you. What's this about? Caspar's been dead for seven years. Thanks to you lot.'

Patrick leaned in. 'Whatever happened to Doyle, he did to himself.'

Denise folded her arms, perhaps not realizing how ludicrous she looked, trying to act hard in her factory smock and hat. 'Whatever. I ain't done nothing.'

'So you said. But you can tell us more about this nothing at the station, Miss Breem.'

Two hours later, Patrick stormed out of the interview room, slamming the door behind him. He went straight to the incident room, shoulder-barging the door, taking off his jacket and flinging it across the room. He picked up an empty coffee cup and chucked it against the wall, then kicked it as hard as he could.

He punched the wall.

'Fuck!' He yelled out with pain and frustration and fury. He whirled round and saw the three children staring at him from the wall, talking to him with their big, beautiful eyes. Frankie's in particular seemed to be calling to him.

Help. I'm scared.

He was letting them all down. All of them, and their families. The whole community, the people he was meant to serve, meant to protect. 'I'm sorry,' he whispered to the pictures on the wall. 'I'm so sorry.'

The door opened and Suzanne came in, eyes wide.

'Patrick, what's wrong? I heard a commotion coming from in here.' She saw his face. 'Oh, please tell me Breem isn't another dead end.'

He sat on a folding chair and sank his face into his hands. When he eventually lifted his head he said, 'She has an alibi. She took great pleasure in telling us where she was when Liam was abducted. She was at work, in the factory, standing beside that conveyor belt all day with ten other women.'

'You've called to check?'

He nodded wretchedly. 'And we checked Mike's theory, that maybe she was scouting out kids for the old family lodger, McLean. Turns out he died of cancer two years ago.'

'Oh, shit.'

'We're back at square one.' His gaze turned towards the photos of the children again. 'Maybe I'm not the right man for this job. Maybe I shouldn't be leading the investigation. I'm tired. So fucking tired after everything that's happened in the last couple of years.'

Suzanne pulled up a chair and sat down beside him. 'Patrick—'

'Perhaps you should let Winkler take over. He's gagging to.'

She put her hand on his forearm. It was warm. 'No, Patrick. Don't be so hard on yourself. You just need a break.'

'Yeah, a long bloody holiday, preferably somewhere tropical . . .'

She smiled. 'I don't mean that kind of break, you idiot. I mean a break in the case. Some luck. Listen, we've got the photofit now, which we didn't have this morning. We'll go back over the lists from the Dads' Club. We'll talk to the travellers again. Whatever it takes. We're going to find them. You're going to find them, DI Lennon.'

His phone started ringing. He glanced at the screen – his mum – and silenced it.

Suzanne said, 'I have faith in you, alright?' Her hand was still on his arm. It felt good there. 'Now stop feeling so fucking sorry for yourself. That's an order.'

He pulled himself straight. 'Okay. No more feeling fucking sorry for myself.'

After she left the room, he took out his phone and saw he had a voicemail from his mum. Thinking it might be something about Bonnie, feeling that familiar lurch of anxiety in his stomach, he listened to the message.

'Patrick, it's me. Listen, I just had a call from the unit. It's Gill. She's asking to see you.'

Chapter 19
Patrick – Day 3

In the eighteen months since Gill had been locked up, Patrick had tried to visit her four times, and each time she had refused to see him. Each time, he'd been both upset and relieved. He had not set eyes on her since she stood, head bowed, in the dock, and the sight of her had shattered his heart into irreparable pieces.

Patrick realized that he could barely recall the way they had been together when they were happy. He remembered bits and pieces – arms round one another on the sofa, her whispering 'don't die' urgently into his ear as he laughed and told her he had no intention of doing so. Their shared jokes and rituals. Singing *Take That* songs in the style of elderly pub singers. The way she had to turn the duvet round so the end with the poppers was always at the bottom. Taking baths together. Date nights and movies and weekly supermarket shops. Normal, happy married life.

After a year apart, he stopped wearing his wedding ring. He wondered if she still wore hers.

It still seemed impossible that everything had changed so irrevocably, so quickly.

When he thought back to it, the first warning sign had been the departure of Gill's sense of humour, flying away on stealthy black batwings, so quietly amid all the chaos of Bonnie's birth and first couple of months that it took him a while to realize it had gone. At the time, of course, he put it down to the veil of tiredness that had settled over them both. Neither saw much of the funny side of anything – how could they, when sleep only came in such mean portions? But Gill had always been so funny. It was what had made him fall in love with her; her bone-dry, intelligent, self-deprecating and surreal humour. Tiredness used to bring it out in her – after a long, tough day in court she would stagger back in through the door and within minutes they would both be roaring with laughter at her impressions of the hapless jurors or the jobsworth court clerks.

After the seventh consecutive day of him coming in from work to find Gill sobbing, he realized he hadn't heard her laugh about anything in almost a month, even though the five-month-old Bonnie had a giggle that would melt the heart of Attila the Hun. Once she had stopped crying, Gill would list their daughter's new achievements every day with just a tiny almost-sad smile, relating escapades that would previously have had her in gales of laughter.

But postnatal depression was normal, wasn't it? They had talked about it, and the three of them went to see the GP together. Patrick carried Bonnie in her Baby Bjorn, loving the feel of her warm fluttery breaths on his chest as the GP got Gill to complete a checklist of symptoms: Irritability – check. Tearfulness – definitely. Inability to cope with simple daily tasks – yes. Mood swings – check. Difficulty sleeping – well, duh. Lack of appetite – the weight had dropped off her.

Gill cried steadily throughout the appointment, and added a couple of extra tick boxes of her own to the bottom of the list: Guilt. Hopelessness.

Patrick looked over the top of Bonnie's head at his weeping wife, her lank hair, unmade-up face, grey complexion and thought, *I don't even recognize her any more*. For a split second, he resented Bonnie for taking away the wife he adored and replacing her with this sad, grumpy shell of a woman.

'Have you ever suffered from depression before?' asked the GP, scrolling through screens of Gill's medical records.

Gill wiped her hooded eyes and nodded slowly. 'When I was at law school,' she whispered, looking away. 'I took an overdose. Had to get my stomach pumped.'

The doctor, a plump Indian lady with half a dozen noisy gold bangles and a kindly face – a locum, not Gill's regular GP – scribbled a note on a pad shielded by her elbow so that Gill and Pat couldn't see what she was writing. Pat could imagine, though.

'I didn't know that,' he said incredulously. 'How could I not have known that?'

Gill turned back to face them, and her face was bleak and empty. She opened her mouth to speak and Pat waited for the shamefaced apology – not an apology for trying to top herself, but for keeping such a huge secret from him, when he thought they had no secrets.

Instead she narrowed her eyes and spoke to the doctor:

'Could you take off those bloody bangles, please? They're doing my fucking head in.'

Pat and the locum both gasped. 'I'm so sorry,' the locum said evenly, sliding off the offending bracelets. She stacked them neatly on her desk, and for a moment all three of them gazed at them, saying nothing. Pat felt numb.

Then the doctor seemed to snap out of her reverie. 'Mrs Lennon – may I call you Gill? – I think it's pretty clear that you are suffering from postnatal depression – PND – but what I want to be very clear about is that this is a *temporary* condition, and with the appropriate treatments you should feel completely recovered again, hopefully in a very short time. Many women go through a bout of it, especially with a first child – you must never underestimate the physical and emotional stress you have both been placed under, suddenly having responsibility for a newborn baby. Add to that the lack of sleep, pressure to be good parents, and for you, Gill, drastic hormonal changes. Personally I'm amazed that more women do not go through it.'

Pat buried his face in the fluffy crown of Bonnie's warm fragrant head. He suddenly wanted to cry too.

Over the next month or two, Gill did start to feel better. She had a course of cognitive behavioural therapy and went on to anti-depressants and she, Pat and Bonnie settled back into a new kind of routine. Bonnie was such a delight to them both that, if he was honest, Pat could not understand how Gill could possibly be depressed. She had all day to herself, coffee with friends, play dates with Bonnie, gym sessions while Bonnie was entertained in the crèche. She said she welcomed the break from the Bar, along with its endless case notes to be read and briefs to be prepared.

She didn't cry nearly so much anymore – but then a new, and possibly even less appealing emotion took precedence, one that she didn't want to inflict on Bonnie, so she saved it up for Pat instead. He'd just be through the door making an innocent enquiry about their day, and it would start:

'What did I do today? Well, let's think – I slept in till noon, had a long boozy lunch with the girls at Oxo Tower, came home, entertained my twenty-five-year old lover – what do you fucking *think* I did? I changed eight nappies, ironed a pile of clothes that can be seen from space, scraped carrot mush off the floor and fed some ducks.'

'There's no need to be so sarcastic,' became Pat's new catchphrase.

He tried to be patient. But he was tired too, sleep-deprived and working as hard as ever at the station during the day – harder, as he'd recently been promoted to DI and it became a matter of principle to be better than Winkler at his job. He felt as though he was mourning the loss of his happy marriage, his happy wife, their sex life. So he threw all his energies into work instead.

Until the day he came home and found Gill sitting on the stairs, and Bonnie half-dead in her cot.

It was four months before he went back to work after that. For the first few days he stayed with Bonnie on the paediatric ward of Kingston Hospital, watching her bruises fade and her colour slowly return. The look of bewilderment in her eyes was more heartbreaking than the bruises around her neck.

'She had a lucky escape,' the doctor said. 'There's no lasting brain damage. Good thing you weren't doing overtime that night.'

Patrick had shuddered. He had indeed been so close to staying late that evening to pore over some witness statements, but at the last minute hunger and a burning desire to hold his baby daughter had propelled him out of the office and into his car.

Gill was arrested, sectioned, and locked in a mental ward in Hanworth. Pat had not gone to see her for three weeks. He couldn't. Whenever he thought of that day, bile rose in his throat. It was as though he had become physically allergic to his own wife. When he did go, she refused to see him.

His mother did visit her, though. Mairead reported back that Gill was heavily sedated, under 24-hour suicide watch, and not speaking at all. Gill had been told, of course, that Bonnie had survived and would be fine, but she became hysterical whenever either Patrick or Bonnie was mentioned.

Gill's trial took place at Kingston Crown Court. Attempted murder on the grounds of diminished responsibility. She was found guilty and sentenced to be indefinitely detained in the local secure mental hospital.

People say, of things like that, that it was 'all a bit of a blur', but unfortunately for Pat, it wasn't. Every detail of the trial was etched indelibly into his brain, and snapshots would pop back up in his mind with traumatic regularity at all hours of the day or night, regardless of what he was doing. It had got a little better of late, especially seeing Bonnie so hale and hearty, seemingly happy with the arrangement of living with his parents. Time was doing its much-trumpeted healing thing. He could only hope that the same was true for Gill.

But whether it was or not, he was really glad that she had finally decided she would see him. There were things that needed to be said.

Chapter 20
Winkler – Day 4

The Philips bird was fit, in a damaged goods way, like a little sparrow that had fallen from its nest and needed looking after. DI Adrian Winkler had always been attracted to women like that. Vulnerable, with wounds that needed licking. Not *mental* birds, though, like Lennon's missus. *She* was way beyond the pale, a proper nut job who'd tried to kill her kid, the type who should be sterilised and locked up forever. Though he supposed he could understand her going gaga with Lennon as her husband, probably writing down everything she said in that poncy notebook of his, not to mention having to contend with his massive crush on DCI Laughland. He almost felt sorry for the poor bitch. And another thing: if it was down to Winkler, tattooed Goth weirdoes would be barred from joining the Police even if they were ex-Goth weirdoes and kept the tats covered. It was a sure sign of not belonging, of not being normal.

He stopped thinking about the Lennons and focused on Helen Philips' arse, snug in a pair of designer jeans, as she led him towards the study, pausing only to look at his reflection. He found it impossible to walk past a mirror without gazing at himself, and who could blame him? If being handsome was a crime, he'd have to arrest himself. He smirked at his little joke and ran a hand through his thick black hair.

'Um . . . Detective Inspector?' The Philips woman stood in a doorway, checking him out. 'The computer's in here.'

He knew this was going to be a waste of time. Some internet troll pretending to know what had happened to the missing kids. What next – a clairvoyant who was receiving messages from the dead? He'd just wanted an excuse to come and meet the Philips family, do something productive, get away from the fucking search teams. The need to push this investigation forward, to achieve a breakthrough, made Winkler's bones ache. Lennon was a screw-up, especially since his wife had gone infanticidal. Anyone with eyes could see that – but for some reason the guv was blind where Patrick was concerned. Well, he was going to show her what a real detective looked like. He was going to solve this case, even if he had to do it on his own. Thinking about it made him feel like a maverick cop in a movie, the hero bucking the system, the rebel outsider. He drifted into a reverie in which his colleagues stood and applauded him, the papers called him HERO COP, the Prime Minister invited him to Downing Street to ask him what could be done about crime. Maybe the PM would make him a Tsar. He fancied himself as a Tsar . . .

'Are you alright?'

'Huh? Oh, yeah. I was just thinking what a nice place you have.'

'Right. Well, thanks. But do you want to see the messages I received on Facebook?'

He gave her his most charming smile. 'I certainly do.'

He followed her into a study, crammed full of smelly books – Winkler was proud that he didn't have a single book in his own house – along with overflowing manila folders almost toppling from shelves, with posters from art exhibitions and postcards stuck all over the walls.

Helen sat down at an iMac and navigated to Facebook. Winkler stood behind her, breathing in her scent. He wondered idly if she preferred to go on top, or if she liked it from behind.

'This is the message, detective.'

He leaned forward and read the words from the obvious nutcase who'd contacted Helen. Clearly the work of some sad sack who lived on her own with a dozen semi-feral cats and the crime channels playing all day long. Winkler's own mum bought all of those real life mags and cut out her favourite stories – all the ones about child abuse and honeymoon murders and ritual killings by love rats and wicked stepfathers. She was always on Facebook, calling for the castration of some child murderer or the torture and slow death of a woman who'd put a cat in a wheelie bin. There were millions of them out there: Winkler had heard something on the radio about it, about how these people were 'punishers', how they played an important role in society but the internet had allowed them to get out of control. Helen's troll was worse – she actually wanted to make contact with victims, maybe even believed in her twisted mind that the kids who lived happily with their parents next door were actually kidnap victims.

'Fascinating,' he said, biting down on a yawn.

'Do you think there's any truth in it?' Helen asked. She had that wide-eyed *I want to believe* look but she wasn't thick.

'I'm going to look into it,' he said. 'Don't you worry.'

'But do you think it will lead anywhere?'

'Mrs Philips, I don't want to get your hopes up. But I'm going to need you to give me your Facebook log-in details so I can make contact with this woman and try to track her down, find out who she is.'

'Really? My log-in?'

He nodded. 'Don't worry, I'm not going to go poking anyone you don't want me to.'

That didn't raise a smile. But she very reluctantly said, 'OK,' and wrote them down for him on a scrap of paper.

'It won't take me long,' he said. 'As soon as I'm done, I'll let you know and you can change your password. In the meantime, don't make contact with her, OK?'

She looked a bit sick, but that might have been desperation to find her daughter. He said, 'Right, I'll be in touch, then.'

'Thank you.'

He walked back to his car, imagining how sick it would make Lennon if Winkler cracked this case. He knew Lennon was convinced that the stepsister, a foxy little piece of jailbait, was lying, that she and her boyfriend had been up to something. Well, it didn't take a genius to figure out that while the parents were out, the daughter was indulging in some heavy more-than-petting with her chavvy bloke. He also knew that Lennon had abandoned that line of inquiry. So what if the daughter had been breaking the law in her bedroom while the little kid was being snatched? Did it make any difference? Well, what if this boyfriend had something to do with it? Yeah, it was unlikely, unless he had some connection to the other two kids as well. What about the parents? Cases, like this, the parents were usually involved. Maybe there was some kind of weird connection between the three sets of parents, like . . . they were all members of a Satan-worshipping cult who had sacrificed their kids in return for money and success. Weirder things had happened.

He took a look at himself in the rearview mirror, blew himself a kiss, then drove off whistling, Helen's Facebook log-in hot in his back pocket.

Chapter 21
Patrick – Day 4

Patrick transferred the bunch of lilies briefly into his armpit, and wiped his palms on his legs. He felt like a fourteen-year-old going on his first ever date, except that the excitement his teenage self would have been experiencing had been syringed out of him, to be replaced by a flat white panic. He had bought the lilies from the M&S at his local petrol station at nine that morning wondering, as he paid for them, if Gill still liked lilies. Wondering if she would still like *him*, and whether he even cared. He tried to see everything through her eyes – had he owned these jeans when she last saw him? Would she think he'd aged, or that the Buzzcocks retro T-shirt he wore was too young for him? She wouldn't have seen this T-shirt before.

Would he start mentally comparing her to Suzanne Laughland when he saw her? He twirled the unfamiliar-feeling wedding ring around the fourth finger of his left hand. He'd had to search through all the drawers of the bedside units in his mum's spare room to find it, and then polish it with a jewellery-cleaning cloth so Gill wouldn't be able to tell that he hadn't worn it for over a year. Would she still be wearing hers? Why was he worrying about it?

Holmwood House looked, from the outside, like an old folks' home – apart from the high barbed wire-decorated perimeter fence – one of those Eighties-built institutions that appeared as though someone had designed it in Lego. The entrance sported a porch with bright green painted metal poles supporting a corrugated plastic pointed roof, and Pat thought how much Gill would hate the look of it. She liked muted colours and stylish architecture. But then, how often did she get out? Perhaps she never crossed the threshold. He had a fleeting image of what he would find when he came into her room – a hunched, prematurely aged figure, the colour leached from her waxy cheeks, dry frizzy hair, dressed in some kind of nylon tabard . . . He shuddered. No, surely not, that was prison. Gill wasn't in prison, at least, not a physical one.

As he stretched out his finger to press the door buzzer, his mouth went dry. Despite his years of police experience, he'd never been inside a secure unit before. A surprisingly perky-looking receptionist was sitting behind a melamine desk in a lobby area with a locked double door leading into the main house. She looked up when he came in, and he saw her eyes briefly flicker with appreciation when she gazed at the tattoos on his upper arms and then up at his face. It felt like a long time since a woman had done that, even though this one was in her late forties, with unbrushed straw-like hair and lipstick that had bled into the wrinkles around her lips. She was quite pretty when she smiled, though, and Pat felt slightly more at ease.

She handed him a sheet of paper pinned to a clipboard with Holmwood's rules and regulations on it and a dotted line at the bottom for him to sign on. He saw with dismay that one of the first rules was 'All mobile phones to be left at Reception'.

'Damn, can I really not take my phone in? I just wanted to show my w – er . . .visitor, some photos on it.'

He felt immediately flustered and ashamed that he hadn't been able to say the word 'wife'. Why had he said 'visitor'? *He* was the visitor, not Gill. Still, he'd have sounded even more of a twat if he'd said 'my visitee'. The receptionist looked at his wedding ring and smirked very slightly, enough though to make him not feel so flattered at her initial reaction.

'Sorry, you can't,' she said tartly. 'You have to leave it, and all your other possessions, in one of those lockers over there.'

Pat couldn't help wondering if she was punishing him for being married to one of the patients. *Stop it, you moron*, he told himself. *As if!* He skim-read the rest of the rules and signed his name at the bottom, far more clearly than his usual scrawled signature: *DCI* Patrick Lennon. He left his thumb near the DCI in the hope that when he handed the clipboard back she noticed it. She did, and her expression switched back to the original flirtatious one, this time with added respect.

'Oh – keys,' he said, noticing another clause he'd skipped over. He put down the lilies and delved into his jeans pocket. His house keys were on a ring with one of those photographic fobs – a picture of Bonnie, her eyes shining with glee on being presented with a Peppa Pig cake on her first birthday. 'If I take this off, I can take the fob in, right, and leave the keys?'

The receptionist nodded. 'Is that your little girl?' she asked, reaching out a hand with long scarlet fingernails to tap the photo of Bonnie's face. 'She's *so* cute.'

Pat smiled – more at Bonnie than the receptionist – and put his stuff into one of the small bank of lockers in the lobby. The receptionist walked out from behind the desk, handed the lilies back to Pat, and produced a hand-held metal detector that she passed up and down the length of his body. When it passed over his crotch and beeped, she inhaled with surprise.

'Is that..?'

He nodded, willing himself not to blush.

'Well. I'm sure you know the score, Detective Inspector,' she said. 'We're all set. Let me show you through to the visitors' room.'

She pressed four numbers on the keypad by the double door – 5786, Pat noticed – and ushered him through. He followed her down the corridor as she greeted two white-clad female colleagues with a high-pitched '*Alright?*', which was echoed and replied to in the exact same pitch by both recipients, with the exact same words. Pat wondered if it was the requisite staff greeting. His gut twisted and he thought he would have to ask to stop and use the nearest loo, but before he could speak, the receptionist slowed and turned left, just past a large dayroom with nobody in it.

'Here we go!' she sang, opening a door into a small room like a hospital relatives' room, pastel walls adorned with bland prints. 'I'll just fetch her for you. Have a seat. Won't be a jiffy!'

Pat sat down in a pale green velour chair that was either very new, or had just been cleaned. When Gill came into the room, he was rubbing the nap of the velour the wrong way with his forefinger and on seeing her, his first thought was that it was he who had been detained indefinitely in a secure mental unit, and she was visiting *him*.

She couldn't have looked more different to the broken wreck of his imagination. She strode into the room with her jaw set and her determined expression on, the one she had worn in court. She was dressed casually but neatly in jeans, trainers and a Superdry lumberjack shirt, and her hair even seemed to have fresh highlights in it.

She looked exactly the same – no, Pat thought, much *better* than he had seen her look since Bonnie's birth. Not happy exactly, but gone was the pale, anxious face she'd worn in the first few months of Bonnie's life. If he had had to pick one word to describe her, it would be 'relieved'. For a second Pat felt resentment – no wonder, she's probably had eighteen months of unbroken sleep – and this was immediately replaced with a flood of such strong emotion that he had to stare at one of the halogen spotlights in the ceiling to stop tears flooding into his eyes.

'Hi Patrick,' she said, and he flinched. She only used to call him by his full name when she was cross with him.

'Hi Gill*ian*,' he replied, standing up and smiling at her to let her know that he was joking by reciprocating with her own unabbreviated moniker. Nobody ever called her Gillian.

'Pat,' she corrected, and a brief return smile flickered across her face. They were at eye level with one another. Pat could hear his heart thrumming in his chest, but couldn't tell if it was from anxiety or love. He handed her the lilies.

'These are for you.'

'Thanks,' she said, sniffing them deeply and getting a little bit of orange pollen on her nose. 'I love lilies.'

'I know.'

Of course he knew, Pat thought. They'd had lilies at their wedding.

'But you know that,' she added, and he felt a tiny bit better. She put the lilies on a small table and turned back to him.

'Are you going to give me a hug, then?' she asked, and for the first time, he saw the vulnerability in her eyes.

'Of course,' he said, and drew her into his embrace. She wrapped her arms around his chest and hugged him so tightly that he had to pant slightly to be able to breathe. She wasn't crying, but then she'd never really been much of a crier, at least not until the PND.

'Oh, honey,' he said. She didn't smell like his wife anymore. Not unpleasant, just different. 'You look great,' he added, after a couple of minutes. He pushed her gently away so he could scrutinize her, and he saw that, close up, she did look older and paler, but it was all so much better than he'd feared that at first he hadn't been able to tell any difference.

'Nice T-shirt,' she commented with a slight smile.

'Thanks. You've got pollen all over you,' he said, licking his thumb and wiping it off the tip of her nose. She blushed and broke away, rubbing vigorously at her nose herself.

'You expected me to be a total wreck, didn't you?' she blurted.

He shrugged, a bit sheepish. 'Maybe. Because you wouldn't see me. I thought you must be in a bad way.'

'Well. I was. It's hardly been a barrel of laughs. But I feel a lot better than I did a year ago . . .'

'When can you come—' He was about to say 'home?', then realized that this was getting way, way ahead. He didn't know whether he wanted her home, or whether she did either. 'Out?' he finished instead.

'I'm not sure,' she said, and the slight embarrassment in her voice made Pat aware that she also knew there was a lot to discuss, before anything should be assumed regarding their future. There was a long, long silence.

'Let's sit down,' he said. They both sat, still in silence. 'Talk to me, Gill?' Pat pleaded, feeling the panic rising in him again.

Gill looked at the ceiling, and spoke in a blank matter-of-fact voice: 'At the last review, they said there had been a noticeable improvement, but they wanted to give it another six months to make sure it wasn't a blip. Because I tried to kill myself after I'd been in here for four months. So I was considered a danger to myself. Do you want a drink? Coke? Tea?'

Pat felt as though someone had sucked the air out of his lungs, although the news didn't come as a complete surprise. He had wondered if this was the case, because she'd been in there so long. They only kept you in secure units if you were a danger to yourself or a danger to others, and Gill was clearly not going to be a danger to anybody else.

'No thanks, unless you happen to have any Jack Daniels handy . . . Oh Gill. I'm so sorry. Why didn't you tell me?'

'Why do you think?' Her hand touched the arm of his chair without touching his skin, and he noticed that she was still wearing her wedding ring. He had to swallow the lump in his throat that had risen again.

'You did bring photos of Bonnie, didn't you?' she asked abruptly

'I've got tons on my phone, and videos – but they took it off me when I got here. I'm sorry, I should've realized they'd do that.' Pat extracted the key fob from his jacket pocket, thinking that he ought to stop apologizing, and held the key-ring out to her. 'Got one on here, though, but it's from her birthday and so not that recent . . .'

When he saw the eagerness in her eyes, he wondered how on earth she could have coped for eighteen months without seeing a single picture of Bonnie. 'Have you seen any?' he asked, unable to contain his curiosity.

'No,' she said brusquely, gazing at the tiny photo of Bonnie with her small silky pigtails. Last time Gill had seen her, Bonnie had had very little hair, certainly not enough to put in pigtails. 'How could I have?'

He shrugged. 'Maybe your mum brought some in?'

'I haven't seen my mum either.'

'Seriously?' Pat was shocked. He himself hadn't heard anything from Gill's parents, and his occasional emails went ignored. He had assumed it was because they were too devastated by what Gill had done. He hadn't imagined that they had not been allowed to see her either.

'I can't explain it, Pat, but it was better for me when I was ill to cut myself off completely, just to try and start again. I couldn't bear to see anyone.'

She did not take her eyes off the key fob, gently stroking Bonnie's Perspex face. 'Oh God, she's so beautiful.' Her voice cracked.

'I know,' Pat said, trying to contain himself. Seeing Gill appear so relatively normal was almost harder than what he'd steeled himself for, and reminded him with a painful jab of what they had all lost over the past year and a half. Bonnie had been without a mother. When he'd imagined Gill as a nervous wreck, incapable of cleaning her own teeth, he'd consoled himself with the knowledge that

Bonnie no longer had a functional mother. And he'd been right, if she'd tried to kill herself. But that was a year ago, and now he was confronted with the fact that Gill had been here ever since, still Gill, healing slowly and depriving him and Bonnie of their rightful family.

'Shit, this is hard,' he said. 'She's started to ask about you, you know. Not properly, of course, she only has a few words. But she says "Mummy?" to most people around her at some point or another. Even me.'

Gill didn't reply, just stared at the key fob. After a long silence, she eventually spoke, tension vibrating in her voice. 'Can we talk about something else, something that's not about Bonnie, or this place? How's work?'

'Work's OK. Bit tricky . . .' He'd been about to say 'juggling everything' but managed to stop himself. He didn't want her to think he was having a go.

'Any juicy cases?' For a second, she sounded like the Gill he remembered, and his heart gave a small nostalgic flip.

'Grim one at the moment. Three kids, all under four, kidnapped in the last month from houses in the Teddington area. One found dead in a traveller camp, no sign of the other two. Only one lead so far, that woman called Denise Breem who was implicated in the Caspar Doyle case but nothing ever pinned on her. But she seems to have a solid alibi.'

Gill made a face. 'I wondered if you might be involved in that – I read about it. We're allowed a newspaper sometimes, and the odd bit of supervised internet access, if we're very good . . . The Child Catcher. I remember Breem from that case. Trafficking ring, do you think?'

'Could be. We know that at least one of the kids was taken by a woman.'

At that moment in the corridor outside they both heard a terrible screaming and wailing. The door burst open, an alarm went off, and a young, emaciated woman with a half-unravelled knitted sweater in pink wool and bandages on both wrists literally ricocheted off the doorframe into the room, like a human pinball, trailing a long pink wool thread behind her. She headed straight for Gill, shouting at the top of her lungs:

'YOUBITCHI'LLKILLYOUYOUTOOKMYFAGSAGAINIKNOWYOUDID . . .'

Gill and Pat leaped up and Pat grabbed the woman in an armlock as two security guards ran in and took over, frogmarching her out again. The alarm was silenced. 'Shit,' Pat said, feeling shaken. 'Does that happen often?'

'All the time,' Gill's voice was calm. 'Usually with her. She hates me. She thinks I nick her stuff. I don't. I mean, I don't even smoke.'

Pat just stared at her. 'It's awful in here, isn't it,' he said flatly.

'Yeah.' Gill didn't meet his eye, but gazed at the horrible print on the wall behind his head, a bucolic scene of lavender fields he'd noticed on his way in, thinking how inappropriate a picture it was for people who were so confined. If he had to look at badly executed paintings of lavender every day when the closest he ever got to it was a plug-in air freshener, he was sure that it would drive him even more insane.

'There are loads like her. They're always trying to kill themselves.'

Pat was glad that she had said 'they' instead of 'we'.

'We have to use plastic cutlery and everything. That mad cow somehow managed to get into the kitchen and break a bottle a few weeks ago and hide the bits of broken glass everywhere, in toilet cisterns, behind pictures, in her shoes, everywhere. They search the whole place every single day but she still keeps appearing and slashing at her wrists with a new shard. She's always in the Supervised Confinement Room – 'solitary', to you. Killed both her kids because her ex was trying to get custody, then tried to hang herself with a belt. She's only twenty-eight, and she's been in here for six years.'

Gill sat up straighter and met Pat's eyes again. 'I know trafficking's the obvious thought, for your case, but if I were you, I'd be looking for someone like her. Recently released but probably still insane. Desperate. May have lost her kids already. Nothing else left to lose . . .'

Pat stared at her.

Nothing else left to lose . . .

Why on earth hadn't he thought of that before?

Chapter 22
Patrick – Day 4

The air outside the secure unit was thick and tense with the tar and brimstone smell that rose up from the pavement before a storm. Sure enough, as Patrick reached his car the light dimmed as an armada of black clouds drifted over the sun and the heavens opened.

He sat in the car, watching fat raindrops bounce off the windscreen, sucking hard on his e-cigarette. The tip winked green to indicate the battery had died and he threw it angrily into the footwell of the passenger seat. He would give his right lung for a real fag right now.

He held his hands out before him. They were trembling. While he'd been in the room with Gill he had kept his emotions locked down tight, trying to pretend they weren't there, ignoring them as if they were a crowd of rioters yelling abuse at him. And now – well, it felt like an emotional riot, so many conflicting feelings rampaging through his head and stomach, where he felt it most, that he couldn't process it. He simply didn't know how he felt. There was relief, that she had seemed so stable. Sadness, when she had asked about Bonnie and all he had to show her was his stupid key-ring. What else? Mostly he had felt awkward and tense. Not so long ago,

Gill was the one person in the world that he felt fully comfortable with. Today – and he knew this shouldn't surprise him – it had been just like talking to an ex-girlfriend.

He had wondered so many times if their marriage, their relationship, could ever be healed after what had happened. Now, after seeing her, the prognosis was as uncertain as it had been yesterday or last week. And the thing was, he didn't even know if he wanted them to get back together. Of course, he wanted her to be well. He wanted Bonnie to have a mum. But could he imagine them being together again as husband and wife? Maybe. But just maybe.

He turned on the engine and watched the windscreen wipers fight against the raindrops. He pressed play on the CD player and The Cure's 'The Same Deep Water as You' came on, a song that always soothed him. He smiled and ran a hand through his hair. *I probably need to see a therapist*, he thought. *Talk through my feelings. Listen to music other than The Cure*. He clenched his jaw. A therapist? A psychiatrist, more like. And as the rain slowed to a rhythmic drumming on the glass, he remembered what Gill had said. Over the past months he had conducted a thousand imaginary conversations with her, but had never dreamt on their first encounter they would talk about one of his cases.

What she had said though. It was like a break in the clouds. She had always been good at that, shining a light through the fog. And as the rain slowed and he reversed out of his parking space, he realised how keenly he had felt her absence from his life. How much he had missed her.

'What are we looking for, sir?'

Carmella pulled a chair up to his desk as Patrick tapped at the keyboard.

He concentrated on the screen. 'I'm looking for women who were committed to secure units for harming or abducting children.'

He felt rather than saw Carmella's stare, knowing exactly what she'd be thinking. *Women like your wife.* And maybe she would be thinking why he hadn't thought of it before. But, of course, they hadn't known that the person who'd taken Liam – and, they had to assume, Frankie and Isabel – had been female, and as soon as Bowie had given them that explosive piece of information they'd set off after Denise, straight down an investigative cul-de-sac.

As Patrick entered search terms into the HOLMES database, he felt a presence behind him and heard an unwelcome voice.

'Don't tell me,' Winkler said, 'you're about to crack this case wide open.'

'Fuck off, Adrian,' Patrick said without turning round.

'Ooh. Someone's prickly. In a bad mood, are we?'

Patrick gripped the arms of his chair, counting to five beneath his breath.

'I'll leave you to it,' Winkler said. 'Don't want to disturb the great brains of the Met. Beside, I've got some proper investigating to do.'

After he was gone, Patrick shook his head. 'It's not just me, is it, Carmella?'

'No sir. It's not just you. That man is a twat of the highest order.' She crooked her little finger. 'I've heard he should be called Winklette rather than Winkler.'

Patrick couldn't help but smile. 'Who told you that?'

'That would be telling. But he tried it on with me once, when I first worked here. He seemed convinced he could convert me.'

Patrick laughed, and scrolled down the screen. 'Arrogant bastard . . . OK – let's crack on. Don't want to give him a second's more head space.'

After an hour, he sat back, Winkler forgotten. 'Right, these look like the most promising pair.'

They had identified two women. The first was called Sharon Fredericks, a 42-year-old resident of Richmond. Nine years ago, she had attempted to snatch a baby boy from a hospital, had only made it as far as the exit before she was stopped, at which point she had pulled a knife and threatened to kill both the baby and herself. A hospital porter had tackled her, getting himself stabbed in the process, but they had managed to rescue the baby without him getting hurt. At the trial, the judge had ordered Fredericks – who, it turned out, had suffered the devastating blow of SIDS twice, losing two baby boys in as many years – to be committed to a secure unit, the same one as Gill. She was released eighteen months ago. The photograph they had on file was of a pasty, hunched woman with frizzy hair, who could easily be the woman Bowie had described.

The other woman looked similar. Her name was Andrea Hertz, she lived in Teddington and, like all women in this area who were committed, she had also been in the same unit as Gill. Hertz had kidnapped her own children after custody of them was given to her ex-husband, who had convinced the court that Hertz was an alcoholic and an unfit parent. She had locked herself and the children in her car, connected a hose to the exhaust, fed it through the window and turned the engine on. Her ex had found them and smashed the car window with a brick. Andrea Hertz was still breathing, but the two children, a boy and girl, three and five years old, were both dead. This had happened twelve years ago and Hertz had been released last year.

'Heartbreaking,' Carmella commented.

Patrick tried not to picture the bodies of the children in the car. He said, 'OK, Hertz is closer – let's go talk to her first, then Fredericks.'

After two minutes talking to Andrea Hertz, Patrick knew she wasn't their woman. She nervously invited them in to her tiny flat and offered them a cup of tea. Not wanting her to know the real reason for their visit – as it was, at this point he merely wanted to scope her out – Patrick said they'd had reports of teenagers causing trouble in the area and wanted to know if she'd had any problems. As she replied, stumbling over her words, his eyes fell on the framed photographs of two smiling children, a gap-toothed girl and cheekily grinning boy, on the sideboard.

Andrea Hertz was like a walking corpse, her spirit as emaciated as her flesh. Her hair was white; she looked twenty years older than her true age. Nothing like Bowie's description. Carmella asked if she could use the toilet while Patrick chatted to her, so she could have a quick look round. When she returned she subtly shook her head and they left.

'That poor, poor woman,' Carmella said as they got back into the car.

'Her poor children.'

They didn't talk about it any more on the way to the address they had for Sharon Fredericks, a small terraced house on an estate on the outskirts of Richmond. The sun was shining again, the air clear and fresh following the earlier storm. As they stood outside the house waiting for someone to come to the door Patrick felt a tingle in his veins. They were on the right track now. He felt sure.

But there was no response.

He pressed the doorbell again and waited. Nothing.

'Wait here,' he said, pushing open the side gate and going into the back garden. The grass was overgrown, daisies and weeds choking the garden. The curtains were drawn across the back windows, but through a side window he could see into the hallway. Mounds of junk mail were stacked up behind the door.

He went back round to the front. 'Looks like she hasn't been here for some time.' He checked the time. Five o'clock. He felt torn: he was sure this was important but he was desperate to see Bonnie, especially after everything that had happened today.

As if she'd read his mind, Carmella said, 'Why don't I go back to the station, try to find a new address for Fredericks, and you can get back and see Bonnie before she goes to bed?'

'I don't know . . .'

'Go on. It won't take both of us to look up an address.'

'Have I ever told you what a great partner you are?'

'I don't think you have, actually.'

'Well, I should have. I'll go and see Bonnie and then meet you back at the station. Unless you want to get home.'

Carmella put a hand on his arm. 'I'll see you later.'

Patrick told Carmella to take the car and called a taxi for himself. While he waited he took the printout with Fredericks' details from his inner pocket and scanned through it. Her psychiatrist's name was Dr Catherine Hudson.

Patrick called the secure unit and asked to speak to Dr Hudson, but was told she'd gone home for the day.

'It's extremely urgent,' he said. 'Can you give me her phone number?'

After a few minutes of arguing about confidentiality, the receptionist agreed to give Dr Hudson Patrick's number, and would ask her to call him. He had no choice but to agree.

Ten minutes later, his phone rang. Finally, someone who didn't enjoy obstructing the police. Dr Hudson told him she was at home and that she would be happy to talk to him there.

Her house was a five-minute drive away, not far from Helen and Sean's place. Another detached property with a ridiculous price tag. Not for the first time, as he waited for the psychiatrist to come to the door, Patrick muttered to himself that he was in the wrong game.

Two minutes later he sat in Dr Hudson's home office, surrounded by stacks of paper and hundreds of academic books with titles that made his head hurt. Dr Hudson was a good-looking black woman in her late forties, with smooth skin and an amused look in her eyes.

'Thank you so much for agreeing to talk to me,' he said.

He wondered if she knew the connection between them. There were a lot of doctors at the secure unit, and Dr Hudson probably wasn't treating Gill, but there was a good chance this woman had encountered his wife or at least knew of her. He decided not to bring it up.

He explained that he was trying to find Sharon Fredericks.

'I know there are proper channels, and that you're probably going to cite patient confidentiality, but I'm going to be open with you. I'm investigating the so-called Child Catcher case—'

Dr Hudson's eyes widened.

'—and this is very urgent. I need to find Ms Fredericks ASAP, so we can eliminate her from the enquiry.'

Catherine Hudson perched on the edge of her desk and ran her forefinger across her chin thoughtfully. 'Hmm. Well, yes, there is patient confidentiality, of course. But I couldn't help you with her whereabouts anyway. I referred her on to another practitioner very shortly after she was discharged. Someone who I thought could do more for her.'

'Can you give me their name?'

She rocked her head from side to side and said, 'Hmmm.'

'Come on, Dr Hudson . . . please?'

Without replying, Hudson went over to her vast bookcase and scanned the shelves. 'Uh-huh,' she said to herself, taking down a thick book with a white spine and laying it on the desk.

'I'm sorry, detective, but I can't tell you.' She looked at the book meaningfully and Patrick smiled, picking it up.

'I know this book,' he said. It was *The Snapping Point* by Dr Samuel Koppler. He had a copy under his bed at his parents' house.

'Really? Is this the kind of thing they get you to read when you join the police?'

'Not exactly.'

She gave him a curious look. 'Well. I'm sure if you didn't find it useful before, you will now.'

Patrick laughed to himself as he left Dr Hudson's house, enjoying her sneaky way of telling him who she had referred Fredericks onto. He had asked Hudson if he could borrow the book, even though he had a copy at home, thinking it would be a useful icebreaker. In his experience, people who regarded their opinions highly enough to fill a book with them usually responded well to flattery.

Samuel Koppler's office was located in a large, converted townhouse. Patrick pressed the buzzer and waited, wondering if the doctor would have already gone home for the day. But as he was about to give up, the door opened and a middle-aged woman came out. Patrick caught the door and went through, climbing the stairs to the third floor.

He found the outer door to Koppler's office and went through. There was nobody behind the reception desk but he could hear classical music coming from behind the door to what he guessed must be the psychiatrist's consulting room.

He knocked and the door was immediately opened.

'Yes?'

'Doctor Samuel Koppler?' Patrick flashed his warrant card and introduced himself. 'I was hoping to talk to you about a former patient of yours.'

Koppler turned to look Patrick up and down. The psychiatrist was in his early fifties, almost completely bald, and huge: around six foot four, with a slight stoop. He frowned and tilted his head from side to side, before finally saying, 'You'd better come in. Though I was just about to leave for the day.'

'Understood. But it will only take a moment.'

The office was similar to Catherine Hudson's: dark wood, a couple of comfortable chairs, certificates on the wall. A computer sat on the desk beside a huge stack of papers held in place by a chunky paperweight. There was a distinctive smell in the air too, acrid and smoky, like Koppler had been burning something.

Koppler had spotted the book Patrick was holding, and Patrick followed his gaze to the large letters on the cover.

'I first just wanted to say, Dr Koppler, that I've read *The Snapping Point* and, well, it was an illuminating read.'

The psychiatrist raised his eyebrows, as if amazed to find that police detectives could read. The frown remained in place but he was visibly pleased.

'Thank you, er, detective . . .'

'Patrick Lennon.'

Patrick had a feeling Koppler was wondering if he was going to ask for an autograph, but had decided that would be laying it on a bit too thick.

'Anyway, this patient,' Patrick said. 'Her name's Sharon Fredericks.'

Koppler pressed the off button on his iPod dock with a long finger. 'You've no doubt heard of doctor-patient privilege.'

'Yes, of course I have. I'm not asking you to reveal anything sensitive.' Although what he really wanted to ask Koppler was whether he believed Fredericks was capable of abducting a child. 'Have you had any contact with Sharon Fredericks recently?'

The psychiatrist picked up the paperweight and weighed it in his hand before replacing it on the stack.

'Can we do this tomorrow?' he asked. 'I have tickets for the theatre and I really need to get going.'

Patrick tried his most charming smile. 'It's very important, Doctor.'

Koppler's face creased with irritation. 'I'm sorry, but whatever it is you need to know, I can't help you.' He looked at his watch then turned away and began shoving papers into his bag.

'We believe she might be in danger,' Patrick said, hoping to get a reaction. Koppler grunted.

This was frustrating. 'Dr Koppler, do you have an address for her?'

This time the doctor audibly snorted. 'I already told you I can't give out confidential information.'

Patrick decided to appeal simultaneously to the doctor's better nature and baser instincts. In his experience, most people loved the idea of being involved in some way in an investigation into a high-profile crime. Murders and child abductions were exciting – he imagined Koppler meeting his wife at the theatre and saying, 'You'll never guess what happened to me as I was leaving the office . . .'

'This is confidential, sir. But I'm sure you've heard about the Child Catcher abductions.'

Koppler finally turned back to look at Patrick. 'You think Sharon – Miss Fredericks – has something to do with that? Ridiculous.'

'She does have a history of trying to abduct children.'

Koppler shook his head vehemently. 'No. Not Sharon.'

Patrick waited a beat. 'Sharon? Were the two of you close?'

The psychiatrist was flustered now. This was interesting.

Koppler stood up. 'I really do need to go.'

He came around the desk, ushering Patrick towards the door. Patrick stood his ground. 'Listen, Doctor Koppler, what makes you so sure Sharon Fredericks wouldn't do it again?'

Koppler had gone pink and sweat patches were spreading on his shirt beneath his arms. This was *very* interesting.

'Anything you can tell me about Sharon—'

Koppler swept his hands forward in a shooing motion. 'Please, I must ask you to leave. I have to get going right now.'

'When did you last see Sharon Fredericks?'

Koppler pulled open the door and waited. Patrick paused. There wasn't much he could do right now without arresting the psychiatrist and he had no grounds for that. He would leave now and think about what to do.

Once out of the office he turned around. 'I'd like to talk to you in more—'

Koppler shut the door in his face.

Patrick counted to five in his head, then jogged down the stairs. *You haven't seen the last of me, Doctor Koppler*, he thought. He was about to exit onto the street, keen to get home to see Bonnie, when he remembered where he knew the strange smell in Koppler's office from.

It was the same smell that had clung to Isabel's clothes.

He turned around and raced straight back up the stairs, determined to ask the psychiatrist some more probing questions. He knew he ought to call for back-up but he wanted to talk to Koppler right now, and get another whiff of that smell, just to make sure.

He reached the top of the stairwell and knocked on the office door.

'Who is it?'

'It's DI Lennon. Please open the door, sir.'

The door swung open and Koppler filled the doorway. The smoky smell was even stronger now. Patrick was about to start talking when he noticed that Koppler had one arm outstretched above his head, an object glinting in his hand. It was the paperweight from the desk. Before he could raise his own arm to protect himself, everything went white, as pain exploded inside his head, and then black.

Chapter 23
Patrick – Day 4

Patrick didn't want to open his eyes. The screaming pain in his head and the taste on his tongue – a mix of sand and metal shavings – told him he must have had too many snakebite-and-blacks last night. He remembered dancing to Nine Inch Nails around the tiny dance floor at The Crypt, slime dripping from the ceiling onto his backcombed hair, the heat in the club making him sweat the white foundation from his face, and he'd met this girl called Lucretia, which definitely wasn't her real name, who had black hair with a white stripe running through it. Through his pulsating headache he tried to remember what she looked like. He couldn't remember, but he could definitely recall going back to her friend's bedsit in a taxi and spending a long time trying to unbuckle her enormous boots and peeling his off his own jet black drainpipes before having disappointing sex with her on the sofa. His piercing had alarmed her but she had wanted to take a photo of it. Would she still be asleep? Could he get his clothes back on, remove the film from her camera and escape before she stirred?

He opened his eyes, and was shocked to find he wasn't in a bed-sit in 1999. It was fifteen years later, he hadn't listened to Nine Inch Nails for years and he was lying on the floor of an office.

He sat up, clutching his head as the pain bloomed inside his skull. He gingerly felt his cranium – a lump the size of a baby's fist had sprung up on his forehead. Then, in a whoosh, everything came back to him. Doctor Koppler. The paperweight. Sharon Fredericks. He checked the time. He'd been out for thirty minutes. Not good.

He found his phone in his inside pocket. Carmella picked up on the third ring.

'Carmella, I need a car to pick me up *now*. And get me the DCI. We're going to need a lot of back-up – a PSU, commissioner's reserve, all the bells and whistles, OK?'

'I'm on it, boss.'

'Did you bring the painkillers?' were Patrick's first words fifteen minutes later when Carmella arrived. She had volunteered to pick him up herself. She handed him a packet of ibuprofen and a bottle of water. He took three, thought about it, then added a fourth.

'I ought to take you to the hospital, get you checked out.'

'I'm fine. Please don't fuss.'

'I'm not fussing. I just don't want you passing out on me. I make a terrible nurse.'

He took a swig of water, wincing again at the throbbing in his head. 'You've got Koppler's home address?'

'Of course. The PSU should be there already. He lives a mile away, in Parsons Road.'

On the way there, Patrick filled Carmella in on what had happened in the office. 'This is my guess. Koppler must have formed a bond with Fredericks when he was treating her. A romantic bond, most likely. She could very well be living with him. And somewhere along the line they became desperate for a child but, I'm guessing, couldn't conceive. With Fredericks' record she would never be able to adopt, so . . .'

His phone rang. It was DS Mike Staunton. 'Sir, I'm at the Hollisters' place. I've shown Sharon Fredericks' photo to Bowie and he says he's pretty sure it's her that he saw taking Liam out of the car.'

'Good work, Mike.'

'One more thing, sir. We also showed her photo to Liam's parents. Mrs McConnell recognises Sharon too. Sharon used to work as a waitress at Viva Pizza in Teddington. They used to go there every Friday with the kids. I've just checked with the Hartleys and they go to Viva Pizza a lot too. I haven't asked Mr and Mrs Philips yet . . .'

Patrick ended the call. Viva Pizza hadn't been on their list, but he had been right. A place that connected the children. That was why Liam hadn't protested when Sharon had got him out of the car. He probably thought she was going to feed him. Viva Pizza was a local business, cheap and child-friendly, the kind of place that didn't bother CRB-checking their employees, most of whom were probably paid cash in hand.

'We're almost there,' he said to Carmella.

'Yeah, it's just round this corner.'

He smiled. It was too soon for the painkillers to kick in but the adrenalin was doing the job for him. 'No, I mean we're almost *there*. Let's just pray Koppler and Fredericks haven't done anything even more stupid.'

Parsons Road had been cordoned off at both ends, the hostage negotiator's articulated lorry and trailer already *in situ* – colloquially known as DB1, thus named by the Head of Negotiation Unit at the time the first one was brought into service: 'That's the dog's bollocks, that is.' They'd been known as DB1s ever since.

Crowds of the curious added a triple layer to the barrier. As Carmella eased the car through the melee, they saw the DPA press officer, a skinny woman whose name Patrick never remembered, frantically shouting into a digital Dictaphone. He was relieved to see that there didn't seem to be too many journalists there. Major incidents were often on Twitter before even the police knew about them – the moment the officers turned up to tape off the road, it would have been all over the social networks – but storm-chasing hacks these days knew better than to run around with cameras and mikes, aware if they did that they wouldn't get a sniff next time anything went down. The biggest risks of leaks to the press often came in the form of some muppet Community Support officer on the cordon, freely doling out his opinions on the proceedings to anyone who'd listen. It drove Patrick potty. He glanced at the cordon, but the two CSA guys there were standing impassively, arms folded, keeping the small crowd at bay.

They pulled up behind DB1 and a white van outside Koppler's house that Patrick knew would contain those of the PSU not immediately visible on the scene; one inspector, three sergeants, and twenty-one constables, all with multi-roled experience of surveillance, hostage situations, riot policing. It would be a solid team.

Standing behind the van, Suzanne was talking to two guys: a black man with a thin moustache and a pudgy white man whom Patrick had seen before. As he walked over with Carmella just behind him, he looked up at Koppler's house. The curtains were closed and there were no signs of life within.

'This is Sergeant Luke Hardy,' Suzanne said, introducing the first man. 'He's leading the armed response unit. And this is Sergeant Tony Fraser, our negotiator.'

That was where he knew the pudgy man from. Fraser had become a minor celebrity for a few days last year when he had successfully negotiated with a man who had taken his estranged wife and their three children hostage. The husband had, famously, exchanged one of the children for two packs of cigarettes, before eventually giving himself up.

The hostage negotiator's job was basically to keep Koppler talking and engaged so that the rest of the team could work out how to get the hostages out of there. 'Have you already talked to him?' Patrick asked.

Fraser nodded. 'He's demanding safe passage for himself and his family, as he calls them.'

'Or?'

'His exact words were, "If we can't live together as a family, we'll die together as a family. I've got a gun. I'll do it, you know."'

'Shit.' He looked back at the house, just in time to see a curtain fall back in one of the upstairs bedroom windows of number 20, catching a glimpse of a figure that might or might not have been Koppler. The house was red brick, lovely, the garden well-kept, a thrush hopping about on the lawn. The sun was shining. The headlines, if this were all to go wrong, wrote themselves: *Horror in Suburbia.*

'It's not going to go wrong,' he said under his breath.

'At the moment, Koppler is refusing to talk anymore. He won't answer his phone.' Fraser paused. 'We're listening in to the phones of both Koppler and Fredericks—'

'You've established she's definitely in there?' Patrick interrupted, glossing over the legality of what Fraser had just said. It was strictly illegal to hack into anyone's phones without written permission from the Home Secretary, as Fraser would well know. But this was a life and death situation, and it was unlikely he'd had time.

'Yes. Koppler named her when I first spoke to him. But they've both been quiet. No calls to or from their mobiles or the landline, no texts. If you'll excuse me, I'm going to try to call them both again, hope one of them answers.'

Suzanne said, 'OK, let's debrief.'

She looked tired, Patrick thought. Tense. She was the ranking officer here, and Patrick knew she would be in constant contact with ACPO. If they fucked up, if Koppler was able to go ahead with his threats, she would be the one who took the flack. It made him even more determined to get those kids out of there safely.

Suzanne ushered a group of them into DB1 where they could speak privately. She addressed them all – Patrick, Carmella, Mike, Sergeant Hardy and five of the PCs from the PSU, as Fraser stood a little way away, the phone glued to one ear, his finger jammed in the other one to block out their voices.

'I don't need to spell this out,' she said, 'but our priority is to get those children out safely. Second, we need Koppler and Fredericks out of there alive. We have no knowledge of whether Koppler would carry out his threat, or if he even does have a gun. But we know from what happened to little Isabel that they *are* capable of murder.'

'Plus she tried to steal a baby from hospital, didn't she?' Mike said, referencing the crime for which Sharon had been put away. 'She's nuts.'

The look Suzanne gave him could have turned him to stone. 'That's not helpful, sergeant. Except, yes, we do know that she has a history of instability. And Koppler attacked one of our own officers this afternoon.' She rubbed a hand across her face and shot a sympathetic look at Patrick, whose head throbbed in acknowledgement. 'Sergeant Hardy, can you brief us on the situation with your unit?'

'Yes. We've evacuated this whole end of the street and the houses directly behind Koppler's. We have ten armed officers here on street level, plus four to the rear of the house, concealed in the back gardens. We also have two rifle officers upstairs in the house behind us with long-range rifles trained on number 20.'

All through this talk, Patrick felt uneasy and fidgety, his head still pounding. He didn't like the silence, the lack of action.

'Shouldn't we be doing something right now? Why are we sitting around waiting? Koppler was highly agitated when I saw him. He must have thought I'd be knocked out for longer – enough time to get home and get Sharon and the children out. But we've got him trapped and he's going to be panicking. They could be in there killing the kids, and themselves, right now. They might have already done it.'

'Detective,' Hardy said with a smile, 'in my experience, that's very rarely the way it plays out.'

'And you've handled situations exactly like this one before, have you?'

The smile vanished. 'No two situations are exactly alike.'

'Precisely. These people are desperate. That's why they took the children in the first place. I don't think we should be out here waiting for them to make a move. We need to get in there. Now.'

Hardy turned to Suzanne. 'That would be a mistake. We need to wait, re-establish contact. We're not going to go barging straight in there. This isn't the movies.'

'I know it isn't the fucking movies,' Patrick interrupted. 'In the movies, the kids always survive.' It was his turn to appeal to the DCI. 'We need to do something. I really think it's a mistake to sit and . . .'

Fraser saved Suzanne from having to make a decision. He waved them over, clutching the phone to his ear with the other hand. He had the phone on speaker so they could all hear.

'. . . let you tear apart my family.' It was Koppler, his voice strained and angry.

'Doctor,' Fraser replied in a soothing voice. 'No-one wants to do that. We want to make sure you're all alright. Is there anything you need us to get for you?'

'You know what I want.'

'I meant any food, drinks, medical equipment?' For a moment Patrick thought Fraser was going to offer to send in a carton of cigarettes.

'No. All I need is to get my family out of here.'

'We're working on that, Dr Koppler, as hard as we can.' He paused. 'Would it be possible for me to talk to Sharon? I'd like to see how she's doing.'

'No! She's very . . . fragile at the moment.'

In the man's voice, beneath the veneer of arrogance, Patrick could detect fear. It was the voice of a man who was way out of his depth, who was probably wondering how the hell he had got himself into this situation.

There were several types of criminals. There were the career criminals, who knew exactly what they were doing. They might be street-level thugs, gang bosses or white collar fraudsters, but whatever level they were at, they were in this game and fully aware of the rules. Then there were the criminals who filled films and books and front pages: the psychopaths, the serials, the cold-blooded and the insane. They were the rarest type and the most slippery.

Finally, there were people like Koppler. People who, for whatever reason, be it circumstance, bad luck or love, found themselves breaking the law, doing stupid things. Whether it be the girl who stole much-needed cash from the till at work, or the guy who ruined his career by getting drunk and in a fight after a stressful day, or the professional who got drawn in to an insane plot, cooked up by two desperate people. Patrick was sure this was Koppler's category. He had embarked on a journey with no comprehension of where it would lead, no idea that it would end in a house with two kidnapped children, surrounded by armed police. Koppler was not an idiot. He must know there was no way he and Sharon were getting safe passage out of here. He must know his career and reputation were destroyed, that he was going to spend the rest of his life in jail. The only alternative was death. And that was why Patrick was so scared about what was going to happen here.

'Let me talk to him,' he said to Fraser. It was hot in the trailer, and the air was becoming humid with their perspiration.

The hostage negotiator shook his head but Patrick turned to Suzanne. 'Please, tell him to let me do it. I understand him and I'm the only person here he's met, even if it did end with him whacking me with a paperweight. I'm the only one he's got a rapport with, however messed up. Let me try to talk him round.'

The DCI hesitated for a moment then said to Fraser, 'Let him.'

Fraser acquiesced, informing Koppler that he was handing over. He passed the phone to Patrick, who had to resist a brief temptation to wipe the sweat off it first.

'Dr Koppler,' he said. 'This is Detective Inspector Patrick Lennon. How are you feeling?'

The psychiatrist didn't answer straight away and Patrick thought he might have hung up. He knew this was risky. Then Koppler said, 'I should be asking you that, detective.'

'Oh, don't worry about me. My head is made of steel.'

'What are you trying to do, detective? Talk me round? Try to be my friend?'

Patrick was keenly aware that everyone was watching him. Carmella, Suzanne, Fraser. Hardy, still with his arms folded, a deeply sceptical look on his face.

'No,' Patrick said. 'None of that. I just want to give you the chance to talk, and I'll listen. Because I bet you never get the chance to do that, do you? In your profession, others tell you all their problems, and you listen to them. But I reckon you deserve the chance to do the talking for once. Let others know how you feel.'

He felt foolish speaking the words, they sounded so clichéd and ridiculous to him, and for a moment he wished he hadn't insisted on trying to do Fraser's job for him. If Koppler was a bona fide psychiatrist he wouldn't for a second buy all that guff – he was a highly intelligent individual who wouldn't be taken in by impassioned rhetoric.

But to Patrick's surprise, Koppler seemed to take the bait: 'You don't know what you're talking about.'

'Oh, I do, doctor. I know what it's like to find yourself in a situation that you think there's no way out of. When all you can see ahead of you is darkness. But I found a way through the darkness – and you will be able to as well.'

'What makes you think I'm facing darkness? Ahead of me I can see the thing I've always wanted. A family. A bright future.' There was a smile in the psychiatrist's voice and it struck Patrick that maybe he'd got it all wrong. He had assumed that it was Sharon, with her history of losing her family, who would be so desperate to replace her dead babies that she would have pulled Koppler along with her. But what if it was the other way round? If Koppler was the driving force, the one who wanted the children? To do it, he would need a woman to help, and when he met Sharon he saw the perfect, damaged female, someone who would go along with it.

She was the weak link. She was the one they should be talking to, trying to reason with, not Koppler.

He groped for something to say, to keep the conversation flowing, but before he could, he heard Carmella gasp and turned around to find her staring at the house on one of the TV monitors in the lorry, pointing at movement behind a window. A shot was fired – they heard it even from inside the artic, a sharp pop – and the curtains billowed outwards on the grainy monochrome monitor. A small boy crawled onto the balcony.

'Go!' yelled Patrick, and they all piled out of the trailer, running full tilt towards the house.

Chapter 24
Helen – Day 4

Helen could sense Alice's mood as soon as she walked into the kitchen to start making a dinner that, in all likelihood, none of them would do more than merely pick at. But she and Sean had decided that they had to at least try to keep a grip on normality, and regular meals were a part of that. Sean had even been in his study most of the day, attempting to catch up on some of his backlog of work emails. That's what he said, anyway, but every time Helen had stuck her head round the door, he had been staring blankly at his screensaver, a rotating collage of photographs of Frankie and Alice.

Alice had her back to Helen, but Helen could tell the sort of day she was having by the way that Alice was angrily spooning instant coffee into her favourite One Night Only mug. She was still wearing her sleep T-shirt and her black hair was all matted at the back, even though it was five in the afternoon.

'Hi sweetie,' Helen said, opening the freezer and wondering if she could defrost and marinate pork chops in the next hour. Remembering how much Frankie liked pork and, in the next second, wondering if someone out there was hurting her. The speed at which her thoughts always immediately returned to Frankie made Helen feel dizzy with pain.

'You been in bed this afternoon? Thought you were studying.' She winced as she spoke the words, realizing immediately that they would be perceived as a criticism. 'I'm not criticizing,' she added, taking out the chops and unwrapping them.

Alice's shoulders were as stiff as the pork chops as she poured boiling water into the mug. 'Get off my back, Helen,' she muttered.

Helen gritted her teeth. 'I'm not on your back, Alice, I was making conversation. Are you having dinner with us?'

Alice snorted. 'You, Dad, me and Nan sitting round a table in silence? No ta.'

'It's not easy for any of us, Alice.'

'What – it's not easy for you to sit at a table and look at me, the person responsible for letting Frankie get taken out of her room while I was in the house supposedly babysitting? That's what you mean, isn't it. You hate me, don't you? Why don't you just come right out and *fucking say it!*'

Alice was already screeching, looking like a mad girl with her black hair all tangled and her face twisted with a rage that had slashed across Helen's landscape, tearing it up without warning like a tornado. Normally Helen would have fallen over herself to placate Alice, murmuring platitudes and denials, but as she stared at her stepdaughter, something switched in her head. She was not going to be held hostage by an obnoxious fifteen-year-old, not any more, not with so many far worse things going on in her life. She put her hands on her hips and stared coldly at Alice, strangely feeling more in control than she had at any point since the night Frankie disappeared.

'I don't hate you, Alice. But I'll tell you something – I'm not joining your little pity party, not this time. In fact, since you brought up the subject, why don't you tell me exactly what you *were* doing that night? What was so absorbing for you and Larry – yes, I'm not stupid, you can tell the police or your dad till you're blue in the face that Larry wasn't there but I bet you anything he was – that neither of you noticed someone break into our house and steal my baby from under your noses? What was it? Sex? Drugs? Drink? All three?'

Alice's mouth fell open and she stood frozen to the spot, with the black coffee in her hand. Helen idly wondered if she was going to throw it at her. Had anyone ever challenged Alice that directly before? She was pretty sure that neither she nor Sean had. A Tiny Tempah song came on the radio, one of Alice's favourites. It seemed to snap her out of her reverie and she walked up to Helen, still holding the coffee, her teeth clenched in fury and stress.

Helen wondered which way it was going to go – confession, a plea for understanding, apology – or a resumption of the tantrum?

'You miserable *bitch*,' Alice hissed, slamming the mug onto the kitchen table and spilling coffee all over it. *Ah, OK*, Helen thought, *so it's back to the tantrum.* Foolish of her to expect anything else. Alice was standing so close to her that Helen could see the faint constellation of spots on her forehead and see the sleep still in her eyes. Would they fight? Helen itched to slap her, but forced her hands to stay glued to her side, afraid that if they started they wouldn't stop.

'You can't handle your guilt, can you, that you left your precious little baby girl with me while you and Dad swanned off to a fancy restaurant because you're too tight to pay a proper babysitter?'

Helen couldn't even be bothered to point out the illogicality of that question. Alice would have kicked up a massive fuss if they had got a 'proper' babysitter in when she was at home herself.

'I don't have anything to feel guilty about, Alice. Do you?'

Helen had been so determined to keep calm but, face to face with Alice and her rage, she could feel something seismic shift inside her, and the control she'd felt only moments earlier was beginning to desert her. Alice's question about guilt echoed the words of many of the trolls on the Facebook page, adding velocity and heat to Helen's rage. She hadn't taken Marion's advice; she still found herself compelled to read the comments in the way a tongue will repeatedly poke at a painful tooth.

Helen took a step forwards until her and Alice's faces were inches apart like soap-opera protagonists.

'I asked you a question, Alice: Do you? DO YOU HAVE SOMETHING TO FEEL GUILTY ABOUT? I think you do, don't you? I'm going to ask you again – what were you doing that night? Do you have something to do with Frankie's disappearance? How could you not have noticed someone stealing her? HOW COULD YOU NOT HAVE NOTICED?!'

That was it. The point of no return. Helen was screaming as loudly as Alice had been.

Alice made a noise, a sort of primal, guttural moan. 'I fucking hate you, Helen, I really, really do. You're an evil witch and a shit stepmother and I thank God you aren't *my* mother. Frankie probably just *ran away* because she hates you so much! My dad regrets marrying you, I know he'll never get over my mum, and if she hadn't died he wouldn't have looked twice at you and if you think I'm staying here in this house a minute longer with you then you're deluded, I'm going—'

'GOOD! I'LL HELP YOU PACK!' Helen screeched back, and they made a lunge at each other just as Sean came running into the kitchen and stood between them.

'What in God's name is going on?' he bellowed. 'I could hear you through my headphones!'

'Dad!' wailed Alice, tears now streaming down her face, 'Helen's being such a bitch! You said she didn't blame me for Frankie, but she does! She just screamed at me for no reason and said she does blame me!'

'I didn't say that, I just asked what she was doing that night. Perfectly reasonable question, I'd have thought.' Helen made a monumental effort to regain control, not wanting Sean to see her lose it in front of Alice. She walked over to the sink and picked up the blue sponge, wiping up the spilled coffee on the table with shaking hands. Sean folded his daughter in his arms, and she collapsed into his chest, sobbing dramatically. Helen gritted her teeth.

The phone rang, and she rushed into the hall to answer it, desperate to get away from both of them. When she picked up she immediately wished she hadn't – it was Eileen. The last person she needed to speak to. But when she managed to decipher what her mother-in-law was saying, she felt all the blood rush from her head and she had to cling on to the wall to stop herself fainting.

'I'm round Margaret's.' Margaret was a woman who lived nearby whom Eileen had befriended. 'Have you seen it, Helen, on TV? It's on the news, turn it on, quick, there's a siege, they're saying the kidnapped kids are there, it's only up the road from you in Richmond, oh my goodness, Frankie's there, somebody's holding them hostage . . .'

Helen dropped the phone and ran back into the kitchen, all her rage gone. 'They've found her! She's in a house in Richmond, quick, let's go, Alice – bring the iPad and let's find out where they are on the way, we have to go now, they're saying that she and Liam McConnell are both there being held hostage – oh God, oh God, please let her be OK – come on, please, please . . .'

Chapter 25
Patrick – Day 4

Sharon Fredericks backed up to the edge of the balcony then stopped, looking behind her then down at the street, a dazed expression on her face. Liam McConnell wailed, and she picked him up, holding him fiercely. It was then that Patrick spotted the huge knife in Sharon's free hand. His heart sank. They were both wielding dangerous weapons, the pair of nutters. And where was Frankie? In the room Sharon had just come out of? Patrick had a terrible feeling that she was going to hurt Liam, then go back to get Frankie. Or worse, that somehow it had been Frankie on the receiving end of the bullet they'd just heard fired.

Patrick became aware that the voice on the phone still held to his ear had gone silent. 'What's going on? Koppler? Are you still there?'

He thought he heard a reply, but in the heat of the moment couldn't tell for sure.

The knife glinted in the sunlight as Sharon raised it above her head, a deranged High Priestess on her second-floor sacrificial altar. Suzanne, Carmella, Mike and Fraser approached the house and stood beneath the balcony, calling up to Sharon, imploring her not to do anything stupid.

'Here, you talk to him.' Patrick shoved the phone back at Fraser and legged it after the armed police, pushing aside the swinging bashed-in front door. He heard Suzanne call his name but ignored her. He heard barked orders from upstairs, an officer demanding that a door be opened, then a crashing sound, splintering wood, a yell – and more gunshots. Patrick ran up the first flight of stairs and pushed past the half-a-dozen armed police who filled the hallway. At the end of the hallway, an office door had been kicked in. On the floor inside the office, Koppler lay on his back, his shirt blooming red across the chest, a trickle of blood tracing a line from the corner of his mouth to his ear.

'Shit!' At least it wasn't Frankie.

He heard men's voices and a child's scream from the next floor, where Sharon was, threw himself back down the hallway and up the second flight of stairs.

Four armed officers stood in what was presumably the master bedroom. French doors were wide open, revealing the balcony, curtains undulating in the breeze. One of the officers was ordering Sharon to put down the knife she was still holding, but now her hands were shaking so much that she could barely hold either the knife or the child in her arms.

Patrick raced to the French doors, ignoring the protests of the black-clad officers. 'Sharon,' he said. 'My name's Patrick. I've come to help you.'

She turned her head towards him. Her face was twisted with confusion, pink and wet with tears and snot. Her expression reminded Patrick of a documentary he'd seen in which a cow was led into a slaughterhouse.

'Where's Samuel?' she demanded.

'He's downstairs. Everything's OK, Sharon. We're your friends.'

She sobbed.

'Put Liam down and come back inside. No one is going to hurt you. I promise.'

'Don't lie to me,' she screamed. 'They shot Samuel. I heard it.'

'No, he's fine. Just put . . . the boy down and let's talk.'

She shook her head vehemently. 'I'm not going back to that place, that hospital. I don't want to be locked up. I don't want them to pump me full of drugs again, make me feel like I'm evil. I'm not evil.'

'I know you're not, Sharon.'

Her voice was choked. 'I'm a good mum. I was always a good mum.'

'I'm sure . . .'

'They're not taking me back there.'

And in one fluid movement, she turned and spread her arms wide so that there was distance between the knife and the crying child. He was sure that she was just planning to put Liam down on the balcony – but one of the marksmen inside the room clearly thought otherwise, as another shot was fired from inside the room, whizzing past his sleeve. Sharon's body jerked backwards, a look of surprise on her face, and Liam was suddenly in mid-air. Patrick lunged forwards and caught him before he hit the floor of the balcony. In one swift movement he handed the shocked boy to one of the armed police. 'Get him out of here.'

Hardy entered the room. 'Nice work, detective,' he said, clapping slowly as they both surveyed the splayed body of Sharon Fredericks, the hole in her belly pumping red. Patrick rubbed his hands together in a washing motion, trying to wipe the blood splatters off them. His head pounded afresh and he had to swallow hard to prevent himself vomiting.

'Shut up,' he managed. 'Get the paramedics up here, now. Where's the other kid? Frankie?'

'There's no sign of her.'

'What do you mean?'

Patrick turned and pushed past Hardy, ignoring his throbbing head and churning stomach. He raced from room to room, looking under beds, in closets and wardrobes. He pulled open the attic door and poked his head inside, and half-fell down the stairs in his haste to find Frankie. As he ran around he noticed that smell again, the one that had been on Isabel's clothes and in Koppler's office.

Opening one door, he found Koppler's body, zipped into a body bag, momentarily abandoned where the paramedics had rushed upstairs to see to Sharon. The mobile phone Koppler had been talking on to Patrick still lay where it had fallen when he'd been shot.

There was no sign of Frankie. In the room next to the dead man, Patrick found one bedroom that had clearly been occupied by a child: a single bed, Disney characters on the walls, stuffed toys, a pair of child's pyjamas on the pillow.

One child. As he exited the house into the warm evening sunshine, his blood felt cold.

Sharon was brought out on a stretcher immediately afterwards – a stretcher, not in another body bag. For a moment, Patrick felt a flash of hope. Carmella rushed over and crouched down on her haunches beside the injured woman, at the same time that Patrick shoved the paramedics aside and joined them.

Sharon was still alive, just. The blood that trailed from mouth to ear formed a terrible symmetry with what Patrick had seen upstairs on her lover's face.

Patrick leaned close to her. She was trying to talk.

'He . . . promised me . . . a family. I couldn't have a baby of my own. They were too fragile . . .' Her voice faded and she closed her eyes. Patrick was sure they'd lost her. But her eyes opened. 'I'm so . . . sorry . . . about the little girl. When Samuel brought her to me it was like . . . like a wonderful gift. He wanted to make me happy. But it all . . . it all went so wrong . . .'

'What happened, Sharon?' Patrick asked, keeping his voice low, respectful of witnessing a life coming to an end, the guttering of the candle that was her spirit.

'She wouldn't stop screaming. We tried to give her . . . a bath. But she screamed and . . .' Again her words trailed off. 'It was Samuel. He was worried . . . the neighbours would hear. He pushed her under the water. Just for a minute.'

Tears rolled from the dying woman's eyes.

'And Liam?' Patrick asked. 'He was a replacement?'

Sharon's eyes said yes. 'We just wanted a child. Someone to love. I saw him in the car and recognised him. Such a sweet boy. His so-called mother didn't care about him . . . She just left him in there, didn't even lock it . . .' She broke off, gasping and coughing.

So Liam's mother, Zoe, *had* been lying about not leaving the car unlocked. Patrick would allow himself to feel angry about all the hours wasted hunting for the man who supposedly bumped her later.

Patrick leaned closer. There wasn't long left. 'And what about Frankie? Where is she?'

'Who?'

'Frankie Philips. The other little girl.'

Sharon's face was a mask of confusion. She opened her mouth to speak but, instead, took in a long, rattling breath and lay still, her eyes still open, staring as if she would be confused for eternity.

Patrick and Carmella exchanged a long, fearful look. As Patrick pushed himself to his feet, his knees crunching as he stood, he saw a woman with soft black hair running full pelt towards them, a uniformed PC in pursuit. The woman had broken through the cordon.

'Oh shit,' he said. 'It's Helen Philips.'

'Where's Frankie? Where is she?' Helen gasped as she pulled to a halt beside them, the PC catching up and grabbing hold of her. She shook him off. Her face twisted with contempt as she looked at the dead woman on the stretcher, the paramedics preparing a second body bag. There was not an ounce of compassion or fear at being witness to such recent death. 'Is that her? Is that the bitch who took my baby?'

Then her eyes widened and Patrick followed her gaze. Liam McConnell was sitting in the back of an ambulance with two police-women. His own eyes were like saucers and he was pale, but he was alive, found. Whereabouts known. Tonight he would be back with his family. Whatever else happened now, Patrick told himself he had to remember that. They had reunited one family with their lost child.

'Where's Frankie?' Helen insisted. 'She's not still in there, is she?'

Patrick steeled himself.

'Mrs Philips, I need you to remain calm. Frankie's not here. It doesn't look like she was ever here.'

Chapter 26
Patrick – Day 4

As soon as he could get out of DB1, Patrick headed back to the station. He'd only intended to go there to pick up his car, but once he was through the doors, he sat down at his desk and found he couldn't move. To give himself an excuse to stay at his desk, he switched on his computer and surfed around news and social media websites reading all the breaking news reports with their differing slants and conclusions: 'SIEGE ENDS IN DISASTER – POLICE SHOOT TWO DEAD' 'LIAM MCCONNELL FOUND, FRANKIE STILL MISSING', 'FRANKIE PHILIPS' MOTHER DISTRAUGHT' . . .

The only person who was happy right now – apart from Liam's parents – was Wesley, who was already back at the travellers' camp, having been immediately released from custody.

Eventually Patrick's hand stilled on the computer's mouse and he surrendered to his exhaustion. His eyes closed and he tried to empty his throbbing head. The noise of the door opening made him jump. It was Suzanne.

'Didn't think you were still here,' he said, wearily squinting at her through one eye.

'Nor should you be. Particularly not with that egg on your forehead. You look like you either need a drink or medical attention, and, call me selfish, but personally I think the former is the preferred option. Swift half before we wend our ways home?'

Patrick grinned weakly. His head was still pounding, and if he was honest, he knew he probably should be checked out for a mild concussion – but Suzanne was inviting him for a drink? He'd have to be missing a limb to turn that down.

'I'm fine, boss. The Nurofen are kicking in. You're right – I need a drink *way* more than I need to sit in Casualty for four hours.'

'Let's go.'

Patrick had a moment of doubt. What if Suzanne was only asking him for a drink so that she could give him an off-the-record bollocking about how much he'd fucked it all up?

Have I fucked it up? he wondered as they entered their local and Suzanne headed for the bar. Frankie was still missing and two people were dead – but Liam had been found, and they knew what had happened to Isabel. Grim swings and roundabouts. And besides, he hadn't been the hostage negotiator . . .

He headed for a table at the back of the cool dark bar. After the harshness of the fluorescent station strip lights and the dramas of the day, he needed somewhere dark and quiet for his head.

And for his heart, if he was honest. The darker and quieter the better. In all the years he'd worked with Suzanne, they had never socialised together apart from office Christmas parties and people's leaving dos, at which she had always been unfailingly professional – apart from that one time about a year ago, in her office when Suzanne had unexpectedly produced a bottle of whiskey and two chipped mugs and they'd proceeded to get pissed like two teenagers with their first bottle of Thunderbird. That night, Patrick had opened his heart about Gill and what had recently happened with Bonnie, and Suzanne had started talking a little bit about her own marriage. That night was seared into Patrick's memory: the way their chairs had inched closer together as the drinks went down, the heat in the room that led Suzanne to pop open the top two buttons of her blouse, the fizz in the air . . . and how Suzanne had suddenly stood up and told him it was time for them to go, like she'd shoved a knitting needle into his bubble.

Because it had never been spoken of since, Patrick sometimes wondered if it had really even happened or if he'd just imagined it.

Suzanne came back with the drinks, handing Patrick a pint. 'How are you feeling now?'

He swallowed a mouthful and, despite his headache, felt the cold lager help ground him, restoring a sense of normality to the insanity of the day.

'Better,' he said. 'Definitely better.'

'How's Bonnie?' Suzanne suddenly asked, fiddling with a beer mat and not meeting his eyes, as though she had just propositioned him or something.

'She's fine . . . well, basically. We're still living at my mum and dad's, which is pretty . . . interesting . . . and I think they're struggling with the childcare. Especially as she's developed quite a strong personality.'

'What – you mean she has tantrums?'

'All the time, apparently,' Patrick said glumly. 'I feel so responsible. My folks should be enjoying their retirement, not conducting damage limitation for a narky two-year-old. They're knackered.'

Now Suzanne looked him full in the face. She knew, of course, all about Gill and what had happened, although rarely mentioned it. Not since that session with the whisky in her office. Her eyes were tawny and flecked with gold. 'It's hardly your fault, is it? And presumably it won't be forever – won't she go to nursery soon?'

'She could do. But it's so expensive, and I just feel she should be around people who know her really well . . . I'm probably being over-protective but . . . you know . . .'

'I do know,' Suzanne said with sympathy. 'For what it's worth, I think you're doing an amazing job.'

'Really?' Pat said, with genuine surprise. He constantly worried that his slightly haphazard methods and sudden disappearances home to troubleshoot the latest Bonnie crisis had marked him down as unreliable in her books. 'That's great to hear. Thank you. I'll feel a lot better when I find this Philips kid, though.'

'If anyone can, you can,' she said. 'Right, that's enough blowing smoke up your arse. Another pint?'

He noticed that she had already finished her G&T.

'It's my round,' he said, and got up, staggering very slightly. 'Lovecats' by The Cure came onto the jukebox and he grinned, quashing a fleeting notion that it was A Sign. Suzanne, he reminded himself, was not only his boss, but a married woman. And he was a married man – technically, at least. Waiting at the bar, he turned around to look at her, sitting with her back to him, engrossed in something on her phone. He liked the way her long blonde hair tumbled over her shoulders and down her narrow back.

When he came back, there was a glint in her eyes as she put her phone away and accepted her second G&T. 'Now, Lennon. We could talk about what just happened and what the ramifications of it all are – but you know what? I really don't want to. What I would really like to do is to sit here with you and get quite drunk. I think we've earned it. Tomorrow we'll be back at the grindstone, and today was hell, but this evening is neither one nor the other.'

Patrick appraised her, his head on one side. God, he wished he didn't have such a headache. He sensed that this was not an opportunity that would often present itself again.

'Fine by me,' he said. 'Are you sure everything is OK?' He wanted to add 'at home', but it felt too personal.

She immediately changed the subject as though she hadn't heard him – something she often did at work when someone said something she disliked. 'Tell me about those,' she commanded, reaching her forefinger towards his arms. The tip of her finger traced the swirl of the darkest of his tattoos, and her touch sent an electric shock straight to his groin.

He shrugged. 'Had that one since I was eighteen,' he said, pointing at an abstract shape on his right arm, just above the elbow. 'I got the rest over the following ten years, one a year. I stopped when I met Gill because I didn't want to end up like one of those freaks who get every spare inch done, even eyelids. It's very addictive. And Gill didn't like them.'

'They look sort of Maori,' Suzanne said. 'I've often wondered about them but you usually have long sleeves at work.'

'They're Maori-inspired, but not actually the traditional Maori *kori*, because those aren't tattoos done with needles like these ones are. They're actually carved out of the skin with little chisels. I just really liked the shapes. This one,' he showed Suzanne a spiral on his left bicep, 'is based on a *koru*, which is a fern shape.'

'It's lovely,' Suzanne said. Was he imagining it, or did she have a slightly dreamy expression on her face? Patrick wondered if she'd have used those same words if she hadn't been halfway down her second double gin – 'impressive' or 'interesting' were more the sort of words he would have expected her to use. 'Thank you.'

'Are they just on your arms?' Her eyes flickered over his whole body, and he thought, *fuck me, she is. She's coming onto me!*

'Arms, over my shoulders, and one on my calf,' he said, pulling up his jeans leg to show her. 'Do you have any?'

She laughed. 'Me, with tattoos? No. I'm far too much of a wimp. I'll stick to admiring yours, thanks. Besides, like Gillian, Simon would hate it.'

Patrick couldn't help it. He leaned forward slightly and put his elbows on the table. 'Do you always do what Simon wants?'

She mirrored his movement. They were inches apart, and he could smell her perfume, something musky and subtle. He forgot about his headache.

Her phone rang. She pulled it out of her bag, examined the screen, made a face – but took the call anyway. 'Hi darling . . . Yes, I'm fine, don't worry . . . Did you? What channel? . . . Shit. Well, as you can imagine, there's a lot of debriefing to do, so I'll be late. Don't wait up. Thanks honey. See you in the morning . . . You too.'

She put the phone away briskly. Patrick noticed the 'you too' cop-out. In his experience, 'you too' was what you said to someone who'd just told you they loved you when the feeling wasn't reciprocal. But perhaps he was just extrapolating more than was strictly necessary, or even fair.

Her mood changed a little over the course of the next two drinks each, as the pub filled up around them. She was still friendly, but a distance had crept back in. There were more silences – in which they could then clearly hear that most of the conversations around them involved the siege, the found toddler and the dead couple. After a while Pat tried not to listen.

He felt disappointed, but didn't let it show. He had started to experience a weird sort of euphoria – survival relief, perhaps. The after-effects of the earlier adrenalin. His headache had greatly subsided, he was getting drunk with his sexy boss, and Liam O'Connell had been found alive and well.

Things could be a lot worse.

A thought popped into his head. 'You know that smell at Koppler's house? Any idea what it was?'

Suzanne lifted her glass. 'Sage. I only know that because someone bought me some sage incense sticks once. It's used for cleansing, purifying.'

Patrick nodded. He could picture it: Koppler and Sharon burning the sage after accidentally killing Isabel, thinking it would help remove the stain of what they'd done. Clearly, they felt so tainted by it that they continued to burn it at home and Koppler filled his office with the smell. Or perhaps it was something they had always done.

Sometimes it's easy to ascribe meaning where there is none.

'Have you got a picture of her?'

'Of who?' Patrick was startled, thinking Suzanne meant of Gill, for some reason.

'Bonnie, of course! I haven't seen any of her for ages. She must have changed loads. Is she walking?'

Flustered, Pat fished out his phone and tapped into Photos. 'Oh yeah, she's been walking ages. She's almost two now.'

Suzanne shrugged. 'I don't have kids. How would I know?' But she said it in a down-to-earth rather than a bitter manner. He was pretty sure he'd heard her say she didn't want children. The thought flashed through his mind, for just a second, that perhaps she wouldn't be any good as a surrogate mother to Bonnie if . . . things ever changed . . .

As if!

As he scrolled through the pictures, holding out the phone to Suzanne, she wriggled closer to him. He almost dropped the phone, then reciprocated until their arms were pressed together. 'Aw, Pat, she's *adorable*!' she cooed, and he laughed, with pride and amusement at how different she was when inebriated.

A text vibrated his phone and he groaned when he saw that it was from his mum. WILL YOU BE BACK SOON? B NOT SETTLING AT ALL TONIGHT.

'Oh hell. My poor mother's been stuck with Bonnie all day and now she won't go to sleep. Ma will be furious if I stink of beer when I get in.'

They both collapsed with laughter at the irony of big, muscular DI Lennon getting told off by his mum for coming in late smelling of drink. 'You'd better go, then,' Suzanne said.

Suddenly she leaned her head against his chest. 'This has been nice.'

'Really nice,' he agreed, instinctively sliding his arm around her shoulders.

'Back to normal again tomorrow, though,' she said warningly, looking up into his eyes.

'Yes boss. Understood.'

'In that case, perhaps we could risk a quick if rather unprofessional . . .' Her lips were moving towards his, her eyelids floating blissfully closed and he could smell her scent and the appley shampoo she wore . . . He bent his head towards her, risking one last glance around and then—

'Oh shit,' he hissed, jumping away from her as if stung. 'Don't look round. Winkler just came in.'

'Winkler?' she snapped, immediately back in sharp focus, sharp-tongued Suzanne, all the soft edges erased. 'Did he see us?'

'No, thank God. He's got his back to us. But I think that's my cue . . . Thanks for the – decompression. It was much needed.'

'Indeed,' she said gravely. 'I very much enjoyed it. Goodnight, Pat.'

'Goodnight, boss.'

She laughed. 'One more thing,' she said, as he swallowed the dregs of his final pint. 'This will never be spoken of. Agreed?'

'. . . Agreed.'

We're still in London, and Frankie is locked up safe and sound while I go out to buy supplies. She's still not eating properly and her body is starting to look like a bundle of sticks. I remember seeing a documentary about this once, a child who missed her mummy so much that she became depressed and stopped eating. As I'm walking round the supermarket I think about Sean and Helen and how they are to blame for the poor child's mental frailty, and as if my thoughts have conjured them I look up and there they are.

On the TV. I mean, on the banks of TVs in the electrical department. The sound is turned down on all of them, but from the headlines flashing on the screens, the shots of the house and the police cars and the stills showing the children, it isn't hard to work out what has happened. They've found whoever it was who took Liam and Izzy.

I'm so pissed off by this latest development that I leave the supermarket without buying anything and walk back to the van, thinking hard.

All the while the police thought all three children were taken by the same person, I was protected by the smokescreen of their ignorance. But now they know Frankie has been abducted, to use their word, by someone else. Right now, they will be trying to work out who, and why. Maybe they will talk to that stupid girl, find out what happened that night.

But they will never reach the truth, which is this:

I love this child.

I have taken what I deserve.

And I would rather die – that we both died – than be alone again.

When I get back to the van, having read news stories on my phone all the way home, I let her out of the cupboard and give her a Fruit Shoot, which she gulps down. I think the sugar in these drinks is the only thing keeping her going. Without saying a word, she plods over to the table and sits down in front of her drawing pad. A crayon rolls onto the floor and she quickly snatches it up before I can shout.

I sit and watch her. I'm concerned. If they find us they'll try to take her away from me. They won't believe that I love her, that she belongs with me.

I know what I should do. Get far, far away from here. I keep driving out into the country, into Surrey and Kent, trying to escape the city, but something always draws me back, a compulsion I can't fight, despite the danger.

I know exactly what it is that pulls me back here . . .

Or exactly who.

I notice that she has finished her drawing, is staring into space. I get up, take the single step over to where she sits, and look at the picture. It's a woman with long black hair, exaggerated eyelashes and a big smile on her face.

'Who's that, sweetie?' I ask.

'Mummy,' she whispers. 'My mummy. I miss her.'

I take the picture and screw it into a ball. 'Shut up,' I say, when she starts to wail. 'Shut up! I need to think.'

I have to decide what to do. Because things simply can't continue like this.

Chapter 27
Helen – Day 5

Helen tried to tell herself that this was just like going to any coffee shop to meet any friend for a latte, like she might have done on any normal day off work. When Frankie was back, she would make an effort to meet up with her friends more often – well, at least the ones who'd bothered to contact her with offers of sympathy and assistance. It rankled that she had only had calls from a few, even after the fiasco of the siege yesterday. But she didn't want to think about that. The weight of disappointment that landed on her head when she realized that Frankie wasn't there had been like a cartoon anvil, squashing her into a pancake. She felt exhausted, and foolish too, yelling at everyone in front of TV cameras and all. All those people on Facebook would think she was a maniac who deserved to lose her child.

Was she a maniac? Meeting this woman now, without telling anyone, was probably a mad thing to do. But that creepy Winkler hadn't got back to her, so he was obviously discounting the messages too. She had to do something. She had tried to call Winkler but hadn't been able to get hold of him, so had decided to take matters into her own hands.

Maybe this was why her friends weren't in contact. They thought she was crazy. Several had emailed cautiously, the 'if there's anything I can do, don't hesitate to ask' sort of message, but not since yesterday. Helen had felt like emailing back: 'Yes. How about actually phoning, or coming over to give me a hug?' But she hadn't. Stiff upper lip, and all. She didn't have time for anyone else at the moment anyway. Marion from the gym had sent a few messages but even she had been quiet for the last couple of days.

She walked into the Marks and Spencer's café. On autopilot she bought a large skinny latte, just like a normal person out for a normal coffee – although as if she cared whether she had skimmed milk or full fat! – but then had to bite her lip to stop herself crying when the rotund lady behind the counter carefully dropped the small round of shortbread onto the saucer next to it. Frankie loved those little shortbreads. It was the reason that Helen always came to M&S for her coffees.

It felt weird being here without Frankie. It felt weird being out of the house, with make-up on, in public, when the red-top newspapers on the stand not ten feet from her featured photographs of her missing daughter, and an announcement of a £100k reward.

Everything felt weird.

She sat down in the corner of the small café furthest away from the window, with her back to everything, keeping her large dark glasses on. She didn't want anyone to recognize her – except Janet Friars, of course, who presumably already knew what she looked like. With every fibre of her being, she was thrumming with desperation that this meeting would lead to Frankie's safe return. *Anything. I'll do anything*, she whispered to her shortbread. She checked her iPhone – but it was switched off. Damn. She'd forgotten to charge it again. Janet Friars was four minutes late, and if she'd Facebooked to say she couldn't make it, Helen wouldn't be able to check. *Please don't blow me out.*

She glanced behind her, and her heart lurched when she realized that a woman was approaching. The woman was older than her by maybe ten years, haggard and tired, with a wary look in her faded green eyes. Her ill-fitting baggy shift dress hung badly off her shoulders, and her blonde hair looked like it needed a wash. She wore massive 50's-style film star sunglasses pushed up on top of her head.

'Hello Helen,' she said flatly.

Helen's heart jumped into her throat and she tried hard to keep the desperation out of her own voice. 'Are you Janet?'

The woman nodded.

'Can you tell me what you know? Please?'

The woman sat down opposite and regarded her, her gaze cool and appraising, answering Helen's question with another question. 'Why did you choose this place to meet?'

Helen twitched one shoulder in a shrug. 'Most normal place I could think of. Public, in case you're a psycho. Please tell me where they are.'

Janet tipped her head to one side and said nothing.

'Please. If it's money you want, you'll get the reward, you know. Why don't you go to the police? Why did you want to talk to me instead?' Helen had to sit on her hands, both to stop them shaking and to stop herself throttling it out of Janet, who was now pursing her lips at her.

'So many questions,' she stated. 'Slow down. We got plenty of time.'

Her accent was odd, thought Helen. Not English – not entirely, anyway.

Janet dropped her big sunglasses back down over her eyes. Helen studied her face carefully, trying to commit it to memory in case she had anything to do with Frankie's kidnapping, but the woman was fairly unremarkable in appearance. The most noticeable thing about her was her skin colour, a pasty white, as though she never went in the sun. She reminded Helen of a toad.

'Why did you contact me?' Helen repeated.

The woman smiled. 'Cos I feel for you, darling.'

Something about the way she said it made Helen shudder. It was as if the woman was putting on a voice that wasn't her own. Helen was starting to get a seriously bad feeling about Janet Friars. Her next utterance didn't help, either:

'How is your husband coping?'

Helen frowned at her. 'My husband?' She was about to say 'None of your damn business', until she remembered that Janet might, just might, be able to help her. 'As well as can be expected.'

Janet leaned forwards across the table towards her and removed her shades, just for a moment, to squish a finger into the corner of one of her eyes, as if something had irritated it. Then she hastily put the glasses back on, perhaps realizing that she hadn't intended to do that. Helen noticed that the whites of her eyes were yellow and sickly-looking. Perhaps she was jaundiced, or worse, suffering with liver cancer.

'I hope you are still having relations,' she said conversationally. 'Very important for a man to feel cherished. I saw his photo in the papers. I think he's a man who needs much intercourse, am I right?'

Helen jerked back in her chair and put up both her hands in an angry gesture of surrender. 'That's enough! If you have something to tell me, tell me now or I'm walking right out of here and going to the police.' She wished her phone was switched on. She could have taken a surreptitious snap of her.

Janet Friars was almost certainly a nutter.

'Chill out, sweetheart.' Janet confirmed it, with a wide smile. 'I don't mean any harm, or disrespect. Just tryin' to help.'

'Then *help* me,' Helen hissed. Inside her head she repeated a small mantra, over and over again: *Don't cry. Don't cry. Do not cry. Don't cry.* 'Where is Frankie?'

Even as she said it, Helen knew it was hopeless. This woman had no more idea of where Frankie was than that fat lady behind the counter did.

'You don't know, do you,' she said flatly.

'No darling. I'm sorry. I don't know anything. I just wanted to see you in case I could help in any way.'

'You can't.' Helen pushed her chair back and stood up, leaving most of her latte, and the little round shortbread. She turned to leave, then turned back.

'Yes, actually, you can. Don't break my heart by giving me false hope. Don't waste my time by sending me stupid dramatic Facebook messages when you don't know *anything*. I could report you to the police, you know, make an official complaint. They already know about you. I showed them your messages. You'll get a caution, for harassment. For wasting police time.'

The effort of keeping her voice down in the public place made Helen speak in what was almost a squeak of outrage, and she couldn't prevent tears plopping down from underneath her sunglasses. *I am an idiot*, she berated herself. Especially because she had thought Janet describing Frankie's pyjamas had meant something. The truth was, the description of what Frankie was wearing had been in all the papers. Helen had known this really, but had been so desperate to believe this woman might know something.

Janet shrugged and smiled that infuriating smile again. 'Don't think so, darling, because we haven't wasted any police time, have we? But I promise you, and I mean this most sincerely, I will watch out for your baby, and the others. I want to help, I really do. That's why I contacted you. I knew you wouldn't see me unless you thought I knew something. But, the thing about me, I can't bear it when people make other people suffer. Whoever took your—'

Helen turned and ran out of the café without waiting for the woman to finish her sentence.

She wished she hadn't bothered telling Winkler – her instincts had been right. It was a waste of time.

She was an idiot.

As soon as she got home she sat at the computer, deleting all the messages between her and Janet, erasing all trace of her stupidity so she would never have to be reminded of it. After that, she felt a little better.

Chapter 28
Patrick – Day 5 – Afternoon

Patrick strode through the corridors of the station aware that every person he passed was staring at him. He kept his head down. The last time he'd experienced anything like this was when Gill had tried to kill Bonnie, and everybody knew – not just what she'd done but that he'd arrested her – and he'd felt then like an alien who'd crash-landed on this planet, not understanding this peculiar place or its gawping inhabitants. This wasn't as intense as that (he prayed nothing ever would be) but today he should have been walking the walk of triumph. Case solved, criminals caught, justice – of the roughest sort – done.

As he'd turned to walk out of the pub last night, Suzanne had caught his arm – her touch, even in moments like this, sent a little jolt through his body – and said, 'You did well today, Pat. You should be proud.'

And it was true. Right now, the McConnells would be the happiest and most relieved parents in the world. That was down to him. Although Zoe McConnell would have some explaining to do to her husband over the fact that she had lied about locking the car, and Patrick was tempted to get her to do some explaining to the police.

Maybe later. For now, while there was still one child missing, he needed to put all his energy into finding Frankie. He wouldn't rest until Frankie Philips was back with *her* parents.

If she was still alive.

He entered Suzanne's office and shut the door behind him. She had organized an urgent state-of-play review with the most senior members of the team plus, on Patrick's insistence, Carmella.

Unfortunately the other senior detective on the team, who sat smirking at him now, was Winkler. Pat wondered if he'd spotted Suzanne and him in the pub last night.

'Patrick, take a seat,' Suzanne said.

He took the empty chair next to Carmella and waited for his boss to begin.

'First,' she said, 'I want you to know that the Commissioner has spoken to me this morning. He backs us, he understands why we have pursued the investigation in the way we have, and he asked me to pass on his gratitude for finding Liam McConnell.'

Patrick nodded, trying to ignore Winkler. If he didn't remove that smirk from his face soon . . .

Suzanne went on. 'But the media are not congratulating us on the good news. They want to know why we have failed to find Frankie Philips, and how we can justify our officers shooting two people dead.'

'Who can blame them?' asked Winkler.

Carmella swivelled in her chair and glared at him. 'I suppose you knew we were going down the wrong path with Frankie all along but chose not to say anything, huh?'

'Well, if I'd been leading this investigation you can bet your beautiful ass I would have made damn sure the cases were connected. I wouldn't have just *assumed*.'

Carmella's mouth dropped open and she pointed a finger in Winkler's smug face. '*My beautiful ass*? I can't believe you—'

Suzanne banged her desk. 'Enough! Adrian, lay off the sexist bullshit. And Carmella, I want you to calm down. This is not the time for us to start blaming one another.'

'But we didn't blame him,' Carmella protested, her voice rising an octave. 'There hasn't been anything to blame him for because he's done sweet FA in this investigation.'

'That's what you think,' Winkler muttered.

'Both of you – stop. Now.'

Patrick had never seen the DCI so angry. Her face was scarlet. They were all losing the plot, the whole team.

'How can we be sure that Koppler and Fredericks didn't take Frankie?' Carmella asked. 'Maybe they killed her and her body is somewhere else, like Isabel's was?'

Sadness replaced the anger on Suzanne's face. 'Not unless they never took her to the house and didn't use either of their cars. The SOCOs were working all night. They've been through the house and both cars. Fredericks' house too. There's no evidence at all that Frankie had any contact with them.'

'Like I said,' Winkler piped up. 'You were barking up the wrong tree all along.'

Carmella visibly bristled but Suzanne said, 'We were all barking up the wrong tree. We don't have unlimited resources. We were absolutely right to follow the path we did.'

She looked at Patrick. He hadn't spoken throughout this whole exchange. 'Isn't that right, Patrick?' she said.

'No,' he replied.

The other three stared at him.

'It's my fault,' he said, looking down so he couldn't see what would no doubt be an expression of surprised delight on Winkler's face.

'What are you talking about?' Suzanne asked.

He sat up straight. 'Alice Philips and her boyfriend, Larry Gould. I interviewed Alice the morning after Frankie disappeared and we knew she was lying about something, including the question of whether Larry was there that night. We had a witness who said they saw a young man who matched his description near the house. Carmella and I went to interview Larry but he stonewalled us. I made the decision that it wasn't worth pursuing that lead, that the two of them probably just didn't want Alice's parents to know that he was round the house, but nothing more.'

'And what makes you think that isn't actually the case?' Suzanne asked.

'He's probably got a hunch,' Winkler said.

Patrick ignored him. 'Nothing. I mean, I don't have any new evidence. But I made a mistake by not pursuing every lead. I was blinkered. A good detective always keeps every option open, explores every avenue. I wasn't a good detective.'

'Come on, sir, you're being too hard on yourself,' Carmella said. 'It must be that crack on the head you took yesterday. We followed the path that seemed most likely. Anybody would have done the same. I completely agreed with you.'

Patrick was glad, now more than ever, that he didn't have someone like Winkler as his partner. It would be easy for Carmella to stab him in the back, try to advance her career by claiming that she had pressed him to pursue the Larry lead. Because it was true, she *had* wanted to talk to him more. She was loyal, though. No matter how regretful he felt at this moment, he was grateful to her.

Suzanne sighed. 'Alright, I'm not interested in self-torture and if onlys. All I care about is finding where Frankie Philips is. As far as I'm concerned this is a new investigation. Patrick, do you want to lead it?'

He might have said no, let someone else take it on, if he hadn't seen Winkler almost bounce out of his chair. Did he really want someone like Winkler leading this case? Winkler didn't really care about the victims of crime. He saw every investigation as a chance to accumulate points. This wasn't mere speculation: Winkler had once told Patrick that himself, back in the days when they had got along reasonably well.

Plus, Patrick wanted the chance to make amends. He knew that he was still the best chance the Philips family had.

'Yes,' he said. 'I do.'

'Good,' Suzanne said.

'For fuck's sake,' Winkler hissed.

Suzanne gave him a look that would freeze oil. When she turned back to Patrick, her face was warmer, but businesslike. 'Patrick, tell us everything we know so far.'

He recounted the scant facts, his ears whistling as he went through the details. The stress was causing his tinnitus to go crazy. Last night when he'd got home he had dragged his quilt and a couple of cushions into Bonnie's room and slept on the pink furry rug beside her bed, listening to her breathe and make little snuffling noises in her sleep. Gill used to do that too, though they were more snores than snuffles.

Lying on his daughter's bedroom floor he had drifted back in time to the days when his wife was pregnant, during the second trimester, before the discomfort and constant urge to pee kicked in. He would lie behind her, his arm draped over her, resting lightly on her swollen belly, and they would talk about names and all the exciting things they would do with their daughter when she was born. Some days, when he allowed himself to think about it, he felt furious with Gill for robbing them of that life. Last night though, he had simply felt an ache in his chest, grief for those lost experiences.

Eventually, he'd fallen asleep and was awoken by his mum coming into the room, asking what on earth he was doing, Bonnie already sitting up in bed giggling at her silly daddy.

'So we have the fact that Alice was almost certainly lying about Larry being there that night. We have the unlocked back door and the strange drawing of a face looking through a window – though that may be of no significance whatsoever.'

'What's your feeling about what happened, Pat?' Suzanne asked.

'I think there are three possibilities. Firstly, abduction by a stranger. It seems like a huge coincidence that we could have two sets of child abductors active in the same small area at the same time.'

'Unless it's a copycat,' Carmella said.

Patrick nodded, although he had previously dismissed that option. 'Someone who got the idea, or felt inspired by, what had already happened to Liam and Isabel. Or there's the chance that we have a predator who knew we would assume that the children were all taken by the same person and saw an opportunity – a ready-made smokescreen.'

'What are the other two possibilities?' Suzanne asked.

Patrick was momentarily distracted by the pigeon that had appeared on the windowsill behind her.

'The second possibility is that Sean and/or Helen are involved. We need to look at them more closely. And the third, which to me is the hot favourite scenario, is this: Alice and Larry killed Frankie, maybe accidentally, and covered it up.'

They fell silent as they contemplated that possibility. What could it have been? A prank that went wrong? Did they leave drugs lying around which Frankie had found and overdosed on? Maybe she fell down the stairs or out of an open window. Or did she wander out of the open back door while her sister and her sister's boyfriend were having sex in her room? How far would a three-year-old go on her own? Patrick could picture it all too clearly: the accident, the desperation, the panic. And yet Alice, whilst obviously upset, hadn't seemed utterly distraught when he'd interviewed her. She'd have to be a consummate actress to have pulled off that level of composure if she had just disposed of her little sister's body.

'What do you think Adrian?' Suzanne asked. 'Have you got any theories?'

Winkler pulled a face. 'I don't know. I can't see the teenagers having the bottle to cover it up.' Patrick felt irrationally irritated that he'd echoed his own thoughts.

'But you haven't got any better ideas?' Carmella said.

'Don't start,' Suzanne warned. She turned her attention to Patrick. 'I think your third scenario sounds plausible. Let's get Alice and Larry in now.' She glanced at the clock on the wall and smiled wryly. 'We could have this wrapped up by teatime.'

They agreed that Patrick would drive to pick up Alice while Carmella went to get Larry. They didn't want to give either teenager the opportunity to warn the other.

Thirty minutes later, Patrick pulled up outside the Philipses' house. He felt better now they were moving again. *Call me DI Shark,* he thought, ironically. *Keep moving or die.* The Philips residence was silent and still, but Helen answered the door almost immediately.

In a low voice, Patrick said, 'I need to talk to Alice.'

Helen Philips had been stripped of her sheen. Her skin was dull, her clothes rumpled, and her eyes were bloodshot and puffy.

'So do I,' she replied. 'Alice has gone.'

Chapter 29
Alice – Day 5 – Late Afternoon

Alice awoke, drenched in sweat inside her sleeping bag. She knew immediately where she was; her brain didn't allow her a moment of respite from the truth, from the horror of her situation. She needed to get out of this disgusting, stinking sleeping bag. But her body wouldn't obey her brain. Instead, she lay helplessly as scenes from earlier that day replayed inside her mind.

The dual carriageway was empty as she'd trudged along it with her head down. Her backpack had felt as though it was full of paving slabs, even though it actually only contained a few clothes, her passport, phone and iPad and chargers. Tears of fury were dripping off her nose, mingling with the sweat on her face. She licked her top lip and tasted the salty drops. When she'd checked her watch she had seen that it was one thirty in the morning. Would they have noticed she'd gone yet? They wouldn't care, even if they had. She hated them all: Helen, Eileen, her dad – they all blamed her! Her two best mates had deserted her: Larry by refusing to come with her, and as for Georgia, she'd *tried* to talk to her, but she was just being really selfish at the moment. How could Georgia be so worried about her folks cutting off her allowance, when her best friend's little sister had been kidnapped? The tears of fury turned into tears of outrage.

Alice thought of her squidgy little sister, her soft feet and tiny pearly teeth, the way she giggled in the bath and the smell of the back of her neck when Alice nuzzled her head into it, and it made her cry harder. Oh god . . . it was all bound to come out, what they'd done. She shivered in the evening warmth, thinking about the consequences. About what her dad and Helen would say when they found out.

She'd walked for an hour towards Heathrow, thinking that she might have enough cash to jump on an Easyjet flight to Spain or somewhere, but hadn't been convinced by that idea because that would leave a trail and make it easy for her dad to find her. But then she had an idea. There were loads of empty flats on the Kennedy Estate. As long as she kept well away from Jerome's block of flats she should be OK.

Alice had pulled out her phone and risked switching it on, ignoring all the alerts for missed calls, voicemails and texts from her family that immediately appeared. So they'd noticed she'd gone? *Astonishing*, she thought, sarcastically. She knew she needed to be quick – they'd be able to trace her by her phone if she left it on for long. If they'd even alerted the police, which they might not have done. Maybe they'd think she'd been kidnapped by the same person who stole Frankie. The thought gave her a guilty little thrill, as she imagined her face on the ten o'clock news, filling the screen. Hopefully they'd use a nice picture of her, maybe that one of her in her sarong on holiday in Tuscany last year sipping a mocktail, hopefully not a naff old school photo in blazer and tie with hardly any make-up on . . .

She had speed-dialled Larry's number with a sudden pang of anxiety that he wouldn't speak to her. She'd been pretty brutal to him earlier when he refused to run away with her – she'd called him quite a few mean names. But he answered immediately. 'Al! Are you OK?'

'Hi Larry, I can't talk long, don't want them tracing my phone . . . soz for what I said earlier, babes, I didn't mean it. I don't really think you're a spineless plank or a twat, honest, I was just upset. I need your help, right—'

Larry interrupted her. 'Where are you?'

Alice laughed hollowly. 'You think I'm telling you that?'

'No, serious, you need to tell me right now, 'cos I'm coming with you. I've already left. Got all my stuff, straight up, sleeping bag and everything. Been trying to find you for the last three hours.'

A wide smile spread across Alice's dirty tear-stained face. 'Babes! That's awesome. What made you change your mind?'

'You're my bird, babes! I can't leave you to handle all this on your own. If I'm honest, you're right, I was being a total fucking wimp. Anyway I reckon the cops will be back, poking around with their questions and shit. Best we just take off, I reckon.'

Fresh tears sprang to her eyes, gratitude and anxiety mingled. 'But now we're running away they're definitely going to think we had something to do with it!'

'I know, right. But we totally didn't. Listen, you should get off of your phone. Where are you now?'

'Walking down the A316, near Whitton. I was ringing to ask if you could help me break into a flat on the Kennedy. There's tons of empty ones, on the far side of the estate, away from Jerome's gaff.'

'Perfect. I'll meet you at the Wayfarer pub in Whitton, round the back, in, like, twenty minutes? I'm not far from there either. Then we can figure out what we need to get into one of those flats.'

'Awesome,' Alice said, feeling much happier. 'Whistle when you get there so I know it's you.'

Ten minutes after that she had dumped her bag on a picnic bench in the dark garden of the Wayfarer, the shadowy shapes of plastic playground equipment looming above her as she looked nervously around, rolling her shoulders to ease the stiffness from the heavy backpack. Climbing over the fixed seating part of the bench, she had a pang of guilt about her dad and how he might be feeling right then. But then she dismissed it – he knew that she was capable of looking after herself, unlike poor little Frankie. He'd understand. She would send him an email from an internet cafe as soon as she could.

It was a clear, starry night, the sky a bluish-black beyond the edges of the sodium haze of the city behind her. The silence was eerily intense, and Alice began to long for Larry's slightly malodorous but comforting presence. What if someone had stopped him? What if he wasn't coming? She had only been away from home for three and a half hours, and already she was craving her soft bed and a hot shower. Suddenly the Kennedy Estate didn't seem like such a great idea. In fact, it seemed like a horrible idea – the prospect of a dirty, syringe-littered squat that stank of piss, when only four miles away was her lovely nest of a bedroom . . .

A soft whistle broke into her thoughts. Larry was whistling Bruno Mars's 'I Think I Want to Marry You,' and it made her smile.

'Psssst,' she said. 'Over here!'

There was a rustle and quiver in the bushes, then the thin silhouette of Larry emerged. He swore as he banged into the next table in the dark.

'Ow! Shit!'

Alice had jumped up and hugged him hard. He was so thin that her arms reached all the way around him and the army duffel bag on his back. Sticking out of the pocket of it she felt something small and furry and, puzzled, closed her fingers around it. Then she laughed.

'No *way* have you brought Spesh the tiger!'

'Shut up,' Larry said, and she could feel the heat coming off his face. 'Don't tell anyone.'

'Don't worry, I won't. It's sweet. You're awesome,' she replied, finding his lips in the dark and kissing him as though it was the last kiss she would ever experience. Just as she was contemplating dragging him into the kids' play area and shagging him on the bark-chipping carpet underneath the rope bridge, he pulled away.

'Are you serious about hiding out in the Kennedy?'

They sat down together, holding hands like an old married couple. 'Yeah. No. I don't know. What do you think?'

Larry pondered. 'I mean, we need somewhere inside to sleep, don't we? Somewhere they won't think to look for us. Have you got your sleeping bag?'

'Yeah. And Helen's yoga mat. And an inflatable travel pillow that my dad bought for long-haul flights.' She couldn't keep a note of pride out of her voice. Then she sniggered. 'And you've got Spesh, so we've got a guard tiger. We're all sorted.'

'Fuck off,' he replied, tickling her until she wriggled away, laughing.

'We'll need a crowbar or something, won't we, to open the door?' Larry said. 'I can get one from that big B&Q when it opens at eight. But how will we know which flats are empty? I mean, I can't exactly go round crowbarring open people's gaffs. Jerome would be bound to find out and be on us like a ton of spuds.'

They thought about this, and Alice couldn't help but hear the words 'mixed metaphor', spoken in the voice of her creepy Drama teacher, drift through her head. In fact this whole escapade seemed more like a piece they'd have devised for their Expressive Arts GCSE rather than reality. The obvious thing to do would be to ask Jerome, as he seemed to know the business of everyone on that estate – but he was the last person they needed to know they were there.

'A boarded-up one. That's what we need. Remember when we went to see Jerome before? We passed loads on the way up to his flat. We should just go into another block, up to the highest floor we can, then wait to check no-one's around and crowbar it open.'

'You're a fucking genius,' Larry said, and they kissed again.

They spent the night in the pub garden, zipping together their sleeping bags and putting Spesh the cuddly tiger – ironically, of course – in between them like a child. Alice wished it was Frankie. At five-thirty they woke, with bark chippings in their hair and dew on their sleeping bags.

By eight twenty they were at the Kennedy, having gone via B&Q for a crowbar, a machine coffee, a quick wash in the toilets and a Snickers bar each for breakfast. They'd decided on the twelfth floor of Block G, fairly sure that it didn't contain any other residents – all three flats at that level were boarded up. After an hour with no movement, even after they had knocked on each door as loudly as they dared, Larry set to work with the crowbar. The wooden planks splintered noisily but surrendered with ease, and to their delight, the door underneath hadn't even been locked. It opened immediately and they grinned at each other as they stepped inside.

Their smiles faded a bit as they took in their new home. The previous occupants had clearly left in a rush, and the flat stank of musty carpets and old takeaways. But it had an ancient sofa in it, and one saucepan in the kitchenette. The toilet was filthy but usable.

'This is *fine*,' said Alice doubtfully.

'It'll have to be,' replied Larry, equally doubtfully.

'I'm so tired,' Alice moaned. The few hours' sleep they'd managed had hardly been refreshing. Plus the situation made her feel exhausted, like all she wanted to do was lie down and retreat into dreams where everything was happy and normal. 'I'm going to lie down for a bit.'

Now here she was, marinating inside her sleeping bag, forcing her stupid brain not to go back in a loop, to replay the events of the day again. Larry was still asleep, lying on the floor by her feet like a faithful Labrador. Alice wanted to get up, to tell him to wake up too, but she still couldn't move. Moving would mean facing reality. And she wasn't ready for that. Not yet.

She could hear a baby crying somewhere close by. The cry sounded familiar and for a delirious moment she thought it was Frankie. Before she could think about it further, exhaustion dragged her back down into sleep.

Chapter 30
Patrick – Day 5 – Late Afternoon

Helen Philips wordlessly invited Patrick in, turning and drifting towards the living room, head drooping and shoulder blades sticking out. She reminded Patrick immediately of poor Fiona Hartley, who had answered his knock at her front door in exactly the same defeated manner. Not remotely alike physically, it was as if they had morphed into identical grief-stricken twins.

Was it possible for someone to shed pounds in just a few days, he thought, looking at the bones in her skinny back showing through her T-shirt. Yes, of course. He himself had lost a stone and a half in the weeks that followed Gill's attempted murder of Bonnie, but he pushed down the memory of his hollowed-out reflection the moment it bobbed up. He didn't have space right now in his head to think about Gill and what her apparent improvement might mean. The problem lurked like an uninvited guest at a party. He would have to deal with it soon, but not today.

Helen perched on the edge of her designer sofa and chewed her fingernails as she looked up at him. Here was a woman who was losing hold. The TV was tuned to Sky News, the volume turned down low.

'When did you last see Alice?' Patrick asked, his back to the TV.

She gazed around the room as if the answer might lie behind the pot plant or beneath an armchair. 'Yesterday evening. We had . . . we had a huge fight, and then Eileen came in and told us about the hostages.'

Their eyes met and Patrick had to look away.

'When we got back I was so upset I went straight to bed. Sean and Eileen stayed up. They were drinking – I found an empty bottle of gin in the bin this morning.'

A man choosing to sit and get drunk with his mother rather than comfort his wife. Patrick wanted to note that down in his Moleskine but would have to do so later.

'When I got up this morning I went to Alice's room. I thought I should apologise, drain some of the poison from the air. She wasn't there. Her bed looked like it had been slept in though that doesn't necessarily mean anything. She never makes it. Sean and Eileen say they didn't see her last night. Too busy getting pissed.'

'You've tried ringing her?'

A tiny nod. 'Yes, several times. Her phone is going straight to voicemail, like it's switched off.' Her frown deepened. 'Why do you want to talk to her? Oh my god, do you think she had something to do with Frankie?'

Patrick dodged the question. 'Where are Sean and Eileen now?'

'Eileen's gone out somewhere and Sean is in Alice's room "looking for clues".' She made air quotation marks, her voice dripping with sarcasm.

Patrick was about to ask Helen to fetch her husband when he heard footsteps on the stairs. A moment later, Sean Philips appeared in the doorway. His sandy hair stuck up above his round, pale face in clumps. He blinked at Patrick.

'Detective.' Sean glanced at his wife who sat staring straight ahead. 'Have you got news about Frankie?'

'I'm afraid not yet. Would you mind taking a seat?'

Sean sat beside Helen and tried to take her hand. She pulled hers away like his was covered in slime. He *did* look damp and sweaty, Patrick thought, his skin resembling wet putty. Patrick had also noticed that Sean had buttoned his shirt incorrectly so there was an extra inch of shirt at the bottom on one side. Like his wife, Sean Philips was falling apart, though the husband was making a doomed effort not to show it.

Patrick cleared his throat. 'Firstly, I wanted to assure you that we are still doing everything possible to find Frankie and in the light of what's happened in the last twenty-four hours we're going over everything again from the beginning. I need to ask you some more questions about the night she disappeared.'

'We've told you everything we know already,' Sean said.

'I'm sure, but—'

Patrick's words were interrupted by a sharp intake of breath from Helen. Staring intently at the TV, she grabbed the remote and turned up the volume, as Patrick turned round to see what had made her gasp.

Liam's parents, Zoe and Keith McConnell, were on the news channel. There was a shot of them standing in their substantial front garden, the car from which Liam had been taken in the background, hugging their son tightly and beaming at the cameras. Neither of them looked like they would ever want to let go of him again, and Patrick could imagine Liam's future – his parents never letting him out of their sight, hovering over him day and night, smothering him with love and concern. But he was safe; that was what mattered.

Then the McConnells were being interviewed in their living room, a room very like this one: straight out of *Home and Garden* magazine, all that creamy, expensive furniture, a huge family portrait hanging behind the sofa.

'I just can't express how I feel,' Zoe McConnell said. Her eyes met the camera lens. 'I want to say an enormous thank you to the police for finding him for us, and—' Her voice broke with emotion, and it sounded like she was there in the room with them – until Patrick realized that the crying noises were coming not from Zoe on the TV, but from Helen.

She sobbed, her entire body trembling with distress, her fingers clawing at the upholstery, grabbing a cushion and pulling it to her, hugging it against her belly. A terrible keening noise came from her and she stamped her foot on the carpet, her face pink and streaming with tears.

'Frankie, oh Frankie,' she cried, a tsunami of grief making her body buck. She kept uttering her daughter's name over and over. Sean tried to take hold of her but she shrank away and he hovered at the edge of her, stricken and useless.

'We're never going to find her.' Her words trembled in her throat. 'She's gone, gone forever.' She sounded like someone was shaking her.

She lifted her face and looked directly at Patrick. Behind him, the McConnells continued with their public display of joy. Helen pointed a finger and said, 'You said you'd find her. You've failed us. You've failed Frankie.'

'Helen, that's not fair,' Sean said weakly.

'Fuck you,' Helen spat.

Patrick stood there and took it. Her words made him go cold, but he couldn't blame her.

'We will find her,' he said. Not adding *or what happened to her.*

A fresh wave of tears broke and, finally, she let her husband pull her into an embrace. He stroked her hair and whispered to her as she continued to cry, clutching the back of his badly buttoned shirt.

Patrick had never felt so awkward.

'I'll put the kettle on,' he said.

While he waited for the kettle to boil, his phone rang. It was Carmella.

'Guess what,' she said.

'Larry's done a runner?'

'Alice too, eh? I got there and his mum was being all "leave my poor little boy alone" on the doorstep for about five minutes until I eventually persuaded her to let me in. Larry's nowhere to be seen. His mum admitted she thought he was just having a lie-in, but she hadn't actually clapped eyes on him since last night. She said his backpack was gone, along with a toy tiger he's had since he was little.'

'Bad man, huh?'

'I know, right? Bless. She said it never leaves his pillow. The last time he took it out was on a camping trip with the Scouts when he was twelve.'

Patrick couldn't help but laugh.

'They're *bambinos*,' Carmella said. 'Him and Alice. They think they're all grown up but they're just children.'

When Patrick returned to the living room a few minutes later, holding two steaming cups of tea, each containing three spoonfuls of sugar, Helen was wiping her face with a tissue, the TV was off and the couple sat with their hips touching, facing forward. There was a large wet patch on Sean's chest.

'I'm sorry,' Helen said in a raw voice.

Patrick put the mugs of tea on the coffee table and sat in the armchair opposite. He put his hands on his knees and leaned forward.

'I'm going to need to ask you those questions. We may have covered some of this before but it's important now we're looking at everything from a different angle.' He deliberately avoided using cold words like 'case' and 'investigation'.

Both Philipses nodded.

He paused for a moment before deciding how to begin. He didn't want Sean to leap to his daughter's defence from the first moment. 'How often did you go out leaving Alice looking after Frankie?'

Sean answered. 'Once in a blue moon. We hardly ever get out.'

'I'm never going out and leaving her again,' Helen said quietly.

'So it was an unusual event? You didn't have a regular night that somebody else might know about?'

'God. No, not at all,' said Sean.

Patrick had his notebook out. These were warm-up questions whose answers he didn't expect to be illuminating, but he made a show of noting them anyway.

'Who knew you were going out?'

Sean said, 'I don't know. I think I told a couple of people at work, made a comment about how we were actually going to go out for a change.'

'What about Facebook or Twitter? Did you announce it on there?'

Helen and Sean looked at each other questioningly. Sean said, 'I hardly ever update my Facebook. I don't think I put anything on there. And I only use Twitter for business.'

'I'm sure I didn't either,' Helen said.

'So the only people who knew you were going out were you – the family – plus a couple of friends and colleagues? Did you pre-book the restaurant? Go there in a cab?'

'Yes to the booking. No to the cab – we walked. It's only ten minutes' walk. It was a nice evening. We gave you those details before.'

'Of course. But bear with me.' Patrick knew that they had already spoken to the restaurant, checked out the employees, and that no-one else was under suspicion.

'So the only other people who would have known would be those who Alice told,' Patrick stated. 'Which could be any number of her friends.'

'I guess so,' Sean said. 'But we can't ask her at the moment, can we?'

Patrick scrawled a line in his pad. 'Let's come back to that. Alice told me that her boyfriend, Larry Gould, didn't come round that evening. Do you believe her?'

Sean said, 'Yes,' and Helen said, 'No.'

'A difference of opinion.'

Sean said, 'She was told not to invite Larry round that evening. Why should we disbelieve her when she says she didn't?'

'Why did you tell her not to invite him? Don't you like him?'

Sean laughed humourlessly. 'I like him as much as any father likes his teenage daughter's boyfriend.'

Patrick waited for him to say the obvious, and Sean didn't disappoint. 'I know what boys are like at that age.'

'He's actually a nice kid,' Helen said. 'He's a bit rough round the edges, very "street." But he's always very polite and quite funny. I can understand what Alice sees in him. She's at the age where boys who seem a little bit dangerous and different to what their parents approve of are very appealing.'

Patrick was impressed by how quickly Helen had pulled herself together. She was in that calm state of mind that people often go into after a big emotional episode.

'So why didn't you want him coming round while you were out?'

'Because,' Helen said, 'I know what boys *and* girls are like at that age. I didn't want them making loads of noise and disturbing Frankie. Maybe it's because I'm not Alice's natural mother, but I'm not that bothered about the thought of them having sex in her room. I mean, they're obviously doing it anyway.'

'*What?*' Sean said, appalled.

'Oh, come off it, Sean,' Helen said. 'They've been together six months. Of course they're sleeping together.'

Sean looked sick and Patrick had a horrible vision of himself in thirteen years' time, going through the same with Bonnie.

'But despite your warning, you think Larry did come round that night?' Patrick asked Helen.

'I'd be amazed if they could resist. And I bet that's what they were doing when Frankie . . . was taken.' Her face darkened again. 'Alice was too busy screwing her boyfriend to look after her sister.'

Sean stood up and pointed a finger at his wife. 'Don't talk about Alice like that. None of this is her fault.' His face shifted from white to pink to purple before Patrick's eyes. The truce between the Philipses was over.

'Please,' Patrick said. 'Mr Philips, sit down.' He waited till Sean had taken his seat, at the very edge of the sofa, before asking, 'Do you know if Larry and Alice are into drugs?'

He expected the 'yes'/'no' conflict again, but while Helen thought about it, Sean said, 'It wouldn't surprise me. Like you said about the . . . sex thing, they're teenagers, aren't they? I'm sure they smoke a bit of dope.'

Patrick hadn't heard it called that for years. Feeling old, he said, 'What about harder stuff?'

Sean sighed. 'I don't know. No parent really knows what their kids get up to, do they? But I *do* know that Alice didn't have anything to do with Frankie's disappearance. She would tell us if she knew anything. She loves her sister more than anything.'

'So why has she run off?' Helen asked.

'Because,' he said in an exasperated tone, 'she's sick and tired of everyone blaming her. As am I.'

Silence settled over the room. Patrick thought hard. All this speculation wasn't getting them anywhere. Helen and Sean didn't know a thing. Alice was a teenager; it was like having an alien living in their house, a being they would never fully know or understand. The police had to focus on finding her.

'OK . . . Any idea where she might have gone? Does she have access to any other properties? Any distant friends or relatives she might have gone to stay with? Anywhere at all that you can think of?'

The answers were negative.

'What about her phone?' Sean asked. 'Can't you trace it?' Before Patrick could reply, he added, 'I've tried ringing her a dozen times, and her phone is going straight to voicemail, as if it's turned off. But can't you trace phones even if they are switched off?'

'We can. But not if the battery has been removed. We'll try though.'

His own phone rang. It was Suzanne, no doubt wanting an update. He rejected the call and said, 'That's it for now. If you think of anywhere Alice might have gone, or if you hear anything from her, please let me know immediately. And it would also be useful to have a list of her friends.'

'I'll do that for you,' Helen said. She looked completely drained.

'Thank you.'

He left the house and walked a little way down the street, before calling Suzanne back. As he waited for her to answer, he looked back at the Philipses' house. A week ago, it would have been vibrant, noisy, full of mess and energy.

Now it was a silent, empty nest.

Chapter 31
Winkler – Day 5

Winkler stood in the station car park and watched Lennon and his bitch of a sidekick, Carmella, drive off in separate cars. He was still smarting from the way that lesbian had spoken to him in the meeting, but most of his fury was directed at Lennon. How the hell was he still the lead on this investigation? He couldn't work out if he was actually fucking the DCI or if they merely had the hots for each other. It had to be one of those, and one of these days he was going to find out and expose the pair of them so everyone could see how corrupt this department was. But first, he was going to put Lennon in his place by finding the kid and showing the tattooed twat up for the crap cop he really was.

He drove home, made himself a cup of green tea – it was important to keep his body in tip-top condition – and sat down at the computer. He rested a hand on his belly, feeling his taut abs, and ran a hand through his lovely hair. *Oh Lord, it's hard to be humble.* He resisted the urge to visit the Japanese fetish site he'd become addicted to lately and went to Facebook, logging out of his own account then logging in, for the first time, as Helen Philips.

Lennon reckoned that the teenage duo, Alice and Larry, were responsible for what had happened to the kid but, like he'd said in the meeting, he couldn't see them having the guts or gumption to pull that off. The girl would have crumpled during her first interview.

No, Winkler was now sure the parents were to blame. An accident, maybe. Or straightforward infanticide. Shit, you'd think Lennon would be able to spot a child-killer a mile off, being married to an attempted murderer. But look at the odds – in cases like this, after they'd discounted the neighbourhood child snatchers, it was always the parents. Behind that middle-class veneer of respectability, Sean and Helen Philips were hiding something dark. He could smell it on them. The thought of Helen, with that perfect peachy arse, having a wicked secret gave him a semi. Maybe he'd find some flesh-bearing shots on her Facebook page.

He was disappointed. Pretty much every picture in Helen's Facebook albums was of Frankie, along with a load of pictures of bracelets she'd made in her spare time (all of them with tons of likes from her girly mates) or boring close-ups of bees and flowers she'd taken with 'my fab new macro lens' in the park. Interestingly, there weren't many photos of Alice or Sean, apart from a few Christmas snaps in which Alice looked pouty and Sean appeared pie-eyed. There certainly weren't any pictures that revealed her to be a member of a Satanic cult or anything juicy and incriminating like that.

Her status updates were as vanilla as his ex-wife's sexual tastes too. Lots of sharing of LOL-tastic pictures of cats and 'nom nom'-inducing shots of cakes, plus loads of 'hilarious' (i.e., completely unfunny) things that Frankie had said or done.

Still, he hadn't been expecting to find much on here. What he was really hoping was that, like many people, Helen's Facebook log-in was the same as her email. There could well be something illuminating on there. Before, checking that out, he decided to take a look through her messages.

There wasn't much. An exchange with an old friend, arranging a play date. A couple of gossipy exchanges with some woman from the gym. A mutual moan-fest with another chick about the challenges of parenting toddlers. Apparently, Frankie had bitten some kid at nursery and Helen was in a total panic about it, though 'Sean doesn't see it as a big deal. He says it's just a phase.' Interestingly, there was also a string of exchanges, from about 18 months ago, with a friend who lived in Switzerland, Sara, bitching about their respective mother-in-laws. Helen had really gone off on one about Eileen.

'She turned up out of nowhere and told me about how I was too soft on Frankie, that I need to be stricter with her or she'll end up going off the rails like Sean. I asked her what she meant, coz as far as I know Sean has never done anything bad – nothing I know about anyway!! – but then she clammed up and said she didn't mean anything by it. I tried to press her but she said she just meant Sean was a bit naughty at school, nothing to, in her words, get my knickers in a twist about. When I asked Sean about it later he said he had no idea what Eileen meant.'

That was interesting. Sean Philips had a dodgy past. What did they know about him? He'd been brought up by a single mum, Eileen, in Braintree where Eileen still lived. Gone to study business at uni in Birmingham, then come to London to work in the City. Done well for himself, and set up his own management consultancy firm about five years ago. The Essex boy done good.

Winkler made a note that he needed to talk to Eileen, or maybe go back to Essex and find some old mates of Sean's.

There was another interesting message about Eileen from Helen, writing to her friend Sara.

'She's such a racist. Even though I'm mixed race, I overheard her once saying she didn't think Frankie should go to the nursery she goes to because there are too many of "them". Can you believe it? Has she not noticed that Frankie's mixed race too?!?'

Sara made some horrified statement and Helen continued:

'I reminded her that both her granddaughters are mixed race and she said, "Exactly".'

Winkler pressed print and waited for his shitty printer – was there ever a more temperamental piece of technology? – to grumpily awaken. That could be interesting too. Was Eileen's reference to Sean going off the rails merely something about him fathering a child with not one but two black women? If Eileen was some kind of BNP nut, that would no doubt be seen as a terrible sin to her. He sighed. That probably was it, in which case the reference to Sean going off the rails when he was younger wasn't going to lead him anywhere. It was just the ranting of a racist old woman.

There was no sign of the messages from the woman who had apparently contacted Helen saying she knew where Frankie was. He guessed that this woman had come to her senses and deleted all her messages.

He was about to move on to try to log in to Helen's email when the little chat box in the bottom corner popped up with a new instant message.

It was someone he hadn't heard of before, someone called Hattie Styles. Not one of Helen's existing Facebook friends. Styles' avatar was a mean-looking black and white cat. Winkler immediately smelled a rat. And the name . . . he was no fan of recent pop music, but even he had heard of One Direction and Harry Styles. It was an obvious play on that name. Did that mean he was dealing with a teenage girl here?

I knew Frankie wouldnt b in that house, the message read.

Winkler paused, his fingers poised over the keyboard. He typed, as Helen, How did you know that? Who are you?

The reply came back immediately. U need to look closer to home . . .

What do you mean?

He paused. He felt tense and excited. He added, Please tell me. I need to know what happened to Frankie. I'll be so grateful if you can tell me anything.

There was no immediate response. Shit, had he frightened her off by being too needy? Maybe the best tactic would be to play it cool. But he wanted 'Hattie' to believe that she had power, make her want to show off. Of course, it was highly unlikely she actually knew anything, but it was worth a try.

Finally, the reply came back. You have a demon livin in ur house.

This was interesting. Was 'Hattie' talking about Sean?

He typed, What are you talking about?

Ur stepdaughter. She is evil. An evil bitch!!!

He responded with ???

Alice killd little Frankie. She is a devil. Her and her boyfriend. They are evil and r goin 2 ROT IN HELL for wot they have dun.

Winkler smiled. An obvious nut. Probably seen a picture of Alice in the paper and taken a dislike to her face.

Don't be ridiculous, he wrote. Alice is a nice girl.

Immediately the response came back: That's wot YOU think. I can prove she is evil. And enyl that evil could EASILY kill a little kid. I KNOW wot she is like.

He typed, I thought you had real info for me but you are talking nonsense.

'Hattie' came back with, I can proov it. Im sending you a link to a video that ur stepdaughter made. REMEMBER evil Alice did this. SHE IS GUILTY!!!

Winkler waited for what seemed like forever and was starting to think that 'Hattie' was bluffing or had chickened out, when another message popped up, with a link to an external site.

He clicked it. As 'Hattie Styles' had promised, it led to a video. Winkler clicked play and started watching it.

'Well, fucking well,' he said.

Chapter 32
Helen – Day 5

Helen sat in the office with her back to the door, but kept an eye on the laptop screen for a movement in the reflection that would signify Sean's approach. It would only make things so much worse if he spotted the contents of the email discussion she was having with Marion. After returning from the encounter with Janet Friars, Helen had got home to find an email from her gym-buddy, asking her how she was doing. Quickly firing emails back and forth, Helen had asked Marion what she was up to that evening and her friend had replied that she had a date with a guy so hot he made Brad Pitt look like Shrek. Sex was, apparently, very much on the cards.

I actually can't imagine ever having sex with Sean again, Helen replied. She paused and stared at the photo montage on the wall above the desk, a selection of the best photos from their last few holidays, of her, Sean, Alice and Frankie, mostly on beaches with wind-whipped hair and summer-dark skin, only Sean pale and freckly next to the mocha skin tones of the three girls. She wondered, not for the first time, if Alice minded the fact that she, Helen, could pass for her mum.

Then she added, *How depressing is that?*

Marion had replied immediately. Try not to worry, honey, you're under so much stress. Sex is probably the last thing on your mind.

Helen crossed her legs, squeezing them tightly together. No, she replied, typing furiously, her fingers pounding the keyboard. I'm gagging for it, to take my mind off everything. Seriously. But every time I think of Sean and I doing it, the way he is now, so cold and distant, it just turns me off again. And I feel so guilty for even thinking about it, with F missing . . .

Helen hesitated before hitting 'send'. Perhaps she was 'over-sharing', something she knew she was prone to doing, usually after too much white wine. She *was* over-sharing, she decided. She deleted the last few sentences and instead wrote, Yeah. Not really in the mood these days . . . Anyway, got to go . . .

She was unwilling to admit the reason – that her Diazepam was about to kick in. It had been her only chance of getting any sleep since Frankie had gone.

. . . Thanks for messaging me. It's good to hear from you.

Marion replied, See you at the gym, honey. You'll get your princess back again soon. Hang in there. XXX

Sure, said Helen, brushing away a fat tear that dropped onto her keyboard. Bye XXX.

Then she sat still for a long time, thinking about the words she had almost sent her friend in a moment of honesty. She wanted sex so badly; craved its oblivion – but her only available option was currently staring blank-eyed at the TV screen downstairs, an almost-empty bottle of red wine beside him, his tongue stained black. Last time she had popped down to get a cup of tea, Sean had been watching *Britain and Ireland's Next Top Model*, a programme that Alice loved, but that Sean would, under normal circumstances, rather scoop out his eyes with a spoon than watch voluntarily.

When had they last made love? It took her a moment to recall: it had been the day before Frankie was taken, a middle-of-the-night wordless quickie. The next evening in the restaurant she remembered wondering if she could already be pregnant. She recalled her feeling of pure heady happiness at the thought of another baby, sanctioned by Sean, a confirmation that their marriage was working and their family putting down deeper roots – and then, less than an hour later, everything was in pieces, as though a giant wrecking ball had come long and bashed their lives to shit, its huge hard smooth surface blotting out all light and future and hope . . . at least until Frankie came home.

She didn't bother saying goodnight to Sean. Overcome by a huge tiredness, so great that she couldn't even summon up the energy to trudge downstairs and tell him she was turning in, it just seemed easier to close her laptop lid, give her teeth a perfunctory brush, strip off all her clothes and collapse into bed in a drug-blurred haze.

She awoke several hours later in the pitch dark, lying on her side, not quite sure if she was dreaming the prodding sensation in the area of her coccyx. Not entirely sure if she was even awake. Sean's breathing was light and fast on the back of her neck and the prodding became more insistent. Instantly aroused, she moved her bottom up and back, returning the pressure, feeling the tip of his cock slip between her naked buttocks. Perhaps because it was dark, perhaps because she had her back to him, and she didn't have to see the naked grief in Sean's eyes, or maybe because of her lustful thoughts earlier on, she felt almost overwhelmingly turned on. Everything in her focused on his penis, the softness of the head of it as it probed her, squeezing briefly, tantalizingly, towards her anus, then further down, slipping in, shoving hard into her wetness . . . Helen felt her breathing change too, and she moaned.

'Sean,' she murmured. 'My darling.'

He came almost immediately, pushing deep inside her and shuddering. 'I love you,' he said.

Only now, she noticed the smell of stale alcohol coming off him, and before she could decide whether to say something about it, his breathing changed. He was asleep.

Helen lay in the dark, her eyes open, staring at the digital clock, wondering where Frankie was right now, if she was warm. If she was suffering. Sean shifted against her in his sleep, muttering something. She felt more alone than ever before.

Chapter 33
Patrick – Day 5

Patrick opened the door to his parents' house and let himself in, surprised to hear Dora the Explorer urging Swiper to stop swiping from the TV in the living room. He peeked in – Bonnie was propped up on the sofa, the new cuddly monkey he had bought in a petrol station during a moment of parental guilt clutched to her chest. The stair gate that acted like a prison cell door was shut and Bonnie's eyelids were drooping despite the noise coming from the TV. Plastic toys and brightly coloured books were scattered across the room, the aftermath of the toddler-sized hurricane that swept through the house every day and that Patrick's mum, Mairead, spent hours clearing up. She wouldn't let Patrick hire a cleaner, despite his protestations. For the ten-thousandth time he felt a pang of guilt, followed by a stab of resentment aimed at Gill.

He found his parents in the kitchen, sitting at the table, half-empty cups of tea in front of them.

'What's wrong?' he said, reacting to their glum faces. 'Has something happened?'

'Oh, decided to pay us a visit, have you?' Jim's expression was dark.

'Leave it, Jim.' Mairead forced a smile. 'Would you like a tea, Pat?'

Patrick ignored the question and addressed his dad. 'You know I'm in the middle of a very intense case. You should also know that I feel terrible about you having to look after Bonnie all the time.'

Normally, his dad would have told Patrick not to worry about it, but today he said, 'And so you should. Your mum is exhausted. We both are. We love Bonnie to bits but we're retired now. We should be out enjoying our retirement, but we're stuck in this house every day.'

'Jim!' Mairead protested, but Patrick felt a chill run through his veins. It was pretty obvious that this was what they'd been talking about, why they'd left Bonnie sitting on her own in the other room. And he didn't blame them. Instead, the guilt he'd felt a minute ago intensified and took away all his strength. He sat down with a thump at the table and rubbed his face.

'I know. I'm really sorry. I feel terrible about it.' His eyes stung with emotion.

'Now look what you've done,' Mairead hissed at her husband. 'Pat, my darling, don't worry – your dad and I are just having a bad day, that's all. Bonnie's been playing up, having tantrums. She chucked an entire bowl of Cheerios over the floor, went crazy in Tesco because I wouldn't buy her any sweets and has basically spent the whole day refusing to do anything we tell her to do.'

'She's spoiled rotten,' Jim muttered.

'We're the ones who've spoiled her.' Mairead stood up and went over to Pat, resting a hand on his shoulder. Pat had a flashback to when he was a kid, coming home from school with another lousy report saying he needed to try harder, that he was 'so laid back he's nearly laid out'. Jim would tut and shake his head and lecture Patrick about how he was never going to fulfil his potential if he didn't buck his ideas up. But his mum would almost always be calm and reasonable, making him his favourite dinner to help him feel better. But then, as now, he could tell what she was thinking, the emotions she was too kind to express.

Patrick said, 'Dad's right. I've been asking far too much of you, taking you for granted. I need to sort something out – get a nanny or something. Bonnie can go to nursery.'

'That's so expensive, though, Pat. We really are happy to look after her. I don't want you to spend all your money on childcare.'

'I'm happy to help pay for the childcare,' said Jim. He added hastily, 'Not because I don't love spending time with Bonnie but . . . We're too old for this. We just need to be able to cut down on how much we do.'

Patrick nodded. 'I know, I know. Listen, as soon as this case is over, I'll sort something out. I promise.'

The three of them fell quiet. The only sound was a singing guinea pig from the TV in the other room.

'What about Gill?'

Both Patrick and Mairead looked at Jim. He usually refused to speak Gill's name.

'She can hardly look after Bonnie,' Mairead said.

'I know that. I don't want her anywhere near our granddaughter. But do you know what's happening there? When are they going to let her out? Is she going to be allowed access?' Before Patrick could respond, his dad fired another question at him. 'You went to see her the other day, didn't you?'

'Yes.'

'And how was she?'

'She seemed . . . better. A lot happier. More her old self, in fact.'

'So, what? Are they going to let her out? What are you going to do when that happens?'

Patrick sighed. 'I don't know. I really don't know.'

'I don't know why you haven't divorced her . . .'

'Jim!' Mairead finally snapped. 'For goodness sake, shut up.'

Jim pouted like a pre-schooler. 'Alright. But if and when they do let her out, you'd be mad to take her back, son. As mad as her.'

Down the hallway, Bonnie started wailing. Mairead immediately moved towards the door.

Patrick stopped her. 'No, Mum. I'll go.'

He hurried off toward Bonnie calling out, 'Don't worry, sweetheart, daddy's coming.' At the same time he thought about his dad's questions. Why hadn't he divorced Gill? And what was he going to do when they discharged her? Did he still love her?

It was a bigger, more difficult puzzle than any missing child.

He waited until Bonnie was fed, bathed and in bed before heading back to the station, leaving his parents in front of the TV, his dad frowning at his Sudoku while his mum watched *Coronation Street*. Through the day, Carmella had updated him on the lack of progress and their failure to locate Alice and Larry.

When Patrick got to his desk and checked his email, he found that Helen had emailed him the list of Alice's friends. At the top was Alice's best friend, Georgia, followed by around forty more names. How did girls have so many friends? He imagined her Facebook friend list was considerably longer but, according to Helen's email, these were her real friends.

This was the kind of job he ought to delegate to a lower-ranked member of the team, but Patrick wanted to hear the voices of the girls and boys on the list. He wanted to hear any hint of a lie or cover-up. He picked up his desk phone and started dialling, beginning with the name at the top of the list.

It was going to be a long night.

For the second time in a week, he awoke with daylight penetrating the room and the sound of the cleaner's hoover buzzing in a nearby room. He unpeeled his face from the desk and sat up, rubbing at his scratchy eyes.

The buzzing stopped and was replaced by another sound: shouting. He got up, ignoring the moans of protest from every muscle in his body, and walked out into the corridor. Someone – a woman – was yelling and screaming obscenities, the sound coming from the direction of the front desk.

He decided to check it out, see if they needed any help. When he got there, he found two PCs trying to usher an old woman out of the building, while she continued to yell about 'babies' and 'those kids'.

One of the constables appealed to her to be calm, at which point she threw herself to the floor, just as Bonnie had apparently done in Tesco earlier.

'They tried to kill my baby,' she screamed, thumping the ground.

It was time to step in and help.

'Come on,' he said, kneeling beside the woman. He looked up at the PC and said, 'It's alright, I'll take over from here.'

'Are you sure, sir?'

'Yes, don't worry.' He gently coaxed the woman from her prostrate position. 'We know each other. Don't we, Martha?'

Chapter 34
Winkler – Day 6

St John's was one of the biggest and best secondary schools in Richmond, the kind of school that sent property prices in the surrounding streets soaring as parents who couldn't quite afford to go private clamoured to get into the catchment area. This was the school that Alice Philips attended along with her boyfriend, who lived in one of the Local Authority houses that the middle-class parents wished could be moved to allow space for more of their little darlings. If those parents knew what Winkler had just watched, they might think about putting their overpriced houses on the market, start looking for a different school.

It was dynamite. After the girl – he assumed it was a girl – calling herself Hattie Styles had sent him the link, he'd watched the video it had led to with a slack jaw, so stunned and amused by what he was watching that his brain forgot to send the signals to his body that porn usually elicited.

In the ten-minute clip, a boy and girl – or should he think of them as young man and woman? – shagged each other in what was actually a pretty vanilla way. A strip, a quick blow job, followed by missionary position sex and a bit of doggy style on a double bed.

As porn went, it was at the softer end of the scale. What made it remarkable though was the fact that, until they stripped, the fornicating couple were wearing school uniforms, and on their heads they wore masks to conceal their identities. Because he couldn't see their faces, Winkler couldn't tell exactly how old they were, though he would guess from their bodies, and from their voices as they spoke a few lines of clichéd dialogue, they were no more than fifteen or sixteen. A quick Google image search told him the uniforms were, as he suspected, from St John's.

By the time he'd finished watching the video, Hattie Styles was no longer online. He printed out all her messages – and, more crucially, his own replies masquerading as Helen – then deleted them from Helen's Facebook inbox. Then he sat back and thought about what all this might mean and how it could be connected to the investigation. The girl in the clip was definitely white, so it wasn't Alice. But 'Hattie' had said Alice was responsible for the video. So . . . what, she'd filmed it? Were she and her boyfriend amateur porn directors? Good grief, teenagers today. When he was a kid, the worst things he ever did were shoplifting seven-inch singles from Woolworths and getting into the odd scrap with lads from the rival school. The closest he came to porn was passing round a contraband copy of *Penthouse* with his mates and marvelling at the bushes. Now, though, he lived in a world where women didn't have pubes and every teenager in the western world had instant access to every variety of hardcore porn ever created. He sighed. This generation was so fucking lucky.

Now, he walked across the grounds of the school towards the reception. It was that time in the summer term when most pupils had finished their exams and there was a giddy quality in the air. Winkler felt like he had a hand grenade in his pocket that would destroy all that carefree good feeling. Pull the pin and *boom!* He had a Tigger-ish bounce in his step as he buzzed for the receptionist to let him in.

Five minutes later he sat in the head teacher's stuffy office drinking a lukewarm glass of tap water. The head teacher, Hazel Fletcher, was a smart white woman with a golden bob who reminded him a little of Helen Mirren. A silver vixen. He felt only slightly guilty about ruining her day.

'I've found out something involving a couple of your pupils that might shock you,' he said.

Hazel Fletcher gave him a wry smile. 'I've worked with children for almost thirty years, Detective Winkler. I don't shock easily.'

'Do you have internet access on that computer?' he asked. 'And do you have a firewall that prevents access to adult material?'

She did. Winkler waited while a guy with a head that was balder than a baboon's bum fiddled with the settings on Hazel's computer. After Baldy had left, Winkler read out the URL of the porn clip, then sat back while the head teacher watched it. Her face gave nothing away. He wondered idly if she was slightly turned on by it. She'd never admit it, and neither would he, but when it came down to it humans were animals. The whole lot of them were only a few social niceties away from tearing off their clothes and cluster-fucking in the streets.

Winkler told Hazel what he knew about the source of the video. 'And Alice Philips and Larry Gould are currently whereabouts unknown.'

He expected her to start spouting off about how Alice and Larry were model pupils and how she couldn't possibly imagine how they could have done such a dreadful thing. But he guessed she hadn't been exaggerating when she'd said she'd seen it all.

'So you think Alice and Larry made this video with some other . . . children from this school.' She grimaced at the world 'children'.

'We don't know that for certain, Mrs Fletcher.'

'Ms Fletcher.'

Of course she was. 'Sorry. I was always getting into trouble with the headmistress when I was at school.' Tumbleweed rolled in the space between his sentences. 'I need to find out everything I can about this video and who knows about it.'

'Is it a criminal offence, what Alice and Larry appear to have done?'

'It depends. If the kids in this video are under sixteen, it becomes a lot more serious.'

She nodded grimly and picked up her phone. 'Sarah, can you get Danny Clarke in here? Yes, I saw him earlier. He's here today. For a change.' She put the phone down and addressed Winkler. 'If anyone knows about this, it's Danny Clarke. He knows everything that goes on at this school.'

Shortly afterwards, the receptionist escorted a five-foot-nothing boy with a fringe that flopped over his eyes into the office. Winkler had been expecting a member of staff, not a kid. But Danny Clarke was, as Hazel now explained, a Year Ten student. Winkler almost laughed. It appeared that the head teacher used Danny as the equivalent of a police informant. Danny sat down and his leg immediately started to jerk up and down; he had the worst case of restless leg syndrome Winkler had ever seen. His leg gave off enough kinetic energy to power a small town for a week.

Hazel fixed Danny with a serious look. 'Danny, this is Detective Inspector Adrian Winkler.'

Danny sniggered.

'What's so funny?'

'Oh, nothing,' he said innocently.

Winkler wondered if Danny had broken any laws recently and if he could find an excuse to arrest him and give him a proper scare.

Hazel pressed on. 'We need to talk to you about a very serious matter. We have learned that an . . . explicit video may have been made by some students here.'

Danny grinned. 'The St John's porno? Yeah, everyone's seen it. It's a bit vanilla for my tastes but still pretty cool.'

Vanilla? Winkler wondered if this kid had read his mind.

Hazel had gone white. 'Everyone's seen it?'

'Yeah. Well, I guess there are a few totally lame kids who've missed it but everyone I know has watched it. Curtis was showing it to everyone on his phone at lunchtime.'

'Today?' Winkler asked.

'Nah, a few days ago. It's old news now.'

'Do you know who the kids in the video are?'

Danny's eyes widened. 'No! It's a total mystery. Nobody knows. I mean, there have been a lot of guesses and accusations going around. James Peach reckons the girl is India Ripley, said he recognized the mole on her bum. But I'm sure he's bull – I mean lying.'

'And do you know who made the video?'

He squirmed. 'I don't want to grass no-one up.'

'It's alright, Danny,' Winkler said. 'We know who made it. How did you hear about it?'

'It just kind of went round school. Viral, you know? There was a Facebook group that you had to ask to join, and once you were approved you could get the link. But everyone had the link anyway.'

'And can you remember when you found out about it?'

He scratched his chin. 'Yeah, it must have been last weekend. It went live on Sunday night. I remember because I was round Jack's and we watched it together. Not in a gay way, you understand.'

'Yes, Danny,' Hazel sighed.

Winkler smiled at him. So it appeared that the video had been uploaded and sent out on the same night – the night Frankie had disappeared.

This was great. Because if Alice and Larry had been busy messing around with online videos and sharing them with their mates at the time Frankie had vanished, there was no way they would have had time to do anything else. And it also explained why they had been so reluctant to confess to Larry's presence at Alice's house and why they had done a runner now. It was because they didn't want any adults to know about the flesh flick.

'One last question,' Winkler said. 'Do you know anyone who calls herself Hattie Styles?'

Danny laughed. 'Yeah – she's this mental Year Ten girl, completely obsessed with 1D. Her real name is Emily Foggett-Hayes.'

'And do you know any reason why she might have it in for Alice Philips?'

'Alice? Why do you ask that?'

'I'm asking the questions, Danny.'

The boy thought about it. 'I dunno. A lot of girls hate other girls for completely random reasons. Maybe she dissed 1D or something.'

Winkler smiled. He would have shaken Danny Clarke's hand if he didn't suspect where it had been. Now he had something to tell the DCI that would prove to her that Lennon was heading off in the wrong direction again. OK, so he might not have any great leads of his own, but here was a chance to make Lennon look even more stupid and there was no way he wasn't going to take it.

Chapter 35
Patrick – Day 6

'Here we are again,' Patrick said.

Carmella craned her neck towards the tops of the tower blocks, where Adidas tops and Primark knickers flapped in the soft summer breeze. 'At least when it all goes horribly wrong and we find ourselves living here, we'll know our way around.'

They walked over to the building where they had encountered Martha and her dolls, just over a week ago. A group of teenage boys in sportswear and an emaciated girl in a belly top that showed off the tattoo that snaked around her midriff watched them from across the street. A young man with a Staffordshire terrier stood a little way apart from the group, also watching them, a sneer on his lips. Patrick recognised him: Jerome Smith, a small-time gangbanger who'd been up on a number of charges, none of which had stuck.

This morning, Patrick had taken Martha into an interview room, wishing dearly that he had a cold so he couldn't smell her, the reek of layer upon layer of body odour and uncleaned teeth, mixed with cheap alcohol. She was barely coherent but, between rants, she told an interesting tale.

'Them kids – the boy tried to take my baby – and now he's living next door with his girlie-friend. I saw it, I saw it in a paper – someone's been stealing children, and now they want mine.' She screwed up her filthy face and hugged the doll she'd brought with her, kissing its scraggy head.

'Can you describe these kids, Martha?'

'Yeah, the girl is, whatchamacallit, half caste, and pretty. Very pretty. The boy, he's . . . white. He's tall and he's got these little eyes that look right at you and make you feel like he's stripping you naked.' She gasped. 'That's what he wants. He wants to take my babies and then have his wicked way with me.' She squeezed the baby so tightly that Patrick thought its head might pop off.

'And how long have they been there?'

'Since . . .' The pause that followed was longer than the gap between Stone Roses albums. 'Yesterday. But I saw them, them and their friends, that evil boy and that other pretty girl.' She began to sob. 'Please, sir, you have to help me.'

Patrick assured her that he would.

'So what are we going to do if it's not Alice and Larry?' Carmella asked as they stepped into the building.

'I don't know. But it will be. I bet you my rare picture disc of *Disintegration*.'

Carmella wrinkled her nose. 'Wow, now I really hope it's not them.' Then, 'What's a picture disc?'

'You youngsters. You missed out. You probably feel nostalgia for cassettes.'

'I don't really remember them either.'

They reached the top of the stairwell and headed towards the flat where they'd found Martha last time. According to her, she'd moved back in a day after they'd chucked her out. Patrick wondered why she wasn't in a hospital somewhere, how she had slipped through the cracks of the system. He wished he could do something for her, make sure she was taken care of. But that was something for another day, and if he was honest it was something he was unlikely to ever get round to. Now, all he cared about was finding Alice and Larry – and, he prayed, finally finding out what had happened to Frankie.

They stood outside the door of the vacant flat next to Martha's. There were no sounds coming from within. Somewhere in the distance a baby was crying; a real one this time.

Patrick knew the flat had no back exit. The only way out was through this door or one of the front windows. He rapped on the door and waited, not expecting a response. None came.

He nodded at Carmella. *Ready?* She nodded back.

Patrick lifted his leg and kicked the door with all his strength. It gave immediately, swinging inwards and thudding against the wall. He ran into the room, Carmella behind him.

'Police!' he shouted, entering the first room he came to, what would have been the living room. No sign of them – but there were sleeping bags on the floor, a couple of empty pizza boxes, bottles of water, fag packets. The room was skin-meltingly hot and stank like a teenager's bedroom turned up to eleven.

He heard a noise from somewhere in the flat and gestured for Carmella to follow him.

They found them in the gutted kitchen, standing against the back wall, holding hands. Alice looked terrified. Larry was trying his hardest not to look scared, but he was shaking.

'Alice,' said Patrick. 'And Larry. Remember me?'

'We haven't done anything,' Larry said.

'A lot of people are looking for you two. Like your parents. They're worried sick.'

'I doubt that,' Alice sneered, though her boyfriend wore a guilty expression, like he was concerned about his mum.

Carmella said, 'We need you to come to the station to answer a few questions.'

'What about?' Alice asked, squeezing Larry's hand like she was trying to break it. 'We don't know anything.'

'Anything about what, Alice?'

'About . . . I don't know.'

Carmella took a step towards them, her arm outstretched, and Larry stepped in front of his girlfriend and pulled out a flick-knife. Carmella froze.

'Larry? What are you *doing?*' Alice cried.

Patrick and Carmella both put their palms up. Larry moved the knife from side to side, his eyes wild and shining with panic. 'Leave her alone.'

'Come on, Larry,' Patrick said quietly. 'Don't be a dickhead.'

'I'm not scared to use this,' Larry said, jerking the knife from side to side, but his voice betrayed him.

'Do you really want to go prison? They'd love you in there. Nice boy like you.'

Larry stopped swinging the knife and Patrick saw his opportunity, going in fast – grabbing the wrist that held the knife, grateful that his instincts were correct as Larry put up little resistance. Patrick pulled the boy's arm behind his back and pushed it upwards, making Larry gasp in pain and drop the knife. Carmella darted in and snapped handcuffs over his wrists.

'You got any weapons?' Patrick asked Alice, who stood trembling by the filthy window.

She shook her head meekly.

He held up his handcuffs. 'So I won't be needing these?'

As they led the teenagers out to the car, Patrick caught the eye of the guy with the staffie. Jerome Smith. He had a wicked smile on his lips. He noticed Larry looking at him too.

'Friend of yours?' he asked.

'No,' Larry said quietly. 'He's a twat.'

Patrick put his hand on Larry's head and eased him into the car. When he looked back up, Smith was gone, leaving just a steaming dog turd on the pavement to show he and his terrier had been there.

Patrick leaned on the coffee machine, wondering why he still bothered drinking this muck when its placebo effect, which relied on the drinker believing it was real coffee containing real caffeine, had long ceased working.

'Patrick.'

It was Suzanne. She looked like she needed a hug, gorgeous and vulnerable. He stared at her lips then inwardly admonished himself. What was he thinking?

'Update, please.'

He pulled the coffee out of the machine, some of the diarrhea-brown liquid slopping over his fingers.

'Of course. We've got Alice Philips in interview room two and Larry Gould in four. We're waiting for the appropriate adults to turn up. Last time, Alice had her neighbour but now she wants us to provide someone. Same with Larry. I'm going to alternate interviews.'

'OK, good. Keep me posted, alright?'

She headed back to her office and Patrick checked his watch. He was pleased that the appropriate adults weren't here yet. He wasn't rushing to talk to the two teenagers – he wanted them to have time to fret, to imagine the worst. He took his coffee back to his desk and waited.

Winkler walked past and gave Patrick a wink.

'Still think those kids did it?' he said, pausing by the desk.

'Piss off, Winkler.'

'If you insist.' He walked off, that smirk on his face again. Patrick took deep breaths.

Finally, the adults – a social worker called Janice Swift for Alice, and a youth worker named Colin James for Larry – were present and ready. So was Patrick. He gave Carmella the nod and they headed to interview room two first.

Alice sat slumped in her chair, her shoulders drooping. She looked exhausted but wore the same sullen, defiant expression as last time. She smelled bad, her hair was a mess and without her make-up she looked like a child. He couldn't help but feel sorry for her but stronger than his pity was his need to do the job. To find out what had happened to her half-sister.

After checking the video camera was recording, Patrick said, 'Alice. I expect you'd like to get home, have a hot shower.'

She grunted.

'I'll take that as a yes.'

He had an A4 file on his desk and he made a show of opening it and looking over his notes. There was a photo of Frankie on top and he left the file open so Alice could see it, right in front of her. He saw her glance at the picture and swallow.

'Alice, last time I interviewed you, you told us there was no one else present on the night of June ninth, the night you babysat Frankie. Are you still sticking with that story?'

She nodded.

He stared at her, not speaking. One of the techniques he commonly used was to leave long silences. Most people hate silence in conversations; they rush to fill them. But Alice remained mute.

'We've got a witness who saw your boyfriend, Larry Gould, in the vicinity of your house on the night in question. As you know, we're also talking to Larry today. Do you think he's going to tell the same story as you?'

'Come on, Alice,' Carmella coaxed. 'Answer the question.'

She shuffled in her seat. 'Yeah, he will. Because it's the truth.'

Patrick sighed. 'Come on, Alice. Pull the other one. We understand why you don't want to tell us the truth about him being there.'

A flicker of fear in her eyes.

'But do you understand the seriousness of lying to the police? I expect you've heard of perverting the cause of justice?'

'Larry didn't do anything,' Alice insisted. 'How many times do I have to tell you?'

Carmella asked, 'How do you know he didn't do anything if he wasn't with you?'

'What are you doing, trying to confuse her?' Janice Swift said, leaning forward.

Patrick chipped in. 'To be honest, it's us who are confused, Alice. We don't understand why you're lying to us. Unless, of course, you have something to hide.'

The muscles flexed in Alice's jaw as she bit down, a sign she was trying not to cry. Patrick leaned closer and stared at her until she was forced to meet his eye.

'Where did you hide the body, Alice?'

She flinched like he'd tried to hit her. 'What?'

'Frankie's body. What did you do with it? You can't have gone far, though I suppose she was pretty light. I'm guessing the park down the road from your house. A shallow grave. Won't be hard for us to find now we know where to look.'

'No!' Alice yelled. Now the tears came. Janice tried to pass her a tissue but Alice angrily waved her away. 'Frankie's my little sister. I love her. I'd never do anything to hurt her.'

'So it was Larry?'

'Oh my God, this is so fucked up. Larry thought the world of her too. He'd never hurt her either.' She looked from him to Carmella and back. 'You have to believe me. Please.'

Patrick said, 'I'm suspending the interview.' He stood up. As he was about to open the door, he looked back and said, 'Why do you keep referring to Frankie in the past tense?'

He and Carmella left the room, closing the door on the sound of Alice's sobs.

Larry Gould's demeanour was very different to Alice's. He sat up straight, trying to keep any expression from his face. But he was scared, that was obvious. A sheen of sweat coated his face and he kept knotting and unknotting his fingers. The skin around his thumb was bleeding where he'd been chewing it. The youth worker, Colin James, well known in the community for working with teenagers and diverting them from a life of crime, was leaning back in his chair with his arms folded over his muscular chest, watching Larry intently.

'You were at Alice's house the night of June ninth, the night Frankie disappeared, weren't you?' Patrick began.

To his surprise, Larry nodded.

Patrick and Carmella exchanged a glance. Carmella said, 'You're admitting it?'

'I don't want to lie to you any more,' he said. 'I'm sorry I denied it before. I didn't want Alice to get into trouble with her parents.'

Patrick paused. Either Larry was about to tell them the whole truth, or he was being clever. Confess to the stuff the police already know and make yourself look cooperative. It was a smart tactic.

'So tell us what happened that night.'

Larry took a sip of water. 'Alice told me her parents were going out and that she was babysitting Frankie, and I asked if I could go round. She was a bit, you know, reluctant because she didn't want to get into trouble, but she gave in.'

A smiled twitched at the corners of Carmella's lips. *She must be thinking the same as me,* thought Patrick. This is Larry being chivalrous.

'And?' Patrick said.

'There isn't much to tell. I went round about eight, saw Alice, then went home at about eleven before her dad and stepmum got home.'

'What were you and Alice doing?'

Larry squirmed. Patrick thought he was probably torn between wanting to tell him to mind his own and the desire to show off.

'We went to her room,' he said. 'To . . . you know.'

Carmella asked, 'Were you in her room the whole time you were there?'

He shrugged. 'Pretty much.'

'What did you do in her room?' Patrick asked.

Larry avoided his eye. 'I already told you.'

'No you didn't. You said "you know". You need to elaborate.'

Now Larry looked straight at him. 'We had sex, alright? Do you want to know what positions we did it in?'

'And that's the only reason you and Alice didn't want us to know you were there that night?'

'Yeah.'

'Do you really think that Alice's parents would be so freaked out by the thought of you and their daughter having sex that you had to lie about it, when you knew how important it is for us to know exactly what happened in their house that night?'

Larry gnawed on his thumb before replying. 'I knew we should tell you I was there. But I didn't see anything. I don't know anything. So I didn't think it would make a difference.'

'Did you see Frankie that night?'

'No. She was in bed when I got there.'

'You didn't hear her?' Carmella asked.

'No. I didn't hear or see nothing. As far as I could tell, she wasn't even there.'

Patrick barely gave him a chance to finish before asking, 'Were you and Alice drinking that night? And I don't care about you being seventeen, by the way.'

'No. Well, maybe a can of beer each. But that's it.'

'What about drugs?'

Larry's answer was a rather unconvincing, 'No.'

'You sure about that? You don't sound very sure. Not even a bit of weed?'

'Nothing. I swear.'

'What about Alice?'

Larry shifted in his seat. 'Alright. We ate some brownies. Hash brownies. But just, like, one each.'

Patrick was tempted to laugh. He remembered eating hash cakes when he was in his teens. It was the closest he'd ever come to having a psychotic episode. No wonder Alice had been passed out on the sofa when Helen and Sean got home.

'Who baked them?' Patrick asked.

'I did. Alice is crap at that kind of thing.'

'Alright, Larry, thanks for finally being honest,' he said, and suspended the interview. It was time to go and talk to Alice again, let her know what her boyfriend had admitted.

They found Mike Staunton waiting for them outside in the corridor, pacing anxiously.

'DCI Laughland wants to see you urgently, sir.'

'What's it about?'

'Sorry, sir. She just said to get you to go straight along as soon as you came out of the interview.'

Patrick frowned. 'Carmella, do you want to grab a drink or something and I'll meet you outside interview two in a minute?

Assuming Frankie hasn't been found safe and sound – in which case we can all go home and put our feet up.'

He knocked lightly on Suzanne's door and went in. His heart sank when he saw who was sitting on the near-side of the desk. Winkler, that insufferable smirk on his handsome, slappable face.

'Alright, Pat?' he oozed.

'Patrick,' Suzanne said. 'Take a seat.'

'What's happened?'

'DI Winkler has unearthed some important information about your young suspects. You'd better fill him in, Adrian.'

'My pleasure, Ma'am.'

As Winkler told him about how he had discovered that Alice and Larry had made a porn video starring two other kids and that on the night of Frankie's disappearance, they were editing the video, Patrick's head filled with the high-pitched tremulous hum of his tinnitus. Winkler went through the whole thing, from being contacted by a girl on Facebook to the interview with the school stool pigeon.

'And that,' Winkler said, leaning back in his chair and showing off his damp armpits, 'is the real reason why your number one suspects don't want anyone to know what they were up to that night. Not because they accidentally killed the kid and buried her in the flowerbeds. I mean, I hate to say I told you so . . .'

Patrick looked over at Suzanne, at her tight lips, the worry in her eyes as she no doubt pictured herself telling the Commissioner this.

He put his face in his hands and rubbed his brow. Then he lifted his head and said brightly, 'Thanks, Adrian, that's brilliant.'

Winkler's expression changed in an instant. 'What?'

'That's exactly what I needed. You're a true star.'

He stood up and patted Winkler on the shoulder as Suzanne looked on, shocked.

'Right, I'm going to get these interviews wrapped up. If there's nothing else . . .'

Before either of them could respond he pulled open the door and left the room.

As soon as he heard it click shut behind him he let out a silent scream.

He found Carmella waiting outside interview room two, swigging from a bottle of water.

'Come on,' he said. 'This is it. Do or die. The last chance saloon.'

'What are you talking about?' she asked. 'What happened in there?'

'Someone tried to shaft me,' he replied. 'We're about to find out how successful they were.'

He sat down opposite Alice and started the interview again.

'The time for bullshit is over,' he said, forcing her to meet his eye. 'One, we know Larry was there that night. He just told us. He said that you and he spent the evening having sex.'

'No way.'

Patrick almost said, 'Yes way,' but stopped himself. Instead, he said, 'Two, and more importantly, we know about the video.'

Alice blanched. 'What . . . video?'

'The video starring two pupils at St John's that you and Larry made. Don't even bother denying it, Alice. We *know*. So, I have good news and bad news. The good news is that I believe you when you say you aren't directly responsible for whatever happened to Frankie. Indirectly – well, yes, you are. But that's not a crime.'

He willed Alice to refrain from crying before he finished. Her lip wobbled and she swallowed several times, but no tears came yet.

'The bad news is that making and distributing pornographic material featuring minors is an extremely serious crime, one for which you and Larry could face a pretty lengthy prison sentence.'

This was a gamble. Winkler had said he didn't know how old the kids in the video were.

Alice let out a terrible keening sound and started to sob. 'No . . . No . . . It's not fair. I didn't know how old they were. I didn't find them, I hardly even know them. I thought they were sixteen.'

'So it's all Larry's doing, is it?'

'No. He didn't know them either.'

'What are you telling me? That they just walked in front of your video camera one day and started getting it on?'

Alice wept into her hands. Janice reached out to comfort her and Alice shrugged her off violently. 'Get off me!' But this time she accepted the tissue Janice offered, blowing her nose loudly.

'It was . . .' She hesitated. 'It was Georgia.'

Patrick checked his notes quickly. 'Georgia Hardy-Wilson? Your best friend?'

'Yes. She persuaded the kids to do it. She said they'd get a share of the profits. They were, like, a couple of real, you know, chavs. They don't actually go to our school – she met them on the Kennedy Estate and lent them the uniforms. Jerome knew them. But Georgia told me they were sixteen.'

Patrick believed her. She was just a silly girl, who had got herself mixed up in a stupid scheme. He couldn't stop the anger burning in his veins, though.

'So, what, Georgia found the kids and then you and Larry did everything else?'

Alice blew her nose again. 'No, she was there through the whole thing.' Her eyes glistened. 'She was there.'

'Tell me that again.'

'She was there that night. At my house.' And she dissolved into another round of wet, gasping sobs.

Chapter 36
Georgia – Day 1

Georgia stood behind Larry and Alice as they stared with a mixture of hilarity and revulsion at the writhing naked limbs on the screen of Larry's MacBook, a half-eaten hash brownie in her hand. Alice's dad and stepmum were out but Alice kept looking nervously at the door, flinching whenever she heard a noise in the house, in case they came back early. They'd all seen the video loads of times before, but Larry's final edit perfectly captured the grossness and ignominy of the whole performance.

'Oh my god, he's got a huge zit, on his arse,' said Alice, clapping her palm over her mouth in horror.

Larry tilted his head to one side. 'Do you think anyone will be able to recognize him?'

'What – from the arse zit?' Alice giggled. 'Nah. Those bags on their heads work a treat. In fact, they should wear them all the time, they're so ugly.'

'Don't be so mean,' Georgia said, although she knew she was usually the first to make rude personal comments about people in school.

Alice raised an eyebrow at her in acknowledgement of this fact. 'Er – pot . . . kettle?' she said. 'What's up with you today, George? You've been in a right strop since you got here.'

'Nothing,' Georgia said sulkily. Her phone vibrated in the back pocket of her jeans, a reminder of the reason for her panicked state. That would be Jerome's fifth text in the last hour. She sat back down on Alice's bed, waited until Larry and Alice were tinkering around with their video, then slipped out the phone to have a look, bracing herself as she opened the text.

COME ON BITCH, DON'T THINK YOU CAN TALK YOUR WAY OUT OF THIS ONE. AND DON'T IGNORE ME OR YOU'LL REGRET IT. I KNOW WHERE YOU LIVE.

Tears leaped into her eyes.

Georgia was used to feeling in control. She'd never before been in a situation that she couldn't either charm or buy – with her parents' money, of course – her way out of. Why oh why were her bloody mum and dad being so unmoveable about her allowance? She'd thought they were joking when they said that unless she got at least four Cs in her mocks, they were stopping her allowance and freezing her savings account until she was twenty-one. And now, the one time in her life when she really, really, really needed money, urgently, she had none. And she could hardly go to them and say 'Mummy, Daddy, I need four grand to pay off a violent drug dealer that I've upset by losing the weed I was meant to be selling for him, and he's going to actually kill me unless I come up with the dosh in the next couple of days . . .'

She couldn't even bring herself to tell Alice and Larry. She told herself that she was 'doing the right thing' by not wanting to involve them, but closer to the truth was that she didn't want to admit her stupidity. Who was thick enough to leave a bag of weed and pills on the bus? They'd think she was a total moron. Every time she opened her mouth to tell them, her tongue became immediately paralysed at the thought of how much they would laugh at her. And if there was one thing Georgia hated even more than being skint, or having to do homework, it was being laughed at.

Plus, she was afraid that if she told Alice, Alice would do something insane like telling someone, the police or her dad, and then they'd all be even further up shit creek. It would be bad enough if anyone ever found out they were behind the movie.

Georgia managed a brief smile of pride at the thought of her movie brainwave. It was unlikely to raise anywhere close enough to the amount of money she needed to get Jerome off her back, especially when it had to be split three ways, but it was shaping up to be a nice little earner. Everyone at school was talking about it, speculating as to who the shaggers were – before the video had even gone live! There was a special secret Facebook group set up to discuss it, and over three hundred kids had already joined, all of whom seemed completely willing to hand over the ten quid it would cost them to join the Facebook group, watch the movie and place their bets on the identity of the faceless participants. It had been a genius idea. Coerce two gullible kids from the Kennedy into getting high, getting naked and putting paper bags over their heads, and then film them having clumsy embarrassing sex, promising them a share of the profits. Georgia was sure that apart from charging kids at school to view it, they could sell it to some big porn site, maybe in America, and make more than enough to wipe out her problems in one stroke.

Larry had spent ages editing the footage. Alice had done the marketing and PR, anonymously of course. Georgia had been the creative director.

'Total shame we can't submit this for our Media portfolios,' Alice said. 'We'd get straight A's. I can't believe we're ready to go live! Kind of exciting, don't you think?'

Larry nodded. He kissed Alice's cheek and snaked an arm around her neck and down her front to caress the side of one of her practically non-existent boobs.

Georgia felt sick. 'Oh, get a room, you two,' she snapped. Her bottom vibrated with yet another text. Jerome wasn't going to leave her alone.

She was a dead girl.

'Georgia! You're really getting on my nerves tonight. What is WITH you?'

Georgia jumped off the bed and grabbed her bag. 'You know what? I'm going. I'm sick of playing gooseberry to you two.'

Alice put a hand on her sleeve but she snatched it away. 'Seriously, babe, what's the matter?'

'Nothing. I'll see you around, OK? I've got to go.'

Georgia felt as though Alice's blood-red bedroom walls were beginning to close in on her. Her heart was beating faster than it had done that time she took speed, and she couldn't breathe.

'Alright. Maybe it's best that you do, since you're in such a foul mood. I'll call you tomorrow.' Alice's voice was cool and unfriendly, and she turned away without giving her a goodbye hug. Georgia knew that they would bitch about her the moment she left – but so what? She had more important things to worry about. Like trying to stay away from Jerome before he killed her.

She stomped down the top flight of stairs from Alice's attic room, swinging joylessly around the banister and opening the stair-gate. She felt so faint with fear that her bowels clenched and she realized she had to go to the bathroom, urgently. Her head was swimming too. How much hash had Larry put in those brownies? Swearing under her breath, she dashed into the Philipses' bathroom, mindful even in her panic of closing the door quietly so as not to wake Frankie, asleep in her room next door.

Sitting on the toilet, she put her head in her hands, rocking back and forward. Why the hell had she eaten Larry's fucking hash cakes? She caught a glimpse of her reflection in the mirror opposite and was horrified. Her complexion was greenish instead of its usual, much-praised, English Rose peaches and cream. Her beautiful strawberry blonde hair was matted and dull. Her face looked puffy. She thought of what Jerome might do to it with the Stanley knife she'd seen him with, and moaned out loud. Oh god . . . The porno wasn't going to save her. Nothing would. She was going to have to run away, leave the country. She had enough to get her to France, and maybe from there she could hitch south, head for Spain where she could get a job in a bar or a club. She imagined herself for a happy moment sunning herself on a beach – then the vision warped into one of her being forced to work as a stripper or a prostitute, shaking her tits for drunken British tourists and disgusting old men.

Gulping in air, she sat there until her bowels had emptied and her gut spasms started to relax their iron grip on her belly. A recent copy of Metro caught her eye, left on the wicker basket full of toilet rolls next to the loo. She picked it up and stared at the headline: SUN NEWSPAPER OFFERS £100,000 REWARD FOR SAFE RETURN OF LIAM AND IZZY.

One hundred grand? She read on. The £100K wasn't even for physically finding the kids and returning them to their families, it was for 'information leading to the safe return of either of them.' Georgia thought hard. Obviously she didn't have any idea where Liam and Izzy were. She entertained a brief fantasy that Jerome had snatched them and she not only got the reward – would it be two hundred grand for the two? – when she told the police that the kids were in the estate somewhere, but she also managed to get Jerome locked up . . .

Well, that wasn't going to happen. But a plan started to form in her mind. She made a mental list:

1. The police think Liam and Izzy have been snatched by the same person/people – which they could well have been, since they were both taken from this area.

2. What if another toddler of the same age happened to vanish, from around here? It was obvious what conclusions the police would draw.
3. If *The Sun* were offering £100K when two kids had gone, how much more would they, or another tabloid, offer once a third one disappeared?
4. The reward was for 'information leading to . . .'
5. What if she had that information?

Her stomach clenched again – this time with nervous excitement. She knew how she could get her hands on the reward – and save her own miserable life.

Chapter 37
Patrick – Day 6

Patrick had chewed his e-cigarette so hard on the drive over to Georgia Hardy-Wilson's house that there were teeth marks in it. He chucked it onto the dashboard, left the blissful air-conditioned sanctuary of the car and stepped out into the suffocating heat. It was 32 degrees in London, even with the evening drawing in.

A middle-aged woman with long blonde hair and a golden tan was in the front garden of what was yet another huge, expensive house, attacking an overgrown vine with a set of shears. Sweat streaked her face as she hacked at the plants, the way she wielded the shears making Patrick want to cross his legs.

'Mrs Hardy-Wilson?' He spoke to her over the gate.

She turned and pushed her sunglasses onto her head. 'Just Hardy. My daughter's the only Hardy-Wilson. Yes?'

A flash of his badge. 'DI Patrick Lennon. It's your daughter I'm after, actually.'

She dropped the shears into a flowerbed and came closer, waving away a bee that zig-zagged across her path.

'Georgia? She's not here . . . Has something happened?'

Patrick pushed open the gate and went into the garden, finding a patch of shade beneath an apple tree. 'I need to talk to her. Nothing to worry about. Do you know where she might be, Mrs Hardy?'

The woman scrutinized him, looking him up and down in a manner that made him wonder if he'd forgotten to put his clothes on that morning, then smiled. 'Call me April, please. Georgia went out for a run – crazy, in this heat.'

'Would you be able to call her for me?'

'I suppose so.'

She led him inside the house, where a golden Labrador lay panting on the stone floor of the kitchen.

'Lemonade? I made it this morning. Excellent with Pimms but I suppose you're on duty.' Her quietly wicked smile made him warm to her immediately. He could picture her when she was younger – the naughty public schoolgirl, secretly sneaking a fag in the school grounds. From what he knew of Georgia, she had probably inherited her rule-breaking side from her mum.

Without waiting for a reply, April poured him a glass – it was sharp and sugary – then fished her phone out of the pocket of a pair of shorts that showed off a great pair of legs.

'Let's see.' She pressed the screen and held the phone to her ear.

'Hmm. Straight to voicemail. I'll text her. She usually answers straight away, unless she's with a boy.'

'Does Georgia have a boyfriend?'

She sent the text and laid the phone on the marble kitchen surface. 'Oh no. Georgia's attention span isn't long enough for her to have a boyfriend. She's more like a butterfly, flitting about, taking what she needs.' She laughed and fluttered her hands in imitation of the insect.

'Do you let Georgia have a lot of freedom, then?'

April took a step closer. 'She's sixteen, detective. She needs her freedom to be able to find out who she really is. We've always encouraged that. Although we've had to curb her spending recently, make her take responsibility for her own money. She'll get access to her trust when she's twenty-one. We're very strict about that.'

'Have you got any reason to think Georgia has been in need of money recently?'

April leaned against the worktop and smiled with one corner of her mouth. 'Am I being interviewed? This hasn't happened to me since the late seventies when I was arrested for smoking a joint.'

'I'm not interviewing you, April. Just making conversation.'

Her wicked expression returned. 'Shame. There's a *very* naughty cop in my new novel.'

'You're a writer?'

'Yes. Well, I guess there's no reason why you'd have heard of me.' She gestured towards a framed poster on the wall. *Enslaved, by April Hardy.* 'That's my new one. I used to write what were called bonkbusters but now it's all about erotica.'

Patrick blinked. 'Has Georgia replied to your text yet?'

She checked her phone, her brow creasing a tiny amount. 'No. Hmm, she has been a long time.'

'You didn't answer my question about money,' Patrick said, sipping his lemonade.

April thought about it. 'She always wants money for something or other. I know she wants us to get her some swanky car when she passes her test. But she hasn't been begging us for cash any more than usual.'

'Do you know Alice Philips and Larry Gould?'

Her face lit up. 'Yes. Of course. Alice is Georgia's best friend and Larry is her adorably chavvy boyfriend.'

'Has Georgia said anything to you about them recently?'

'No. Well, there's that dreadful business with Alice's little sister, but Georgia doesn't like talking about that, says it upsets her too much.'

'We really need to talk to Georgia, April.' He put his empty glass down. 'It's serious. It's connected to Frankie's disappearance.'

'What? Why?'

'Georgia was at Alice's house the night Frankie disappeared.'

'Oh. I see. And you want to ask her if she saw anything. Well, I'm sure she would have said something to me if she had.'

'I still need to talk to her.' He was itching to tell her about the video that her liberated daughter was responsible for making. Would she be shocked? Was it prudish and old-fashioned of him to be shocked by it? Online porn, celebrity sex tapes and viral videos depicting acts that Patrick didn't even want to imagine were, to Georgia's generation, as commonplace and ordinary as reality TV and wi-fi. He guessed April would be relaxed about it too – as long as it wasn't her daughter actually starring in it.

'I'm not sure how I can help you further, detective.'

'Can you try calling her again?'

'Yes. You know, I'd lost track of time but she's been gone for *hours*.' She picked up her phone. 'It's still going straight to voicemail.'

'As if it's switched off?'

'Yes. It's unusual, to be honest. The phone is like an extension of her. She normally replies to texts within seconds.' She crossed to the window. 'I hope she hasn't collapsed in this heat. Maybe she's gone to the flat.'

Alice had told Patrick that the porn video had been filmed at Georgia's parents' flat.

'It's on her usual route,' April said, 'and she's got a key. I'm worrying now.' She chewed her lip. 'Maybe I'll nip down to the flat to take a look.'

'I'll come with you.'

Patrick followed April in her top-of-the-range Discovery, thinking about his interview with Alice as he drove. In the final minutes, after she had told them about Georgia, another mystery had been solved: the mystery of why she had been unconscious on the sofa when Helen and Sean got home that night.

'We ate hash brownies and I got totally paranoid about the video – as soon as it went live I got convinced everyone was going to find out that it was us and that we were going to get in loads of shit. So I took a sleeping pill. Helen has some in her bedside drawer and I nicked one. I've never had one before. I didn't realize it would knock me out that much. I was well out of it.'

He followed April for ten minutes before she pulled up outside a large converted Victorian house and got out.

'I haven't been here for ages,' she said. 'Our tenants moved out about six months ago and we can't decide whether to get new ones or sell it. Tenants are *such* a hassle. But, anyway, I know Georgia comes here sometimes to chill out.'

Not just that, Patrick thought.

She fiddled with the keys for ages before finally opening the door. It was cool inside the hallway. April stooped to pick up the mail, tossing it onto the side before leading Patrick up the stairs to the first floor, where she spent another age unlocking the door of the flat.

So this, according to Alice, was where the teenagers had made their dirty movie. They went into the living room, April's sandals clicking lightly on the wooden floor as she walked across the room, calling Georgia's name.

'She's not here. No sign she's been here either.'

She took her phone out and tried to phone her daughter again. She looked properly anxious now.

But Patrick's attention had been seized by something lying on the coffee table. He crouched and picked it up, turning it over in his hand. A small teddy bear, the kind you would give to a newborn baby. Bonnie had one similar, except hers was a pink rabbit, much-cuddled, always filthy.

Helen Philips had described this teddy to him. He'd seen it in a photograph.

Frankie's Red Ted.

'What's that?' April asked.

His heart was thumping now. 'April, I *really* need to talk to your daughter.'

His phone rang. It was Carmella. 'Sir, that girl you went to talk to, Georgia Hardy-Wilson . . .'

As he listened to Carmella, he couldn't meet April's eye. These were the moments he lived for and dreaded as a policeman. The breakthrough, the sudden parting of the clouds. But these clouds had parted to reveal a hot, vicious sun.

'April,' he said, after Carmella had hung up. She was staring at him fearfully. 'You might want to sit down for a moment. It's about Georgia.'

Chapter 38
Georgia – Day 6

Georgia let herself out of her house, her Nike sun visor keeping both the evening sun and her long ponytail out of her eyes. Her earphones were plugged firmly into her ears, and Bruno Mars was being delivered right into her brain via her iPhone. She set off at a slow jog towards the park, almost immediately feeling short of breath – it was the first time she had been out running for days now. But she was feeling so guilty about the amount of stress-induced Cokes and sweets she'd been shovelling into herself recently that she was forcing herself to try and jog some of it off.

Yesterday she hadn't eaten all day, and had been so starving by the evening that she had consumed a Big Mac and large fries followed by a Chinese takeaway and half a tub of Häagen-Dazs with her folks two hours later when she got home. *And* her nails were bitten to the quick. Her life may be going down the toilet, she thought, but she was determined not to let her arse get huge on top of everything else. She needed to be in control of *something*.

She ran through the main gate of the park, already feeling slightly better. It was a beautiful evening, cooling down after a hot day, a welcome breeze on her face. Deer lay in indolent groups under the trees, and the sweet scent of cut grass filled her nostrils. She took the path around the edge of the park to avoid the deer, which scared her – you were always hearing stories about how furious stags chased people round and round trees, sometimes for hours, sometimes killing them. A big kid on one of those small bikes rode past her and she veered to the side of the path to avoid him. But he suddenly slewed his bike sideways and blocked her path.

'What the fuck?' she said, yanking one of her earbuds out so that Bruno was in mono. The kid was her age, but she didn't recognize him. He was a right little chav – low-slung jeans, too-large baseball cap, big diamond stud in his ear. He and Jerome obviously had the same fashion advisor, she thought with a shudder. She ran around him, but he got back on his bike, pedalled after her and did the same thing. This time, he walked up close to her.

'You have to come with me,' he said.

A worm of fear crept into Georgia's belly. 'What do you mean? I don't have to do anything you tell me to.' She was aware that she was using her poshest voice. She sounded like her mum hectoring the traffic warden who put a ticket on the windscreen of the Discovery when she'd only stopped for five minutes to go to the Post Office.

'Yeah right. You won't be saying that when Jerome has finished with you.'

Georgia swallowed hard. 'Have you been following me?'

The boy sniffed. 'Only enough to find out where you live, in that big fancy house. So, come on, you need to follow me. Jerome wants to talk to you. He's over there in the car.'

He gestured towards the car park, a couple of hundred metres away through the trees. Georgia thought she was going to vomit. She looked desperately around her – the gate she'd come in was just visible, but there was no-one around, and even if she sprinted, this horrible boy would be able to catch up with her easily on his stupid bike. And he knew where she lived! She fingered the iPhone in the side pocket of her jogging bottoms – but who could she call? If she dialled 999 she'd be dropping herself right in it too. She could just hear the conversation: 'Right, miss, so you're saying you need rescuing from the man to whom you owe four thousand pounds for losing the drugs you were supposed to be selling for him? I see.'

'What does he want?' she heard herself saying. As if she didn't know.

The boy shrugged. 'Dunno. But he ain't happy. Come on. You run that way. I'll follow.'

She had no choice. He got back on his bike and jerked his head impatiently for her to lead the way.

Fuck. *I'm so dead*, she thought, and tears filled her eyes. Would Jerome really kill her? Of course not. She was just being a drama queen, like her mum was always telling her she was.

If I get out of this, she thought, *I'll be such a good girl. I'll never touch weed again, let alone agree to sell it. I'll study really really hard. Please let me get out of this.*

In a way, it was almost a relief to know she was going to meet her fate. The past few days had been unbearably stressful, jumping at every knock at the door and face in the street. Things are never as bad as you think they're going to be, she chanted in her head, a mantra her dad always used.

But it didn't feel that they could get much worse.

In minutes they were at the car park, a large open space near an artificial lake. Georgia was relieved to see that although it was far from full, there were still plenty of cars parked and – oh thank God – a few people walking dogs in the distance. If she screamed loudly enough they would hear her.

Jerome's car wasn't what she'd expected. It was a battered and rusty plum-coloured Honda that looked like someone's nan's car. If she hadn't been so terrified she would have smiled. Jerome was sitting in the driver's seat glaring at her, and the expression on his face was enough to make Georgia wee herself, just a little bit. She turned to the boy on the bike and said quietly, 'He's not going to hurt me, is he?'

The boy grinned, made a gun shape with his fingers, pointing them at her and mouthing '*Pop pop*,' then cycled off. Georgia watched him go with a pang of almost regret. She was on her own.

Jerome wound down the window – the car was too old for electric windows.

'Get in, sugar-tits,' he said, flinty-eyed, gesturing to the passenger seat.

Georgia opened the door, glancing down at her pale peach short tracksuit bottoms to check that the bit of wee wasn't visible on the crotch. Could dogs smell human pee? 'Your dog won't attack me, will it?'

'She. You don't call RiRi *it*.'

'Sorry. Will she?'

Jerome shrugged and turned round to address the dog, which sat malevolently on the back seat. 'Not unless I tell her to.'

She slid hesitantly into the car, closed the door and sat with her back pressed against it, shrinking as far away from Jerome and the dog – softly growling – as she could. The car's interior stank of weed, wet dog, cigarettes and Jerome's cloying aftershave. She wondered what songs her family would play at her funeral. *Goodbye Yellow Brick Road* would be a good one. Her mum used to sing it to her when she was a baby.

'I'm really sorry, Jerome, but I promise I'm going to pay you back. It won't take long, I had a bit of a hold up because my parents won't let me get my savings out of the bank, but right, seriously, I know how to get my hands on a ton of money. I might need your help, but if you help me, we could split it, so you'd actually end up with, like, twenty times more than I owe you . . .'

Jerome raised one artfully shaved eyebrow. 'This better be good, bitch, 'cos I am well running out of patience here.'

Georgia took a deep breath – which she immediately regretted, because of the smell. 'I'm just gonna wind down the window, OK Jerome? I'm feeling a bit faint.'

The fresh air calmed her slightly. She had a moment of doubt – was she crazy, admitting to Jerome what she'd done? But she had no choice. Best just to come out with it.

'I kidnapped Alice's sister, for the reward, so I could pay you back, ' she said in a rush to the air-freshener swinging from the rear view mirror.

Jerome sucked his teeth and laughed. 'No way! You're gonna have to come up with something better than that. Crazy bitch.'

'I did. I swear.'

He scowled. 'So where's the reward then? And where's the kid?'

'There was a problem.' She told him what had happened after she'd left Alice's house with Frankie.

Jerome listened, as Georgia spoke in a silence broken only by the sound of RiRi licking herself enthusiastically. 'So it ain't that insane doctor guy and his mental missus, the ones who took the other two kids, then she topped herself?'

Georgia shook her head. 'No. But I still know how we can get the money.'

She explained. Jerome nodded slowly. The cogs were almost audibly whirring behind his eyes.

'Can I go now?' she asked timidly, after some time.

Jerome was lost in thought,

'Text me that photo before you go.'

She whipped out her iPhone and immediately obliged. Jerome scrutinized the photo on his Galaxy.

'You better not be shitting me,' he said suspiciously. 'If I find out this is just some random photo, you're a dead girl. You know that, right?'

Georgia nodded vigorously. Something about the expression on his face made her involuntarily release more urine, and she cringed. She'd left a wet mark on Jerome's seat. Thankfully he didn't seem to notice.

'You got yourself a reprise. Temporary, anyway. A week, tops. And if I don't get that four grand in a week, the interest's up to fifty per cent. Understood?'

Once Jerome had driven off, Georgia's legs refused to hold her any longer. She sank onto the sandy gravel of the car park, the wet patch on her crotch liquid fear. She had no idea if she'd just taken steps to get her out of the shit, or dropped herself further into it.

She put her head into her hands and howled like a baby. Just like Frankie had, the night she had taken her. She cried so long that she didn't notice that all the other cars had gone, and the deer had vanished into the dusky long grass to sleep for the night.

Nor did she notice the distant sound of a car returning and parking a little way away. She didn't hear Jerome's heavy footsteps until he was almost next to her, and Rihanna started to snarl. She jerked her head up and scrambled to her feet, but it was too late. For a moment they stood opposite one another. Jerome's face was implacable.

'Changed my mind,' he said. 'Thought about it for a while, didn't I. It'll look better if you ain't involved. Oh – and you pissed in my fucking car.'

Then, almost matter-of-factly, he stooped and unclipped Rihanna's lead. It was then that Georgia saw the flash of a blade in his other hand. She turned to run, but knew it was futile. The dog was airborne on a fang-first trajectory straight towards her throat before she'd even remembered the first line of *Goodbye Yellow Brick Road.*

Her.

Not *it*.

Chapter 39
Helen – Day 6

Helen found herself spending more and more time alone in Frankie's bedroom, sitting on the oatmeal carpet with her spine pressing against the rail on her toddler bed, seeing the view of what Frankie ought to be seeing from her pillow vantage point, her bookcase and whirling magic lantern, the decals of Babar the Elephant on the walls, as if somehow she would be comforted by Helen seeing it when she, Frankie, couldn't.

Sometimes Helen climbed onto the bed and curled up into a foetal comma, pressing her nose into the brushed cotton sheets, desperately trying to keep her scent in her nostrils as well as in her soul. Her only comfort was that Red Ted was missing too – Frankie must have been clutching him when she was taken, unless the kidnapper was particularly considerate. Helen hoped so. She prayed, with varying degrees of hope, to cover all bases with a God she wasn't sure existed but figured she had nothing to lose by asking, begging Him to return Frankie unharmed, to keep her safe, to leave her unscarred both physically and mentally, that Red Ted was still with her.

Today, as Helen lay there, too traumatised even to move, she thought about the detective, Lennon. 'Call me Patrick,' he'd said when he'd first introduced himself. That was less than a week ago but felt like an eternity in Hell.

Sean had just come rushing in clutching his iPad.

'You won't believe this,' he said, ignoring the fact that Helen was lying with her feet hanging over the bottom of Frankie's little bed, tears sliding silently down her cheeks. 'I Googled him, that Lennon bloke, and you'll never guess what.'

Helen wanted to punch him in the throat for thinking she might be remotely interested in playing guessing games concerning the detective entrusted with the search for their most treasured possession.

'What,' she stated baldly.

'He was all over the papers a couple of years ago. Well, not him, but his missus. She was that one who suffered from such bad post-natal depression that she tried to kill their baby. Over near Hampton Court. Do you remember? We watched it on the news one night. You commented on it because they live so close to us. She got locked up.'

Helen sat up slowly, her blurred eyes open wide and her voice thick with tears. 'Oh my God, yes, I do remember. We were really shocked – he arrested her, didn't he? I thought he looked vaguely familiar when I saw him. I felt so sorry for them. Are you sure? That's really him?'

She didn't know what to think. Was this a good thing? He might try harder to find Frankie because he understood the pain of almost losing a child, of things falling apart so spectacularly. But on the other hand . . . it was only two years on . . .

'What if he's not up to it?' she blurted.

Sean squeezed in next to her on the tiny bed, patting her thigh. 'He must be. There's no way they'd have let him have the case if he wasn't. Think how badly it would reflect on the Met if he was allowed back to work all screwed up . . .'

Helen stared into space, fighting the urge to push Sean's hand away.

'I thought that other detective seemed pretty competent. What was his name? Winkle?'

'Winkler. He was looking into the person who contacted me on Facebook but I haven't heard anything. I suppose it came to nothing.' She still couldn't bring herself to admit the wasted journey to the M&S café to find out for herself that Janet Friars was a nutter and a timewaster.

'Maybe we should ask for him to be put in charge of the case.'

Helen wriggled away from Sean's touch. She couldn't stand it any more. 'You think we could have any influence?'

'I bet we could, if we kicked up a stink.'

'I don't know. I trust Lennon. That other guy . . . I'm sure he was checking me out.' *And*, she thought, *he never bothered to get back to me.*

Sean smiled. 'And who can blame him?'

She didn't see the funny side. 'Don't.'

They stared at the wall in silence.

'Anyway,' said Sean. 'If DI Lennon doesn't get anywhere in another twenty-four hours, I'm going to talk to his boss. And if that doesn't work, I've a good mind to go to the papers, tell them how much Lennon's ballsing up. After the fiasco of that siege I'm sure they'd bite my hand off for the scoop.'

It kept going through Helen's mind, long after Sean had left the room (he didn't like to stay in Frankie's room for long, as though her pain and Frankie's absence collided in there like two particularly noxious gases). She didn't feel all that sorry for Patrick – not as sorry as she felt for herself, for Patrick's baby had survived, but she conceded it must have been horrendous. As she roamed around Frankie's little bedroom, trying to find things to do, she idly wondered if she would dare broach the subject with him. Patrick was a strange sort of guy, for a policeman, even though he was really good-looking. Hair a bit too long, glimpses of all sorts of tattooed tendrils creeping under his shirt collar. Not to mention a kind of hooded reticence in his face that suddenly seemed to make more sense to her.

She could hear Sean downstairs, tipping ice into a glass. Within an hour, she knew, he'd be drunk again. She was tempted to join him in oblivion.

She opened a red plastic drawer in a stack of three primary-coloured ones, like huge Lego bricks. A sheaf of Frankie's paintings had been stuffed in there, the thick mix of poster paints rendering the cheap off-white paper almost corrugated. Sifting through the usual toddler daubings, she found a few of the 'naps' she had drawn on Frankie's insistence, and caught her breath.

Frankie loved maps, which she referred to as 'naps'. She'd gone through a big phase recently of demanding that everyone around her draw her special 'naps', and Helen loved her daughter's world view this afforded. The 'naps' were a mixture of fantasy and reality, a collision of fact and fiction along dotted lines denoting imaginary borders.

The first one she pulled out took her straight back to the afternoon she'd drawn it for Frankie, a few weeks ago, as she sat astride on one of her legs, leaning forward on the table to keep her balance, her finger tracing the lines she drew and crowing with delight as Helen added each of Frankie's suggested landmarks:

'There, Mummy,' pointing with a tiny forefinger, 'that's where the three little pigs live.'

Helen remembered drawing three pink faces with snouts, and carefully inscribing *Little Pigs' House,* which was a few doors down from *Frankie's House.* 'And up here is really really actually Heaven.' So she had written *Really Really Actually Heaven,* with an arrow pointing skywards, towards the clouds. It made her smile, but with a pain like a sharpened icicle simultaneously stabbing her gut. The other landmarks on their map included *An Orchard, Ross's Car* and *The Cold Place Where They Make Ice-Lollies.*

She picked out another one, one she hadn't seen before, in Alice's rounded handwriting. NAP OF MY ROAD. The word had become part of their family's lexicon.

'Oh Frankie,' Helen whispered. 'Draw me a nap to tell me where you are?'

Both of them gone, Alice and Frankie. But Helen wasn't so worried about Alice. She'd be home soon enough, after her diva tantrum had deflated and her money run out. She was with Larry – Larry's mum had rung in tears that morning and Helen was ashamed that she had felt little about the plight of Alice and her scrawny boyfriend, and had almost had to pretend to sound half as concerned as the hysterical woman on the end of the line.

Helen turned her attention back to the NAP OF MY ROAD. Alice had drawn a picture of their blue front door for Frankie, and the garden path, with shapes of cars outside that she had got Frankie to attempt to colour in. The picture was annotated with big X's over several of Frankie's random instructions: *Fluffy cat from Number 18, Max's house, Sandpit, Where Red Ted's Eye Fell Out.*

Helen's own eye fell on something she hadn't noticed before. There was an X on the far side of the road, as drawn by Alice, and underneath it were the words *Cross Ghost Who Lives in the Lamp Post.*

Cross ghost who lives in the lamp post? What did that mean? Helen got up and went to Frankie's window, hauling up the roller blind to look out. The place across the road Alice had marked with an X was outside number 26, where an elderly gay couple had lived until recently, when one of them had been taken ill and they had both moved to a nursing home. The house had been empty since, so no cross ghosts there – or anywhere else in their street, that Helen was aware of. She frowned. So many of Frankie's comments were fairly nonsensical, and that had become part of the adults' enjoyment of the 'nap' drawing game. But they usually had some sort of basis in reality, or a recollection of something that had happened to her that day.

Who was the cross ghost and what was it doing outside her house? Helen stared at the nap for so long that the dotted lines began to undulate, swirling slowly before her eyes. And that other drawing, the one of the man looking in through the window that they'd found the night Frankie had been taken – where had that come from?

'What were you telling us, Frankie baby?' Helen spoke out loud, an idea springing into her head. Sean had put a whole box full of Frankie's artistic efforts up in the loft just a couple of weeks earlier – naps and finger paintings and bits of macaroni glittered and glued onto wrinkled craft paper. He'd been all for chucking them out with the recycling, but Helen had put her foot down, and the loft had been the compromise. What if someone had been watching Frankie for weeks, and this has been her way of trying to tell them?

She walked up to the second floor, Alice's domain and, out of habit, frowned at the dirty washing and creased wet towels that Alice had dumped on the landing, not even bothering to move the two paces necessary to reach the laundry basket. The pole that opened the loft trap door was lying by the skirting board behind the basket. Helen picked it up, hooked the end into the catch, and pulled down the ladder. From below, she could hear Sean shouting at the TV.

Fifteen minutes later she climbed back down the ladder, her feet blindly trying to find the treads, and her mind blindly trying to process what she had just seen.

Chapter 40
Patrick – Day 7

Patrick had seen some unspeakable things over the course of his career, but something about the sight of the swollen, bandaged girl lying motionless in the hospital bed moved him so much that he had to turn his face away from the porthole window of the room, tears actually coming to his eyes and his throat catching.

Perhaps it was that her appearance was so at odds with the beautiful photograph of he'd seen of her the day before on the kitchen wall of her house, which had immortalized her as someone she would never ever be again – a vibrant teenager at the tipping point between girlhood and womanhood, her skin flawless, apricot-rosy, her eyes shining with the assurance of her beauty.

Or maybe it was a paternal instinct, that this could be Bonnie, twelve years from now. It was the same dreaded unbidden thought that he awoke to suddenly at night. Recently, it had been whoever took Liam and Izzy might come for Bonnie too. In the dead of night, all the children on whom horrors and tragedies were visited wore Bonnie's face, and Patrick could never save her.

Georgia's eyes were open – just barely. They looked like two puffy black water-wings. She lay listlessly on her pillows with her hair spread across them like the Lady of the Lake. Patrick suspected April had arranged it that way, probably to distract from the awful swollen abomination that was once her daughter's face.

April herself was sitting on a camp-bed next to Georgia's hospital bed, looking as though she hadn't had a wink of sleep. Scratches, from the gardening she had been doing the day before, still decorated her legs beneath her shorts and criss-crossed her forearms. 'Hello, detective,' she said flatly. 'Can't keep you away?'

He smiled sympathetically at her, wishing he'd had the common sense to bring her a coffee and a croissant or something. Carmella would have done.

'I need to ask Georgia some questions, I'm afraid,' he said, gesturing towards one of the horrible blue vinyl hospital armchairs on the other side of the bed. 'May I?'

She nodded, and he sat down. He took out his Moleskine and a pencil and leaned forward. 'Georgia? How are you feeling today?'

Stupid question. A tear popped out from the slit between her eyelids, at the exact same moment that a drop of fluid dripped out of the IV bag into the tube running into her arm.

'Can you talk?'

'Yes,' she whispered. Her eyes were so swollen that Patrick couldn't tell whether she was looking at him or not.

'I'm so sorry you've had to go through all this. I understand you were found in Bushy Park? What were you doing there?'

'Went for . . . a run.' Another tear. Another drop of antibiotics.

'Can you tell me what happened?'

She tried to take a deep breath, but moaned with pain at the exertion. Her mother caressed her fingers and frowned at Patrick as though accusing him of bullying her daughter.

'Take your time,' he said patiently, giving April what he hoped was an encouraging smile.

A deep sigh. 'It was . . . a guy called Jerome. I don't know his last name. He lives on the . . . Kennedy Estate.'

'Jerome Smith?' She nodded. 'Why would he do this to you?'

'He . . . hates me.'

'Why, Georgia?'

Patrick could see that the girl was trying to work out lies in her head, trying and failing to internally muster up a convincing story. She bit her lip.

'Georgia, you do realize that all you can do now is tell the truth?' He spoke as gently as he could. 'The chips are down. It's time to start being honest. I promise you, things will be so much better for you in the long run if you tell the truth now.'

A long, long pause. Patrick shifted on his vinyl armchair and the seat squeaked, breaking the silence.

April blew her nose, then spoke: 'Georgie, sweetheart. If you're in trouble, we can fix it. I won't be cross and nor will Dad, I swear. Whatever's gone on, you're our girl and we love you more than anything in this world. We'll stand by you.'

They were both crying now.

'Mum . . . where is Daddy?' Georgia turned her head slightly as though her father had been there all the time, silently holding up her drip bag.

'He's on his way, darling. He's on a plane back from his conference in Singapore – he came as soon as he heard. He'll be here later.'

They were going off-piste. Patrick tried to steer them back. 'So, Georgia, why did Jerome want to hurt you?'

She moaned again. 'I owe him money. He . . . gave me some drugs to sell and . . .' her voice became almost inaudible, 'I left them on the bus and he's been after me for the money.'

Georgia couldn't quite believe this was happening. A couple of years ago she used to have fantasies about being in hospital, leg in plaster after perhaps a car crash, or an incident in which she had rescued a baby from a burning building or something. In her imagination she would lie there while all her friends and family crowded around her bed, cooing with sympathy. One Direction would come and visit her themselves, in person, and bring flowers because she was a heroine. Zayn would fall in love with her and they'd become a couple. She'd be in the papers.

But now it was really happening, this was the last place she wanted to be, and she wouldn't want any of her friends, and certainly not One Direction, to see her lying like this, bandaged up like an Egyptian mummy. Every part of her body hurt, but particularly her face and her belly. She couldn't move.

And now her mother was staring at her with the sort of horror she had never seen on her face before, ever, as though she, Georgia, was an alien freshly landed from Mars. Who said that telling the truth was a better option? She had just confessed to the drugs. To Jerome trying to kill her. *Oh my God,* she thought. *Now I've grassed him up, he's definitely going to kill me.*

But then a fresh wave of pain reverberated through her body. Her face was going to be scarred for ever – how could it not be, when she could feel the stab and itch of every stitch holding her cheeks together? It felt as though there were hundreds of them. She was ruined. So what if Jerome killed her? She would kill herself before he got to her. There was no way she was going to live being a scarred freak that everyone felt sorry for. No way.

Then she felt a stab of something equally sharp: regret. She couldn't top herself without confessing what she knew about Frankie. She had to say something. Surely things couldn't get any worse? The nice detective was sitting gazing at her with his pencil poised over his notebook. If she didn't tell him now what she knew, then she might never get the chance. Alice would never speak to her again either way, but so what? She, Georgia, wouldn't be around, so what did it matter?

'There's something I need to show you,' she whispered, before she changed her mind. Her mum looked like she was going to be sick.

'Yes?' the detective asked.

'It's on my phone . . . last photo on there . . . It's of the person who took Frankie.'

Her mother and the detective both gasped, and her mum lunged for the iPhone in the bedside cabinet.

'Tell me, Georgia. Tell me everything.' The detective didn't sound so calm now.

This was it, thought Georgia hazily. Now it was all coming out, it didn't feel too bad. It was all like a dream, anyway, a half-waking nightmare. Nothing left to lose.

She forced herself to remember. She'd been on the loo at Alice's; that was when she first got the idea . . .

It was a brilliant idea.

She could pay Jerome back – and buy a car to have driving lessons in with the leftover cash! She was dying to have a Mini Cooper, a red one with a black sunroof. The gripes in her stomach ceased. Georgia sat very still on the toilet, staring at the words ***'£100,000'*** *in bold black newsprint. It was a dead cert that if they were offering that for the other two missing kids, there'd be a similar reward if a third child went missing, maybe even more.*

Frankie knew Georgia. She wouldn't object if Georgia took her on a little adventure. Georgia had the keys to her parents' flat in her pocket because that was where they'd filmed their movie. Her mum and dad never went to the flat. Every couple of months her mum muttered something about 'getting round to renting it out again' – but they didn't need the money, so they never did get round to it, and the flat stayed empty. It was only five minutes' walk from here.

It was a no-brainer.

Georgia felt a new and exciting rush of optimism. She'd found a solution! She flushed, washed her hands and crept back onto the landing and halfway back up the stairs towards Alice's room. As she'd suspected, all had fallen silent, but when she listened hard she could hear a few little moans and gasps. Excellent.

She tiptoed back downstairs and found a Waitrose carrier bag in the kitchen into which she put a couple of the plastic sippy cups and a bottle with a teat that she selected from the dozens in the cupboard. Helen was the sort of mum who stockpiled stuff in the kitchen like nuclear war was about to break out any minute – the cupboard next to the fridge was packed full of long-life milk, cereal bars, boxes of raisins and Pom-Bear crisps. She found night-time nappies under the sink, and took half a dozen of those. Nobody would notice a few things missing, and tomorrow she could go out and get some more supplies if she stole cash from her mum's purse. She glanced at the huge clock on the wall – 10:05 P.M. They wouldn't be back till probably eleven at least, and Alice and Larry would likely be in bed for half an hour.

She left the bulging Waitrose bag by the back door and crept back upstairs. Frankie was wearing pink pyjamas with Tinkerbell on and was breathing steadily around the thumb plugged loosely into her mouth. She was hot, and little spikes of black hair were plastered to her forehead. She looked so sweet.

Georgia had her first moment of doubt. Would Frankie sleep alright with her in the double bed in the flat? What would she do with her, when she had to go out to get stuff? She could hardly take her with her. But, she reckoned, it was only for a few days, and she wouldn't leave Frankie for long when she did have to go out. Nobody would hear if she cried – it was a garden flat facing away from the road, and as far as Georgia knew, nobody was living in the first-floor flat, and when they'd been there the other day to make the movie, post for the people on the top floor was all piled up in the hallway, so they must be away . . .

Should she? She looked down at Frankie again. Helen would go out of her mind with worry. Perhaps there'd be some way she could let her know Frankie was safe? No, don't be stupid, she thought. It would be fine. It would just be for a couple of days, then she could march into a police station carrying Frankie, saying she heard crying in the park, went to investigate and found her abandoned there, of course recognizing her immediately because she was her friend's little sister. Everyone would be ecstatically happy with her. She'd get the reward – and, undoubtedly, her allowance reinstated. Helen and Sean would be so grateful! She smiled, already bathing in the glory of it all. Already picturing herself driving to college in her new Mini. She'd be able to afford the road tax and driving lessons and everything. All for the sake of two days of discomfort for her and Frankie, and worry for Helen, Alice and Sean.

Yes, it was more than worth the risk.

She scooped Frankie out of her cot and Frankie snuffled, opening and closing her mouth like a goldfish. There was a baby monitor on her chest of drawers, but it wasn't switched on. Georgia knew that this was because she so rarely woke up any more, once she was asleep, and if she did, her voice was plenty loud enough to alert her parents without additional amplification.

'Come on, sweetie-pie,' she whispered. 'We're going for an adventure. You up for it? It would really help me out if you are.' She hoisted Frankie up in her arms so that her head was on her shoulder. Wow, she was heavy. She considered taking the pushchair, then dismissed the idea – surely real kidnappers wouldn't do that. Frankie babbled something, then went straight back to sleep, still clutching her weird thin little teddy bear. Excellent.

Georgia tiptoed down the stairs and out the back door, picking up the carrier bag on the way. When the cool night air hit Frankie's fat hot cheeks, she jerked her head up and wailed briefly, and Georgia had to clap a hand over her mouth. She froze in the shadows of the back garden, staring up at Alice's bedroom window, but there was no movement. Alice was obviously too busy with Larry to have heard anything. The neighbouring houses were dark and silent on both sides.

She hurried down to the end of the garden, Frankie's weight already making the small of her back hurt. Thank God the flat wasn't far away. But how would she avoid being spotted on her way? Once Frankie was reported missing, someone was bound to report seeing her being carried away. Georgia hadn't thought about that. She paused by the back gate, thinking fast. She knew the area well – she and Alice used to play on their bikes in the maze of back alleys that people put their bins out in, the thin arteries connecting all the big houses. Once she crossed the road, it was, she realized with joy, possible to get all the way to the flat just through the alleys.

She waited in the dusk by the back gate to make sure nobody was about, no silent dog-walkers or those bloody insane joggers who seemed to be running around at all hours. Frankie opened her eyes and looked at Georgia with surprise, so Georgia stroked her soft head and pushed the teddy up to her face for her to cuddle.

'It's OK, Frankie, go back to sleep,' she said. A VW campervan rolled very slowly along the road, as though its driver was looking for a parking spot, and Georgia shrank back against the gate. But to her horror, the driver, a black woman, stared straight at her. Shit shit shit, she thought, closing her eyes. Fuck!

She couldn't believe it. The first person who'd passed by had seen her! Her heart rate accelerated and she thought she was going to cry. Should she just take Frankie back now, forget the whole thing?

But the woman couldn't have got a clear look at her – and may well have not even spotted that she had Frankie on her shoulder. It was almost dark now. She shouldn't worry. She was probably just being paranoid.

She waited a few minutes. No more cars came by, and when Georgia stuck out her head, there was no sign of joggers, or anybody else. The street was dark and quiet now, just the lingering smell in the air of a dying summer's day. A sudden movement startled her, but it was just a fox, slinking silently along the pavement.

Georgia made her move, rushing across the road and a few houses down until she reached the next alley.

She didn't notice the woman, following her at a discreet distance. She had absolutely no idea that she'd been followed at all, until she was fiddling with the keys outside the secluded front door of her parents' flat.

The voice hissed in her ear, taking her by complete surprise, so much so that she almost dropped Frankie, and Frankie dropped her teddy.

'Give her to me. Now.'

Patrick sat in stunned silence for a few moments after the clearly exhausted Georgia finished telling her tale. He stared at the photo on Georgia's phone. The woman was in her late thirties, he would guess. She looked a little like Helen Philips – the same skin tone, almond eyes, Cupid's bow lips.

'Did she see you take her photo?' he asked.

'Yes. And she grabbed my phone and deleted the picture.'

'I'm confused.'

Georgia gave him a look that made him feel very old. 'I have my phone set to save pictures directly to the Cloud. You know, online. So there's, like, a copy on my phone and one on the internet. That means I never lose them, and I can publish the ones I like on Facebook or whatever.'

'That's amazing,' Patrick said.

The first thing he needed to do, after making sure every cop in London had this photo, was show it to the Philips family, see if they recognized this woman.

'Why didn't you come to us, tell us what you'd done? You could see the pain you caused Alice and Helen and Sean. How could you bear it?'

Georgia turned her face away, unable to meet his eye. 'I couldn't tell them what I'd done. Alice would hate me forever. Everyone would hate me. And I thought I'd go to prison.' She rolled her head on the pillow, looked at him at last. 'I was scared.'

Patrick shook his head.

'Detective?' Georgia said quietly. Patrick felt terribly sorry for her. She had done something unutterably stupid, and compounded it through selfishness and fear, but now her face was ruined. Her life would never be the same. Her life would never be as good.

'Yes, Georgia?'

'If you find her . . . If Frankie is alright . . . Will I be able to claim the reward?'

I've got my period. For years, every time it arrived I would cry with frustration and rage. I knew I could get pregnant, that there was nothing wrong with me. The doctors confirmed it. Howard's sperm count was low-to-average, but they were there, wriggling away inside him and several times a month, without fail, wriggling inside me too. They just never did their job.

And for years – though I could never tell my husband this – I knew deep down why I never got pregnant. It was because of what I'd done. Of what had happened to me. This was my punishment. Every month the blood would arrive, reminding me of the terrible secret I forced myself to forget the rest of the time, that I blotted out with pills and dope and sunshine.

My shame. My past.

Today, though, the arrival of my period doesn't make me sob or scream. Because now I finally have a child of my own.

Once again.

I will never forget the look on that idiot girl's face when I confronted her and took Frankie. I knew the teenager wouldn't scream or cry out. She wouldn't want to attract attention to what she'd done. She was trapped with her terrible secret.

I didn't intend to keep Frankie at first. I was going to take her straight back but once I'd got her in the van I realized something: I wanted to spend some time with her. Quality time, getting to know her. She wasn't scared that night. She was too sleepy and confused. She went to sleep almost immediately and I sat and stroked her hair, thinking that she was beautiful.

When morning came she wanted to know where mummy and daddy were. I promised I'd take her home, and even set off towards their house, planning to drop her off nearby, sure she would find her way home.

But the nearer we got to the house, the more I realized I couldn't do it. I couldn't take her back.

She was so perfect. The child I'd always dreamed of. I deserved her and Sean and Helen didn't. It was as simple as that. Why should they have everything while I had nothing?

So I kept driving. Out of the city. We drove for miles and miles.

I knew the police would think that Frankie (and I would change her name, as soon as I could) had been taken by the same people who had taken Izzy and Liam, the children who were all over the news. Unless that teenage moron confessed – and I couldn't see that happening – the police would be on the wrong trail.

It was so easy. For the first time in my shit life, I had a stroke of luck.

I used to think God hated me. Now, it seemed, He was finally on my side.

Until they caught the people who took Liam and killed Izzy. Since then, I've been worried. Any day now they are going to find out what happened. That teen is going to crack and confess. Or someone will see us.

The more I think about it, the more determined I am that we will never be torn apart again. I can't let that happen. I lost everything once, and now I've got what I've wanted all these years, I would rather die than lose it again.

I insert the tampon and wash my hands. Frankie is lying on the bed, her hair matted and filthy. She flinches when I reach out a hand to stroke it.

There's a newspaper lying on the floor, one I picked up earlier. There, on page five, is the familiar photo. 'Helen and Sean Philips with their missing daughter, Frankie.' I touch Sean's face then fold the paper over so Helen, on the far left, is removed.

A voice behind me says, 'Daddy.'

The van stinks. I'm sick of living like this. Sick of running.

I know what I have to do.

I sit beside Frankie and stroke her soft hair. 'How would you like it if we were together forever and ever?' I whisper.

Chapter 41
Patrick – Day 7

It was 11:15 in the morning and Sean Philips smelled of drink – not the stale morning-after fumes Patrick had detected on his last visit to this house, but the fresh stink of spirits on his breath. His eyes were watery and unfocused and when he said, 'You again,' there was a noticeable slur.

'You'd better come in,' he said, walking into the living room and slumping down on the sofa. The TV was on, playing a rerun of *Columbo*. Sean giggled. 'Got one more thing to ask me, eh?'

Patrick took a seat. 'Are you alright, Sean?'

'Oh, never better!' His head jerked around like he was looking for something, before he deflated back into the folds of the sofa.

'Where's Helen?' Patrick asked.

'Don't know. She took off first thing this morning, before I was even up. Probably sick of the sight of me, and who can blame her? She thinks I'm useless. You saw us arguing the other day. It's like that all the time now. She sleeps so close to the edge of the bed that I keep thinking she's going to fall out. I think I disgust her. She just sits on Facebook all day. She was on it when I went to bed last night. Marriages don't survive this kind of thing, do they? And Alice's staying at Larry's. I've driven them all away.'

'Come on, Sean . . . At least you know Alice is safe, anyway.'

'Yeah but you're never going to find Frankie, are you?' He stared at Patrick with red-rimmed eyes. Before Patrick could respond, Sean buried his face in his hands. Patrick promised himself that as soon as he got out of here he would get a FLO back here. Get Sean Philips to a counsellor.

Sean looked up. 'When I met Helen, I thought she was the best thing that ever happened to me. I mean, I love Alice but . . .' He swallowed hard. 'But when Frankie was born, it was like, like . . . *I* was born. Reborn.'

Patrick waited.

'She was so beautiful. It was a difficult birth, you know? Helen was in labour for nearly two days after being induced. We thought the baby was never going to come out. Helen was exhausted and when she was finally having proper contractions they gave her an epidural. She clung to me as they stuck the needle in her back. There was a tear . . . it rolled down her cheek, splashed on my bare arm. I've never loved her more than in that moment.'

'I understand.' Although privately Patrick thought Sean was being sentimental from too much alcohol. He would never have spoken to another man in such soppy terms.

'And the epidural didn't work. She was screaming with pain. The midwives were running in and out of the room. Finally, they got another anaesthetist in who did the epidural properly. Then we waited all night until Frankie finally came out. Nine pounds, she was. A bruiser.'

A smile flashed on his face then vanished as quickly as it had appeared. 'Frankie. From that first moment, I knew how special she was.' His voice dropped to a whisper. 'She was my redemption.'

He sniffed loudly and wiped his nose on the back of his sleeve. Patrick saw Sean make a deliberate effort to pull himself together. His hands were trembling. 'And now she's gone.'

'We *are* going to find her,' Patrick said. He wondered how many times he'd said that in the last week. How many times he'd really believed it.

'No,' Sean said. 'She's gone forever. I've been reading up on it. The odds . . . they were long before, but now we'd need a miracle.'

'Sean, something has happened. We're making progress.'

'What?'

Patrick took out his phone. 'I'm going to show you a photograph. I just need to know if you've ever seen this person before.'

He crossed the room and, crouching down, showed Sean the photo Georgia had taken with her phone.

Sean stared at the picture for a long time. His hands, Patrick noticed, were trembling more violently now. Finally, he said, 'No. I have no idea who she is. Why?'

Patrick tried not to let his huge disappointment show. 'She's someone we want to talk to, that's all. Are you one hundred per cent certain you don't recognize her.'

Sean shook his head. 'I've never seen her before in my life.'

Patrick put the phone away. 'Can you ask Helen to call me when she gets back?'

The other man stared into the middle distance.

'Sean?'

'Huh?'

'I asked if you can get Helen to call me when she gets home.'

Sean Philips nodded and Patrick still wasn't sure the words had got through. He sighed and got up. 'I'll talk to you again soon, OK?'

Sean said, 'You've got a kid, haven't you?'

'Yes. A daughter. She's almost two.'

Sean leaned in close, his alcoholic breath warm on Patrick's face. 'Look after her, whatever you do. Keep her close.'

Patrick paused by the open front door, feeling shaken. He needed to sort out some help for Sean, but the best thing he could do was find Frankie. He just had to find the woman who had taken her from Georgia – and pray that she hadn't murdered her.

He heard Sean walk through the house and into the kitchen, listened to the unmistakable sound of ice clinking in a glass, the rattling of bottles as Sean opened the fridge.

Patrick closed the door behind him and walked down the front path.

There was a stout woman standing on the other side of the wall, smoking a cigarette, a couple of supermarket carrier bags at her feet. It was Sean's mother. She was wearing smartish clothes, the sort of clothes that Pat's own mum wore – M&S or BHS or Next – but looked as though she would be more comfortable in a shell suit. What was her name? Eileen, that was it. Watching her smoke made him crave a real cigarette and he had to use all his willpower, and a couple of sucks on his e-fag, to stop himself from cadging one off her.

'Mrs Philips?'

She scrutinised him. 'You're that detective.'

'That's me.'

'Are you any closer to finding her yet?' She coughed and took another drag, the wrinkles around her lips deepening.

He didn't want to get her hopes up; there was still plenty of opportunity for this all to go wrong.

'Not yet.'

The older woman frowned and dropped her cigarette, grinding it out with her toe. 'Do you believe that people can be cursed, detective?'

He was taken aback by the question. 'Cursed?'

'Yes. Like a family, I mean. Cursed by bad luck. People might look at Sean's nice house and think he's been lucky. He came from nothing, you know. We were so poor you couldn't imagine it. But he's worked bleedin' hard to get all this.' She gestured around her. 'And now look what's happened. Poor little Frankie snatched by god knows who, Alice gone off the rails . . .'

Patrick wondered how much Eileen knew about what Alice had been up to, or if she knew about the arrest, and that Alice had chosen not to come home after the police had released her.

'I don't believe in curses, Mrs Philips. But I get how people can start to feel like that, that everything has gone wrong for them.'

Eileen picked up her shopping. 'I'm wondering if anything's ever going to go right.'

'Hold on, before you go.' Patrick produced his phone. 'Can you take a look at this picture for me, see if you recognise the woman?'

She rolled her eyes like it was a terrible hardship. At first she glanced at the photo. Then she snapped her head back to look at it again. After that, she stared, her mouth open, her yellow teeth on full display.

'Oh my word,' she said, her voice deep with shock.

Patrick tried to contain his excitement. 'You recognise her?'

Eileen Philips fumbled in her bag for another cigarette and lit it. Like her son five minutes before, her hands shook.

'That's Sean's ex-wife.'

'*What?*'

'That's Alice's mum.'

'Are you alright, Mrs Philips?'

The older woman grimaced. 'I need to sit down. When was that picture taken?'

'Last week.'

'In . . . in London?'

'Yes. Very close to here.'

She shuddered. 'And you think she's got something to do with Frankie's disappearance?'

Patrick was itching to get back inside to talk to Sean. Why had he lied about recognising the woman? But he wanted to get as much out of Eileen as he could. He was holding a box full of family secrets here, and in her shock Eileen was allowing him a glimpse inside. He needed to take a proper look before the woman became guarded and slammed the lid shut.

'I thought Sean's first wife died when Alice was three,' Patrick said. It suddenly occurred to him that this was the same age as Frankie was now.

Eileen puffed on her cigarette. The way her mouth puckered made him glad he'd quit.

'That's what he told Alice. He didn't want her to know her mum had run off and abandoned her.'

Patrick studied her as she took a magazine out of one of her shopping bags and fanned herself with it. She was lying about something. But before he could quiz her further, she said, 'I really do need to sit down. And I think you should talk to Sean about this. Oh my Lord, he's going to . . . I don't know how he's going to react when he finds out Penny is . . .' She trailed off.

'That's her name?'

She nodded.

'Let's go inside,' he said.

Eileen used her key to unlock the door. The house was silent, the TV turned off. Patrick stuck his head in the kitchen but it was empty, a half-drunk bottle of vodka on the worktop.

'Sean?' Eileen called. There was no reply.

Patrick checked the living room and dining room. A feeling of unease slid into his veins, the same kind of sick tingle he'd felt that day he'd come home and found Gill sitting on the stairs.

'Sean?' he called. Again, there was no answer. 'He was here just now – wait here,' he commanded Eileen.

He jogged up the stairs. The first room was Frankie's. He walked straight past it and knocked on the door of the master bedroom before pushing it open. No one there. He called Sean's name again. Had he slipped out the back door while Patrick was talking to Eileen? He checked the bathroom, then the office and Alice's room. All empty.

One more room to check. Frankie's. Patrick went inside.

'*No!*'

Sean Philips was hanging from the light fitting, his belt tied around his neck. His feet swung a couple of inches above his daughter's little bed.

Patrick jumped onto the bed, threw his arms around Sean and hefted him up, grunting with exertion. But it was impossible to reach the belt while holding Sean, who was hanging limp. Patrick let go and reached up with both hands to detach the belt from the light fitting. Sean's body dropped and landed with his lower half on the bed, his head and shoulders on the floor. He wasn't breathing. Patrick knelt beside the body just as Eileen entered the room, saw her son and started screaming.

Fifteen minutes later, after a futile attempt at CPR, with Eileen's screams drilling into his skull as he tried to bring her son back to life, Patrick had managed to get Eileen out of the room and onto the sofa, where she sat staring into space. Patrick called the station and told them what had happened.

Sean Philips had lied about recognising his ex-wife, then immediately hanged himself. What was he hiding? Was he somehow involved in Frankie's disappearance? Patrick had looked around the house but there was no sign of a suicide note. No explanation other than the one that turned Patrick's insides to ice. That seeing the picture of his ex-wife on Patrick's phone had pushed Sean over the edge.

Patrick needed to talk to Eileen more, and he also had to urgently find out where Helen was.

He went back into the living room. Eileen was in deep shock. He sat down opposite her and reached out a hand. She looked catatonic, barely breathing. She held her cigarettes in her hand, as if she intended to light one but was frozen. For a moment Patrick was afraid she might have had a stroke. She was in no fit state to talk now.

Do you believe that people can be cursed?

Frustration gnawed at his insides. He now knew who had taken Frankie, but not if the little girl was alive or dead, or why Sean's ex-wife, Penny, had done it. Where the hell were they?

Too many questions. Did Helen know the truth, that she wasn't really dead? Was it only Alice who had been kept in the dark?

He needed to talk to Helen urgently. For one thing, she needed to know what had happened here. But he also had a feeling she held a vital piece of the puzzle.

He heard cars pull up outside, the slamming of doors, heavy footsteps coming towards the house. Soon, this house of horror would be sealed off for the second time in a week, and Sean's body would be taken away.

Where was Helen? He was about to try to call her again when it struck him. Sean had said Helen sat on Facebook all day, that it was the last thing he'd seen her do last night. Helen had told Winkler last week that a woman had been in touch with her saying she knew where Frankie was, but Patrick had dismissed it out of hand, assumed it was a troll.

What if it hadn't been a troll?

A fresh wave of nausea hit him. He knew who he needed to talk to.

Chapter 42
Patrick – Day 7

'Where's Winkler?'

Carmella looked up from her computer. 'Patrick! I've just heard about Sean Philips . . .'

'Later. I need to talk to Winkler right now.'

She cupped her mouth with her hand and yelled out. 'Hey – anyone seen Fonzie?'

Patrick suppressed a smile. He'd forgotten that was Winkler's nickname, one which wasn't meant affectionately. One of the PCs at the other end of the room called back, 'I think he went to the gym.'

'Of course he bloody has,' Patrick hissed. He stamped across to Winkler's desk and sat down. It was the most clutter-free desk he'd ever seen, not a scrap of loose paper, no science experiments in mugs like on Patrick's own desk. Anyone would think Winkler never did any work. The computer was locked and Patrick started typing in random password guesses:

ilovemyself
happydays
winkler

None of them worked. He started to type in another when a familiar voice said, 'What the fuck are you doing?'

It was Winkler, his thick hair still damp from the shower, his skin gleaming with sweat, biceps bulging.

'You've got access to Helen Philips' Facebook account. I need to take a look at it, now.'

Winkler's eyes twinkled. 'Uh-uh. I don't think I should do that.'

'Why the hell not?' Patrick felt hot and prickly; he could actually picture his temper fraying.

'It's private, isn't it? Besides, there's nothing else useful on there. I've been through it all.'

Patrick took a deep breath. 'When was the last time you checked it?'

Winkler shrugged. 'Dunno. A couple of days ago. All she's done is like dozens of posts on the "Find Frankie Philips" pages.'

'She was on it last night. Sean told me. I need to take a look – now.'

Winkler waved a hand dismissively. 'I'll check it out later.'

That was it. Patrick saw a flash of red and, barely knowing what he was doing, grabbed the front of Winkler's shirt with both fists, two buttons popping as he yanked him forward so their noses were almost touching.

'Give me the log-in,' Patrick said in a low voice.

Winkler brought his hands up and apart, breaking Patrick's grip. 'You arsehole. This is a fucking Ralph Lauren shirt . . .'

Patrick threw himself at the other man, catching Winkler off balance so they both tumbled to the floor. Patrick rolled on top and grabbed Winkler's shirtfront again, getting a fistful of chest hair.

Winkler cried out and brought his knees up fast, connecting with Patrick's thigh. Patrick loosened his grip and Winkler pulled away, getting up into a crouching position and aiming a punch at Patrick's ear. Pain seared across his head but he was able to block the second punch, balling his own fists, ready to throw a punch of his own.

He felt hands on his upper arms, pulling him backwards, shouts, Carmella whispering to him, though he couldn't hear what she was saying through the roar in his ears. Two other cops had grabbed Winkler and were pulling him off.

'What the hell?'

It was Suzanne. From Patrick's place on the floor she appeared eight feet tall.

'Get up. Both of you.'

Patrick slowly pushed himself to his feet, panting, and Winkler did the same. With one hand, Winkler held his gaping shirt together; with the other he jabbed a finger towards Patrick.

'This dick attacked me.'

Patrick counted to five in his head. He wasn't going to sink to the level of a schoolboy. But he felt like one when Suzanne snapped, 'Both of you. In my office, now.'

As soon as the door shut behind them, Suzanne demanded, 'What the hell was going on out there?'

Winkler said in a loud voice, 'Lennon went for me, ma'am. He grabbed me, pushed me to the floor, attacked a fellow . . .'

'Why?' she interrupted.

Taken aback, Winkler said, 'Huh?'

'Why did he do that? I am guessing he had a very good reason.'

Winkler's expression shifted. 'Oh, I see. Taking the side of your boyfriend. I should have fucking known.'

'Shut up,' Suzanne shouted. 'I am sick of listening to you.'

Winkler looked like a dog who'd been told off for trying to steal its master's dinner.

'Patrick, tell me what happened.'

He explained, as calmly and evenly as he could manage, about Winkler's refusal to hand over the log-in to Helen's Facebook account.

'Give it to him,' she ordered Winkler, who sighed and huffed before finally scribbling it down on a piece of paper and holding it out so Patrick could take it without the two men having to look at each other.

'This,' Suzanne said, gesturing to the two of them, 'is to be continued. I can't have two colleagues on the MIT acting like bloody Tom and Jerry. But right now, there are more important things to concentrate on. Adrian, go home, change your shirt, then get back here. Patrick, sit down.'

Winkler left the room, grumbling to himself.

As soon as he'd left, Patrick said, 'Which one am I?'

'What?'

'Tom or Jerry?'

She didn't smile, so he quickly rearranged his own face.

'Come on, then,' she said. 'Let's have a look at this Facebook account.'

Patrick went behind her desk and brought up the Facebook site, typing in the email and password Winkler had given him. He found himself on Helen's wall. He quickly scrolled up and down but couldn't see anything interesting. As Winkler had said, she had done nothing but like and share posts about Frankie in the past few days.

Then he went to her inbox and read her most recent messages, Suzanne reading over his shoulder.

'Oh my god,' she breathed in his ear.

They stared at each other and Suzanne said, 'Go. *Now.*'

Chapter 43
Jerome – Day 7

Jerome had the new Chase and Status album turned down low on the car stereo, not wanting to draw attention to himself, not wanting to hurt Rihanna's sensitive ears either. He turned and looked at the dog, sleeping like a baby on the backseat. She'd been all sensitive and twitchy since yesterday, after ripping that little bitch's face off. If Georgia survived – and Jerome needed to keep an eye on that situation, though he was pretty damn sure she wouldn't dare rat on him – she had better get used to doing it doggy style, because no guy was going to want to look at that wreckage of a face while he was banging her.

Last night, soon as he'd got home, he'd called up his boy Snowglobe – named because he had the worst case of dandruff in TW11 – and instructed him to put the word out that he was looking for a VW Camper Van with the registration number that could clearly be seen in the photo Georgia had taken.

'A VW Camper?' Snowglobe said. 'That's like that fucking thing that Benny had on the front of his T-shirt?'

'That's the one.'

'Nice. What, is it like a mobile meth lab or something?'

'Just put the word out to everybody. This is priority one, you get me? Five hundred to the person who spots it and reports back. But I don't want no one going near it, alright?'

He thought it might take days for someone to spot the van, but he got lucky. This morning he'd got the call. Some muppet mate of Snowglobe's called Niall had spent the night in Richmond Park with some piece of ass who was well into outdoor sex. As Niall had staggered off into the morning light at the crack of dawn he'd spotted the camper. It took the twat three hours to get round to reporting back, which meant his reward was going to be halved, but what the fuck. Jerome had a sighting – it was outside the Grant's Hotel by the park gates – and he was on his way to check it out.

£100k. What would he spend the money on? He had his eye on a black Jeep that he saw most mornings when he was walking RiRi. Or he could take the boys to Ibiza for a few months, live it large, fuck some models and shit.

Except he wasn't going to blow it. Guys like Snowglobe would do that, spend the lot on beer and trainers. Jerome was smarter than that. This £100k was going to be seed capital for his new venture. £100k could buy a lot of drugs, enough product to get Jerome properly into the game. Fuck messing around with a bunch of kids, the smalltime weed-dealing he'd been planning. Even before Georgia told him about the reward he'd decided against using Larry and the other posh kids; they were too much of a liability, although the posh-kid market was highly lucrative. He could make a fortune selling skunk and coke to the middle-class schoolkids of TW9. He could turn £100k into £500k easy. And then . . .

'This time next year, RiRi,' he said, 'we'll be millionaires.'

The dog groaned.

Jerome pulled up on the edge of the car park and looked up at the hotel. This place was alright, but when he was a millionaire he'd have a suite at the motherfucking Savoy.

There was the VW camper, right in the corner of the car park. He said, 'Wait here, alright,' to Rihanna and strode over to the van, weaving between the Beamers and Mercs and Audis – a lot of fucking Audis – and finally approaching the camper cautiously. The curtains were drawn across the back windows and the front cabin was empty. He peered around. There was a guy out front of the hotel lobby but his view of Jerome was blocked by the van. No one else around. He pressed his face against the glass and tried to peek behind the curtains but couldn't see a thing. He tried the door, just in case the crazy bitch had accidentally left it open – which happened a lot in his experience – but it was locked up tighter than a nun's pussy.

Was the kid in the camper now? He tried to think what he'd do if he'd snatched a little kid, which was not the kind of thing he'd ever do, no way. Though if it came down to it today, snatching this brat from the crazy kidnapper woman might be necessary. He had a pleasing vision of himself as a one-man liberating army, storming the hotel in a Call of Duty *stylee*, grabbing the kid and busting out of there, straight to the police station where he would collect his one hundred K and be a hero, all those feds standing slack-jawed and stunned that Jerome Smith had done what none of those lame motherfuckers could manage.

But first, he had to find her.

He took a walk round the back of the hotel. Going in the front wouldn't do him any good. He imagined some snooty stuck-up fag behind the desk, the kind of person who looked at Jerome and put his guard up higher than a Kennedy tower block.

There was a young woman standing outside the back entrance, the door through which, Jerome guessed, they wheeled laundry and groceries. She was smoking, her free arm clutched tight around her ribcage. She had dark, spiky hair and dark eyes, kind of Eastern European looking. Pretty hot.

He walked up to her just as she flicked her cigarette away.

'Hey.'

She eyed him suspiciously.

'You gotta light?'

He pulled out his cigarettes and extracted two from the pack as she searched in her pockets for her lighter. She lit his cigarette for him, leaning in close enough for him to get a whiff of some kind of cleaning product, bleach or something, and he offered her a cigarette.

He smiled at her in that way that always worked. 'You work here?'

She nodded.

'You like a receptionist?'

She laughed. 'No. A cleaner.' He had been right about her being Eastern European. Her accent was sexy and he thought maybe, when this was done, he'd come back here, flash some cash, see what her voice sounded like when she was moaning his name.

He guessed she was paid minimum wage, probably less. As an expert in the black economy, he knew all about these poor suckers who came over here and did the crap jobs no other fucker wanted even though half of them were doctors and shit.

'Want to earn some easy money?'

She looked him up and down. He gave her that smile again, one million watts of Jerome Smith charm.

'What do I have to do?'

'I'm looking for somebody.' He took out his phone and showed her the picture Georgia had shared with him. 'This woman. You recognise her?'

The cleaner hesitated then nodded slowly.

Jerome said, 'Cool. A guest here, right? I need to know what room she's in. If you can find that out for me I'll give you a hundred quid right now.' He showed her his wallet and counted out the money.

The cleaner licked her lips. 'Two hundred.'

Jerome beamed. 'You know what room she's in?'

'Yes. I clean her room.'

'Nice. OK, two hundred.' He pinched the money between forefinger and thumb and held it up.

The woman snatched it. 'She's in the honeymoon suite, top floor.'

'She in there now?'

'I don't know.' She had already stuffed the cash deep into her pocket. 'But she was there one hour ago.'

'Nice one.'

'You go in that door,' the cleaner said, 'and take the stairs to the top.'

Jerome stubbed out his cigarette and winked at the woman. Then he went in through the doors and started to climb the staircase. This was going to be the easiest £100k anyone had ever made.

He reached the top of the staircase, out of breath and sweating, and stuck his head out the door. This wasn't the freaking honeymoon suite. It was some kind of garden – a roof garden, loads of trees and shrubs and shit, a pretty cool place. He decided he'd like one when he owned his owned penthouse. The parties would be immense.

Trotting back down the stairs he went through another door and found himself standing at the end of a short, cool corridor with springy carpet beneath his Nikes. Cool. This must be it.

He took out his phone. All the way up, he'd been figuring out his plan. He needed to see the kid. He would look pretty damn stupid if he called the cops now and, when they turned up, she wasn't there. He couldn't see any way he could eyeball the girl without going into the hotel room.

This was going to be easy, though. The woman in Georgia's photo was old. It wasn't like she was going to fight him. All he had to do was get in the room, lock it and call the police. Maybe even make a motherfucking citizen's arrest. He could imagine the feds' faces when they rocked up and found out who the big hero was.

He rapped on the door.

From within, a woman said, 'Who is it?'

This was exactly like being in a movie, one in which he was the star. That was another thing he wanted to do when he was loaded. Make a film, one with loads of guns and cars and money and boobs.

What would he say if this was a movie? 'Room service.'

'I didn't order anything.'

'I brought you some champagne, madam.' He suppressed a laugh. 'Compliments of the manager.'

He waited, and for a moment he thought she wasn't going to buy it. But then she opened the door.

'You don't look like—'

He barged past her, pushing her aside and slamming the door behind him. The crazy bitch started yelling at him, asking him who the hell he was, but he ignored her, scanning the huge room. There was a large lump in the bed. A kid-sized lump. He walked over to the bed, ready to pull back the covers.

'Stop right there.'

He turned around, preparing to grin at her, but his smile was stillborn.

She was holding a gun.

He put his hands up. Shit, he hadn't been expecting *that.*

'Who the hell are you?' she asked. She had a weird accent, kind of Essex mixed with a bit of Australian. 'Are you police?'

'Police? Uh-uh. I'm a friend.'

'A friend of whose?'

The gun was trained on his face. He said, 'Hey, I'm no one. This was all a bit mistake, alright? Put that thing down and I'll walk right back out of here. No drama.'

The woman looked past him at the bed. Jerome stole a look over his shoulder. The lump in the bed wasn't moving, despite all the noise.

The phone beside the bed rang.

'Get over there,' the crazy bitch commanded, jerking the gun towards the far wall. He obeyed, striding over with his hands still aloft, keeping his distance from the gun.

The woman picked up the phone, said, 'OK, thanks. Tell her I'll be down in a minute.'

The woman looked down at the phone, thoughtful, taking her eyes off him.

This was his chance. He rushed her, but as he tore across the carpet he realized he'd underestimated the distance and her head came up and with it, the gun.

Pain exploded in his shoulder. *Oh my fuckin' days, I've been shot*, he thought. *I've actually been shot.* This really was like a movie. Except in a movie, he'd spring to his feet, or roll and trip the woman standing over him now with the gun pointed at his head.

Her face was twisted with anger. 'You stupid arsehole. You've fucked everything up.'

He watched, paralysed, as her finger tightened on the trigger. His last thought, before she blew his head off, was of Rihanna. She was locked in the car, all the windows up, the hot sun rising in the sky. He opened his mouth to plead for the woman to stop, because otherwise who was going to save his dog?

He didn't even get the first word out.

Chapter 44
Helen – Day 7

Helen pushed open the heavy revolving door leading into Grant's Hotel. Even before the door had finished the half-revolution necessary to spin her into the interior, she smelled the difference in the air inside: lilies, furniture polish, wood panelling, expensive luggage. This was the hotel where she came to the gym, but she hadn't stayed in a hotel like this for quite a while. It reminded her of her old, pre-Frankie life, of romantic weekends away with Sean in exotic European capital cities, enormous king-sized beds with nothing comprehensible on the wall-mounted TV except Sky News, going to sleep sated with sex and the monotone lullaby of the air-conditioning. Although she wouldn't want to do it again, not without Frankie. When they got her back, Helen thought, she would book another of those weekends, and this time they'd take Frankie with them. Vienna, perhaps, or Madrid. It could be just as romantic as when they'd first courted. More so.

Helen sat down on a vast square chocolate-brown suede sofa near the hotel lift. Its seats were too deep for her to be able to lean against the back of it, not without her legs sticking straight ahead of her like a child's. So she perched on the edge and waited, her palms flat on her knees to try and stop them trembling. She was five minutes early, and still not entirely sure why she was there.

That moment, up in the attic, when she had found the photographs . . . it had been unreal. Like she had suddenly developed Alzheimer's or something – just utter, total incomprehension.

She had climbed gingerly across the exposed beams of the loft, yellow loft insulation covering the floor between the beams like mashed potato on a pie – boarding it up had been on Sean's To Do list for years now – over to the box of Frankie's paintings that Sean had chucked to the back of the attic next to a baby car seat and another box containing her wedding dress. The boxes bobbed about on the sea of insulation like cargo out of a sinking ship.

She'd crouched down on her haunches and opened the box, flicking through them all, but nothing else had leaped out at her, no more 'naps', no more faces peering through windows.

She had been folding the flaps of the box back in, and about to swing her legs through the loft hatch to descend the ladder again, when the corner of something unfamiliar had caught her eye. It was a photograph album, one she didn't recognize, almost completely hidden by the insulation. She pulled it out and opened it up curiously – and thought she was about to have a heart attack.

Sean had always told her that he'd got rid of all the photos of his ex-wife Penny after she died, that it was 'just too painful' to keep them. Of course it was possible that he had overlooked this one album, had forgotten he'd stuffed it under the insulation, perhaps to spare Alice from hurt – although no, that was bollocks. Helen herself had heard Alice expressing sorrow to Sean that she didn't even have any photographs of her mum, and Sean apologising.

No, what was absolutely, blood-drainingly even more inexplicable than the continuing existence of this album of pictures of

Sean and a woman who, at the age she was in the photos, bore a startling resemblance to Helen herself, laughing and kissing and then, later, holding the bundle that was baby Alice – was that Sean's supposedly dead wife was her own friend, Marion. The woman she'd trained and chatted with at the gym, the woman she'd almost confided in about her sex life. She'd only known 'Marion' for a few months, but had quickly come to think of her as one of her best friends.

What a *mug*.

Helen had sat in the stuffy yellow heat of the loft for half an hour, her breathing shallow as though the insulation was asbestos, choking her, gazing at the photographs.

Could she be wrong?

No. It was definitely Marion. What the fuck was going on? Did Sean know she was still alive? Did *Alice?* Maybe that's where Alice had disappeared to. Helen remembered how Marion had once acted oddly when Helen told her Sean was picking her up from the gym, how she had suddenly announced that, instead of leaving, she was going to try out the sauna. It had suited Helen to have a friend who didn't know her husband, but on any occasion when the two of them could have encountered each other, Marion had made herself scarce.

It also explained how Marion's Facebook profile was so minimalist – no photos, very little background, hardly any friends. Marion had called herself a Luddite and a technophobe, and claimed she only joined Facebook so that she could communicate with her brother in Africa . . . a brother who probably didn't even exist.

It seemed inconceivable, but it was true: Marion was her husband's first wife. Alice's *mother*. And yet she hadn't seemed particularly interested in talking about Alice with her, or expressed any interest in seeing her. She'd encouraged Helen in her moaning about how awful teenagers were. She'd been far more interested in Frankie, cooing over photos on her phone and asking lots of questions.

Back in the hotel, Helen sat for seven minutes, according to the big station clock on the wall across the lobby, her nerves increasing with each slow steady sweep of the big hand. What good would it do, to talk to Marion now – she tried to start thinking of her as Penny, but kept defaulting to Marion – with Frankie and Alice both missing? She bit her lip, and thought about leaving again, going home, to see if there was any news. Frankie was her only priority now. She pulled her phone out of her handbag to check it, but the screen was blank. Damn – she'd forgotten to charge it last night, yet again. Or rather, she'd plugged it in, but not noticed that the switch was off at the wall.

And yet she knew she wasn't going to wimp out now. She couldn't. There were questions she had to ask: why had Sean lied to her, and to Alice, all these years? Since Penny wasn't dead, had they ever even got divorced? Was Sean a bigamist? When the registrar had asked he'd said he'd never been married before, and they hadn't checked up. Helen twisted her wedding ring around her finger and gulped. If Sean could lie to her about something this important, what else was he hiding? She had to talk to Penny, or Marion, or whatever she was called now, to get the facts before confronting Sean.

As soon as she'd come out of the attic the night before, she'd checked to see what Sean was doing. As she suspected, he was passed out on the sofa. She had stared at him like he was a stranger. Then she'd gone to the computer and sent Marion a message telling her she knew who she was.

She'd sat at the computer until the early hours, awaiting a reply, but none came. But when she'd got up this morning and checked Facebook, there it was, a reply, just a single line asking Helen to meet her here at the hotel.

She was brought out of her reverie by a strange popping sound from somewhere in the building, then sudden movement caught her eye across the lobby. The fixed door to the left of the revolving door was flung open with a bang, and two dark-suited security guards ran, fast, across the lobby, shouting into walkie-talkies. One disappeared straight up the stairs. Everyone's heads shot up, including Helen's. The other guard ran over to the reception desk and spoke quietly and urgently to the two receptionists, who both clapped their hands across their mouths in horror. One of them immediately got on the phone, a plump young woman in her early twenties. Helen could see her trying not to cry as she forced the words out. Helen lip-read 'police' and 'gun' and 'Grant's'.

A short bald man who had been standing at the reception desk with a large suitcase next to him, presumably a guest checking in, walked towards her, his eyes wide with shock. Helen jumped up off her sofa and approached him. 'Excuse me. What's going on? What did he say?' She gestured towards the security guard, who had followed his colleague up the stairs, taking them two at a time.

The man leaned towards her as though telling her a secret. 'Awful. Someone's got a gun . . . top floor . . . The roof . . . There's been a shooting. Police are on their way . . .'

Somehow, Helen knew what he was going to say next before he said it. And she wondered, before he'd said it, how she could have been so stupid as to not make the connection before, when she was sitting in the loft like a bird on an empty nest, staring at those photos and wondering why Penny had come back.

Now she knew why Penny had come back, and why she'd wanted to meet her at the hotel. Why she always asked about Frankie.

'. . . it's a woman. And she's got a little girl with—'

Helen had run for the stairs too, before the man had even finished the sentence.

'Come on Frankie,' I say. 'Time to wake up.'

Her eyes flicker open for a moment, before she closes them again and tries to slip back into the sleep, the tranquillizer that I emptied into her bedtime drink heavy in her blood. Warm milk with sugar – the same drink Mum always gave me before I went to sleep. My adoptive mother, that is. Not the jackal who gave birth to me.

'Frankie. Wake up . . .'

She stirs, opens her eyes, looks confused, probably wondering why we're outside, why the sky is so close.

I lift her onto the bench, stroke her hair. She's so pretty. She looks so much like Alice when she was three, frozen in time, as if she was waiting for me to return. It's as if my Alice is here. Three years old. Exactly as I left her. She never turned into the scowling, slutty teenager I've seen coming and going from Sean's house.

'What are we doing?' little Frankie asks, looking around. 'I want Mummy.'

'I'm your new mummy.' I try to hug her but she beats at me with her little fists, catches me in the tit, making me gasp. I raise a hand to slap her but restrain myself.

'We're waiting,' I say.

'What for?'

I could tell her we're waiting to say goodbye. But I really don't want to see her cry again. So I sit beside her and think about the past, letting my life flash before my eyes in a way I can control. Starting with The Mistake.

The Mistake changed my life. Reeling from the truth about who I really was, about everything, I fled. I erased myself – the only thing I could do, scorching the earth upon which I stood.

I travelled to the other side of the world, to a nondescript suburb of Brisbane, Australia, where I set about living the most nondescript life possible. I changed my name to Marion, I met a nice man called Howard, who was thirty years older than me, with enough money to compensate for his tubby gut and stubby dick. I told him I was an orphan, that I had no family, that I was all alone in the world. He liked that. He wanted to be my world. Like most men, he had Handsome Prince syndrome.

We got married. Nobody asked about my past, so I didn't tell them. We moved into his house. It had a pool in its big garden, a succession of state-of-the-art barbecues and, not having to work, I passed a decade swimming and sunbathing, stoned out of my mind on anti-depressants and cannabis, staring at the flat blue surface of the pool, day after day, nothing to do except suck Howard's stubby dick at night, until it stopped working properly, and prepare meaty dishes for him and open his beer.

I forced Alice and Sean from my mind. Did everything I could to forget they existed.

The only thing I wanted was a baby. But I couldn't get pregnant, no matter how hard we tried. Later, Howard blamed his impotence on my constant nagging desperation. Later still, I went out looking for young studs in local bars. One afternoon, Howard came home to find me riding a twenty-year-old called Chesney, trying to fill myself with his sperm. I continued to fuck young Chesney even as Howard writhed on the floor, the heart attack killing him right there in our bedroom while Chesney tried to get out from under me.

I still wasn't pregnant.

With Howard's money – some of which I had to give to Chesney to keep him quiet about the circumstances of Howard's death, in case his family tried to contest his will – I was able to pay privately for IVF. But it didn't work. After the third attempt the doctors told me I needed to accept it, that I should get on with my life, which could be rich and fulfilling without children.

I went home, stocking up on booze from the supermarket and pills and weed from my dealer on the way.

Six weeks later, I awoke from my solo bender on the patio beside the pool. I was naked. My inner thighs were bruised and there was blood in my hair. The booze and drugs had run out. I couldn't remember the last six weeks at all, just fragmented snapshots of flesh and water and the taste of bourbon and weed.

But I knew what I had to do.

It was time to go home – to England.

Finding Sean was easy: fifteen minutes searching on the internet and I knew where he worked – he had his own business now – and where he lived. I flew to Heathrow via Dubai, and took a train to Richmond.

I had plenty of money so I rented a hotel room. But I didn't like it – it made me feel trapped – so I bought a camper van, a classic VW, a vehicle I'd dreamt of owning when I was a girl. I would park it on Sean's street sometimes and watch his house, making sure he didn't see me.

I watched the teenage Alice come and go. I expected to feel a rush of maternal longing for her, but I felt nothing. She was almost an adult, a stranger. She wasn't what I wanted.

I saw Sean – he had gained weight and lost hair but was still as handsome as the day we'd first met; part of me wanted to drag him into the van and watch him gasp as he realized who I was. In my fantasies he would be thrilled, and he would undress me slowly like he used to, whispering my name, telling me he didn't care, it didn't matter, we couldn't and shouldn't fight it . . .

That could never happen.

When I saw his new woman I almost suffered Howard's fate. She looked like me. Another black woman, dressed in a prissier way, smaller tits, skinny arse. But we could have been sisters.

That made me laugh.

I found out which gym she went to and signed up, stood on the cross-trainer beside her and struck up a conversation. She was eager to talk, which made me think she was lonely, lacking in friends. We even exchanged emails and Facebook messages during which she told me about her and Sean's sex life, which sounded so different to the incredible sex Sean and I used to have. I made up stories about a pop star father and a glamorous life with a lucrative job and swanky flat. She talked about her daughter, Frankie, incessantly. I had seen Frankie, of course, watched from across the road as Sean and Helen took her out. She was perfect, beautiful. Seeing her made my ovaries ache. She was the child I had dreamt of all these years. The child I had left behind, the child I wanted in my future.

The injustice made me sick. Why should Sean get to have his perfect family while I was all alone? Frankie should be mine.

The universe owed me. And Sean, who had got off so lightly, deserved pain: to feel some of the suffering I'd been through.

I watched them, and I waited for an opportunity. I sometimes stood outside their house at night. Frankie saw me from her window once or twice, standing beneath the lamp post in my hoodie.

Then one night, while I was driving around, watching the house, I saw the other teenage idiot, the redhead, come out with Frankie.

I rescued her. And like I said, I wasn't going to keep her, but the opportunity was impossible to resist. A child of my own at last. And for Sean to finally feel the pain I have endured. By keeping in touch with that fool Helen over the last week I've had a hotline to their pain. It was exquisite seeing her at the gym, the van containing a knocked-out Frankie, parked outside. Thrilling to read her moans about how she wasn't getting any from Sean any more.

So here we are.

I leave Frankie sitting on the bench and walk to the edge of the roof, looking down. Anyone falling from here would be killed instantly.

I can hear commotion below. That boy, the one I had to shoot, using the gun I bought from a shady man in a backstreet pub, has brought the police running. But that's OK, as long as I can see Helen and Sean.

It's time for Frankie and me to say goodbye.

Chapter 45
Patrick – Day 7

On the radio on the way over, they were talking about how this was the hottest day in London for seven years, the temperature busting through the 30-degree mark, and Richmond Park was thronging with picnickers and kids playing with Frisbees; dogs panting in the heat; young lovers lounging on the grass as a lone, wispy cloud drifted lazily across the sky. There were no shadows for Patrick to imagine ghosts in today. No missing children hiding in the city's dark spaces. The sun had emerged to shine a brilliant spotlight on London, to expose its secrets at last. And here, in a hotel on the edge of this urban lung, Patrick knew he would find the truth.

Whether it was too late for that truth to mean anything, he didn't know.

He and Carmella reached the hotel just as the security guards were locking the revolving door. Patrick banged on the glass and held his warrant card up for the guards to see.

A security guard in his sixties unlocked the side door and let them through.

'Blimey, that was quick. We only just called you.'

'Called us?' He and Carmella exchanged a worried look. 'What about? And why were you locking the doors?'

Confused, the guard said, 'Aren't you here about the shooting?'

'Shooting? Show me. Now.'

The guard, whose name badge read Len Hudson, huffed and puffed as he led Patrick and Carmella towards the stairs, several more security staff following behind. The lobby was packed with guests shouting and arguing with staff, wanting to be let out. Nobody seemed to know what to do. The manager was standing on the front desk, waving his arms, appealing for calm. There was no sign of Helen or the woman she had come to meet.

They pushed through the crowd. Len said, 'We've shut down the lifts so we'll have to take the stairs.'

'What happened?'

Len sweated as he climbed the stairs. 'Some young bloke has been shot in the honeymoon suite.'

'Dead?'

'Yes. I haven't seen him but apparently his . . .' Len mimed someone having their head blown off.

'Sweet Mary mother of Jesus,' murmured Carmella, crossing herself.

'Hang on, was this guy staying in the honeymoon suite?' Patrick asked.

'No. There's a woman staying in there on her own, apparently. Bit weird, eh? I asked one of the girls about it and she said the woman told her it was where she and her former husband stayed on their wedding night. Like she wanted to relive the old memories.'

'What's her name?'

'Sorry, I don't know.'

Patrick swore. He should have spoken to them at the desk before coming up here. But it would have taken forever to get to the reception desk. And it had to be Penny. But where was Helen now? And Frankie?

'Did the woman have a kid with her?' They were halfway up the flight of stairs now. Patrick's chest burned. So much for the e-cigs making him healthier.

'Yeah, that's the bit I haven't told you yet. They're on the roof, the roof garden.'

Patrick ignored the burning in his chest and increased his pace, running up the steps, taking them two at a time. Carmella followed, her breathing much easier than his, and they left Len floundering behind.

By the time they reached the top, Patrick was swimming in sweat. He paused to call the station, pantingly checking that back-up was on its way. They went out onto the top floor and found a couple more security guards and a hotel assistant manager standing outside the door of the honeymoon suite, her face as white as the lilies that drooped in a vase beside the door. Her name badge read Elaine Flint.

'Police.'

The hotel staff stood aside to let them into the room, which stank of blood and shit, plus the smell of gunpowder that always reminded Patrick of fireworks. The body on the floor was clearly that of a young man. He was wearing designer sports gear and pristine trainers. There was a dark, bloody hole where his face used to be, bits of brain and skull splattered on the lovely carpet. Patrick crouched and fished in the man's pockets, pulling out a wallet containing a driving licence and about £300 in cash.

'Jerome Smith. Shit.'

'He found her before we did,' Carmella said, shaking her head.

As soon as Georgia had told them about Jerome and his dog, Patrick had sent a couple of officers to his known address but he hadn't been there.

Patrick recalled Georgia's ruined face; he knew what a petty thug Jerome Smith was, suspected of multiple beatings and muggings. He still felt some pity, though, for this young man whose death would be celebrated by the residents of the Kennedy estate more than it was mourned. But it wasn't a great deal of pity.

'Don't let anyone else in this room. Don't touch anything.'

The assistant manager, Elaine, nodded.

'There are more police and an ambulance on its way. I was told the woman who was staying here is on the roof with a child, a little girl?'

'That's right.'

'Had anyone seen this little girl before?'

'No,' said Elaine. 'We have no idea where she came from.' Elaine was in her early thirties, pretty, with an immaculate blonde bob, but stress had added ten years to her face. Patrick suspected she would be off on long-term sick leave for quite some time after what she'd seen today.

'She looks like that girl off the news, the missing one,' one of the guards interjected. 'Frankie.'

Patrick ignored him. 'Would it be easy for someone to get a child into this room without anyone noticing?'

'It's a busy hotel, people coming and going all the time. It wouldn't be that hard.'

'And how long has this guest been staying here?'

'She checked in yesterday.'

Patrick and Carmella stepped aside. 'What shall we do? We should wait for back-up, right?' Carmella said.

'We should – but we can't.'

'You mean you don't want to.'

'It's not a case of want, Carmella.'

Before she could respond, he heard banging coming from within the room opposite the honeymoon suite and someone shouting, '*Let me out!*'

Patrick raised an eyebrow and Elaine looked at him sheepishly. 'A woman tried to get up to the roof just before you got here. We put her in there for her own safety. She was going crazy.'

'Open the door.'

The security guard obliged and Patrick found himself face to face with Helen Philips.

She rushed out of the room. 'Detective Lennon. Where is she? It's Sean's ex-wife, she's not really dead, she pretended to be my friend, she . . .'

'I know,' he said gently, though he hadn't known she had pretended to be Helen's friend. *Oh god,* he thought. *She doesn't know about Sean.* But this was not the time to tell her.

'We need you to stay here, Helen,' he said. 'We're going up. I need to check that Frankie is OK, try to talk . . .'

'What? Frankie? She's *here*?' Stunned comprehension hit Helen like a slap. 'Oh. Oh . . .'

She tried to dash past him, towards the exit, but Carmella caught her.

'Let me go!' Helen was crying now. 'I need to see her. Frankie! *Frankie!*'

Patrick grabbed her upper arms and spoke in a low voice. 'Helen, please, you need to stay calm. I need to you to remain here. More police are on their way. We will get Frankie back for you. I promise.'

She looked up at him, her eyes spilling over with tears. She was smiling and crying, overwhelmed at the news that her daughter was still alive, but still afraid. 'Don't let her hurt my baby. Please. Oh god, I've missed her so much . . .'

Patrick gently guided Helen into the arms of Elaine the assistant manager, who led her back into the room where she'd been locked up.

He walked towards the stairs. So many things had gone wrong on this case. There had been so many mistakes. He knew well that this could be another. But there was no way he could stand by and wait for back-up while Penny was on that roof with Frankie.

They emerged through a doorway into dazzling sunlight. Small trees and shrubs in large stone tubs had been arranged in what Patrick thought of as a kind of Japanese-style garden, with neat beds of grey pebbles in a square pattern that stretched across most of the rooftop. Beyond: London. The great, grey city. St Paul's looked like he could reach out and scoop it up. He could see all the way to Essex, but he couldn't immediately see Penny and Frankie.

A man wearing the by-now familiar hotel uniform of white shirt and navy jacket, his name badge informing them he was called Kurt, hurried up to them.

'Police? Oh thank God.' He looked over Patrick's shoulder. 'Er, where are the rest of you?'

'On their way. Where is she?'

Kurt pointed towards the far corner, which was obscured by trees and a couple of large parasols. 'Over there. She's got a little girl with her. And a gun.'

Patrick took a deep breath. 'Is this the only exit, Kurt?'

'No. There's the main entrance-exit over there. But we're guarding it.'

'Okay. But, listen, if she comes out, you all just get out of the way. I don't want anyone trying to be a hero, OK?'

Kurt put his hands up. 'Hey, don't worry about that. Not on our wages.'

Patrick and Carmella walked slowly past the garden, the sun beating down on them. As they neared the edge of the rooftop, the woman they had been seeking for what felt like a lifetime came into view.

Penny Philips – or Marion Ellis as she called herself now, as he had learned from her Facebook exchanges with Helen – was standing in the corner, her back against a low wall. Frankie Philips was lying, curled up, at her feet. He knew small children had the ability to go to sleep in the most unusual circumstances, but Frankie had to be drugged. If she was alive.

Penny, who had been staring at the concrete in front of Frankie, noticed them, her head snapping up. She lifted the gun and pointed it first at Patrick, then back at Carmella, then at Patrick again.

'Keep back,' she said. 'Don't come a step closer.' She had an accent, a hint of Australian mixed with Estuary English.

Patrick spoke soothingly. 'Penny . . . is it alright to call you that?'

Surprise briefly registered on her face, before she affected confusion. 'My name is Marion.'

'No. It's Penny. But we can call you Marion if you wish. And I know you haven't hurt any . . .' He was about to say anyone but remembered Jerome downstairs with his head missing. '. . . any children. How is Frankie? Is she OK?' He took a step closer. His heart felt like it was trying to escape his chest.

Penny jerked the gun at him. 'I said, don't come closer.'

He stopped. But now he was a little nearer he could see Frankie's chest rising and falling. She was alive. Oh, thank God.

'I'm sure you've been looking after her, right?'

Still keeping the gun trained on him, Penny crouched down and stroked the unconscious child's hair.

'Little Alice,' she said. 'Such a good girl.'

Patrick and Carmella exchanged a look.

'She is a good girl,' Patrick said. 'And we don't want her to get hurt, do we? Why don't you give me that gun?'

Penny ignored him. Instead, she stared down at Frankie. 'My little angel. We're going to be together forever.'

With surprising speed and strength, she scooped Frankie up, the child lying limp in Penny's arms, and took a step backwards towards the edge of the building – and the sixty-metre drop.

Patrick and Carmella took a couple of swift steps towards them. Where the hell was back-up? Penny swung Frankie over her shoulder like she was made of feathers and retrained the gun on Patrick.

'Where's Helen?' she said. 'She's supposed to be here. And Sean – I want to see him too. I want *them* to see *this*.'

Her voice was hard, especially when she said – or spat – Sean's name.

Patrick said, 'Helen's downstairs. She's waiting to see her daughter. You're not going to harm her, are you?'

Penny's face darkened with anger. 'Frankie is not her daughter any more. She's mine. That bitch doesn't deserve a child and neither does Sean. Why should he get to be the one with the perfect life, with the perfect family? I deserve it. *Me*. All I've wanted was a child of my own, someone to love me. No one is going to take Frankie away from me, you understand?' She took a half-step backwards towards the edge of the building, causing Patrick's stomach to lurch.

He said, 'But you have a child. Alice. Maybe we can arrange for you to see Alice, talk to her, if you let Frankie go. *Helen* is Frankie's mother. She's desperate to see her, Penny. You're a mum. You understand that, don't you?'

'Alice? That monster? I don't want her. She's impure.'

What was she talking about?

Before he could formulate an answer, Penny said, 'I made friends with that bitch. Helen. I wanted to see what she was like, why she had everything I didn't. And do you know what I learned? She's not fit – not fit to be a mother. Not fit to be Sean's wife, either. I watched her with Frankie, saw her lose her temper with her, saw her ignore her while she was staring at her phone. She left her on her own in the house while she and Sean went out drinking! Is that something a good mother would do? No. No, it's not.' Her eyes blazed. 'That's why I had to keep Frankie. Because she's mine, you understand me? *Mine*.'

'She's not your daughter, Penny. She's Helen's little girl. And Helen loves her very much.'

Penny shook her head. 'No . . .'

'Frankie!'

The scream made Patrick whirl around. Oh shit . . . It was Helen. She ran towards them across the rooftop. Those stupid hotel idiots. She screamed her daughter's name again and rushed towards her. Carmella caught hold of her, holding her firm, despite how she thrashed and struggled. Penny stared at her, her lip curled with contempt, then she smiled.

'You came,' she said.

'Give me back my daughter,' Helen yelled. 'What have you done to her? Frankie? Oh my god, is she dead?'

'She's fine,' Carmella said, struggling to keep hold of her.

Penny said, 'She won't call me Mummy.'

'That's because you're not,' Helen panted. 'You're no one to her. Or me. I thought you were my friend! But you're . . . you're just a fucking ghost.'

Penny smiled. 'It's because you've brainwashed her. Poisoned her against me. Do you know how hard it was for me to watch you with her, the way you mistreated her?'

'What?'

'I watched you, all of you. And I listened to the way you talked about her at the gym, always moaning about how tired you were, how you wished you could have a break. Well, now you've got what you wanted. And I want you to tell her. You're not her mummy any more. I am. She's mine.'

'No!'

'Mine,' Penny said, almost to herself.

She took another step backwards towards the precipice, then turned her face and kissed the side of Frankie's head – and with that, Helen went crazy. She tore free from Carmella's grip and raced towards Penny and Frankie.

'Give her to me!'

Patrick tried to block her path, but she sidestepped him nimbly, and lunged at Penny, who screamed.

Patrick, who was facing Penny and Helen, felt the bullet graze his shoulder before he even heard the bang. He heard a gasp from behind him and cried out.

'Carmella!'

She was on the floor, blood blooming across her white shirt. But her eyes were still open, her mouth moving. She lifted an arm and pointed over his shoulder. Helen was grappling with Penny, trying to pull Frankie from her grip. Patrick ran towards them – and at that moment, a rush of noise and wind almost blew him away.

A police helicopter rose from beyond the edge of the hotel roof, the *whomp-whomp* of its blades filling the air, hovering level with him and the struggling women. He waved his arms, pointed at Carmella, who was lying still on the ground, tried to shout above the roar, but he couldn't even hear his own voice. The helicopter rotated, the cops inside gesticulating and trying to make themselves heard.

Several things happened at once. Helen spat in Penny's face, the shock making the other woman loosen her grip, and Helen fell backwards with Frankie on top of her. Penny pointed the gun at them and flexed her finger on the trigger.

Yelling, Patrick leapt at her and, swinging his arm, knocked the gun aside. It spun across the floor. Penny stooped to try and grab it but Patrick grabbed at her and she tripped, twisting sideways and toppling over the edge of the roof, clawing at the rooftop and clinging to the raised edge of the building.

She screamed, the noise just audible above the din of the helicopter. Patrick grabbed her arms, holding onto her, preventing her from falling. Her eyes were wide with terror and he gripped her sleeves as hard as he could, but she was too heavy. He couldn't hold her.

Her expression changed, became calm. She knew it was over.

'Don't let go,' Patrick yelled. But he couldn't hold on to her, not without her dragging him with her.

She shouted something in his ear.

And fell, her body tumbling down the edge of the hotel, bouncing off a window ledge and spinning towards the shining roofs of the cars parked below. He turned his head away before she hit the ground.

Chapter 46
Patrick – Day 7

In the calm that followed the storm, Patrick sat heavily on the edge of a huge earthenware pot containing a small palm tree, considering his next move: Carmella, Helen and Frankie had been taken to hospital. Helen still didn't know that her husband was dead. Alice was still at Larry's – she'd have to be told, too. Even though Frankie was safe, Patrick felt numb with shock and despondency. So many lives lost or ruined. Poor little Izzy. Koppler, Sharon Fredericks, Sean. Georgia and her ruined face. Alice and her ruined life.

Jerome Smith – although no great loss there. Even his stupid dog was dead. The residents of the Kennedy Estate would no doubt be heaving a huge collective sigh of relief. One of the officers had found the dog on the back seat of Smith's car. Smith had left the window open a crack, but it hadn't been sufficient in the blaze of an eighty-degree summer's day, and the dog – Beyonce? Jessie J? No – Rihanna, wasn't it? Rihanna had dehydrated, shrivelled up and died.

Then there was Eileen, who would probably never recover. Penny had shouted something in Patrick's ear, just before she fell: 'Tell Eileen it's all her fault.' He wondered why – perhaps Eileen had made their lives hell and that was why Penny had left? Or had she done something else, more sinister?

He stood up, his legs still feeling shaky. He didn't understand why Sean had taken his own life at the sight of Penny's photograph – but he was pretty sure he now knew who could explain it to him. He left the SOCOs flitting around the hotel roof like bright ghosts in paper overshoes, incongruous in the bright sunshine, and headed back to the Philipses' house.

He leaned on the doorbell of the big house, feeling its emptiness in the echoey quality of the sound within. It would be on the market within weeks, he was certain. Helen and Alice probably wouldn't ever want to set foot inside it again. Suddenly he felt grateful for his own life, however imperfect it was. His folks' place was tiny and cramped, and his own house rented out to two Bulgarian dance teachers, but so what? Home was where Bonnie was, and her own beautiful, life-affirming energy. Nothing else mattered, nothing.

He shook his head, at the same time as he spotted a movement through the panels of frosted glass in the front door. He'd have to watch himself – any more of that hippie nonsense and he'd be dressing in saffron with cymbals attached to his fricking ankles, chanting in the streets . . . He bent down and peered through the letterbox. A large wheeled suitcase sat on the chequered tile floor of the hallway.

'Mrs Philips! Is that you? Need a word. It's DI Lennon. Please let me in.'

Everything was still, but he could smell the telltale scent of cigarette smoke, and after a minute, he heard a long sniff.

'Mrs Philips – Eileen – open the door, please.'

Eileen appeared in the dining room door and shuffled down the hall towards him. Even through the small rectangular frame of the letterbox it was clear that she was a broken woman. Gone was the bluster and the attitude, leaving a shell of a person, someone who looked as though all the blood and marrow had been sucked from her bones and replaced by grief and sorrow. Her hair was limp, her face unmade-up and deathly white. Wordlessly, she opened the door and stood aside to admit him, not meeting his eyes.

'There's some good news,' Patrick said gently, steering her into a chair at the kitchen table. 'Frankie has been found, safe and apparently unharmed. Helen's with her now, at the hospital. They're just checking them both over.' Mentioning the hospital made him feel bad that he wasn't there at Carmella's side. But she was a pro. She'd understand. Thank God it was only a flesh wound.

Eileen gave a wan smile.

'Penny had her, didn't she,' she whispered. A statement, not a question.

'Did you know that already?' Patrick turned away to fetch them both a glass of water, not wanting Eileen to see how much her answer mattered to him.

'No. Not until I saw the photo on your phone. Where is Penny now?'

'When did you last see her, Mrs Philips?'

'My daughter—'

'Yes, your ex-daughter-in-law,' Patrick said, handing her a glass of cold water from the tap which she took, clutching it to her chest with a shaking, liver-spotted hand, but not bringing it to her lips.

'No. She was my daughter.'

'So you thought of her as a daughter? You must have been very close, then.'

Oh shit, thought Patrick, *so this will be another bereavement for the poor woman.* He hadn't ever warmed to Eileen, but he wouldn't wish this kind of emotional devastation on anyone, not even Winkler. A sudden noise made them both jump, but it was only a big ginger tom nudging his metal food bowl across the tiled floor in the utility room.

'No. She was my daughter. My real daughter.'

Something in the tone of Eileen's voice made Patrick begin to understand.

'Your . . . *birth* daughter?'

Eileen's chin sank to her chest as she nodded, too distraught for tears. She seemed semi-conscious. Patrick's breath stopped in his chest.

'But – isn't she Alice's mother?'

Another brief nod.

'And Sean . . . he's not your son? Is he your son-in-law?' Patrick wondered how he'd got this all so wrong.

The clock on the wall ticked loudly into the silence, as if it had only just started marking the passage of time. Signifying the collapse of a family.

'Please explain, Mrs Philips, I'm sorry, I'm really confused. I thought Sean was your actual son. How come your name is Philips too, then?'

Eileen began to sit up, and the glass slipped from her grasp, bouncing off her lap and smashing into a million pieces on the quarry tiled floor. Her lap was full of water that dripped through her polyester skirt like she was straining it through muslin. The cat shot straight past them into the hall in a ginger blur of panic, and the sounds of broken glass and dripping water reverberated in Patrick's ears. He knew he should get a cloth, a dustpan and brush, make soothing noises, but he didn't want to break the spell. He was so close to it all making sense, finally.

'Eileen?'

She turned to look at him then, her eyes rheumy and heart-broken.

'Sean is – was – my actual son. My youngest child.'

Patrick opened his mouth to speak but she carried on, flicking ineffectually at the water in her lap with the side of her palm.

'Yes I know I told you I only had one child. But I didn't. I had Penny first, five years earlier in 1970. I didn't mean to. I was only seventeen, and I was in love. I met her dad, Horace, at Butlins. He was the first black man I'd ever talked to. I didn't mean to get pregnant of course, and I didn't realize I was until I was six months gone, and so was Horace. *Long* gone, he was. I gave the baby up for adoption. My mum and dad were furious with me, 'specially when I admitted the baby would be half-caste. Oh, you can't say that these days, can you? *Mixed race.* Load of bollocks . . .'

A trace of her spirit re-entered her voice, just a trace. Patrick sat back in horror, the implications of Eileen's story slowly beginning to make sense.

'Then what, Mrs Philips? Or is it OK for me to call you Eileen?'

Another brief nod. Patrick wordlessly handed her a tea-towel and she arranged it on her lap to soak up the water, like she was in a restaurant and it was a napkin.

'I didn't know,' she said, her voice once more dropping to a whisper. 'I didn't know that her adoptive parents had called her Penny. I'd named her Tracey. I tried to forget about her, married Sean's dad in '73, had Sean the next year. He was a nice man. Hugh was his name. He died when Sean was seven, of an aneurysm. Never knew about Penny. I still miss him. Unlike that black bastard, excuse my French, but I never liked the coloureds after that.'

Patrick tried to hide a wince at the blatant racism.

Eileen sighed, and her lips trembled. 'I reckon that was why Sean never brought her home to meet me, 'cos she was half-caste and he knew I wouldn't approve. I didn't know, I swear I didn't know!' Her voice rose. 'We weren't very close during that period. I didn't even know he had a girlfriend, that they'd moved in together. Next thing she's pregnant, and they run off and get married. I was so upset and furious.'

'What year was that, Eileen, when Sean and Penny got married?'

She thought a moment, tears now rolling unsteadily down her face. 'How old is Alice . . . almost sixteen . . . so that must have been 1997. But I didn't actually meet Alice till a few years later.'

'How soon did you realize who Penny was?'

Eileen took a deep breath. 'I finally went round to see him, fed up of getting the silent treatment. And there she was. She was as shocked to see me as I was to see her.'

'What do you mean?'

'I'd seen her before. She came to find me, see, her birth mother. Turned up out of the blue one day after tracking me down. And . . . I sent her packing. I didn't want to see her, didn't want to know. I didn't want to be reminded of my mistakes. You can't blame me.'

Patrick said nothing.

'She must have met Sean after she left my house. Apparently, after I'd sent her away she went to the pub round the corner because she needed a drink, and Sean was in there. She swore afterwards that she had no idea who he was but . . . I don't know. I read in one of my magazines that people are often attracted to other people who look like them, or who are similar. Maybe she, what's the word, subconsciously recognized something in him. Was drawn to her own blood.'

'So what did you do when you realized they were together?' Patrick felt so sorry for her. So sorry for all of them. Eileen put her head in her hands and shuddered at the memory.

'I screamed at them. I was so angry. If only Sean had brought her home sooner, if he was the kind of boy who kept pictures of his mum around, none of this would ever have happened. I could've warned them then that it was incest, that it mustn't go any further.'

'But he hadn't done, because he knew you'd be upset that she was mixed-race,' Patrick said, understanding. 'What a mess.'

'Yeah. A mess is about right. I told them they were half-brother and sister.'

'How did they take it?'

She laughed mirthlessly. 'Shocked, obviously. Mortified. Penny went mental. I think she was mental already, but this tipped her over the edge. She did a runner, left Alice with Sean saying that Alice was a freak and she didn't want anything to do with any of them . . . She buggered off to Australia and we never saw her again.'

'Why did Sean tell everyone she was dead?'

Eileen dropped her head again. 'He couldn't find her, to get a divorce. He was so upset. He'd really really loved her. I felt so guilty that I'd come between them – maybe I shouldn't ever have said anything. But then they might have had more children, and the next ones mightn't have been right in the head, even though Alice was alright . . . He didn't want Alice to know, obviously, and he didn't want to tell her that her mum had just abandoned her. So he got rid of all the photos and told everyone that Penny had gone over to Australia on a work placement for six months and died in a car crash over there. Alice was only a toddler; it was better for her that she grew up thinking her mum was dead rather than the truth. He used to worry that Penny would show up out of the blue, but she never did. Not until now. I hate her, for what she did to him and Alice, the mental bitch.' Eileen's voice rose until she was almost shouting.

Patrick took a deep breath. Penny must indeed have been mentally ill. He remembered her on the roof, calling Frankie by Alice's name. Perhaps she thought she had another chance, to succeed with Frankie where she'd failed Alice? The two girls looked similar, the way that Penny and Helen were fairly alike.

'She's dead now, Eileen. She died this morning, jumping off the roof in the hotel when we were rescuing Frankie. I'm so sorry.'

'Good riddance,' Eileen said, but the words were drowned out in a storm of sobs that bent her double over her wet lap. All Patrick could do was squeeze her shoulder.

If it was easier for Eileen to blame Penny, then who was he to contradict her?

Finally Eileen sat up again and gripped Patrick's wrists. 'Promise me one thing,' she said, staring right in his face. 'You're the only person in the world that knows now. You and me, nobody else. Promise me you won't tell anybody, ever. Promise me. It would kill Alice. The poor girl's lost her daddy. Don't tell her she's just lost her real mummy too. I don't want her to know that Penny hated her. Do you promise?'

Patrick hesitated. How the hell was he going to write up the report without mentioning this one, crucial bit of information? Eileen would have to give a statement. Her eyes pleaded with him, and he had a sudden, unbidden thought of Gill locked up in her secure mental unit, trapped by one hasty, life-ruining action.

He was torn. He could imagine how devastated Alice would be if she learned the truth. But he was a police officer, a detective. It was his job to uncover the truth.

Eileen stared at him with desperate eyes. 'Please, detective. Please don't tell anyone.'

He walked away, leaving her sobbing. He had no idea what to do.

Chapter 47
Patrick – Afterwards

Bonnie sat on the edge of the bed with her bare feet sticking straight out in front of her and watched, solemn-eyed, as Patrick got dressed. Black suit – last worn at Gill's trial – white shirt, ironed carefully by Mairead the night before, black tie, hastily purchased from Asda for the occasion, shiny black shoes.

'Daddy look 'mart,' she observed, removing her thumb from her mouth to pass judgement.

'Thank you darling. I need to look smart today.'

'Why, Daddy?'

'I'm going to . . . say goodbye to a nice man who had a hard time.'

'Oh. Bring me back some sweeties?'

Patrick smiled at his daughter in the mirror as he straightened the stiff new tie. *Thome thweeties.* He could listen to Bonnie's voice all day long. Perhaps he should record it on his phone and listen to it through headphones when Winkler was being a tit, to de-stress himself. 'OK, if you're a good girl for Nana.'

'I am.' Bonnie graciously inclined her head.

'Excellent,' Patrick said, ruffling her hair as he left the room.

An hour later, he slipped into a pew near the back of the handsome Victorian galleried church, still wearing the shades he was glad he had with him when running the gamut of the paparazzi outside. *The poor Philips women, having to cope with that*, he thought. There they were, up in the front row, the backs of their heads rigid as they stared straight ahead. Eileen and Helen were both wearing big hats, and when Eileen leaned in to say something to her daughter-in-law, the brims clashed and they both leaped back as though scalded.

Helen obviously didn't know, Patrick surmised. She couldn't do, surely, not if she had agreed to have Eileen sitting next to her. The thought of how much more damage Eileen – or he, for that matter – could do to poor Helen and Alice . . . It made Patrick's stomach twitch with anxiety.

Frankie sat on Helen's lap. Even from the back of the church, Patrick could see that Helen kept her arms tightly wrapped around her daughter, who was wearing a pretty floral party dress, a little fabric flower resting in her black curls. It was a little unusual for a child so small to be allowed to come to a funeral, but Patrick was pretty sure that Helen wasn't permitting Frankie out of her sight for a second. He couldn't say he blamed her.

A child psychologist had talked to Frankie shortly after she'd been found, to ascertain how Penny had treated her and to ensure she hadn't suffered any sexual abuse. The poor child had revealed a few disturbing details, about being locked in the dark and something about a 'hurt' kitten, and blood test results showed that Penny had been giving Frankie small doses of tranquillizers to keep her docile and, at the end, unconscious. Patrick instructed the psychologist to ask Frankie about the drawings of the face at the window, but Frankie's answers were virtually incomprehensible. Something about how there was a ghost who lived in the lamp post outside and who looked in at her.

'My assumption,' the psychologist said, 'is that Frankie spotted Penny watching her from outside the house. I asked Frankie if she likes to look out of her bedroom window at night and she said that she did.'

Indeed, the same neighbour who had spotted Larry the evening of Frankie's abduction had confirmed that he had seen Frankie looking out of her window occasionally. Patrick was surprised that Penny would risk being seen by Sean – Helen had confirmed that the woman she knew as Marion had never, in the short time she'd known her, visited their house. But maybe she hadn't been able to stop herself from standing outside, presumably in disguise, watching the family she was obsessed with. After all, she had seen Georgia take Frankie that night.

Patrick returned his attention to the here and now. Alice sat a little way along from Helen, Eileen and Frankie, Larry's arms wrapped tightly around her, rubbing her back as if she was really cold. She kept her face buried into the side of his shiny cheap grey suit jacket, as though unable to face the sight of her father's lily-covered coffin in her line of vision whenever she looked up.

The church filled up around him to the accompaniment of that soft funereal organ noodling that always slightly set Patrick's teeth on edge. There were a lot of couples there, presumably friends of the Philipses, thirty-somethings looking uncertain in shiny dresses or stiff suits. A few went to the front and spoke softly to Helen – he could see her hat dipping in acknowledgement – but most slid silently into pews. Many of the women were already weeping.

God, he hated funerals.

The one thing that consoled him was the knowledge that he hadn't had to endure one himself, a tiny white coffin and a grief that could never have been assuaged as long as he lived. Bonnie was alive, growing and learning and developing from a baby into a little girl. Alive and well.

Patrick had to swallow the lump in his throat. The woman next to him, a skinny glamorous redhead in her forties, handed him a tissue.

'Oh, thanks, no actually I'm fine,' he said, coughing. 'Something in my eye. Really.'

She rolled her eyes at him and continued to proffer the Kleenex, so he took it and stuffed it straight into his pocket, with a sheepish smile.

'Shocking, isn't it,' said the woman. 'Were you a friend of Sean's?'

Patrick nodded vaguely, hoping that she wouldn't press for more details of how he knew Sean. 'Were you?' he deflected.

'I'm a work colleague of Helen's – a fellow editor,' she said. 'Liz Wilkins. Haven't seen much of her since she went off on maternity leave a few years ago, but of course I called her when I heard what had happened to poor Frankie. What they must have gone through! So I gather—' she dropped her voice conspiratorially '—it was Sean's ex-wife who kidnapped her, and she's dead now too?'

It sounded so simple when you put it like that, thought Patrick, nodding again and hoping she would go away. But she carried on, mistaking his silence for collusion. 'Thank God it wasn't those nutters who took the other kids, though, that would've been worse. And thank God little Frankie is OK. I mean, look at her, the little dote. But now she has to grow up without a dad. He was such a lovely man . . .'

Liz's voice cracked and tears filled her eyes. Patrick wordlessly handed the tissue back to her, thinking *you don't know the half of it*. To his great relief, the noodling organ ceased and a young vicar strode in and stood in front of Sean's coffin before Liz could continue her lamentation.

'Welcome to you all, on this very sad occasion,' the vicar said, spreading his arms wide to herald the start of the service.

At one point Alice got up to read a poem, that one that always got read at funerals about stopping the clocks. *Four Weddings and a Funeral* had a lot to answer for, thought Patrick, aching with sympathy for the girl as she stumbled through the first few lines before bursting into uncontrollable sobs and running out of the church, Larry close behind her. The congregation could hear her crying through the double doors that led to the church toilets, and it started several others off. The vicar smiled insincerely and finished reading the poem himself.

Then Helen got up to speak, shifting Frankie onto Eileen's lap and moving to stand alongside Sean's coffin, holding two typed sheets of A4. She looked pretty good, Patrick thought. Her hair was a straight dark shiny sheet under the brim of her hat, and her coral lipstick matched her dress and shoes – the family having eschewed the traditional black in favour of a so-called 'life-affirming' dress code of bright colours. Only the black bags under her eyes gave away her grief.

She hesitated, opened her mouth to read what was on the sheets, then closed it again, screwed up the sheets into a small ball and dropped the ball onto the marble floor. Everyone sat up a little taller when she finally spoke, in a voice that was strong, unwavering – and absolutely furious. She addressed her husband's coffin directly.

'Sean Adrian Philips' – it had never occurred to Patrick before that the deceased's initials spelled SAP – 'I will never forgive you for what you've done to us.' The congregation gasped. Patrick wondered if she'd have said the same if Alice hadn't left the room. Probably not. The screwed-up ball of paper on the floor was almost definitely very different in content.

'We've been through hell in the last two weeks, the worst two weeks of my entire life, and just when we got our baby back, you do this to me? You—' Her lips formed a cat's bum of a B for *bastard,* but at the last moment, she seemed to remember that she was in church. '*Coward,*' she hissed at the coffin instead. 'There is nothing that would make me forgive you for this. Nothing.'

Gasps and sobs bounced off the rafters in the church roof. It was then that Eileen turned around, still holding Frankie, and stared straight at Patrick even though he was almost in the back row, her eyes lasering into him. Other people turned to see what she was looking at, and Patrick shifted uncomfortably in his seat. Her meaning could not have been clearer: *DO NOT TELL HER.*

Do not tell this grieving furious woman, tearless and devastated, that the reason her husband killed himself was because her stepdaughter was the product of incest. Because he'd married his half-sister, because he hadn't known that the same woman had since come back and befriended Helen, because he couldn't live with the guilt and shame of it all coming out. Or worse, perhaps because he realized he still loved his first wife, and couldn't live without her? They would never know.

Patrick stared at the floor. Liz Wilkins poked his bicep. 'Why is Sean's mother looking at you like that?'

'None of your sodding business,' he felt like saying – or perhaps did say out loud. He wasn't sure. Either way, she didn't speak again, and dropped her hand as though his arm had scalded her fingers. His phone vibrated in his pocket and he sneaked it out to have a look. Someone from a blocked number had left him a message. He'd read it later.

Eileen eventually turned back around. Helen stomped back to her seat and grabbed Frankie back, holding the child so tightly that she started to struggle and cry.

Maybe if I tell her, Patrick thought, *she'll understand why he did it, and forgive him?*

I have to tell her. And how can I stop it all coming out in court, at Georgia's trial?

It was nothing to do with that. It didn't need to come out. Georgia's trial, when she was fit enough to stand it, would be on charges of drug dealing and attempted kidnap.

He had to tell Helen.

Sweat broke out on his forehead. They all stood up to sing a hymn – 'Dear Lord and Father of Mankind' – they'd had that one at his wedding to Gill, they'd laughed about it afterwards because of the line 'forgive our foolish ways', as if their marriage was an act of stupidity for which they requested forgiveness.

Forgive our foolish ways. If he told Helen, then maybe she could forgive Sean's foolish ways.

He was going to tell Helen.

Then, as the hesitant congregation broke reluctantly into the third verse, the church doors opened and Alice came back in, still in Larry's arms. He helped her up the side aisle, past Patrick, and she glanced up at him through puffy blank eyes. The look of raw grief on her face spoke more loudly than Helen's harsh words, and in that second Patrick finally stopped wavering and knew what he was going to do.

He pushed past the red-haired woman and left the church as fast as he could without actually running. Outside, he sat on a bench in the churchyard, his heart pounding and the sweat now running down his cheek like tears. He wiped his face, pulled out his phone, and dialled his voicemail.

It was Gill – or at least he thought it was. She never rang him, and at first he didn't recognize her voice, it sounded so different. Light and bright and – excited?

'Pat,' the message said. 'Oh Pat. You won't believe it. They're releasing me, next week. They assessed me and have decided I'm no longer a danger to myself or anyone else. I'm coming home. We're going to be a family again . . .' Her voice became hesitant, slower. '. . . if you still want us to be, of course. We can talk about it. But isn't that fantastic news? I'm coming home!'

Patrick dropped the phone back in his jacket pocket, stood up and headed for his car. There were only two things he knew for certain at that moment. One, he needed to see Suzanne.

Secondly, that he would take Eileen's secret with him to the grave, if he possibly could.

He was never, ever, going to tell anybody.

Acknowledgments

We have a few people to give special thanks to: principally Dr Paul Monks, Simon Alcock, Kate Blumgart and Nik Waites, for generous and expert research assistance (any procedural inaccuracies are our own!).

Hearty thanks to Liz Wilkins for her excellent early feedback, and to our agent Sam Copeland.

Thank you particularly to our commissioning editor at Thomas & Mercer, Emilie Marneur, for her absolute faith in and support for this novel, and to the rest of the T&M team, especially Sana Chebaro and Nadia Ramoul.

To the amazingly supportive and friendly crime writing community both on and off Twitter – so many people who have become good friends. We apologise if we've left anyone out, but we'd like to thank Peter James, Mel Sherratt, Ali Knight, Keith Walters, Susi Holliday, Rachel Abbott, Luca Veste, Elizabeth Haynes, Eva Dolan, Anya Lipska and everyone else who gathers outside the Old Swan in Harrogate every year.

Mark would also like to express special gratitude, and love, to Sara Edwards, not only for giving honest feedback about this novel but for making my half of this whole writing lark possible.

Finally, we would like to give a big, fat 'like' to our fantastically enthusiastic and helpful group of readers on Facebook.com/vossandedwards, some of whom have their names in this book, including Cathy Hudson and Daniel Hamlet, who won competitions on the page. Pete Aves provided the name of Jerome's unfortunate staffie.

About the Authors

Photo © 2014 Mark Earthy

Louise Voss and Mark Edwards are the co-authors of *Killing Cupid*, *Catch Your Death*, *All Fall Down* and *Forward Slash*. They have also written eight solo novels between them, details of which can be found on their website www.vossandedwards.com. Dubbed 'internet publishing sensations' after being the first UK self-published authors to reach the #1 and #2 spots simultaneously on Amazon.co.uk back in 2011, they have had a wildly varied and interesting publishing career.

Mark lives in Wolverhampton with his wife and young family, while Louise lives in Surrey with her daughter. They love talking to readers on Twitter, @mredwards and @louisevoss1, and run a very lively Facebook page at facebook.com/vossandedwards, where they chat, run competitions and offer prizes. Many of their character names have been suggested by competition winners—most notably, a dog called Rihanna . . .